BOOKS BY LEWIS W. GREEN

The Year of the Swan

And Scatter the Proud

The High-Pitched Laugh of a Painted Lady
and other stories

The Silence of Snakes

THE
SILENCE
OF
SNAKES

THE SILENCE OF SNAKES

by Lewis W. Green

JOHN F. BLAIR, Publisher
Winston-Salem, North Carolina

Copyright © 1984 by LEWIS W. GREEN

Printed in the United States of America

Library of Congress Cataloging in Publication Data

Green, Lewis W., 1932–
    The silence of snakes.

    I. Title.
PS3557.R373S5   1984   813'.54   84-16804
ISBN 0-89587-040-1

To Lillie Strain Green,
Georgia Burnett Wyatt, and
Myrtle Wyatt Green
Who stood to their tests

THE
SILENCE
OF
SNAKES

I

THE WINTER HAD BEEN fierce and relentless, but it loosed its grip some as it surged into mid-March. Despite the warming temperatures, it still threw bitter fits throughout the days. Big winds roared along the ridges, and the forest was marked where the tops of some larger trees had broken, and as they took their plunge to the earth they marked the smaller ones. Many limbs had splintered under ice storms, and they dangled by strips of bark. Some of them lay in tangles on the ground. Time had also come for numerous old trees. The accumulations of stress and disease told, and they toppled under the winds. In the subtle time and psychic pressures of a hard winter, some old people also died.

From the porch of the small frame house, voices droned in the chill air of the afternoon, reiterating old beliefs, observations.

"Now, some of them big trees went down late last fall," Big Boy rumbled in his deep, slow voice. "You know what they say, that when the old trees fall, a lot of old folks won't last out the winter. January is always the hardest. They seem to die in threes. I've heard it said time and time again."

His wife, Edith, and his stepmother sat quietly. The older woman, Mrs. Guffey, stared across the forested ridgeline. Then she thought this of time and people: incessant wind through the trees, exposed on a ridge.

A dim, brief perception, it passed like a gust in a dark night.

The girl Loretta was in the edge of the yard next to the brush. She was as pregnant as she ever would get, and she was impatient with the restrictions of it. The winter's confinement in the small house on the mountain with her husband's people had kept her in a state of irritation, and now she was extremely tired of them. She listened to the slow voices, watched the wind in the treetops listlessly. Her small, strong hands ceaselessly folded and unfolded, twisting the cloth of her dress.

Mrs. Guffey raised her head, looked about with a slow, queenly, and tolerant turn, and spoke:

"Well, I don't always hold with the signs," she said, "but it has been a winter to take out the infirm. I know they buried several around here in January, now that you mention it."

"Now, Mama, there is something to the signs," Big Boy said ponderously. Edith opened her mouth to speak, wanted to say something, failed, closed her mouth. Loretta saw it and sympathized. She knew how closed the conversations became. Then Loretta could stand no more. She rose and went into the house, her air of resentment unmistakable. The three of them on the porch looked quickly at each other, then away toward the ridge again.

"Sometimes she hears things I don't say," Mrs. Guffey said, in maddening acceptance of the girl.

Loretta's voice rose out of the house.

"I hear what you say, all right." Her voice was a sharp point, constantly thrust out to hold them back. It held Mrs. Guffey back, but it did not make her retreat.

"Did you say something, Loretta?" Mrs. Guffey asked with a tight smile.

"What? No! No, I didn't . . . ."

But the girl thought that nobody got around Mrs. Guffey, not even Big Boy. He could talk about signs and mean no harm, but the older woman would come behind him and try to make a fool and a liar out of him.

The wind gusted and a high tail of it stayed up, creaking the house. A brief moan trailed off the lip of the chimney. They murmured in surprise, laughed, commented on the tone of the wind.

A moment's silence, then the strong, cracking soprano of Mrs. Guffey's voice began anew, speaking of family, ancestors, old homeplaces.

Loretta took a saucepan from the kitchen, went out the back door and around the house to them. She turned abruptly and held out the pan, timorous and defiant at once.

"I'll pick some greens," she said. "Some are coming up."

They smiled, nodded. She trudged up the narrow, beaten mud of the path to the top of the hill, where beside a road young stalks pushed green and incongruous from the cold and wintered earth. Still she could hear the mumble and purl of their talk.

—Big Boy, gutteral German, his throat rumbling:

". . . all I can say is that she's as big with child as she's going to get. . . ."

—Mrs. Guffey, a shifting soprano, breaking and honking:

"Well, it's Walton's first. My first grandchild with my blood . . ."

A mistake—quickly, quickly, ". . . but you and Edith know that I love yours like I will love this one. You are just like my own son. . . ."

Frowning, sensitive to it, Loretta strained to hear the hurt in Big Boy's voice, but he did not speak. Her stepson. She does not quite let him forget in all these years. He recalls no other mother, but she does not let him fully claim her.

Loretta bent and plucked the tender stalks. Then came the sharp pain in her back. She straightened, dropped the pan, and pushing hard against her kidneys with flat palms, stared into the valley.

Hame Tree Gap, named when some early traveler broke the hame tree on his wagon, was not a true mountain gap at all, but rather a barely noticeable saddle on a ridge. From the gap, a path ran out the ridge spine, meandering here and there as the first travelers (probably game, then Cherokee, then stock) had packed it clean and hard with their feet. The path was used by the few who lived in the Wild Cat area, not so much as a shortcut as an alternative to the clay road to Hollytown, which became a mire in bad weather. The path ran along the spine for two miles and then fell off on the sixteenth green of a golf course. A gravel road also ran between the cliffs and the golf course. The state had provided it because several rich and influential Floridians maintained summer homes near the country club: trim, brown log cabins, or rather, log mansions, with orderly shrubs and flowers and wide, clean lawns. Expensive, well-crafted masonry walls lined the banks, and the trees were cared for by yardmen brought in by the owners. But this zone of affluence was small. The gravel ended shortly past an old Indian burying ground near Wild Cat. A farmer with several hundred acres lived past this point, but since he was a Republican the state kept the road poorly. Past his drive, the state rarely put an earth machine on the road. No wealth resided at Wild Cat.

From where she stood on the hill, Loretta could see the fields in the valley. Already some of them had been plowed, and from the

3

mountain the dark parallelograms, rhomboids, and squares patterned the drab land. Each man cut his field according to the lay of his property and the sway of his mood, and there was no rhyme or form. Bare wintered timber ran halfway down the nearer ridges, and between the fields and timber lay scrubby pasture of varied angle, roll, and slant. The drains that flowed from springs in the pastures were marked by stunted, gray brush. Here and there in the valley rose far, thin columns of smoke, where farmers burned tobacco beds. The scents of burning grass, weeds, and leaves came faintly up the mountain.

Far across the ridge in Hollytown the quitting whistle blew at the tannery. It was a brief blast since it was Sunday, but the echoes ran raggedly and vanished abruptly into the coves.

She listened. The sound disintegrated, like a soul expiring.

Quitting time. Walton's day was in at the tannery. Now he could come home to her.

A sudden bright bird song sounded in the brush near her. She turned to look.

March 21, 1932—the first day of spring. For once the Appalachian weather seemed to keep with the calendar. Out of the chill wind some warmth arose. The bird sang and fluttered about busily. Clearly winter had ended and spring was arriving on schedule.

Still their voices intruded. Loretta strained to hear if they were discussing her, but there was only the rise and fall, ebb and flow of their low, sinuous dialect. She could not distinguish the words. A bolt of pain made her kneel quickly and grab at her sides. She almost lost consciousness, but she did not think the baby was coming yet. She shook her head, the vertigo passed, her senses returned.

—Big Boy's low, rumbling cough. He laughed deep in his chest. His big hands rolled tight cigarettes, but he licked them too much and they never burned well, so he had to suck hard on them with great thick lips which smacked and hissed as he smoked. The voices, high, low, ever ranging the octaves. Now woodsmoke from Mrs. Guffey's fireplace diffused in the stirring air, and the breeze lifted the spruce boughs nearby like great, green fans. The early odors of the older woman's cookery rode in the air, then the wind rose and brought the wild earthy aromas of spring aborning. Shadows from clouds passed over the valley, and the touch of moisture was in the air.

4

Loretta's pan was filled with greens and she was resting when her husband crossed Hame Tree Gap and started up the road toward her. She watched his wide, lurching, mountaineer's gait. His dark hair fell in careless, curved bangs over a thin, serious brow. His overalls were faded from many washings, and the lard bucket he used for a lunch box swung wide as his shoulders rocked in the slight rhythm of his stride. He walked quickly up the rocky, rutted road to her and set his pail on the ground. Then he ran his hand across her stomach and patted the hump of it.

"Not long now," she said, suddenly bright of face.

His eyes filled with her new light.

"Tonight?" he asked.

"I think so."

He bent to her, kissed her gently, rubbed her long dark hair.

"You been picking salat? Bending over won't hurt the baby, will it? Is it a boy, you reckon?"

Her mood shifted. She nodded sadly.

"Listen, if you just knew what I have to go through here," she said.

Walton was quiet, watchful. "Has she said something to you?"

"No, no . . . ."

"Well, what's wrong, then?"

"You know what she thinks. She'll not forgive or forget."

She began crying, and he patted her awkwardly. He looked through the gray, stark trees and the far plowed fields, then he guided her gently to the house.

She would not eat at the table with the others this day, so Walton carried a plate to her in their bedroom. She ate, listening grimly to the ceaseless family conversation. Then she felt the baby's first serious struggle to escape the womb. Her outcry brought them all. Mrs. Guffey arrived first, patted the girl tentatively. For a moment in her pain, Loretta's perception shifted, and she saw that her mother-in-law's soft, wrinkled face was devoid of judgment and her gray eyes had turned into green glitters of alarm.

Walton came. He was calm, masterful, efficient:

—"All right, here, now. Let her lay back. Everything's going to be all right . . ."

Then he wheeled about, eyes wild, unreasoning.

—"God damn it," he shrieked, "get her a glass of hot water."

He whirled again and banged his head into a doorjamb. Big Boy raced for the kitchen. He returned immediately with a sloshing cup of scalding water.

"What is this for?" Mrs. Guffey asked incredulously.

Big Boy's thick lips parted. He rolled stricken eyes and ran his fingers through the early gray in his long pompadour.

"By God, Mama, he asked for it," he replied, chastened.

Walton rubbed his forehead.

"Women with childbirth need hot water, don't they?" he demanded.

Loretta watched them fearfully, her face drawn and wet. Her eyes were bright with pain, and her breath drew down hard and deep.

"I'm going to get the doctor. I mean right now," Walton said. Instead, he removed the owl-globe from the lamp and lit the wick. Then, unaccountably, he dashed the globe to the floor and smashed it. "God damn it to hell," he shouted.

His mother stared reproachfully at him. She went to a back room and brought out another globe, placed it on the lamp, and removed it from the vicinity of her sons. Big Boy stood in the door, his eyes uneasy in a moon-full face. Night deepened. Big Boy licked his lips. Edith turned to him.

"Go!" she commanded. "Go get the midwife. Get her mother. The time is upon her, man."

Big Boy was rooted to the floor. His head, shoulders, and torso turned to go, but his feet and legs were frozen. Walton bent over Loretta, pale.

"Go, I said," Edith yelled.

"I'm going for the doctor," Walton said, raising himself from the bed. "I don't want a midwife. I want Dr. Rawson up here."

At the door he turned again.

"Will she be all right? Oh good God Almighty, Mama, will she be all right?"

Mrs. Guffey nodded with a slightly bemused expression. "Yes, she's going to have a baby, that's all."

Big Boy grew calm. Excitement never remained with him long.

"You go get the doctor, Bud, and I'll go after the midwife. Loretta, do you want your mama to do it?" he asked.

"No, no," she gasped. "It's bad luck."

Edith's eyes were guarded. She stared at Big Boy. Walton pushed past him and ran up the trail. Big Boy shifted from one foot to the other. The women ignored him for a moment, then finally Edith turned to him.

"Git gone," she hissed. "Go git somebody to help."

He trotted heavily up the hill and out the road to Hame Tree Gap, then stopped.

"Hell," he said. "Bud's gone for a doctor. That's enough."

He pondered the darkness a moment. Then he stared at the far scattered lights in the valley at Allen's Creek. Granny McNabb? Too far. Powers beyond his control took over and he resigned himself to them. He turned and hurried up the narrow, muddy, and rutted road that went to Wild Cat Cliff. A mile later he was sweating hard as he lumbered up to a clearing where a large and longish cabin sat.

A man rose up from a squatting position beside the dark trail, like a snake striking upward toward the sky, then hovered quietly in the night before him.

"Ho! Big Boy, that you?"

Big Boy backed a step, put his hands on his sides, and breathed a moment. He sensed others about him in the night.

"Earl, tell you what. Let me have about a quart, I guess."

Earl's voice floated through the night, a power. "Mama, bring us a little jar of that best out here."

The old woman came to the door, held a jar up to the yellow lamplight behind her, and shook it.

"Good bead on it," Earl said.

"Well, pour me a glassful to last me a spell," Big Boy said. "Them women at the house will worry you to death."

"What are they doin'?" one of Earl's brothers asked.

"Wah! Loretta's having her baby. You know how they get."

Earl's mother brought the quart, wiping it with her apron. Her daughters had come with her. She handed the jar to Big Boy.

"A glassful for me, I said," Big Boy reminded her. One of the girls ran to bring the glass. Big Boy unscrewed the cap from the jar, and liquor passed down his rumbling throat.

"A baby? On Earl's birthday!" Mrs. Skiller said in wonder. "H'it's a sign, shore enough."

Big Boy handed Earl a rumpled dollar bill.

"Ah no. No no," Earl politely protested. "Not on the night you'uns is a-havin' a baby."

"I ain't havin' it. Walton's havin' it. Here," Big Boy said, holding

7

the dollar out. "You have to make a living, too. I got a good job at the tannery."

Earl took the dollar. Big Boy turned to leave.

"Wait'll I git my stuff and I'll go with you," Mrs. Skiller said. She ran in the door and wrapped a shawl around her head.

"You done any midwifing?" Big Boy asked.

"She's done some," Earl said. "She's a pretty good hand at it. Ain't Loretta's mama a good midwife?"

"Yeh, but she don't want her. Walton's gone for a doctor."

"Well, why didn't he go git her mammy?" a brother asked. Big Boy now took a deep draught from the jar.

"Hell, Bud wants a real doctor."

"Wait thar jist a minute, now," Mrs. Skiller said. "They'll need me."

Big Boy frowned. There was trouble somewhere in this.

"H'it's Earl's birthday too. I want to be there," she said.

"Well, I don't know if they'll want anybody to read signs," Big Boy said apprehensively. "Mama and Bud is funny about that sometimes."

"Yes, they will want it, too. Ever'body acts like they h'ain't interested, but all of 'em are. They want to know," she said and bounded across the yard. "Send one of the boys atter a preacher," she commanded.

"Do they want a preacher, ye reckon?" Earl asked.

Big Boy swung his head around with a reckless toss.

"Hell yes, git anybody that wants to come," he invited generously.

Big Boy and Mrs. Skiller slid, staggered, and lurched down the slick road. The weather came on now. Clouds gathered on the darkened ridge, and cold mist blew through bare trees. The old woman stopped frequently and stared intently at the trees whipping in the wind. She shook an old shot-pouch made from bobcat skin and filled with a collection of bones, fur, bird claws, frog skins, and items not readily identifiable. A sense of mission lay upon her. In fifteen minutes they reached the Guffey home.

Big Boy barged through the door, leaving Mrs. Skiller outside, where she stood faintly visible in the lamplight. Edith stared out at the spectral crone.

—There or not there?

Then she stared angrily at her husband. Mrs. Guffey came out

8

of the bedroom. Her eyes fell upon the old woman through the window. Displeasure spread across her face.

"By damn, you come in here a minute, Big Boy," Edith commanded.

He bit his wide lip, went with them into the dining room.

"Why did you bring her here?" Mrs. Guffey demanded. Trapped, he cast his eyes about.

"Well, good God Almighty, Mama, you said you wanted her."

"I never said anything like that in my life."

"I said for you to get a midwife, not a witch-woman, for God's sake," Edith said.

"Well, she can read the signs. God A'mighty. God A'mighty, I say."

"Signs? Signs. Yes, and she can sell rotgut likker too, can't she?" Edith barked.

His mouth worked and he rumbled deeply in his chest.

"Well, she's here now. I didn't ask her to come. You better ask her to come in if you don't want them all mad as hell."

Mrs. Guffey went to the front door.

"Come in," she said. "I hope you're all right."

Mrs. Skiller nodded eagerly and skittered in, sidling around until she stood against the wall.

Edith turned to Big Boy and whispered, "I hope you at least brought us all a little drop while you was bringing. God, you didn't have to bring her."

Loretta screamed and Edith rushed to her.

Mrs. Skiller now revested herself with self-esteem and importance. She filled the room with all the vile strength of her presence, although her face was softened slightly by a subdued confusion. Her clothing was old wool, and she stank of many fireplaces. Later, when the clouds came lower and rained heavily and made the atmosphere denser, the reek of her grew even stronger and spread through the entire house until no nostril escaped it.

Silence fell upon the women. Weary with mood, Big Boy sat and ignored them. Then Walton strode through the door, followed by Dr. Rawson and a stranger upon whose fierce face an angry defeat was stamped. Fresh mud was caked up to the knees of the doctor's blue serge suit. The stranger was also muddy to his knees, and there was some mud on his trousers seat where he had fallen. Both men were out of breath. Dr. Rawson stared about awkwardly, then

9

followed Walton into the bedroom. The other man walked to the dining room table and held out his hand to Big Boy.

"I'm Paul Fortune," he said in a weak, breaking voice.

"Howdy do! I'm Big Boy Guffey," he said and looked at Fortune with large, troubled eyes which bespoke a lifetime of trying to be agreeable and being misunderstood at every turn.

Dr. Rawson stepped to the bedroom door. "Get the pot boiling," he commanded. Walton looked about in triumph and vindication. Mrs. Guffey quickly put a zinc bucket on the stove. Walton ran to the well, drew a bucketful, poured it into a small tub, and put it too on the stove. Big Boy filled two iron kettles and put them in the fireplace in the living room.

Rawson watched it all and leaned against the door.

"Good God!" he finally said.

"Well, how much do you want?" Walton asked.

"I just wanted you to make a pot of coffee, son. We might be up awhile," Rawson said and shrugged.

"Well, you're the doctor. Do something about Loretta," Walton said presently.

"There's a time to sow and a time to reap. In between there is the time to wait. It is not yet time to reap."

They drifted about aimlessly, settling into the quiet, slouched, and worrisome mood that fell upon them when they awaited births and deaths—a fixed, inviolate spell of silence. Mountaineers, they were fraught with vague apprehensions about their babies, fears born of lore and of old stories: babies and snakes and spiders; babies upon whose chests sat the cat, sucking the breath from little nostrils, emptying into the child the poisonous, purring catbreath; babies borne away by eagles; babies taken in the night by wandering spirits; babies born marked.

Mrs. Skiller spoke from her dim corner.

"I sent one of my boys to git a preacher."

Rawson turned, stared in myopic surprise.

"What the hell are you doing . . . ?" Then he shrugged in his thin, weary motion of resignation. "What do I care? What is it to me?"

He turned to Walton.

"A preacher?" he asked.

"I don't want no preacher. I didn't order no preacher," Walton said.

"Well, you're a-goin' to git one," Mrs. Skiller croaked.

"Yeah, I'm getting some of everything, ain't I," Walton said, letting his eyes rest blankly on her for a moment. He looked at the doctor, then at the stranger. Big Boy sat across the table from Paul Fortune, satisfied that his brother's anger was directed elsewhere. Edith ran out of the bedroom.

"She's soaking in sweat," she told Rawson.

Loretta screamed. Rawson cocked his ear for another. It did not come. He kept the silence, looked about at them. In the quiet and golden glow of the lamp they stared accusingly at him. He went to the bedroom—not for her but for them.

Indeed! Soaked in sweat. Right on time. He returned to the other room and held up his hand.

"Now listen and don't get excited," he said soothingly. "I am going to need a bit of warm water in a pan to wash my hands."

Nonetheless, several of them ran to the kitchen.

"Is the coffee ready?" Rawson asked without expression. Edith poured and brought it. Big Boy looked at Paul Fortune.

"Do you want a cup of good java?" he asked.

"What?"

"Coffee! Do you want some?"

Paul Fortune's face was uninterested, infinitely depressed. "No, man," he said, "I thank you kindly, but I do not want any coffee." There was a slight retching sound in his throat.

"Are you sick?" Big Boy asked. He asked it from the wisdom gained in a thousand drunken nights and mornings and the nights following the mornings.

"Yes, yes, I am very sick. The good doctor was treating me for a long-standing ailment when that slim little fellow barged in."

"Well, who asked you to come up here?" Big Boy asked inoffensively.

"They did not object. I will need that doctor the very moment you good people see fit to release him."

Then he trembled and licked his parched lips.

Rain sounded on the roof, washed down the windowpanes, and blew in wild spray across the porch and into the open front door. Mrs. Skiller listened, watched. Her red, sunken face, the same weathered, ageless face that she had passed on to her many children, held upon it the calm, unshakable assurance of a perception not given to many people.

11

"H'it's not time fer the child yet. I'll tell ye when. The signs are a-workin'. . . ." Her voice trailed off like a low, far wind.

Rawson glared at her.

"Why don't you get out the graveyard dust and the bones and skulls and let's have a little reading while we wait?" he said.

"Ye'll not laugh! No, ye won't," she said.

"I'm not laughing. Don't put any spells on me. All I wanted was for us to have the benefit of a vision or two while we're waiting," Rawson said.

They covertly studied Paul Fortune. He was immediately recognizable as an outlander, but there was also something else identifiable—a thing wild and uncontrollable, ungoverned and impetuous, mad. They made no secret harsh judgment of the man, these things being also a noticeable part of themselves.

Fortune sat in fever. His hands shook and his eyes were evasive. He made a few attempts at small talk but then ceased. A troubled silence came again over the house. Paul Fortune felt the silence and emptiness, as strange and gray and unmoving as time in a tomb. And in this misery he was acutely aware of the surreptitious glances of the others. Although they said nothing, their self-conscious avoidance of him suggested to him that he was alone and isolated in the universe.

Big Boy loudly slurped his coffee. Edith went to him and whispered, "Get me a tot of that stuff."

He waited a moment, rose heavily, and went to the back door with his cup. Then he returned to her and whispered, "What stuff?"

She stared at him. "What stuff? You know what stuff!"

"Say it. Say what it is."

She tossed her head in exasperation.

"That likker," she whispered archly.

"Aha. Now I understand."

"What are you up to?"

"Well, when the criticism starts later about this, I just want to be sure that you knew it was likker we was drinking and not well-water or grape juice or some such."

Then he went outside to get it. She met him in the kitchen and he handed her a cup. It was half full of corn liquor. She downed it clean and chased it with a dipper of water. Big Boy went to his seat, speculated on Fortune for a moment, then leaned to him and whispered hoarsely: "Would you like to have a little drink?"

Light came to Fortune's eyes for a moment. "Drink of what?"

"Likker."

"Yes indeed, man," he said, "I would. I truly would."

They rose and slipped furtively out the back door. When they returned, Paul Fortune was a changed man. He had a confident, almost smug, set to his jaw, and he was now ready to take an active interest in those about him. More particularly, he was ready to become better acquainted with his benefactor.

Edith was also more affable. She smiled at Fortune, and then she went and crouched beside Mrs. Skiller.

"Nearly time," the old woman said, recognizing the alcohol on Edith's breath. Rawson stared glumly at Mrs. Skiller. Then Loretta screamed again. Mrs. Skiller smiled enigmatically, her secrets her own, and turned her ancient face to the flames in the fireplace. Rawson strode impatiently to the bedroom and shut the door behind him. Walton stared at the door. His mother came to him, took his hand and rubbed it. In his need he allowed it and did not pull away.

There was a knock. Edith opened the door, and they could see one of the younger Skiller boys there. He entered, smiling shyly and foolishly, followed by the Reverend Millard Wharton. He and the Skiller boy were wet, and the preacher was wheezing. The preacher stared about in exaggerated curiosity, his heavy red face as open and friendly as that of a politician. Then quickly and silently Earl Skiller slipped through the door, a brief shadow, and squatted in the darkness beside his mother's chair. Only Walton saw his entrance.

Walton blinked once. Skinny Skillers, the whole bunch. Bloody bones and stringy meat. Raw hell and misery in their eyes. Bones and sinew. That severe landscape of Wild Cat Cliff in their souls. Walton nodded at the preacher and the boy, then went to Earl and bent to shake his hand. Distillery odors rose from Earl—faint, lingering, the aroma of mash, still-beer, and alcohol.

By damn, he got a run off in cold weather, thought Walton. In his daily coming and going to and from his job he had not seen smoke. Cagey, quiet Earl.

Still holding Walton's hand, Earl rose. It was the greeting of men who did not fully understand each other's way but who understood each other's strength—the handshake of two family heads.

"Now, h'it's nearly time," whispered Mrs. Skiller, her voice high with drama and strange authority. Paul Fortune stopped his talk with Big Boy and smiled at her.

"March twenny-first," she said. "Same day and time as Earl was born. Something to think about."

"Well, I say," Fortune interjected, respectfully enough and with interest, "do you read the stars, madam, may I ask?"

"Read stars and ever'thing when I start reading," she said, childishly emphatic.

"Now, I am a man who has some interest in astrology and other occult studies," Fortune began pompously.

Mrs. Skiller's loose lips worked like rubber. Her eyes cut about as though Fortune embarrassed her.

"Shet up!" she spat.

The wind rose suddenly and howled across the lip of the chimney stones. A mighty blast of thunder shook the house and rattled the windows. Mrs. Skiller leaped to her feet. Her chair banged against the wall, and she took their attention. All night they had been afraid to speak loosely, lest in this moment of fate's stress they make an accidental prediction that would come true. At such gatherings they feared their own fey tongues, and they skirted talk of death, sickness, and ill fortune. Yet now they waited to hear Mrs. Skiller. They tensed. Let it fall where it must.

"Thar!" she said as the thunder rolled away to eastern skies. "That's the sign I been a-waitin' on."

Their faces were sallow in the dim, golden light, and they lined the room like a congress of shapeless harpies. Fright and disbelief were upon almost every face. Walton was only uncomfortable; his mother, irritated. Earl's face framed a faint, polite smile. He was slightly embarrassed by his mother, but he watched her and pondered the many mysteries of her.

"First thunder of the year," the Reverend Wharton said.

Big Boy's eyes opened wide with awe and danced brightly with liquor. Paul Fortune wedged his way forward and stared incredulously at the old woman.

The noises from the bedroom hinted that birth was imminent.

"Oh God in heaven. Preacher, pray!" implored Edith.

"Oh Heavenly Father, we ask . . . ," he began, stuttered, then blurted, ". . . first thunder of spring wakes up the snakes, e'god."

A shudder ran through them. They turned to Mrs. Skiller.

"I can tell ye now what ye're a-goin' to say," the preacher announced. "He'll be mean and devilish. Born under a snake sign and marked, mean and bound fer the penitentiary if he ain't killed first."

Anger ran through them. Earl's eyes narrowed, and he fixed them on the preacher. Walton stepped forward, doubled up his fist, and stuck it out so the preacher could see it. The Reverend Wharton shut up. Mrs. Skiller's eyes glittered. The spell of conjuration and interpretation was upon her. Her head went around, lopping loosely on her shoulders. Her hands trembled and she shook the pouch. Big Boy unaccountably grabbed the preacher and shook him.

"Do something about it, God damn it," he yelled.

The preacher held up his hands to quiet him, his eyes fastened on the crone. Lightning flashed, cracked sharply into a tall pine on the ridge. The wind rose and pressed against the windows. Rain came in driven waves. The old woman weaved about, powers pouring through her. She mumbled things unintelligible.

"See!" shouted the preacher. "She's speaking in tongues. That ain't against the Bible. All she does, everything she does, is found right in the Good Book."

Mrs. Skiller turned and stamped her foot toward the fireplace, as if to intimidate the flames. She tottered across the floor toward the kitchen, then turned, ran to the front door, flung it open, and stared outside. The lamp blew out—maybe from the wind, maybe from a spirit. The watchers drew in their breath as one and stared aghast at her wild skeletal frame limned in the doorway by lightning. The wind roared like a demented beast and swept through the house, blowing out the lamp in the kitchen. Now they had only the small dancing light from the fireplace and the blinding lightning. Mrs. Skiller went out into the storm.

"Jesus Christ!" Paul Fortune breathed. He felt a strange and contrary force crackling in the room. "God Almighty damn." He felt he might pass away at the worst, join the belief at the very best. He raced to the door to watch her, pushing the others out of the way.

She rocked about in the sudden white lights from the sky and stared at the ridge above the house. Her head was cocked expectantly, her shawl flapped straight behind her in the wind, and she pointed toward the crest. She staggered further into the yard, where the brightest bolt illuminated her. She cackled in a low, knowing manner, then began to laugh. The terrified pack stood at the door.

15

"Thar!" she yelled above the wind. "I know something now."

She stumbled through them to get inside. They seated her in the chair nearest the fireplace. Big Boy rushed to the fire, took out a flaming brand, and tried to relight the lamp, but he merely smudged the wick, burned his hand, and dropped the torch onto the floor. Earl kicked it back into the fireplace.

"I will not believe this in the American people," Fortune whispered in great strain. "No, by God, I'll not believe it."

They kicked and spread small coals all over the room. Then, amidst billows of smoke, they stamped them out. Walton and Mrs. Guffey stared in glum disbelief, in quiet, deep outrage. The lamp remained unlit. Mrs. Skiller's face was ashine in the firelight, and her eyes glittered in the leaping flames. They crowded in close to hear.

"I declare, I never seed one like this'n before, and I don't believe I could live through another'n. Why, look at the goose bumps on me . . . that means some of the greater powers is near."

She held forth a bony arm in the firelight. The spell was off. She was now nothing more than a friendly, talkative old woman.

"No, t'ain't snakes altogether. But snakes is allus a good sign. First thunder wakes 'em up is right, preacher, but looky here at all the things that went with it. . . ."

They stared, even Walton and his mother.

"That rain is warm, warmest I ever seed this side of June. It'll bring forth the things of the earth early—maybe early enough to get 'em killed by frost."

She stopped and stared about, her eyes profound.

"Remember, thar's allus frost to come from nowhar and kill the growin' buds, the growin' spirit. That has its place, a test of the earth."

Paul Fortune felt the liquor wearing off and the shakes returning. With the protection of the alcohol gone, he began to worry that this night would be more than he could stand.

Mrs. Skiller had her pouch out, shaking it vigorously.

—The skull of a squirrel, the paw of a rat.

—The claws of a bird, found in a vat.

—Dirt from the grave of a man long dead.

—A stone-root dug from a caved-in shed.

"First thunder, all right. Snakes awake, and the devil laughs in some people's heads. Think on this, though, and what it means.

16

That lightning was clost in. H'it's a visit, I tell ye. Who owns the lightning? Come on preacher, who owns it?"

The Reverend Wharton stared at her in dumb fear, his mouth slack.

Paul Fortune rose to participate, shakily. "You'll get no answer from him," he jeered. Every face turned to him, and in that darkened room, dense with emotion, he felt himself in a den of serpents, venom injected from slit, angry eyes.

"The better powers own the earth," she said. "H'it's a visit. Not only does it wake up the snakes; now add that and a warm rain and what do ye get?"

They stared.

"I'll tell ye more signs. Born in fury, live in fury, die in peace? Yes. More things to say. We're unwindin' like a clock spring toward death. Ye hear this house lift and ride in the wind? Did the wind bring the baby? Did the moon? Think on it . . . what does the wind bring?"

"Good Christ! What is this?" Paul Fortune whispered.

"I went into the storm to see if I'd live or die at this young'un's birth, and as ye can see, I live. The storm wuz all around me, and out of it I heard a child with a loud scream. The storm brought it, you see, and it howled back at the storm like the storm wuz h'it's mama and she wuz a-leavin' h'it stranded here.

"But the best and clearest sign, I tell you . . . I went into the storm and lived and looked around and I saw seven big lights . . . seven is a good number, ye see . . . and I saw other lights and heard tongues in the distance and watched strange faces a-meltin' and a-runnin' together in the clouds. . . ."

"Jesus!" Paul Fortune repeated.

And in that space of time, within the strong, wet reek of the old woman, they waited for her to tell. And in that curious ringing voice that carried rough wild poetry and forecasts beyond their ken, they tried to read her answer before she uttered it, and they were afraid of her mind and spirit and soul.

"Trees! Plenty of trees. Hard times and darkness on the mountain. Then what did I see?"

The unholy burnt stink of the woman before them, with stringy hair and raw skeletal face . . . . They waited. She rubbed the pouch absently and spat into the fire.

"She's not conjuring, she's creating," Paul Fortune said. "She's making it up as fast as she can go."

There was no seat for a critic at this performance. He fell silent before their stares. "It's all the same," he offered lamely.

"Beyond the trees I saw the sky, and it was a clear sky beyond the line of trees, and the light is thar yet. Go see fer yeself. Beyond the trees is the light."

They crowded to the high window. The dark clouds rolled. The sky past the trees on the ridge was clean with a filtered light.

"Now c'mere, Walton. C'mere, son," she said. He walked reluctantly to her.

"Ye've got a son. He's been teched. Somehow crazy or wild, I dunno, but he's been teched by sich as I never have seed in my life. And he's gonna be a good 'un and a bad 'un and I can't tell ye what all, but a boy."

The lamp flamed high. They turned to see Rawson holding it. He stared at the old woman a moment, then at Walton.

"You've got a leather-lunged boy, Walton," he said. "He's runty but he's loud."

Then he turned to Mrs. Skiller. "What the hell? You had a fifty-fifty chance to guess what it was. What would you say now if it had been a girl?"

"H'it worrent," she cackled, "besides, the preacher predicted it too."

Mrs. Guffey brought coffee for Rawson. He sat to sip. The others listened for a while to the small cries from the bedroom. In a while they drifted out and were gone. Rawson lowered his cup and looked at Mrs. Guffey.

"How did she know?" he asked.

Big Boy's hulk filled the doorway. The rain pattered gently.

"If you think she's guessing, then she always guesses right," Big Boy said. "Everybody knows she reads signs good."

Rawson snorted halfheartedly, shrugged. He pulled a notebook from his pocket and looked at his watch.

"Walton, how long have you and Loretta been married?"

"Why do you need to know?"

"The birth certificate."

"Two months," Walton said, fiercely candid, defensive. "I don't think that needs to be on a birth certificate, does it?"

"No, I was just curious," Rawson said awkwardly. He turned in his chair.

"Where in hell is that man I brought with me?" he asked Big Boy.

Big Boy stared evasively out the kitchen door.

"I got him another cup of rotgut, and he said he didn't need no goddam doctor and took off with the youngest Skiller. I guess he'll try to get more from them, but he won't get it. Earl don't sell it to jist anybody."

Walton went to Loretta's bed and stared at his child. Loretta smiled drowsily among the old secrets of motherhood. A small fear and lostness came to the face of Mrs. Guffey as she watched them from the kitchen. Now he was making his own family. They were young, and she was nearing sixty.

"Well, I'm glad the first one was a boy," she said, but Rawson was asleep. She covered him with a quilt and went into her own room. When she looked in on him in an hour, he had gone.

2

IN THE WINTER before the birth of the child Logan, Paul Fortune
had staggered stuporously aboard a bus in Asheville, a ticket for
Atlanta in his coat pocket. Clumsily he placed his bag on the rack
overhead, then dropped like a shot buffalo into a seat and closed
his eyes, wheezing and gasping noisily. Again he was trying to leave
Asheville, where he had arrived three weeks earlier in an alcoholic
daze. His purposes after that first arrival, however, had led him to
depart for New York to find and persuade a publisher to advance
him funds on a writing project yet to be announced, and as a matter of fact, yet to be conceived. But he had left the train in Rich-
mond and journeyed by bus to Newport News for no reason he
was ever able to recall. There he came perilously close to sobering
up, somehow overcame that, and entrained for Knoxville. A few
days of hard drinking in a hotel there convinced him that he should
go again to Asheville. But he was arrested for public drunkenness
within a block of the Asheville depot. A night in jail there per-
suaded him that he had better keep traveling until his mind could
come together again.

His flight to the mountain country of the Appalachian region
had begun on the bright wings of drink. He sought a new beginning, away from his latest wife, away from journalism, and away
from the early fears of age coming on. Of his recent days he recalled only the quick, warped images of his varied conveyances
and the flash and flow of dark wintered southlands outside the
windows of bus and train.

Destinations lost and fading. Promises missed, hopes shattered.

Paul Fortune was the only son of a businessman who had risen
from the near-poverty of a prairie homestead to considerable afflu-

ence and influence in Chicago. But when Paul was nine, his father ran away with a woman who worked for him. His mother then had to move her son back to her own family of old uncles and aunts. She spent the rest of her days hating her husband, but Paul went on loving him, even after he forgot what he looked like.

After high school he went to college and studied literature. No sooner had he graduated than the World War started, and he joined the rush of idealistic youth toward the fight. He failed the physical but became a roving correspondent for two magazines and a newspaper. Afterward, he did some teaching and drifting, and somewhere along the line he began taking the big lessons from life. It was as if earlier in life he had failed an important aptitude test, but had remembered the questions well and went into life daily on the alert for the answers. When he finally began learning from life, he found that every idea, concept, theory, practice, was open to question if only one asked the intelligent questions.

He did not realize it when liquor began dragging him down. He knew only that the researching and writing had drained him, and he could not bring his mind to the cutting edge he had sustained for so long. He drank heavily and cultivated the company of people who praised him lavishly. He accepted the praise, grew addicted to it and to the liquor. The praise went away; the liquor remained.

He supported himself for a while by alternating between the pulps and some intellectual periodicals. But he traveled a million streets and worked his way down to newspapers. His disillusionment was complete.

A cold rain sifted down lightly from dreary low Appalachian clouds as the bus pulled out. Passengers left it at small way stations west of Asheville. The mountains grew bigger, crowded closer together. Fortune sat in near delirium, neither sleeping nor awake, but aware of things external and internal. Suddenly he rose, pulled the stop cord, and stood unsteadily in the aisle as the bus slowed. The driver switched on the overhead lights and stared thoughtfully at him in the mirror.

"Here! Let me off here," Fortune pleaded. The rain was muffled on the roof, but it ran thickly down the windows and windshield, where the wipers splashed it off. With the full, weary corporate courtesy of his busline, the driver sidestepped his way back through the aisle and pulled the bag from the rack. Now he could smell the alcohol on Fortune's breath.

"Your ticket is for Atlanta," the driver said carefully. Other passengers raised their heads and looked over seat backs at them.

"Well, is this not Atlanta?" Fortune demanded.

"No sir, we are just barely past Clyde, North Carolina. It's a long way to Atlanta. It'll be daylight when we get there," the driver said, pausing with the suitcase.

"Well, let me off here, then. To hell with Atlanta," Fortune said.

"If that's what you want, all right. If you stay aboard, you'll have to be quiet. I believe you've had too much. Go to sleep and everything will be all right."

Fortune suddenly whimpered and tears ran down his cheeks. "My friend, everything will never be all right again." Profound ruin blotched his face.

"All right, then. Be quiet. The others . . ."

"God damn the others."

"Now, now."

"I said God damn the others. I want off now."

The driver looked toward the front of the bus, where the wipers slowly rubbed back and forth across the glass. "Don't get off now," he pleaded.

"Yes, yes, right now, by God. I want off now," Fortune said, his obstinacy strengthened by the driver's compassion. He wrenched the bag free of the driver's hand and bulled past him. The driver sidled up the aisle behind him, opened the door, then slumped tiredly in his seat.

"I knew there would be trouble with him," he told the woman in the seat immediately behind his. She stared primly at Fortune, then looked away.

"Do trains run through this town?" Fortune asked petulantly from the darkness outside.

"Yes sir, but I don't know their schedule. We compete with them."

"Is it raining here, by God?"

"If you feel something running down your face, that is rain," the driver offered. "Why don't you get back on the bus?"

"No, you move on from here. Get, I say, and get now."

The driver closed the door, then opened it again hopefully. Fortune glared at him. The door remained open. Fortune thrust a defiant chin foward. Wind blew sheets of rain across him.

"Move that goddam bus out of my way," he shouted angrily.

Slowly the door closed, and the motor whined upward through

its revolutions, but the bus did not move. The door opened again, and the driver peered out.

"I wish you'd get aboard."

"I said move. I'll never ride another bus if I live forever. Why, to throw a man off here in this downpour . . . ," he said piteously. The bus moved thirty yards and stopped.

"Move, move, move, God damn you, move," Fortune shouted. The bus moved away slowly, gearing up. Its several taillights glimmered, leaving brief ruby tracks upon the glistening dark pavement. Fortune stood in the rain, staring vacuously into the darkness, blinking rainwater from his eyes.

"What the hell?" He unbuttoned his pants and relieved himself. Then he took a drink from a pint bottle. Alone? He shook his head, then followed unsteadily along the road where the bus had gone. The rain remained steady, but it came down lightly. The chill of wind lay upon him, so he drank all the liquor as he stumbled on. Two hours and many hills later he walked tiredly down a slope, past a cemetery, and toward a lake. False dawn glowed weakly through a mist. The roadside was wet and slick with limp sycamore leaves fallen from great, crooked trees. The earth was healthy here. By now he was filled with self-loathing. The whiskey had burned away, and the shakes were coming on.

Dawn spread weakly in the rain. Paul Fortune was haggard, haunted, and wet. He trudged down the long, sloping street past the hospital at the east end of Wadenton. The light was stronger when he stopped on the sidewalk in front of the courthouse. He set his bag on the pavement and stared about. The low buildings of the small business district were outlined in the early light and fog, and they offered scant contrast to the tone of the weather.

"God!" he moaned, turning and glancing back. He saw that he had passed a small hotel less than a block away. It did not cheer him to see it.

He registered, scrawling his name in shaky, illegible starts.

Paul Fortune.

He contemplated, then scribbled an address.

Chicago.

A small, humped man in an ancient brown suit stared tightly at him across the desk, held out a key, smiled blankly, and pointed toward the stairs. An A-Model clanked by outside. Fortune stared blearily at the little man, who said, "Second floor. It's all there is right now."

"All right. It's all right. Absolutely. I'll go up."

Chilled and wet, he was out of liquor. His arrogance faded as he once more headed into a hole in hell's bleak system of loneliness to shake out one more drunk.

Or die unknown, unmourned.

The following days were spent in purging his system of the worst of the poisonous remnants of the booze. He noted from a remote and debilitated outpost in his mind that the alcohol did not vacate the premises of his body in good will and cheer. Scorching moments dragged it out of the entire system forcibly, and tiny knives and torches left searing wounds along the nerves. Each hour required a month to pass, and strange, dangerous thoughts were born every other minute. The abyss opened at his feet, and wide gulfs lay between his bed and the table that held the most precious water pitcher. Creatures of dense mass, of undefined form, expanded and shrank and moved ponderously under his bed with muted throatchoke noises. Sudden lost voices rang out from the empty closet, and small, extremely bright lights winked in far, empty corners of the room. One moment his skin was wet with sweat; the next it was dry and scaly, and flame looped from his pores.

The third day was the worst. He was convinced that the blow-hole of a whale had appeared in the top of his skull, and with each breath and pulse he felt portions of his brain being spewed onto the ceiling. Yet, with the convoluted reasoning of long experience, a small hope appeared. Relief intertwined with agony. He knew he must now begin the dreaded, epic effort, the long march to clear himself of alcohol.

On the fourth day lucidity returned, held its own, and began gaining. Fortune dressed but did not dare scrape his face with a razor. He slunk guiltily down the steep street at the side of the courthouse, crossed the railroad tracks, and entered the Royal Cafe. Feeling like a creature in a dim aquarium, he struggled to read the ancient menu. He duly noted that wine and beer were available, but he did not answer that invitation. He ate some soup and crackers. With a little nourishment down, he returned to his room and fell clumsily into bed for another night of vivid dreams. The next day he began to believe that he might live on.

He wrote a letter to the railway agent in Asheville, asking in his most ingratiating tone that his three steamer trunks be sent to the Wadenton depot. They were two weeks in coming. In that time he wrote to banks in Milwaukee, Chicago, and Pittsburgh, requesting a transfer of his funds to a Wadenton bank. New hope. A new place. Things fell quickly in line for him. He had the energy and zest for a new beginning. None of the old things could restrain him. Geography made the difference.

During those first weeks he did not enter into social intercourse. He stayed close to his room, occasionally lapsing into intense self-recrimination. After some time he began to scout about. In his meandering he found the even smaller town of Hollytown, which bordered with Wadenton. He liked the feel of the town, and by the time the trunks arrived and money was deposited, he had rented a small house near the center of the village, with an option to buy. Taking form in him was that most treacherous and unreliable urge to begin writing again. He contemplated it one night, and the idea somehow raised to life certain latent miseries. He saw that he had come all this way to find himself marooned once again. The curse descended. Fleeing to a strange and distant land, he had once again met himself.

In one of his trunks he came upon a pint of brandy. The discovery triggered a prolonged bender. The days slipped past in great, looping images. He found new friends at the Royal Cafe, equally as besotted, happy that he had money. Vivants. The last mindless week of his binge was spent with cronies in the brush around Green Knoll Cemetery. Fortune got home, asked someone to go for a doctor. The doctor refused to come. At last, swept by a tide of unaccountable, final energies, Paul Fortune washed ashore in Dr. Rawson's waiting room, where he endured the curious, frank stares of patients with bona fide, respectable ailments. His knees danced uncontrollably from time to time, and he sat upon his hands so that no one could see how they trembled. Each time he turned his raw eyes toward the other patients, he caught them watching him from knowing eyes. At last he turned to a mountain woman— worn, gaunt, browned—in the next chair.

"The weather certainly has been grand, hasn't it?" he asked in a voice that started hoarsely and broke into an unrecognizable squeak. She stared at him for a moment, pursed her lips thoughtfully, rubbed her forearm.

"Why, h'it h'ain't been nothin' but rain fer three solid weeks an' h'it snowed some yisterdy," she said. Others stared at him. He stood, swayed, stared about.

"Hell, where can I get a drink of water?" he asked.

"Ye'll have to wait till ye git into the doctor's office. He's got a sink in there," the woman said.

He sat again, despaired, did not care. Then he leaped up and ran through the door. The doctor was lancing a boil on an old man's neck. He looked up, startled. Fortune ran to the sink and drank deeply from the tap, using no glass. The doctor did not move or speak as Fortune stumbled back out again and took his seat.

"Oh Christ! I'm dying. At last I'm dying," he gasped. Sweat streamed from his scalp, and the odor of it was rich with alcohol. He looked at the woman beside him and saw that her face was not completely devoid of sympathy.

"Clean out ye bowels and eat some sugar or honey," she suggested. "That'll give ye some power, but ye'll have to suffer a sartin amount anyhow."

He looked up, saw Rawson standing in the door. The physician nodded curtly at Fortune, then beckoned the woman inside.

"Come in, Minnie, and I'll take a look at you."

She was in the office only a few minutes. As she passed back through the waiting room, she nodded to Fortune. Darkness came before Rawson waved Fortune in. He sat in a chair beside Rawson's desk and turned resentfully to the doctor.

"I wanted you to come to my room this morning," he said.

Rawson studied him tolerantly.

"You do make house calls, don't you?"

"Most of my practice is house calls."

"Well, why didn't you come to see me?"

"One of my exceptions is drunks. I don't make house calls on drunks. I rarely treat them unless they've been cut up or shot," Rawson said. He made no move to examine his patient; he merely stared at him as if he were trying to decide whether this case properly belonged to the practice of medicine.

"I'm as sick as any man you ever saw," Fortune croaked sullenly, his hands flying here and about.

"I know it. I just don't understand what all I know about it."

Rawson took his wrist, felt the erratic pulse, leaned back, and sighed.

26

"Take off your shirt," he commanded. Fortune fumbled with the garment, unbuttoned, rebuttoned, finally divested himself of it. Rawson put a stethoscope to his chest and listened, his brow furrowing deeper and deeper.

"What is it?" Fortune demanded apprehensively.

"That's the damnedest racket I ever heard in my life."

"Well, what do you think it is?"

"I thought it was a T-Model for a minute, then I thought it might be a grist mill."

"Can you do anything?"

"Truly, you may be dying."

"Don't try any bullshit on me. I'm a sick man. Do you think I'm in trouble?"

"I would be frank with a dying man. How often do you get drunk?"

"Not often."

"Yes, I see. Is not often something like every two months? How long do you stay drunk at a time?"

"Not long."

"Is what you call not long a month at a time?"

"Christ! Cut it out. What can you give me for it?"

"Do you know what's best for you?"

"Well, actually yes. A little morphine ought to help me across the worst of it."

Rawson stared at the wall a moment and shook his head. "You're worse off than I thought you were."

"It's probably the only way I can sleep."

"How long since you had a drink?"

"Three days."

Rawson walked to the cabinet, took out a pipe, and stuffed it with tobacco.

"What are you doing in this country?" Rawson asked.

"It's one place to be out of several million," Fortune said.

"What kind of trade do you follow?"

"Is that any of your business?"

Rawson shrugged. "You're quite touchy about it, aren't you?"

"I'm a writer."

Rawson leaned forward, interested. "Do you write now? Do you get published?"

Fortune glowered. "No," he said. "I'm a sick man now."

27

"Do you like your work?"

"It's frustrating most of the time."

"A man ought not to have to do what is frustrating."

Fortune stared dully at the wall.

"Is that why you drink?"

Fortune studied the floor, the wall, the disordered but curiously clean array of objects in Rawson's office. He shook his head sadly.

"Yes, part of it, I suppose."

"Can't you write now?"

"Maybe I can if I can get straightened out. I have to."

"Are you a man who suffers from depression?"

"Good God yes!" Fortune blurted, staring at the doctor dramatically.

"Well, do you know that liquor is not exactly a stimulant?"

"I don't want to be picked up. I want to be washed on out."

"Can you stop with one or two drinks?"

"If I want to."

"Do you ever want to?"

"No, never. I mean yes, man. Good God. Do I want to?"

Rawson had shown genuine interest and concern. Fortune laughed hollowly.

"I never want to stop once I get started."

"After it's over, do you feel like you've cleaned out your system of whatever was in there?"

"No, it's even dirtier in there. But it keeps the pain back for a time."

"And then do you write?"

Fortune slumped forward. "No, man. Not anymore."

"You might be interested to know that I try to write some, too," Rawson said, uncharacteristically modest. Fortune's head lopped forward on his chest, and he sighed.

Rawson became defensive. "I can write if I want to," he said.

"Yeh, you don't need a license for that, but you do need to do it with some skill or nobody will publish it. Publishers like to know they're going to make some money."

"Well, I want to be able to write well about something I know, and I know damn plenty."

"Is that a fact? Good! I'm interested in your writing. For your part, you might be interested to know that I'm dying. Give me some morphine."

"No."

"I have probably been dead for about three minutes now," Fortune said. "What I feel is not my muscles and nerves tightening, but rigor mortis. I'm the only man who ever had it alive. I can hardly wait to see how you treat rigor mortis. I've been on my way to hell for three or four minutes and you prattle on. Look, you could write a paper on my case and get it in medical journals. You can become famous on my case."

Then he abandoned his plea and looked at the doctor with cunning eyes.

"When do you write, doctor?" he asked calmly.

"I keep a diary. I write some every night. Sometimes I'm too tired, but I try to make some observations every day, and the time might come when I can piece it together."

"Oh, I see. The memoirs of a country doctor, eh? That sounds good."

"Do not patronize me in any way," Rawson said.

"Have I got your attention? Have I really captured your attention?" Fortune asked and held out his hand. "Look at that."

Rawson stared at it a moment. "What?" he asked.

"It's one of the early stages of decomposition. Sometimes it's hard to detect."

Then he trembled and bent his wet face into his hands. Misery returned in jolting force, hard upon his brain and nervous system.

"I wanted you to see about me at my home," he said petulantly.

"I told you, no. Not drunks."

"Why not, man?"

"Usually their homes are a stinking mess, but that's beside the point. I think it is probably good for them to experience the agony and humiliation of walking out into the light before the whole town."

"That's torture. That's sadistic."

"No, I'm a healer. It is therapeutic and it is reality. If you want to call that sadistic . . . but then, the time might come when you want to stop this, and an accumulation of embarrassments, humiliations, lost jobs and friends, lost family, and all the other things that go with drunkenness might add up, and one day you might decide it's not worth the price."

"Well, you don't know how deep it is with drunks, then," Fortune said.

"I want to know. You are articulate and maybe you can tell me something my other patients can't. You can learn very little by observation, in some matters."

"I will certainly be happy to discuss it sometime. Give me some drugs."

"No, but I'll give you something to help."

"Morphine, please."

"How often have you taken morphine?"

"Once. I've always been scared of it. A doctor gave me some once and it helped. But I'm scared now. I need sleep."

"You can't get morphine from me. Minnie told you the truth a while ago."

"What?"

"Clean your gut out and eat something to build up your energy. Then time will do it. Maybe your blood sugar is down. Eat some sugar or honey."

"You think Minnie knows something about it?"

"She knows. She's been married to a sot for twenty-eight years, and she knows that only the passing of time takes it away. Maybe you can learn that."

Rawson went to the cabinet, poured something into a beaker, and handed it to Fortune. "Drink 'er down," he said.

Fortune drained it. His lips wrapped each other and his throat tightened.

"Booze, by God!" he gasped.

"That's the only thing that will help, that I know of. Are you hallucinating?"

Fortune exhaled fiery fumes, shook his head.

"Liquor? This is yours?" he asked.

"Well, I take a drink now and then. Are you seeing things?"

"I expect to in the next couple of days," Fortune said.

"Do you have DT's often?"

"Once is too often."

Rawson arose, stiff and tired. "All right," he said. "Come back tomorrow and see me. Get a pint and try to come down slowly. Be careful where you get it. There's good liquor around here, and there's some of the world's worst."

"How well I know that, good physician," Fortune said, the appearance of slight health returning to his cheeks.

"All right. Give me two dollars."

"What? For one drink of booze?"

"For medical treatment, God damn it."

Fortune paid. It was at this point that Walton Guffey walked in, gaped about, and said:

"Come on. Loretta's having the baby."

Fortune frowned. The three of them left the office together. Rawson and Walton got in the A-Model. Then Rawson shouted at Fortune:

"Hey! C'mon. I might need you."

Fortune got in beside Walton. He looked out the window. The air was momentarily clean and chill. He saw some stars briefly.

Minnie was lying, he thought. Surely it has not been raining for three weeks.

3

APRIL CAME PALE and green. The season's promises swarmed like quick bees. The earth warmed. May heaved sap up, darkened the leaves, feathered soft the fern, fanned the fair and easy winds. Grass shot up, weed and vine uncoiled onto the rich soil. Rains came each day in June's first week, seeped into the rock and root. The heaviest rain fell on a Friday, roaring along the roof, and the wind gouted water in thick sheets off the eaves. Loretta listened, smiling inwardly on her secrets as the clean, wet air ran over her skin. She smelled anew the close and ancient odors of the house. She reclined sensuously on the bed, reached to the baby's crib, and gently stroked his face.

The fourth of eight children, Loretta had been close to her parents only for the eleven months it took the next child to arrive—cared for by a sister until she was old enough to begin the care of a younger one. To survive, she turned at last to defiance. Her life had been and would always be a struggle, because she was a struggler and had no other way. Survival was the main thing—survival with her exaggerated honor and stilted dignity, if possible, but if not, survival anyway.

Small, dark, and vivacious, she showed Indian blood. Often she shied away from those things of love she needed. Walton could tell her that he loved her, but she would not believe it. Yet she needed to hear it. One night while they courted, they got half drunk and happy at someone's house party, and she got pregnant. She was furious at herself and frightened because that was what her father had predicted for those girls who drank, smoked, danced, fixed up their hair, or used lipstick. When Walton had seen the depth of her hurt, he got protective, with a guarded pride in his prowess and virility. He proposed marriage. She fled, grew more unhappy, insisted that she was used goods. He followed and chased, then grew tired of it and moodily withdrew, and that alarmed her. She agreed to marry, found resistance in his mother. But after a while, with her grandchild in mind, Mrs. Guffey gave her consent, and they went to Jackson County and got married in the courthouse.

Now Loretta spent much energy each day cheerlessly protecting a private fragment of her spirit. She felt that it was slipping away and would be lost to her forever. Born at the wrong time, she had married into the wrong family. She had loved Walton; she had not meant to marry the family. She had not meant to live, to raise her child, in a house that was full of the past and excluded her.

The house was gray and weathered, and had but a few remaining paint flakes. The window and door facings had once been painted flat brown. The tread of the years had worn smooth the rough boards which floored the front and back porches.

Part of the back porch was enclosed with planking. This airy room was called the sideroom. It was littered with old clothing and with the records, black bag, shiny steel instruments, and old medicines from the late Dr. Guffey's veterinary practice. Numerous empty fruit jars were scattered about, and the odors from them were sharp and ancient.

A stovepipe in the kitchen ran from a wood range through the high ceiling. In the corner of that room sat a table of indefinite brown, and upon that sat an old ONT thread cabinet, which served as a silverware drawer. In the dining room was a great ugly table with swollen legs. Shelves were stacked high with cheap china and old crystal, and souvenir trash and valuable antiques were displayed with equal pride. A china closet smelled of old butter, cream, and clabber.

In a small bedroom off the dining room was a gray iron cot where the old woman slept. Her husband, the veterinarian, had drunk too much for too long and had come to the payment of it early one morning on this cot in his office in Wadenton.

Even in the room in which Walton and Loretta slept, the smell of history welled up, spilled over. On the wall hung an oval photographic enlargement of two women from another generation. A black desk was stacked with old candy boxes, tobacco tins, magazines. A long drape fell over a closet which held a musty trunk full of Confederate muster rolls and old coins. Mrs. Guffey's past lapped with dim tides into Logan's future. Ancient. Ancient.

The baby stirred as thoughts and images ran through his mind. Haunting reminders surfaced in the old brain's memory: faint slithering in the ancient of souls, a snake, a bird, a prowling wolf.

The cadenced voice of Mrs. Guffey came from the front room; the lazy wet snarl, snore, and wheeze of Big Boy smoking Prince Albert; again Mrs. Guffey in endless recital:

". . . did not hear from him then for fourteen years, Samantha told me. Porter was a strange, strange man. The very drawed picture of his daddy and the same—when he got mad he went straight for his pistol. Now Bascom always went after his man with a knife, and Bill was the one who settled with his fists. He said he didn't have any enemies until he got mad, then he was so anxious to get at whoever made him mad that he didn't have time to go look for something to kill them with. . . ."

Big Boy acceded with a rumble and a grunt. His stepmother's voice trailed on and on. Loretta surged with impatience, irritation. Family, family, all they ever talked about was family . . . hateful, hateful . . . . Endlessly absorbed in old names from other times, other places, they shut her out. Mrs. Guffey continued:

"Yes, it's a strange bunch. They've tried and tried down through the years to make good Christians out of them, but most of them never saw the light. . . ."

The baby blinked, yawned from under a tiny, wrinkled brow, watched the parade of time past the window, saw the light, the light, the light. . . .

Mrs. Guffey's voice again:

". . . now they're good and honest and they won't lie to you nor cheat you, but if you do 'em wrong they'll get you, especially if they're drinking. . . ."

The conversation in the front room ebbed and flowed. Big Boy left for a moment, and when he returned he was more talkative. He stopped his chatter occasionally to sing a verse of the Brown's Ferry Blues. Loretta, drowsing, caught the change, snapped to, and went into the front room.

34

The baby stirred, turned and raised his head, then fell back. He did not look at objects, rather at the way light struck objects and played over them. He saw only light and shades. In thin rims and coronas of light he found the world.

He stared out the window, listened in the flow of low noise and time and eventually heard the clank of stove-lids and pots. Time passed through him in a quick, full current, and he stared at the ceiling. The floor jarred heavily with steps and a great round and ruddy face floated over the cradle, came closer, and kissed the child. When the face left, the odor of alcohol lingered. He looked through the window at the flung rain. It spattered and ran on the pane. Then the early aroma of supper. The child drowsed.

A loud voice.

"God damn it, Big Boy. How much has she drunk?"

"Now, Bud. Buu . . . uuddd. She's all right." His voice was conciliatory, a low, heavy whine.

"Loretta, you're sitting here half drunk and that baby's in there . . . ."

Heavy footsteps to the box. Walton bent, searched the baby's face. He felt the diaper.

A shrill, angry voice.

"See? You think something's wrong? You better not come in here jumping on me. I've had about all I'll stand for, Walton. I warn you. You accuse me of drinking one more time and you'll just see what happens."

"Well, you have."

"Have not, no indeed. No indeedy." A giggle. "Have not. Have I, Big Boy?"

A low, indecipherable growl, neither this way nor that.

"Loretta, by God! Don't lie to me. Are you telling me what I smell or don't smell? I can see. Your eyes, the way you talk when you've been at it. Don't think I don't know—like you was the main star in a picture show or something."

She gritted her teeth, then screamed: "Shut up. Just shut up. Ask Big Boy. Go on, ask him."

"Well, he gave it to you. He keeps a jar handy. I was raised up with him, for God's sake, Loretta."

"You falsely accuse me one more time . . ."

"Don't get me mad, by God, Loretta."

"Oh no, what'll you do? Beat me up? That's how much there is to you. You heard him, Big Boy, you heard him threaten me. . . . Mrs. Guffey . . . ?"

"Loretta!" Mrs. Guffey admonished. "Try not to get so bothered. He didn't say anything like that to you."

"Mama, where did Big Boy put his liquor?" Walton asked.

"Bud! Buu . . . uuddd," Big Boy growled placatingly. "Wait a minute, Bud, and I'll get you a little horn if that's what you want."

"That ain't what I want, God damn it. I don't want her to have no more."

"Why, then she just won't drink anymore, will you, Loretta?" Big Boy pleaded. "Why can't we all have friendly drinks instead of fighting drinks? Why, let's all just feel good about it and forget all this."

"No, I won't drink anymore," Loretta sniffed. "I haven't had any to start with, and I want to put that in now. Have I, Mrs. Guffey?"

"Well, I don't know. I won't say. It smells like you might have."

"Yes," screeched Loretta in outrage. "I might have known which side of the fence you'd land on."

Mrs. Guffey and Big Boy squirmed. Calamity loomed. Big Boy hated the excitement of this argument. Life was to be taken in slower doses.

"Now Loretta, Loretta," Mrs. Guffey said, rising to meet hysteria.

"For God's sake, get your hands off me. Get away from me. I know you didn't want him to marry me."

The older woman stepped back, staring intently.

"Now Loretta, that's not true. I try not to interfere. I promised myself when you came to live with me that I wouldn't bother in any troubles you have."

"So! You heard that, Walton! Yes, you heard it," Loretta shrieked in a high note of vindication. "She's throwing it up. She don't want me here. I want a house of my own, and I want it now."

She sensed that she held them in retreat. No longer was drinking the issue. She advanced furiously.

"To hell with this family. Here I have married into this bunch of hoojers," she spat.

Walton's voice was a quick snake. "Shut up, Loretta."

The proud marshal's lines fell apart. All was chaos. She had crossed into uncharted territory. Hackles were standing on them all. The family, the family, the family. She had only gone against Walton until now. The others had been passive, ingratiating. Now they were joined.

Yet she pushed on rashly.

"Oh, you don't want me to insult your old mother, is that it?"

Big Boy saw the peril. Outside the family, yet inside it, he felt anger rising. But still he sought a compromise, a middle place where all could join him and together they could return safely to reason and affection, because Loretta was also part of the family.

"Now, Loretta," he said. "It ain't that way. Why, we don't try to gang up on you. We want you here. Edith'll tell you that."

"Edith? Why, her and old granny Guffey work against me all the time," she said contemptuously. Then her righteous anger began to unfocus and it occurred fuzzily to her that this escape route was more dangerous than facing up to the liquor.

Mrs. Guffey went into the dining room. Walton called to her.

"Mama, come back in here. I want you to look. See how she is? Just tell me she ain't drunk."

She returned. "Son, I don't want to hear any more. You and Loretta's got a lot of years ahead of you, and you're a-going to have fusses and fights. It's not my place to judge. I know that drinking is wrong, and it's been the bane of the menfolk of this family since I can remember. I don't know where Big Boy keeps his liquor. You know I don't allow it in the house, and I wouldn't stand for your daddy to bring it in . . ."

"Yes indeed!" Loretta interjected. "Indeed, indeed. Drinking is wrong. You know it's wrong, and Big Boy knows it's wrong, and yet he gets it and stays half shot week in and week out. . . ." She stopped, caught her breath, and resumed on a rising swell of victory. "And you, Walton, of all the people on the earth, the way your family has made liquor . . . and don't tell me you don't drink . . . all the times . . . why, if it hadn't been for drinking . . . ."

Walton glowered hopelessly, his anger dimmed, spread over too much talk, directed along too many of the devious paths upon which she had lured them.

"Yes, but I don't get like this when I've got something to do, and by God you've got something to do. You have to take care of little Logan."

"I take care of him. Yes I do," she screamed defensively.

37

Walton shook his head in sadness and loneliness. Defeated, he went to the kitchen, poured coffee, scraped his supper from cold pans. Loretta sat in angry martyrdom.

"What sin, now, is actually worse than judging another?" she asked the house in general. "Yes indeed. Indeed! If we would but remember what the Lord said at the well. Big Boy, Walton has really hurt me this time. I don't know if I can get over this. Would you please bring me a glassful of that whiskey. My nerves are ruined from all the judging and accusing I've had to put up with here tonight."

Big Boy turned to obey. Then his face was stricken with pain as he heard Walton smash the jar into the rock walk in the back yard.

The skies darkened, and rain washing down the pane of the north window glistened softly in the tawny glow from the lamp. The baby Logan opened his eyes, stared at the water, then wailed.

Loretta had periods of tranquillity and harmony with them. At those times she enjoyed the family and listened with some interest to the discussion of kin and ancestor.

Big Boy and Edith and their daughter, Sue Ann, did not live in the Guffey house. They stayed in a two-room cabin on the slope of the property nearest Hame Tree Gap. Saturday afternoons and Sundays, as circumstance permitted, they would join the rest and walk up the road to Wild Cat, past the Skillers' place, and on up a tortuous, steep path to Wolf Pen Mountain. They took a sack of food and some quilts on most of these journeys. Walton or Big Boy would construct an oven from mud and rock, and as the women cooked and talked, the men would squat and stare into the wild beauty of the valleys and feeder coves below them.

Out of the grayness and many streaking colors, Logan came slowly to know. He was aware of the faces, voices, smells, and touches of his family moving about on the mountain, on the paths, on the road, in the pasture. He knew and felt the spread of land in the valley below, the trees and brush, the far ridges, and beyond that, the leaping lines of blue mountains. He saw light play upon the earth. He was fond of sleep.

In the high grass of the yard he played with a rusty toy streetcar which had no wheels. He fumbled with the toy, found a place bent and sharp. Pain came, and blood, the fearful wail . . . . They petted, cleaned the wound, grandmother doting, father concerned. Logan sank again into unmarked time.

On a blanket at the edge of the drive, he saw a snake coiled near him. His mother's face, frightened. She held him close. He watched the snake crawl away.

Gray, timeless ignorance. He was on his back in the box on the front porch. A piece of cheesecloth screened the insects. Early summer's sky was a great sheet of pleasant light. Warm, drowsy silence lay upon the yard, broken now and again by the calls of birds in the shrubs and crows in a far field, but those noises were remote and added to the peace. The child watched the light glance off the leaves of the sarvis tree and play along the rose petals. A slight breeze stirred the leaves, and shadows of them danced along the gauze. A hornet circled above the gauze, then landed on it. The child's hand reached out and knocked the gauze aside. The hornet's wings sang, and the sound lulled the child. The hornet crawled up his cheek and onto his lower lip. Logan opened his mouth and drifted off to sleep. The hornet crawled into his mouth, and he swallowed it.

Logan lay near death on the bed. Loretta dashed about absurdly, whispering loudly to herself, while Mrs. Guffey worked on the child. There had been one loud, pained bleat, then no more. His fever ran high and he heaved with short, shallow breathing. Mrs. Guffey wrapped towels about him, soaked in chill well-water.

"Oh for God's sake, his fever is up," Loretta said. "Don't you know better than to put cold cloths on him? What he needs is something warm."

"Warm? Why?"

"Because I said so. I've always heard . . ."

"No, that's wrong. George was a veterinarian, and if I heard him once, I heard him a thousand times—if an animal is hot, cool it off—and I've seen him wrap feverish calves, colts, and dogs, and one time a bear cub, in cold wet cloths and ice. And this child's body is no more than an animal's. I've heard George say that. If we cover him with heat, then we might roast him to death."

Loretta would not yield. Nothing was simple, logical, or apparent. The answer to any crisis was wrapped in mystery, paradox.

"No, no," she insisted madly, "he's my child. Put heat to him. It'll heat up the outside but cool off the inside. Don't you see? By heating up the skin on him we'll draw the fever out of his blood. That's why we drink hot coffee in hot weather, to cool us off."

Mrs. Guffey continued methodically patting and massaging. She shook her head.

"These cloths get hot about as soon as I get them around him," she said.

"I'm going to heat some water and do it that way. Walton will be here soon and he'll tell you," Loretta said.

"I wish you'd go after the doctor, but if you won't, at least go to the well and draw me up some more water," Mrs. Guffey said.

"I'll not let you freeze my child," Loretta screamed.

Mrs. Guffey pushed the bucket toward Loretta with her foot. "Get it and get it fast," she commanded.

Loretta stared angrily at her, then ran with the bucket through the yard to the well. Mrs. Guffey heard the well bucket banging wildly down the rocky lining of the well. The child had turned darker.

"Do not go now, little boy. Do not leave us," she implored in a whisper, her voice choked in a harsh, unmusical lament. "Stay here," she crooned in rhythm with her kneading, "stay here . . . stay here . . . stay here . . . stay along with us . . . stay along . . . ."

The child was dying, and she did not know what else to do. The baby's eyes had not moved for twenty minutes. There had been only the labored intake of air, and it seemed even that had ceased for seconds at a time.

Loretta pulled the bucket up hand over hand. At last she got it to the top and poured the water slowly into the zinc bucket, as if she were stalling. Mrs. Guffey placed her hand on the infant's brow, then, holding it out, she walked into the next room and placed it on the Bible.

"I have stayed with you when I could, good Lord, and I know that you have remained with me always. I do not go to church as I should, but I will now if that is what it takes, or I will do it anyway. Now I know better than to ask for things, but I will ask

40

anyway. I did not ask for you to sober George up when he was alive, even though I needed him, because I know you have a plan no matter how it confuses me. This is Walton's boy, Lord, and it is the sweetest baby . . . ."

She sobbed and lost the thread of her prayer, then:

"Loretta is not a bad person, Lord. Why take the child?"

Loretta stood in the door to the bedroom, crying softly.

"Mrs. Guffey, I think he's dead."

The older woman turned, her blood in quiet shock, and looked at the pitiful, drawn face of the young mother. Then she ran into the room and bent over the child. There was no perceptible movement. She bent low and stared into the tiny, motionless face.

"Yes, yes. The baby. He's gone," she murmured, and tears welled silently. She looked back through the door at the Bible, its ominous strength. She bent her head in a slight, humble acknowledgement, then turned to Loretta, whose shoulders were hunched and racked with spasms, whose face was tight with a grief that the old woman could not match and did not want to see. She put her hand on the girl's shoulder and patted her gently. Then a low moan came from the girl, and she staggered against the wall.

"Let me alone, please, let me alone," she muttered—then abjectly, to herself, "Walton wasn't even here."

Mrs. Guffey covered the baby's face with a towel, bent slowly, and lifted the bucket of fresh water. Then she turned and looked at the tiny bundle under the towel.

Loretta rushed her, hands open as claws, slaughter in her movement and madness in her eyes. The strength of a dozen was in her.

"You killed my child with your cold water," she said in a strange, dry, and rattly voice as she collided with her mother-in-law. The old woman fell backward and sat on the bed. The pail hung from her hand, and some of the water sloshed gently onto the floor. Loretta beat Mrs. Guffey's face with open hands, and some blood and spittle leaked from the old woman's lips. Then, in the violence of the moment, Mrs. Guffey's hand rose involuntarily, lifting the pail to the edge of the bed. Loretta's knee struck it and spouted the water onto the baby. There was a gasp and a low outcry from the child. The women stared at each other, then at the baby. Together they ripped away the towel, and the child's mouth opened slightly and its lids blinked. They laughed and cried and hugged each other.

41

"The cold water. Yes, that's just the thing," Loretta screeched joyously. "Oh yes, Mrs. Guffey, honey, that's the very thing."

"Yes, yes, dear girl. Go get some more water. Hurry, hurry, hurry," She bent to knead the child's flesh again. "He is still alive. Hurry!"

Loretta ran to the well. The older woman forgot her prayers and tried to pass life from her own will and mind through the conduits of her fingers into the tiny, thin body on the bed. Even as Loretta ran back with the water, Walton strode into the yard.

"What's the matter now?" he asked wearily.

"The baby died once. He's alive again," Loretta shouted over her shoulder.

"What?" Walton asked, rocking on his heels.

"Dead, back alive," she said and ran through the door.

He ran in. "What?"

"I don't know," Loretta sobbed. "He was napping on the porch in his box and we heard him scream. He seemed to be choked or something. He's been like this for a long time."

"Like what? How long?" Walton asked, his face frightened and angry.

"Nearly an hour," Mrs. Guffey answered. She stopped changing the towels and let cold water dribble onto the child in small streams.

"What?" Walton screamed helplessly. "What is it?"

"Go get the doctor, quick," his mother commanded.

Walton ran most of the way to Hollytown, stopping only to tell one of the Skiller daughters on the road what was happening. When he got to Dr. Rawson's office, the nurse sent him to the drugstore, where the doctor was drinking coffee with Paul Fortune.

"What's the matter?" Rawson asked him absently.

"The baby. It's sick."

"What seems to be wrong?"

"It seems to be dying, by God. That's what seems to be wrong." Rawson stirred his coffee.

"Come on now or I'll kill you," Walton said. Fortune raised his head and stared at him.

"I mean it," said Walton.

Fortune's eyes rolled. "This is one of the most insane places on earth," he said.

"How is the road to Wild Cat?" Rawson asked.

"It's slick but your Model A can make it."

42

"All right, let's go."

"Me too?" Fortune asked eagerly.

"Yes, come on."

Rawson drove the clanking, backfiring Ford as fast as it would go, swinging wide around curves. When they topped Hame Tree Gap, Walton and the doctor ran down the trail to the house, with Fortune stepping along gingerly as though a hard stride would roll his head off his shoulders. When he reached the porch, he found Big Boy sitting beside a post, bouncing his daughter on his knee. The girl leaped down, stared at Fortune, and ran inside.

"Ho, boy," Big Boy said, his face warm but crafty. "I ain't seen you lately."

"I've been around town," Fortune said.

"Ah yes. Well, where'd you get to on the night the young'un was borned?"

"There was a family here, you know, the mother made the big show? Well, I went with one of them up a nearby mountain. He made me wait what seemed like half the night in some woods, then he returned and sold me some of the finest—and I mean to say the finest—liquor with which it has been my privilege to severely burn the membranes of my throat."

From the inside, low worried murmurs.

"You don't happen to have a little drink on you, do you? You owe me one or two," Big Boy said.

"No, no. I've quit the damnable stuff. This time I mean it."

Big Boy's face turned moody, depressed. The conversation had ended. Tears came to his eyes.

"Bud's little baby boy is dying, and I'm worrying about pop-skull," he sniffled.

Fortune turned, stared at the house. It brooded with the secrecy of private and isolated death. He wandered to the door of the bedroom and watched Rawson bend to the bed. The doctor was harried and cross, eternally aware of the conflicts, disputes, suspicions, and unpredictability of mountain people. In a vague manner he was also honored that this family believed in his medicine to some extent, so it was not for the baby that he brought forth from his bag the potions, pills, syrups, instruments, gauges, hypodermics, and finally and absurdly, the lens from an old microscope. He laid them all in an orderly row as if he were going to use each of them in turn. He turned to Fortune and said: "If you

43

go into the mountains to doctor, then by God you'd better act like you are doctoring. Now everyone can easily see that I am doing all that can be done within the purview of enlightened medical science."

He paused, then shook his head. "However, I haven't got the slightest idea what is wrong with this child."

He watched the child a moment, then he knelt and felt the faint flick of blood through the arm artery. He put his ear close and heard the slow whisk of breath through tiny lips. He felt the child's heat, but it was not the fever that disturbed him.

The Guffeys began crowding about. For no reason he picked up the old lens and stared through it into the child's ear. Then his finger flew to the carotid, where the beat was stronger.

"Christ! Christ Almighty, what's wrong?" he muttered. He rummaged through the disheveled inventory of his knowledge and experience. He did not know, he could not tell. The child was on the last gray slope and skidding fast. He turned to the family.

"Quickly, quickly, what have you given this child?" he asked.

Loretta leaped forward and knelt with him. "Milk. Cow's milk. That's all he's had. I'm dry, myself."

"Cow's milk? For God's sake. What kind of shape is the cow in?"

"Fresh. She's healthy. She gives enough for everybody."

"Has everyone been drinking her milk in the past day?"

"Yes, I had some in my coffee at breakfast and some—two glasses—for dinner."

When Rawson blinked, his eyes were like those of a harmless freckled bird behind his spectacles. "Has this child been around any poison?" he asked.

"No."

"Do you know if he's allergic to anything?"

"What does that mean?"

"Does anything work against him? Does anything cause him to break out or get sick?"

She shook her head.

"Tell me the truth, now, " Rawson demanded with a fierce set to his eyes.

"He's had milk, that's all," Mrs. Guffey said.

"Sure?" he asked them all again. Loretta turned suspicious eyes toward Mrs. Guffey. The old woman refused to dignify the silent accusation by showing she had noticed.

Rawson unwrapped the child. He searched the body for fang marks.

"Now say again, how long has he been like this?"

"About three hours now," Mrs. Guffey said.

Rawson squeezed the arms, the ankles. He fumbled among the vials on the bed, then left them alone. "What the hell?" he asked himself.

Then he hovered above the child and poked about the legs, the stomach. The child's face knotted. Rawson probed again and drew a low, short wail.

"Good God! Good God!" he breathed. They moved in closer.

"What?" demanded Walton.

"Get back there," Rawson snapped. They obeyed, craning their necks. To the appendix with his finger. No particular reaction. Again he looked at the failing child. He put a needle on a syringe, then picked up the baby's arm. Walton came to his side at once, a great question on his grave, slim face. There was a brief, silent dispute in their eyes. Then Rawson turned to the others: "All right. Everyone get out of here."

He stayed alone with the child for a time and administered the shot. Outside Rawson could hear other voices, and he knew other people had arrived. He walked to the door and saw several of the Skillers.

"There is something toxic. Poisonous. Can you think of anything?" he asked Loretta again. Then in her slow method of detailing every relevant and irrelevant corner of a narrative, she revealed the day moment by moment.

Nothing.

"Where was he when you first noticed something was wrong with him?"

"In his crib, here on the porch. We had put a new curtain over him."

Rawson came onto the porch and looked at the old lumber and vines. A den of dim evils, poison, and disease. He turned and went back inside.

In an hour the shot had worn away and the child had stabilized. Rawson seated himself on the floor beside the door and napped. Big Boy entered the room, fanning odors of sweat, tobacco, and tannery leather and chemical through the house. Rawson, in his drowse, also detected the odor of moonshine. He dropped deeper into sleep, then snapped awake. He arose, picked up the child, slid a medicine dropper of liquid between the lips, and squeezed.

Then he turned to them, his eyes frank and blazing.

"I can't do any more," he confessed in terrible, chilling candor, in the brusque humility that was characteristic of him when he recognized the inevitable. "It wouldn't do any good to take him to the hospital. To be frank, I don't know what's wrong with him, and I'm as good a doctor as you'll find in these parts."

Walton's face grew tight, furious; then he recognized the honesty of it. It was in his soul to try to love the truth.

"All right. How much do I owe you?"

"I'll come back in the morning," Rawson said tiredly. "I've got to get on to some other patients now. I'm late. . . ."

"I want to pay as we go."

"God damn it, I don't know how much it is. I haven't had time to add it up as we go. This baby is bad off. Get ready for the worst."

And with this he had broached the most difficult part of the job. Now to let it blossom in them to its fullest.

Loretta moaned and sank into a chair. Mrs. Guffey started to her, stopped, and said in a low, conciliatory voice: "Well, we're lucky we had him as long as we did. We kept him this far. We gave him up once."

Loretta's face fired with her deep personal rage at the world. "I don't want him for a few more minutes. I want him from now on. I want him to grow up," she said, glaring about with an insane obstinacy. She stomped the floor with one foot. She clenched her fists and gritted her teeth.

"Damn it to hell, I want him to . . . ," she said, and broke into sobs. Mrs. Guffey stared at Walton, who was silent. His face was a glazed mask of wondering pain. Rawson went quickly out the door. He and Paul Fortune were halfway up the path when they came upon a gathering of the Skillers. There was a moment of awkward silence. Finally Rawson said: "Afternoon, Mrs. Skiller."

"Is they anything I can do, doctor?" she asked humbly.

"Oh Christ!" he exploded—then, "Forgive me. Go try if you like. There's no more I can do."

The Skillers passed them by, quietly, with some majesty.

"Listen, I'm going back down there," Fortune said.

"For what? Liquor? Go, damn it. If you want something to write about, go study that bunch."

––––––––––

The friends of the family collected slowly. They were friends to the Guffeys even if they were enemies among themselves, and they observed the armistice of crisis, bringing dark wisdom and harmony to bear upon the visits of death. All factions thought well of the Guffeys—old Doc Guffey had seen to their sick stock in all weathers and hours. Yet it did not seem quite that way to Walton in his sensitivity. He was not comforted and not to be comforted. Death coming? He knew they would not want to miss it. Death would come quietly and no one would see it, but they would see the moment of ruin for the family. He spat.

––––––––––

Mrs. Skiller strode commandingly into the room of sickness. She was now in her time and element. They turned to her, unbelieving in her medicine but afraid of her ominous arrival. Now for a moment they were uncertain: did she truly know both God and the devil? Their minds turned from orderly thought at accustomed levels and toward the signs.

Death? Deliverance? Witch-woman and her granny bag of old mojo.

"Let me see him," Mrs. Skiller said.

Mrs. Guffey's eyes flashed green at the infidel, traveler of dark roads.

"I'll kindly ask you to leave," she said with restraint, but quiet fire scorched her voice.

Mrs. Skiller did not notice. She rattled her bag imperiously. The child did not rise and walk. Mrs. Skiller muttered deep in her throat and gums. Nothing? Well, the doctor had abandoned the ground. The old woman rolled her eyes up and walked onto the porch in her angular, stumping gait. She looked at the weather and at the leaves of the tall Lombardy poplar beyond the yard. Big Boy sat in a chair tilted against the wall, a profound melancholy on his moon face. Paul Fortune squatted in the yard where he could watch it all. Only Earl, hunkered beside a bush in the upper side of the yard, noticed Fortune. He whittled and studied him, scanned the

47

others, listened to the wind. Occasionally Fortune caught Earl's covert stare.

Familiar, thought Fortune, something familiar about that one.

"What did you see?" Big Boy asked Mrs. Skiller softly, believing.

"Wah! H'it'll rain, all right," she said pleasantly, no mood available to her for major predictions. She rattled her fur bag and walked the length of the porch twice, a wake of stench behind her. Big Boy shook his head in slight puzzlement. He was bemused, not an unpleasant state for him since he found it generally with liquor; but now death was nigh with its own mystical finality and promise of cleanness and new beginnings, and he felt these things vaguely for the moment and held a sense of well-being. Mrs. Skiller stumped back down the porch like an angry captain on a bridge. A hornet flew angrily about her head in the gathering dusk. It buzzed a moment and flew away. She turned to look at it. Earl sprang up from his crouch and moved forward to her. He carefully spread the foliage and peered in. Dimly he could see the gray nest built against the roof. He pointed to it. She stared a moment, eyes squinting, then leaped back as if she had recognized her cue.

"Thar!" she said. "I see it now."

She charged back inside to the family in the bedroom.

"He'll make it now, all right," she said. The senseless, vacant hope of it sprang up in Walton.

"How in hell do you know that, Mrs. Skiller?" he asked weakly.

"The hornet. Ask the hornet. I saw it outside. When I first seed that young'un a-layin' thar, the picture of a hornet came to mind. The one I saw outside was a sign."

"Oh Sweet Lord of the very Walking Waters. A sign," Walton moaned in helpless irony.

"Wal, I got a good reading on that boy when he was borned," she declared, her tolerance boundless, "and as ye know, I can see death months away. I didn't see it then and I don't see it now, e'god. I tell you true, he'll be all right. The angels are watching over."

Her sincerity—and the promise, the assuredness—reached even Mrs. Guffey, who thought her to be an ignorant old woman trying to raise hope.

Yet, if she can raise hope, she can raise the dead. Can she?

Earl was in the door, a shy smile on his strong face. Slowly their

48

eyes turned to him as his quiet inner force drew them. He looked at them and slowly nodded.

"She's right. Tell the doctor. H'it's something about the hornets."

Loretta sat numb in her chair and watched Mrs. Skiller leave. The old woman, then Earl and the others, passed among the clusters of people, and as she went she pronounced hope and prophecy to those who believed, those who didn't, those who didn't know.

Dark fell and most of the visitors faded from the yard, including Paul Fortune. The others had neither acknowledged nor disregarded him, but by nightfall he was feeling more an intruder than ever. He passed down the road from Hame Tree Gap in the warm darkness, felt an alien, secret thing brooding back in the trees, felt the ancient sense of mountains, felt faintly guilty as he had in France during the World War.

Guilt? Because death was abroad and it was not after him.

Big Boy took his daughter and returned to his house. Loretta's sister and brother came and bedded down on a pallet of quilts on the floor. Through the night Loretta, Walton, and Mrs. Guffey sat beside the bed. At two in the morning they gave Logan up for dead once more and woke up everyone to tell them. Loretta's brother and sister sat somberly in their quilts and watched her fling a bucket of cold water on the baby. He moved, moaned. They kept the death watch for the rest of the night. Weary, worrisome, toilsome old night of death. Big Boy came again at three. He drank many cups of hot coffee, dipping his long upper lip into the cup and folding the coffee back like an elephant eating hay. He sat on the porch in predawn coolness, thought on the quickness of life, the slow dragging feet of time outside life, the certainty of the end. He heard an owl, attached no significance to it, trilled back at it, and it answered again. The night wore on, and the child held tenaciously to the planet. Short, hard breaths, feeble flickers of pulse. He slept deep in the far shadows of fever, and there was no brightness. Morning came and the tiny dull eyes opened, shone on. Rawson came at ten o'clock, after Walton had decided that he would not. The two of them stood on the porch arguing.

"Well, I tried to come earlier. I wanted to. But I've got other patients, son. I worked all night to keep one going."

"Well, how about my boy? Why didn't you work all night to keep him going?"

"By God, he's alive, isn't he?"

"Not with your help," Walton said in high, formal anger. "All he had was one old witch-woman waving and flapping around, and our prayers."

"That is some bullshit, my boy."

"Well, it looks to me like you could have come back earlier."

"There was no possibility of that," Rawson said. They argued emptily, with no hope of anyone scoring a win. It was automatic, unenthusiastic.

Rawson had not slept, and he heard a faint buzzing. For a second he thought he was hallucinating. He leaned his head against the wall and tried to listen to Walton, but he could only think of how tired he was, and he listened with small attention to the buzzing to see if the noise rose and fell with his pulse and breathing. His palate and tongue were thick with coffee and tobacco. Then he slapped the wall listlessly and felt a sting on his hand. He looked to see a small black hornet pull its stinger out of him. Then suddenly Earl was beside him.

"Did Walton tell you about the hornets?" he asked.

"No, man, no. He did not." His voice rose. "I needed to know it."

Walton shrugged tiredly. "Hornets. I forgot. I want Logan saved."

"That's what's going to save him," Earl said. "The doctor needs to know where they are." Then he pointed up to the grayness of the nest, hidden among the vines. The insects worked angrily around the mouth of the nest.

"Well God damn," Rawson said softly, with wonder and discovery in his voice. Walton saw the nest and backed away. The hornets swarmed out and patrolled the air, and some began attacking. One stung Walton on the ear and another on his cheek. He fled through the yard, cursing and flailing the air.

Three of them were at the doctor's neck. He grinned recklessly. Earl backed into the bedroom. Then Rawson ran to the child's bed and jerked the baby out roughly. Anew he scanned every inch of the little body. Several hornets had entered with him and lit upon the exhausted women, who leaped up, got old newspapers, rolled them, and began swatting at the hornets.

In the midst of it Rawson completed his external examination, then he put his thumb in the baby's mouth and pried it open.

"There, by God!" he shouted joyfully. The baby's throat was red, swollen.

"Has this blessed little baby shit yet today?" he hollered.

Loretta ran to him. Her face was swollen from stings, and one of Rawson's eyes was closing.

"I don't know. He didn't last night," Loretta said. "I just put the diaper on him an hour ago. I just changed it to have something to do."

Rawson pinched the back of the diaper. "Yes, yes, yes, oh by God he has, he has! Has he not? Yes, he has mortally shit his diaper full," he cried happily. Another hornet stabbed his ear lobe, but he didn't react. He quickly unpinned the diaper and jerked it off the child. Then he spread the excrement with his fingers, studying it, smoothing and kneading it.

"So!" he boomed. "Oh God Almighty damn!" He held up a finger brown with lumps, and on the point of that finger rested a partially digested hornet. The door had been closed, and those hornets that had not been smashed by the newspapers had lost their aggressiveness and their organization, and they flitted into the panes. Walton stood beside Loretta's young brother and sister at the inside door of the bedroom. He saw the wide, fanatical smile on Rawson's face and grinned.

"Is he all right?" he asked.

"All right? Hell, no. He's one of the sickest babies on the face of the earth. He may die any minute."

They stared aghast at the man who had so recently raised them from despair with his wild laughing and cursing, only to smash them down again.

"But now we know what's wrong," the doctor shouted.

"What?" they asked in unison.

"He swallowed a hornet."

———

The crisis ebbed slowly, imperceptibly, over the next few days. Through Rawson's careful ministrations the effect of the venom was lessened. Someone was with the child constantly. Loretta's entire family came to do something. The baby's stomach abscessed, and he could hold but scant nourishment. But there was something extremely stubborn about his hold on life. Rawson prescribed breast milk; Loretta had none, but she had a cousin, fresh with child, full with milk. She came and proffered her great jugs to Logan.

Strength returned. Breath and pulse resumed their rhymes and patterns, and finally some color came to his cheeks. The child gained; pain subsided and sank away, adding to all the things he had experienced in his meager sum of days. It remained on the webbed shelves and tilted levels of memory, faintly. Logan swam in the deeps of new thought. Vaguely, as though under a primal dim sea, he began again to sense those things outside—the great plunging dark lines of sky and ridgebacks, valley depths and angles. Light fell from the sky, filtered and seeped, battled with shadow, came and went and returned again.

In bed his eyes shut, but sleep did not come to clean the mind. There were no specific images to occupy him. Color shot spastically through gray cells. He fell up and up, could not sleep or think, whirled, fell upward, the bed spun and he separated from it and fell smiling into the sky behind his eyelids.

Outside, a screech owl trilled its song to the night.

4

THE EARLIEST PART of the moon appeared above the crest of a long, steep ridge near Wild Cat Cliff, its light unbright, strange. Though the heat had broken and the air of autumn was sharp, there were troublesome promises about the moon and its dimension. Earl Skiller stopped his laborious climb and quietly let a tow sack of jars and glass jugs slip off his shoulder. They clinked as they resettled. Then a small, lone cloud crossed the sky to the moon and covered it for a moment, darkening the ridge and dimming the low shine even more.

Earl left the sack and moved silently down the ridge and off to its side, through small, dark pines to a springhead. He scooped it clean, let the water settle for a few minutes, then drank. Returning to the sack, he squatted and slipped a pinch of tobacco into his jaw. He fixed his eyes on a dark spot under the trees, so that if anything moved he could pick it up easier through the corners of his eyes. Looking directly at a movement was not as reliable as looking at one place and not seeing it, yet seeing everything else, particularly movement.

Then he lifted the sack and balanced it over his shoulder. With one hand on his hip he resumed the climb. The wind crossed the ridge with a sharpening edge. The piece of moon sank away to a glow behind far pines, and then Earl was in the oak and other hardwood, his feet on beaten paths.

Earl's trail took him around the side of a cove and down another ridge to a brook, where he put his load down again. He groped in some leaves piled behind a stump until he found a lantern. After he lit it, he studied the flow of water, found no sign of disturbance upstream. He went up the stream about a hundred yards, then downstream for an equal distance, looking for loose sediment in the water. He put his sack behind a stump and covered it with brush and leaves, after which he took the lantern down the cove to a patch of laurel, turned the wick up so that it burned brightly, and hung it high on a limb. He retreated about a hundred feet and crawled under a log to watch the light. He refreshed his chewing tobacco, then pulled an Owlhead .32 pistol from his pocket and placed it on the ground beside him. He covered it with a piece of bark so that he could run off and leave it if he had to. If the law discovered him here, they could charge him with nothing, since there was no liquor still here—only a decoy lantern. It was a simple test. If anyone came to the lantern, he would know who had been talking about his still, because he had mentioned a specific place to only one man.

The law might be led to think he was running liquor tonight because one of his brothers had bought one hundred pounds of sugar from a store on Allen's Creek, and the old Skiller truck had been in Wadenton this day so another brother could be seen buying the things the old woman and the sisters needed—which was a dead giveaway because Earl tried to have the house well stocked for the women in case he and his brothers were caught or killed making moonshine. And if the law had been informed, they would be watching this cove from across on the other ridge, and they would mistake the lantern light for a still fire and move in on it from four sides. He waited two hours, and the oil burned low in the lantern.

"Well, at least it ain't Big Boy," he said softly. The test was worth the time. The ruse was troublesome, but it proved Big Boy out. He got his lantern, pistol, and sack of jars, and took again to the trail.

Earl walked three more miles, then slipped into a gully below Wild Cat Cliff and made his way along a path beneath the overhanging laurel. At the end of that thickety, twisty tunnel was the still. A big dead chestnut tree loomed before him. He stopped and whistled a low whippoorwill, waited a moment, then trilled like a screech owl.

"Aw right, who is it?" a voice asked from close by—from exactly where, no other person would have known until the shotgun went off.

"Earl and jars," he said.

"Earl, Wes Andrews is down there at the still."

"Who let him in?"

"Nobody. H'it's hard to keep anything from him."

"I'll go see."

Earl with sack went quietly down the treacherous stream bed. He came silently to the opening in front of the lean-to. Two of his brothers were stacking wood next to the still; two others were setting the cap on the pot. Wesley Andrews, dirty and bearded, hunched before the small fire.

"Ho, Earl," Wesley said cautiously when Earl entered. The others came to the makeshift table as Earl unloaded the sack of its jugs and jars. Then he placed the pistol on the table. Wesley stared at it.

"I don't mean no harm nor trouble," Wesley said. "I jist come by to see if I could he'p out a little."

Earl did not miss the unease of the man, or the slyness that moved about in Wesley like a strange, unknown animal, dangerous because it was hard to detect.

"I'm glad you come by, Wes," Earl said. "I been wanting to find you and talk a little."

"Why, right here I am," Wes said.

"You been to town lately?" Earl asked.

"Oh no, not me. I sneak down to the golf course once in a while to caddy some on Saturday whilst the law's busy keeping them quiet on the Western Front. I see my old woman once in a while, but mostly I stay here in the woods."

"That gas in Raleigh burns your nose," Earl said. His brothers grinned. Under his beard, Wesley went white.

"Self-defense is what it was," he said.

"The sheriff says first-degree, family says first-degree, witnesses say first-degree, and the warrant says first-degree," Earl said.

"He tried to cut me so I hit him with a rock," Wesley said. They stared quietly at him. The fire crackled and a quick draft blew smoke out from the rocks of the furnace.

"Sonny Bright never pulled a knife in his life," Earl said. "He prayed and worked. He had two young'uns and one full payday in his pocket."

Wesley rolled his eyes about, boxed in.

"Earl, I been on the chaingang and you been on the chaingang," he said, calling on convict loyalties.

"Yes, I been there two times," Earl said, looking at his brothers.

Eager for it, were they?

"It's nothing to be proud of," he said.

"It proves we can stand it," Wesley said.

"I knowed that already."

"Well, we ought to be friends."

Earl shrugged. "You was supposed to be Sonny's friend. Two young'uns and a payday in his pocket. You took the money."

"No, I didn't. Don't jump me, I say. I've got a gun and the nerve to use it," Wesley said, half rising.

Earl glanced at his own pistol. Two of the brothers fumbled in their pockets.

"Well, I've got a gun myself," Earl said, "but I know you h'ain't, and if you did you wouldn't use h'it head-on because you h'ain't mean, just sneaky. You're a coward. You killed one man and that'll do ye fer killin', and you've hid out in these woods till you h'ain't got the spirit of a beat dog left. You jist h'ain't too dangerous. I bet you'd even like to git caught up with. We won't turn our backs on you, but we h'ain't afraid. You're in the wrong bunch to break mean. If one of us gits hurt, you'll die, and you'll wish it was the gas chamber."

"Oh Lordy, Earl, don't gang up on me," Wesley pleaded, tears gathering. "I don't want to get in the outs with you boys. I just came by to see if I could help some with the still. I'd like to help and make a quarter or two to give my old woman."

"All right," Earl said after a pause, "if you work we'll pay you. Making likker is hard work. You don't get to drink any here, either. You know that?"

They turned to work, sorting the wood around the fire and then dipping still-beer from the mash barrels. They poured it into the copper pot, which sat upon a sooted furnace of stone and mud.

Mrs. Guffey tossed in her bed, heard murmurs from Walton's room, sharp voices, silence. She had hoped the cooler weather would bring an end to the growing tension among her family. The summer had been of an intensity and stickiness not known in this century. Obscure resentments had arisen, and they had all carped and sniped and cut at each other. Big Boy got mad at Edith, so he brought Sue Anne to stay with him at Mrs. Guffey's house, although his own small house was upon the same property. Edith was sullen over Big Boy's reluctance to discuss certain matters with her, so it was all right with her if the child stayed with Mrs. Guffey, if Big Boy stayed with Mrs. Guffey, if Walton stayed there, if the whole world stayed there, as long as she didn't have to stay there.

In the reaches of their deliberate minds, the Guffeys refrained from making the final insults that would break them apart. The oppressiveness of this time was attributed to the evil in the moon at its current stage, and serious damage could be averted through discretion. They waited to see if the changing of the moon wouldn't put some of their grievances in another perspective.

Loretta had again stopped speaking, and Mrs. Guffey had gone about the house with her very tread a silent, painful whimper, trying to say or do the thing that would make it all right. But the more servile she became, the more open grew Loretta's scorn.

Walton and Loretta turned about in the bed, each pretending sleep. Loretta was angry because he had not given her the usual allowance. She suspected he had deliberately held it out from her but was acting as though he had merely forgotten it. She would be damned before she asked him for it.

Walton seethed with many things, but mainly because the new outlander foreman at the tannery was trying to assert his authority by giving loud, curt orders when none were needed. The other men were stirring and growling and seeking a leader to express their discontent. Finally, through the dim process of intuition, they had settled upon Walton because open upon his sensitive face and in his eyes was the wildness and strength they tried to keep hidden in their hearts. The silent pressure from them built and flowed into him, and he knew by the same obscure intuitive process that the task was going to be his. When he began to realize it, his instincts flowered painfully into leadership, and against his will he began to wait and watch for the time and the place to challenge the foreman.

Walton turned, groaned in half-sleep. He was edgy because of the job. Every time he lost his temper he overdid it—past all that was comprehensible and tolerable. The shrieking violence of his soul was a force he did not trust or understand, and he never willingly loosed it. He let it wait, like a snake hidden in leaves, until it struck on its own. So he was the rebel leader on the job, and at home he was the chieftan of a clan whose members were getting out of hand, and he could not find the time or place to stop and determine how to rebel in one place and keep down rebellion in the other.

He was angry with Loretta for her sullen childishness; with his mother for her servility; with Big Boy and his family for their troubles. And he was disgusted with himself because the child Logan was healthier, and he had prayed and promised that if the boy lived he would keep peace and order so that the boy would have a good place to grow. Yet he saw that he was so torn with strife that he could do nothing but hold the baby a moment and put him down. Then one of the others would come and pick up the child, so that the baby became a postal drop for their hostilities, and the anger was transmitted to him and he grew cross.

The strangeness in Earl was wilder, of a different strain, from that of anyone else around. He had his claim to Cherokee blood and some lost line of Choctaw, but he was predominantly German, though the line had mingled somewhere with Scotch-Irish. But he was fey. He was dismayed at his mother's practice of witchcraft because he knew most of it was cruel self-delusion on her part. Yet Earl practiced that most dimly perceived of all magic—instinct. In and around him was the hidden net of fatalism and patience formed in those who undergo the forced meditation of being isolated in nature. He dealt in angels and demons and long, slow tides.

He grasped the secret things of people, which his quiet, sad smile hid, so that they became his secrets too. There was no judgment in his eyes, but they flashed quickly with recognition when deceit or falseness was in someone's gesture or words.

The oldest son, Earl had learned the distiller's craft beside his father, but his observations had always been his own. They had not been taught to him. As his years increased, so did his understanding, and it matured quickly when he left the mountains to fight in France in 1917. Earl learned this about the garrison army: whoever controlled a bottle of liquor at the right time also controlled the barracks and the noncommissioned officers and sometimes the officers, and thereby had influence over many decisions. Earl developed the bootlegger's insight into the human condition, and while he was not ruthless, he held to hard and honest agreements. In the army, reports of infractions involving him and his friends had been suppressed simply because he tendered to some regular sergeant a large drink at the right time on a bleary, sick morning.

Earl, unlike many bootleggers, did not seek power at the customer's expense. He did not care to be a father to them, nor did he ask deference from his customers, especially those addicted to alcohol, nor sex from women who showed up needing a drink. He only wanted them to enjoy it. As a poet puts down his lines and a fiddler saws off his tunes, so did Earl give people his best, to enjoy it and to be complimented only for the quality. If they abused liquor, he regretted that. He would have refused to sell it to drunks if that had been the answer, but he did not know the answer.

Earl, the lank, quiet man of mountain poverty, exuded a wealth beyond wealth. His face sometimes melted to unmask elusive sufferings and a disquieting humility. Yet it registered deeper intuitions, and some people did mistrust the shadows that fell from his eyes. There was in him a dark and frightening thing, a suspect air of felony and capital crime, of midnight silence and the quietude of saints and demons, of madness and heresy and heat and anger, the sense of threat found in geniuses, prophets, sorcerers, and other variant personalities who feed their souls on matter outside the bland pabulum sought by the general run.

Then to look again at the man of trust: Earl, dumb Earl, his face blank, with a tiny wry grimace about his eyes, as though he had studied mankind through many men and found not one to whom he could speak about the sad and fragmented perceptions in his own heart.

Earl walked among people seeing and was thought blind. With seeing came revelations, surprises, disappointments. Yet he made no labels in his brain, used no words in his hidden heart. There was a creature in him that moved in all directions, and it watched, watched, watched—a free and wild spirit, fearful of its own destruction, yet aware of its own permanence, watching, waiting, watching, waiting.

For destiny.

———————

At three o'clock Walton left his bed and went to sit on the porch. The moon was a low, dim blade among the boughs beside the yard, and it shone through orange haze and lit the ground with a dead-star strangeness. He did not have to leave for work until five, so he took this hour for himself before Loretta rose to cook his breakfast.

His eyes crinkled as he stared moodily at the moon. But his face held the slack, mute sensitivity that belonged to his family. The air moved, and the flow of it was chilly, so he draped his coat over his shoulders and smelled the leather odors of the tannery upon it. He thrust his finger stiffly into the Prince Albert can, loosened his tobacco, and spilled it carefully into the crimp in the paper. He rolled it and licked slowly along the seam. He lit it and threw the match into the yard. As he sucked in the smoke, Loretta appeared in the door behind him.

"Walton, what are you doing up?"

His sigh was shallow, resigned, tired. Tobacco smoke rose in a flume.

"Go back to sleep," he said. She was faintly visible, shades of white and gray in the dark frame of the door.

"I asked what you are doing up."

"I couldn't sleep."

"Well, couldn't you have stayed in bed close to me anyway?"

"No, I wanted to sit out here awhile before daybreak."

The thrumming night was vibrant with the last noises and signals of dying Indian summer. The moon came through an opening in the trees and lit the porch with sudden brightness. Walton's eyes turned slowly to the side. Far in the valley a rooster raised his cry; one of the Guffey roosters answered. A long gust of wind spread through the brush, and it was chillier. Loretta stepped out the door to him. His hand took hers. She leaned against his shoulder.

"Do you love me more than you love her?" she asked.

"Who? Love who? Mama?"

"Yes."

"Well, I love you in a different way."

"Oh that's it, is it? A crooked answer."

He sighed. "Loretta, Loretta. She's my mama. She raised me and loved me and done for me. What kind of a goddam question is that?"

Her voice rose to sarcasm. "Oh! And now I can't love you and do for you?"

"You do. Yes you do," he affirmed, solemn enough for court testimony.

"Are you tied to her?"

"Don't start in on that. You're as tied to your folks as anybody I ever seen," he said.

She nodded, then her face softened into wisdom and some maturity in the indistinct light. They waited, and soon false dawn broke in the east and some of the insects ceased and the birds began opening up the day. Through those noises they could hear the muted throb and mutter of the tannery in the distance, and it began amplifying its own day. Finally she spoke:

"I want you to get us a house in town so we can start living our own lives."

"Well, maybe before long. I don't want to rent. I want to own my own place."

"That's all right. Whatever you want to do about it."

He nodded. "It's a waste to rent. A man has to have his own place."

"Soon," she urged.

"No. Wait. Just wait."

"No! I mean soon," she said and disappeared inside. He heard her get back into bed.

The Skillers had two stills: the one they were working at any given time, and another hidden away, its components scattered. But they had numerous sites, and at intervals they broke down their rig, cleaned up the area so that it would not reveal them, then set up elsewhere. In pride of craft, Earl saw to it that the liquor was always made in a clean outfit. He had learned his craft from the old foxes who now moldered in deep graves, where gray rocks sink their silent weight beneath the earth. The thought of graves flitted often through Earl's mind.

Barrels for the mash, or still-beer, were kept at equal distances from the two rigs, hidden in a stand of spruce, and the square wooden boxes that held the grain were kept at the house.

Earl's mind was burnt with a picture: down in the earth, the gray rocks in infinitely slow plunge.

When everything was ready for a run, the Skillers moved their supplies and equipment to their site under the cover of night.

Sometimes they used a mule, but then mules often left round, bold tracks.

No man or dog could track Earl, in this world or the world to come.

Because of his high standards, Earl ran alcohol from grain. He sprouted his corn in sacks under the house. The sacks were filled with rich earth and cow manure. Every other day he turned the sacks and watered them. When the corn was an inch long, he pulled it and spread the sprouts to dry in the loft above the kitchen flue. Sometimes he used rye. Old man Jerry Trull, a miller, made the meal for mash from corn grown at Wild Cat, and other places.

From time to time, necessity dictated that Earl make some sugar liquor, but even his sugar liquor was the best of its genre. He did not like to work with sugar. Pure corn was his love. If it was done right, with the alchemist's love for his work and material, he had something to pass on to his customers without qualm or apology. He grinned widely when certain discriminating customers bought it. They were pleased.

A bright one, Earl came early in life to the necessary combination of sense, feel, and instinct for his material. Sometimes he felt the corn as it grew—the rich green juice of it in sprout. After it dried, he beat it into a pulp with a round, flat rock that fitted his hand, mixed it with the meal ground by Jerry Trull, and cooked it slowly. He knew his fire. It obeyed him, responded to the walls and blocks he created for it, followed the sharp drafting of the chimney.

He kept a close eye and ear upon the fermentation of the corn. He let it rise in good activity, and then he put in the crushed sprouts. If the weather was warm, the mash worked well and built up a big head and sounded like pigskins frying slowly.

A distiller must know certain things if he is driven by circumstances to run corn liquor in the colder seasons. The barrels of mash must be handy to the pot. Earl placed them in pits nearby and covered them over with planks. Then he packed cow manure around the sunken barrels, almost to the top, for slow, steady heat. And in the coldest times, Earl heated old, rusted axheads, wedges, horse and mule shoes, go-devils, and whatever else of iron he could get, then strung all that on one wire and sank it into the mash.

Earl, images. Pain in his mind. Sometimes his heart grew heavy and he could not breathe. He did not have bad dreams; they were

62

not necessary. The misery of his life came from clear memory, more vivid and painful than dreams. Worse than dreaming, there was no waking to something different, better. Yet he hated nothing he had seen on the earth. Things came as the world brought them. Each day carried its own.

The brothers got the cap pasted on with wet flour, and the worm was connected. Earl fed pinecones and small twigs of dry ivy and laurel into the coals until the right heat was reached. Wood would have burned too hot and too long in this early building of temperature. It was later that sticks of seasoned oak and hickory were fed into the furnace. As the fire grew to the right heat and brightness, he added green oak and locust for control. Shortly the singlings, or first run, got toward the end of the worm. The careful use of heat kept it from puking out the end in a scorched state. As the stream from the worm broke, Earl caught a cup of it and threw it into the fire. If it no longer ignited, then the singling was done.

Briefly he looked from the fire and out into the night. A light breeze fanned along the mountain, swirled along the creek. He felt his pain, smiled briefly. It never left him for long. There was no distraction. Pain and heaviness. The stricken spirit swept down within him, deeper still. Earl did many things in the World War that he did not like and in later years grew to regret. But the war was not what haunted him. Something else, beside a wet rock, deep in the earth. Great stones are pulled forever downward, deepward. Gravity is infinitely slow, certain. He felt the gravity of fate pulling him toward the future.

The men at the still stopped and rested. Wesley was growing tired. He looked with some yearning toward those few hard-cooked gallons of alcohol. Without a word they rested, then resumed. The air was filled with the aroma of new hot malt. They let it puke out, began proofing it. Then they went outside and breathed the air as it poured up and across Wild Cat in the predawn briskness. They rolled cigarettes and squatted under the laurel and said nothing because Earl was deep in study. Despite the chill of the air, a small, slick film of sweat was upon his face.

Then they began to jug it up. Wesley cast a bleary, eager eye upon the jars.

"You gonna give me a jar, boys?"

"Do ye want money fer ye old woman or likker fer yeself?" Earl asked.

"Well, how much did you plan to pay me?"

"Considering that ye're a-dodgin' and can't make money anywhere else, I thought I'd give ye family about a dollar fer ye night's work."

"That's awful good," Wesley said. "I appreciate it. How about givin' me a quart, too?"

"No. You start drinking and we'll have to watch you like a hawk to keep you from stealing the rest of it."

"I got better sense than that."

"Let's all mosey toward the house. We'll all have a sip or two and then part company. We'll get the money to your wife. You get on down the trail now and wait for us."

After he left they hid the pot, then joined him. Near the cliffs they began to drink. Wesley drank a pint and began to sing loudly and shortly passed out. They dragged him into one of the low caves under the cliffs. Beside him they left a bottle with two good swallows in it, to wake up on. Then Earl went down the road toward Hollytown.

———

Walton arose, flipped the pinched cigarette into the yard. Turning, he saw dimly his mother's pale gown in the other door. Silent.

"Mama?"

"What?"

"How long have you been there?"

"Just a minute. Are you ready for breakfast?"

"Well, I'll be goddamned," he swore weakly and shook his head.

"Do you want breakfast?"

"I reckon so, but I don't want a fight about who fixes it. I'll go on out early today."

"Is something wrong?"

"Just a few things," he said and stepped off the porch. He felt a great need to tell someone about his burdens, but he was grown now, and it was not his to be a boy again to his mother. Suddenly he turned a forlorn face to her.

"I may not be working at the tannery much longer."

"Why? Why on earth?"

64

Now he was his own counsel. The boy was gone from his face. "It's the men," he said.

He went to the well, drew up a bucket of water, and splashed some of it on his face. He returned in a while and listened to the women quarrel about who would fix breakfast. He turned angrily, picked up his dinner pail, and strode out the road.

As he topped Hame Tree Gap dawn was breaking, and Earl came down the road from Wild Cat. They traveled together toward Hollytown, talking about the good crop of squirrels chattering in the trees as they went.

For Logan, the window and the sky. The lonely wind of dawn blew at the corners of the house, and he heard the birds in song.

5

Paul Fortune was in the sixth day of a deep depression. He was driven daily from his rooms to escape the emptiness and doom. He stood at the fountain in the center of Hollytown and talked inanely with anyone who would pass the time. But he knew what he said only as he was saying it, and two minutes later he could not recall a word of it. Then he would run to his room for protection and isolation because a free-floating paranoia convinced him that the people here had perception far superior to any he had ever experienced anywhere else, and that they knew him completely. They knew who and what he was, and this very important information was being withheld from him.

In the nights he faded toward sleep only to come awake. He prayed blankly to know the cause of his melancholia. He asked for the truth about himself and would pay anything for it, but he feared that a wall in his brain would always separate him from the truth, and if he could not find something of worth and strength in his life, then he must eternally play his confounding and varied roles. It was late in life for him to be out in the world lost.

The fear of death was a radiating heat, downward, downward, through his brain. He was not ready. He had done none of the things he had meant to do. Life as he had seen it was not as it should have been. No, nor love, nor war, nor marriage, nor career, nor people.

At thirty-five years of age, he asked: Is it time? My time? No, thirty-five was not a good time to die. One should not have to go before seventy at the very earliest. By then one would have had time to observe life over a good period and see what chickens flew home to roost. Ah God! Fortune was always humbled to see any man's chickens flying home—he had so many out himself. To die before seventy was to cut an experiment short.

Memories of old events and people sailed into his mind like ghostly ships, and dead voices spoke to him in the night and he was afraid. He trembled at the flat, breathless sound of them, but they spoke and he had to listen.

He remembered the death of an uncle in a Chicago apartment. The old man was scared, and the closer death came the more frightened he became, so that in the end it was more ridiculous than sad to Fortune. Not serious, not noble. There was only his uncle cowering and whimpering before the inevitable, then flinching and going, leaving a cold corpse that had curiously demeaned death and robbed it of its great formal dignity. It was hard to forget the image of the scared man facing death. In later years he remembered it as being somehow more human that way, but that was after he had been around a long time.

He recalled the others saying that it was a blessing for the old man to die. Fortune had always doubted that his uncle saw any personal benefits in the coming of death.

Death was the greatest question for Fortune. He could not get it settled. That hidden demon led him cyclically into the reeking oblivion of drink. He lay abed in a stuporous fantasy of his own death, hoped someone would miss him, saw long lines of beautiful women passing his coffin; he called out in his heart for death to come but rose in the morning seeking a drink because he was truly afraid then that he was going to die.

Death, the mother of all. If not for death, there would be no need for birth. The fathers are deep in the ground, their hands folded across their chests, their seed spent. All sons then go to the father, and death is the mother surviving it all. In his brain were the old ancestral, racial eyes which watched time, and he fled from the knowledge of it. Time to love, to fight, to make great decisions, to omit decisions.

The values he had set for himself had proved deceptive. The idealistic lies he had told himself about the world at twenty came back at thirty-five to haunt him. He wanted the world to be more than it was and he needed his days to have come down to more than this. His life must prove out profitable if all the sums were added on any random day. He had compromised himself seriously, but where? At what point on what day had he gone further than

67

compromise and completely sold out? And if he had sold out, for how much?

An emotional person, he distrusted emotional people. A thinker, he held no respect for intellectuals. A spiritual man, he considered religionists misguided at best and retarded at worst. A man of words, he was careless with speech, larded it with vernacular and at times failed altogether in verbal expression.

He went to Rawson's office at noon on Saturday. Rawson was closing for the day.

"I need something," Fortune said.

"I've got to have some time off. I have just got to take some time off," Rawson said. Wearily he returned to his desk.

"I'm way down, blue," Fortune said.

Rawson sat back, cracking his knuckles and staring solemnly at him.

"You writing?" he asked.

"No, I can't even think straight. I'd have to get more optimistic to contemplate suicide."

Rawson nodded sympathetically. "Are you thinking about getting drunk?"

"No, I don't have to think about it. It just comes on me," Fortune said, his hands suddenly palsied, snapping about restlessly.

"You need something to write about, that's what. You come with me. I'll take you somewhere."

"I don't need to see any of your outstanding examples of misery and suffering."

"I'm not going to show you any cases. I want to show you the goddamnedest thing you'll ever see. I've been watching it for years. If you will suspend judgment, you can have quite an awakening in some direction or another. These are not representative of mountain people, but it's a picture of an interesting substratum's social life in a community where a social life outside the local religion is forbidden."

They drove to the Upper End, or Western Front. Rawson parked away from open view, and they walked through some trees beside a little creek and squatted to observe. The place lay just outside the town limits of Hollytown, a congestion of buildings clustered around an intersection and spread more thinly up and down the highway from the crossing. Some respectable small businesses were there, but they were few and overshadowed by the beer joints, honky-tonks, and bootlegging houses. Even the two filling stations dispensed liquor by the shot, bat-wing, pint, quart, half or full gallon, case, or carload if ordered.

Several roads fed into the intersection within a quarter-mile area, including the one from Hame Tree Gap. The section was identified by several names, the more colorful ones placed upon it by dough-boys returning from France in 1918–19. Depending upon who was talking, it was called the Western Front, the Second Front, the Firing Line, or, with a more local flavor, Shootout Flats.

Rawson and Fortune sat under a willow tree. The flow of the scene quickened. Straggling in from all directions were tannery and furniture factory workers, loggers and pulpwood cutters, tan-bark haulers, well-diggers and ginseng hunters, Cherokees and moonshiners.

Stacy Billings, a reputable merchant with short white hair and a pleasant, ruddy face, stepped out of the door of his dry goods store with his apron flapping. Three men of respectable mien, dressed in business suits, followed him. He stepped onto the edge of the pavement and rotated his arm angrily in the air.

Sweatbee Hardy staggered out of Lon Gudger's tavern-cafe across the road and stared boozily about. Alex Fore, stinking and un-shaven, rounded a corner with a tow sack bulging with beer bottles. Free and unpent, he was the local tramp. And then, Joe Felton, dapper in his way, sat down beside some gas pumps, dressed in a suit coat, overall pants and workshirt, dirty tie, and a broad-brimmed hat. He plinked idly, tentatively, on his old banjo.

Music, oh music for the scene. Out of the open door of Lon's place came the juked raw melody of "The Great Speckled Bird."

"There, there, by hell," shouted Stacy Billings heatedly, pointing first at the three and then at the general stirring hive with a wide, inclusive sweep of his hand.

"We've got to rid the place of these. We've got to clean it up, I say. There's the golf course, drawing tourists from everywhere . . . there's the Florida people . . . then, by the most damnable curses ever put upon a man, there's them. . . ." He pointed again at the three men, and his voice carried across the street.

"They are what is keeping the tourists from pouring in here. Them and this snake's den that ought to be torn down and up-rooted from the very ground."

Sweatbee raised his sharp, suspicious face and turned uncertainly to the four men across the street. He reeled a moment on swiveling ankles, then addressed himself to them.

"God damn the tourists," he said. "To hell with them. I hope they all come down with the galloping shits and die in bed of it."

Stacy Billings stared bitterly across the street. His companions shuffled their feet in embarrassment. Alex Fore chewed at his inner jaw. He put his sack of bottles upon the ground and slid his ancient hat back to show the few straggly, long tufts of hair upon his shiny pate. His beard worked fiercely as he chewed. His shifty eyes narrowed to slits.

"Yes," said Alex Fore. "God damn them to hell. And we'll not trade at your place anymore, either."

Stacy Billings swung about. "What?" he shouted. "The thing I feared has now come to pass. But I need this in writing so I can plan on cutting my future budgets. In affidavit form if you will do it—just mark your X on there after I have it drawn up. I think you spent twenty-seven cents with me year before last. I don't know what I'm going to do if I lose your business."

Joe Felton struck a discord on the loose head of his banjo, sang out in a breaking tenor:

"Sweatbee said they can go to hell, go to hell, go to hell. . . ."

Then Sweatbee turned to Stacy Billings. "That goes for you too, you son-of-a-bitch."

The insult hung oppressively over the scene. Stacy Billings held out his hands to the three with him.

"There! You see what I mean. That's it exactly."

Paul Fortune stretched his neck, stared. Rawson nudged him.

"There, you see what *I* mean?" he asked sardonically.

The rich, colorful threads of the life of drinking men on Saturday on the Western Front wove and stitched and wrapped about them. Suddenly a swarthy man came toward them from the road.

"I've been looking for you, doctor," he said.

"What do you want?"

"Mr. Corrigan is in town from Boston and he's sick."

"Where is he?"

"At the dispensary bed at the tannery."

"I'll be there in a while."

The man looked around at the Western Front.

"Christ! What a hole," he said. "I'm a foreman at the tannery warehouse. Those guys there . . . they work for me, a lot of 'em

70

do. Crummy bunch. The scum of the earth. I'm a foreman, and they don't even say 'sir.' Get that? They don't even say 'sir' to the big boss."

"Sir? Sir?" Fortune exploded. "Their very condition says 'sir.' Their very existence makes 'sir' very plain. Why in hell do you have to hear it?"

The foreman fell back, startled. "Who'na hella you, mac?" he asked.

Fortune ignored him. Rawson turned, said, "Go on back to the office. I'll be along."

The man turned and walked away. Once he stopped and looked back resentfully at Fortune. Rawson waited a moment. He stared at Lon Gudger's place, cleared his throat delicately.

"Are you interested in the labor movement, by any chance?" he asked.

"Vaguely. I had my fling with it in the past."

"Are you a subscriber to class struggle?" Rawson asked. Fortune saw that Rawson was suddenly formal, cold, a scientific watcher, and that he was listening aggressively.

"You mean am I a Red?" Fortune asked carefully.

"I didn't ask that," Rawson said, his quick, deep eyes fastened upon Fortune.

"Listen, I'm a drunk and a writer, that's all I know about who I am. I'm no Red and I'm no fellow traveler. I know what you are thinking, but I don't want to organize anyone. I don't know how, and I don't think these people could be organized under any banner."

Rawson's face relaxed. "Well, you do seem to be learning something about mountain people."

"Why did you bring me here?" Fortune asked.

"This is where I often come to observe," Rawson said. "Sometimes I am needed here on Saturdays. I thought you might get something out of it."

Rawson stared straight ahead. "The foreman is not right. These here on the Western Front do not represent the mountain people. They represent, as I said, the drinking men. I felt you might have a high interest in that."

Alex Fore stood now in front of Lon's place with his sack of redeemables and reeked of his many foul odors. He bent his head, turned it to the side, stared into the joint, uncertain of his welcome.

"See him?" Rawson asked. "He had a good trade at one time. He came from a solid family. I don't know what went wrong with him. These things are not the treatable things, as far as his family is concerned. They don't know what's wrong. He sleeps about here and there and won't bathe or take care of himself. There have been insinuations about bestiality," Rawson said, shrugged.

Sweatbee staggered again out of Lon's, another beer in him. He glared about and walked into the next joint. Shortly he emerged, staggered into the highway, into the path of a Florida car. The tourist careened and screeched to a halt. He dismounted and put his hands on his hips.

"Where are you going, fella?" he asked sharply.

Sweatbee swayed about, deeply perplexed. "Why? What do you want to do about it?"

"I might take you down a notch or so, fella," the tourist said.

Sweatbee reeled, glared fiercely, pushed up his sleeves, spat on his hands and balled them up.

"Thar ain't nothing separating you from me but air," he said.

The tourist stared, grinned weakly, got back in his car, and drove on. Sweatbee rocked back and shook a fist in the air.

"No, by God," he shouted. "You'll not laugh at the Sweatbee Hardys of this world. We are dangerous men."

"There, you see," said Rawson. "That is one of the Sweatbee Hardys of this world. They are dangerous men." He thought for a moment. "By God, this one really is. I tell the truth. Why he's not killed someone I don't know."

"Why do you say that?"

"He waylays his enemies, who are legion, and the forces of them are fed anew from every source," Rawson said with an enigmatic grin. "He smites them down in the biblical, which is to say literal, sense. Vengeance is mine, saith the Lord, and Sweatbee is agreeable to that. He is also going to extract his own vengeance no matter what the Lord does."

Walton Guffey came into their sight around the bend, his stride long and heavy for such a slight man. He had worked late at the warehouse.

"You see him?" Rawson asked.

"Yes, the young father."

72

"That's him. He came from one of the backland clans in a county west of here. He's a smart boy. He was taking a correspondence course in draftsmanship, but he quit to get married."

Walton crossed the highway, arms swinging wide. The lid of his lunch bucket glittered briefly as a stray beam of light caught it. They watched him approach a group of men who had emerged from a line of pines. Walton and the men squatted to talk.

Out of Lon's door rolled two men. They wrestled and grunted and cursed. Sweatbee was on the bottom. The other man sat on his chest and hit him savagely twice in the face. Sweatbee bleated piteously for mercy. The man relented and slowly got to his feet. Sweatbee leaped to his feet and scurried around the corner of the building.

"Thar!" crowed the other man. "That'll show the sneaky little bastard. I'll have no guff from the likes of him."

He dusted his hands, hitched his belt, and swaggered in the direction of the next honky-tonk. All activity on the front slowed to a near stop. Everyone stood silently. Stacy Billings edged quietly out his door to look.

It came from behind the building—a big rock sailing in a slow, even arc. Those who saw it marveled at its easy trajectory. It rose and sailed downward, taking the man in the back of the head. He flopped once. They would talk about it for months. It was the longest, most difficult shot that Sweatbee had ever made. His forte was the short, powerful ones in the dark, with only neon and window lights to work with.

"Jesus Christ!" Paul Fortune said. Rawson grinned, shook his head.

"Aren't you going to help him?"

"No, that's what he gets for messing with the Sweatbee Hardys of the world. Besides, he's too drunk to be hurt badly, and I need time off."

Sweatbee skulked back into sight, low-down victory on his face. He stared about, crafty and defiant. Then he walked to the fallen foe and studied his handiwork.

"Yes, you will," he crowed, "you will have some guff from the likes of me. You will have all the shit the likes of me cares to give you."

Then Sweatbee opened his fly and pissed on the man.

"Great God Almighty!" Fortune said. "I find this hard to believe."

"This is Sweatbee's day, all right," Rawson said.

Sweatbee swaggered back into Lon's, pushing those gathered at the door out of the way. He returned to the door several times and cackled. After a while the man got to his feet and staggered down the highway.

Movement resumed on the Western Front. Alex Fore's bitter eye shone out from a window in Lon's place.

Nearby, Joe Felton was ejected from Rob Warren's joint. He landed on his face. His banjo sailed out behind him.

"Joe must be out of money," Rawson observed.

"Why?"

"They just asked him to leave Warren's place. He must have tried to bum a drink or offered to play a tune for a bottle of beer."

Loud noises then came from Warren's place, thumping and bumping. Then a window broke. Out of the babble of many voices came the babble of many oaths.

"Someone has decided it was unjust to ask Joe to leave. They are deciding the case on its merits," Rawson said.

A county car with two deputies passed slowly along the highway. Alex Fore observed them solemnly from behind his pane. Sweatbee broke for cover toward the pines at the golf course. The law passed on, tarried not at the Western Front. The drinking man's dirge came out of Lon's door.

> What a beau . . . ooo . . . tiful thought I am thinking,
> Concerning that great speckled bird . . . .

Walton Guffey rose from his conference with the men beside the road and walked toward Wild Cat. The other men came slowly toward the joints.

"Now here's something to study," Rawson said.

"What?"

"The Skillers, Guffey's neighbors. You recall the old witchwoman? She's their mother."

"Indeed, I recall that bunch," Fortune said. The group came on, rounded the corner.

"Watch up and down the road. Earl keeps scouts out," Rawson hissed. No sooner had the group got in front of Lon's place than another one stepped to the door and signaled them in. Then two more brothers stepped out of the weeds at points on each side of the joint and converged on Lon's.

"That bunch there beats anything you'll ever see," Rawson said.

Fortune squinted. "I keep thinking that I've had something to do with that leader. I don't know where. His face stayed on my mind for days after that child was born."

"I've heard more than one say that Earl gives them uneasy dreams. But to my knowledge he's never been anywhere but here. He did go off to the war in 1917."

"France? I was in France."

"Maybe there. I think he's built time on the roads, too."

"Well, this is one helluva place, all right."

Now it was midafteroon, and Saturday afternoon at that, and the excitement of their time to get drunk was upon them. The Wurlitzers were loaded with nickels, and the music was constant, and they laughed and sulked and fought. Lon's place was packed—a stirring, pushing mass of drunken, ill-clad, and stinking rowdies crowded together along the bar, their speech thick, strands of alcoholic saliva slick upon their lips. The reek of wild fermented blends rose from their collective breath and hovered, pervaded.

Red-eyed, roughshod, and rowdy.

Lon moved along the length of his bar, loose and at ease, big and raw-boned, weary of eye, with thick lips and a hoarse, knowing laugh. At two-thirty he grew tired of fighting with his thirst and joined his customers.

"Set 'em up—on the house," he roared and began opening free beer.

Joe Felton entered the door cautiously. He heard Lon, grinned, pushed back his hat, and struck a note on the banjo. Alex Fore pursed his grimy jaws, narrowed his eyes, nodded wisely at the proprietor's judgment.

———

Rawson stood, stretched his legs. "I'd better go see about the Boston man."

"You've not been in any hurry," Fortune said.

"Well, maybe he's cured by now. Some cases get well quicker if I just leave them alone. Maybe I'll go somewhere and rest. Why don't you stay and watch? For God's sake, if you get thirsty, get out of here. All right?"

75

"I feel better now."

After the doctor left, Fortune sat and watched awhile. Then he went through the weeds, crossed the road, and went into Lon's place. He did not notice that Sweatbee had entered behind him.

"God damn! Here I am," Sweatbee exulted. "I'm a wildcat's kitten and it's my night to howl. Gimme a Ram's Head ale and call the law."

Cries of good will went up.

"Ah, Sweatbee, Sweatbee. You made your mark on the world today," one said.

Fortune stared about, and they quieted some and stared blankly at him.

"Gimme one of those Ram's Head ales too," he said.

He drank with them, and it all came to one point in his mind, and then with about seven of the lagers down he could see clearly that there was a time to sow and a time to reap, and a time to stay sober, and a time for all things in their due season, and indeed, a time to get drunk and it was now that time. How could he have abandoned that great and glorious feeling—the soaring of the heart—when the first two drinks are down, and there is an unlimited afternoon and evening and plenty of cash, and the owner of the bar is also in a corner drunk and singing along with the jukebox? He knew himself to be ruled by the stars because everything came together at a propitious moment, and it was in harmony, and he was in the right place to be drinking away the day in the company of men whose devotion to their drinking was heroic. Though some of them edged away from a yankee flatlander at the bar, most of them did not, and now Lon was lifted out of his good business sense and into generosity by his own beer, and nobody had to pay for anything except those who wanted to, and not many did.

After Paul Fortune had consumed much beer and three blasts of moonshine whiskey and had puked twice, he wandered to the two tables where the Skiller brothers sat. If he had been less drunk, he could have seen that one also stood near the front door and another at the back door, but even sober he would never have seen the youngest of them hunkered down in some weeds behind the place, watching everywhere and everything, patiently.

He talked to Earl, whose face held a gentle smile.

"I've seen you before," he said.

"At the Guffeys', when Logan was borned," Earl said.

"No, somewhere else. Years ago. It keeps coming to mind. . . ."

A shadow came over Earl's face, guarded it.

"Where all you been?" he asked Fortune.

"I've been in every state and half of Europe," Fortune said. All the brothers stared dumbly over their bottles at him. He felt like a rabbit who had wandered deep into a burrow and knew there was a snake in there, but he did not know what kind of snake it was.

"I was in France during the war," he said. "I was over there a long time."

"I was too," Earl said.

"Where? We might have been close together," Fortune said eagerly.

"I was in some towns and places with funny names that I never could say right."

Over the low drunken roar in Lon's place sounded a solitary bird call. Seconds later the warble came again. Earl's eyes went to the back door, then the front. Fortune did not notice that some of the brothers sat on the edge of their chairs and some slumped back, or that the two brothers near the doors had gone to the walls and were watching the front.

Sweatbee was on the floor boasting, drunk and angry. Fortune turned to look at him.

"Somebody's going to beat hell out of that smart little bastard," he said.

Earl's eyes went to the window, saw the county car drive slowly up in front and stop. Sweatbee danced over to Fortune, fists doubled.

"What did you say?" he demanded of Fortune.

"I said you're a silly bastard. I might beat your ass for you."

Sweatbee backed off, stared about myopically. The drinkers were silent.

"Well, start in, then," Sweatbee said, uncertain.

A voice from outside: "Is Sweatbee Hardy in there?"

Sweatbee glared at Fortune. He looked out the front door and saw a deputy about ten feet from it.

"What do you want?"

"Come out here, Sweatbee. I need to talk to you."

"What about?"

"Come outta there, I said."

Sweatbee ran out the back door and into a deputy there. The two eyed each other warily. Then the deputy spoke.

"Sweatbee Hardy, we have a warrant for your arrest for assault with a deadly weapon, to wit, a big rock, on the person of Willie Keever. Will you come peacefully or not?"

"You can kiss my ass or not," Sweatbee mimicked.

"You'll go one way or the other," the deputy said.

"Ha ha ha ha ha," laughed Sweatbee hollowly, snapping his fingers. "You're talking to a man who considers you a piss-ant. You'll do well not to push me in any fashion, nor hinder my comings and goings. It'll only take me a minute to squish you. I might thrash you right now. You are messing with Sweatbee Hardy, in case somebody ain't told you."

"Are you going to get in that car or not?" the deputy asked, red-faced.

"It was a wasted day for your mother the day she had you, but she was a paid whore, and it probably didn't make any difference to her except for the money she lost for a day or two," Sweatbee said.

The other deputy came up behind Sweatbee and brought his blackjack around in a quick, smooth loop. It struck Sweatbee behind the ear and he fell unconscious. Then that deputy quickly rushed the first deputy, whose face was insanely contorted, and who was trying to free his pistol from the holster.

"I'll kill . . . kill . . . killllll . . . ulll . . . ."

"Wait. Wait. Sweatbee is just drunk," the other man said and threw his arms around the first deputy.

"He's going to be just dead, the goddam son-of-a-bitch," the first one bawled. "Did you hear what he said about my mother?"

"I know it. I heard it. He didn't even know your mother, did he? It wasn't true, was it?"

"By God, now what do you mean by that?" he shouted. He broke free, ran to Sweatbee, pointed his pistol at Sweatbee's head, and fired once. Gravel flew an inch from Sweatbee's ear. Then the other deputy hit him with his blackjack, and the lawman fell beside Sweatbee. Sweatbee slumbered on, his mouth open with some dirt in it knocked there by the bullet. The deputy still on his feet turned and looked at the back door of Lon's place. The drunks all stood watching. The deputy looked around anxiously.

78

"I had to hit Sweatbee. He was starting trouble with his mouth."

"He shorely was doing that," Lon said, rocking about. The others nodded.

"He woulda shot him," the deputy said.

"He nearly did," Fortune said, shock and amazement on his face.

"He might yet," said Joe Felton.

The deputy turned to look at the unconscious men. His eye caught movement far on the road.

"Is that the Skillers?" he asked.

"You don't really want to know, do you?" Lon asked, snickering.

"Yeh! They's a warrant out for some or all of 'em."

"What for?" Paul Fortune asked.

"Who in hell are you?" the deputy asked.

Fortune stared blearily about. "I've just never heard so many goddam questions asked that don't get any answers," he said.

"You better answer mine," the deputy said.

"Why? What in hell will you do?" Fortune demanded belligerently.

"I'll stick you in jail for a long time."

"Paul Fortune," he said and went back inside.

Shortly two of Lon's sons came and carried their father, feet dragging, homeward. Then one came back and closed the place. The drinkers drifted off. Paul Fortune went to another place and continued drinking. He left shortly before closing time. He was only four steps out of the door when he heard a movement behind him. Then his mind spun into the stars for a few seconds, and he realized that he was on the ground and that his head was bleeding.

"I got out on bond," a distant voice said. Fortune raised his head enough to see the humped form of Sweatbee scuttling away under a streetlight. Then he sank again as a last stray thought hurtled across the grid of his mind and into the skies: this was the damnedest place he had ever seen, but he owed God at least one favor, because he was no longer depressed.

6

Frost formed silently before morning, and the autumn sun took it away. Winter was not far. In the afternoon Walton worked at the chop block. The axe rose above him, caught the light and glinted briefly on both sharp edges, then flashed down and bit off a great chip. On the porch, Loretta stood with Logan, who stared at his father. Mrs. Guffey cut grass beside the rock garden with a reap hook. The mown grass was curing fast, and the fragrance of it was in the air. Loretta walked past her to the chop block.

"Walton, I need some money," she said in a deliberate manner.

"What for?"

She exploded. "For everything. That's what for. I need money and you haven't offered me any in I don't know when."

"What's the matter with you?" he asked, bewildered.

"I just want some money of my own. You give her a dollar every week, but not a dime, no, not one dime for me. I need fifty cents for some material for curtains in our room."

"Why Loretta, there's curtains in there."

"Those moldy, dirty old rags have been there since this house was built."

His eyes flashed, and he looked quickly to his mother. Loretta recoiled from the intuitive flash in herself, saw again the loyalty he had for his mother. All the agony of her marriage welled up, and she was once more a stranger and alone among these people. She could never escape the feeling that he and his family owned wherever they stood and managed to dominate the scene about them. She detested them at times for the unyielding manner in which they dealt with life. It enraged and terrified her; she felt herself a child with no control over her own life. She sobbed and gritted her teeth, and there arose in her a sudden quiet plea for death to come now and deliver her into the hands of God. But when that involuntary prayer sounded, she was diminished somehow, and she felt she had lost some valuable ground in her battle with the days.

"Are you all right?" Walton asked, leaning to her and holding her arm. She wavered, knew in her strange, lost mood that she had compromised some essential part of herself.

"No, you just keep your money, Walton," she whispered and backed away, a wild and baffling look on her face. A bolt of fright shot through Walton—something had come apart in her and he could not put it back together. She walked listlessly down the trail to the house. He dropped his hand from the axe, opened his mouth to speak, and found he had nothing to say. The women, the women.

Mrs. Guffey swept the hook along the grass, oblivious. She held the grass by the top in bunches and cut it evenly at the ground. Walton wandered aimlessly to the barn, where he sat and stared at the mountain, wondering when he must get the foreman, where he would find another job, what was wrong between the two women, what he had broken in Loretta, wondering . . . .

When he returned to the house, he saw she had been drinking.

"All right, where did you get it?" he demanded.

She tossed her head, laughed dreamily, excluding him. "Get what?"

"Liquor."

"What liquor?"

He took her arm with one hand and balled the other into a fist. She focused slow, drifting eyes upon him. Her face was like a confused child's.

"Waal . . . ton, please, don't hurt me. Don't. I had to have a drink or two. I don't know why. It was some Big Boy had in the sideroom."

Then she giggled, and her eyes drifted off to a world he could not enter. Mrs. Guffey slowly approached.

"Hey!" Loretta said contemptuously, "how come you're always standing around watching us?"

Mrs. Guffey winced. The child cried and Walton went toward it. Loretta moved to intercept him but was bowled over by his rush. She sat, glaring, her face flushed. Then she turned to Mrs. Guffey and gritted her teeth again.

"My baby!" she said, struggling to her feet. "Give 'im here."

Walton hugged the child, chucked its thin chin with a thumb, and handed it to his mother, ignoring Loretta.

"Has she fed him?" he asked.

"I don't know, son."

"Well, feed him again anyway."

Loretta circled him, a fighter now.

"Yes, I fed him," she yelled. "How do you think I treat my own child? What kind of a mother do you think I am? You think I don't love him enough to feed him? Damn it!"

She shook her head frenziedly and shouted:

"God will damn all of you, especially you, old woman. The first thing tomorrow I'm going to pack up what me and Logan has, and we're going off this mountain, and we're never coming back. I'll not live with you anymore, Walton, or her, her, God damn her!"

She saw they were staring at her.

"You're a son-of-a-bitch and she's the bitch," Loretta yelled, "and I'm taking my baby from here, and you'll never see us again."

Then she realized she was shouting into a vast maw of silence. She was being weighed now in that sudden, deadly stillness. Her words echoed in the quietness of the house and returned immediately to haunt her. They stripped away the power and numbness of her intoxication and rang in her skull.

Son of a bitch?

That most terrible insult, supreme, never to be tolerated or taken lightly. More men had died in these mountains over that irretractable utterance than had died over cuckolding or barn-burning, fencelines or hunting dogs; and worse than calling a man a son-of-a-bitch was calling him one in front of his mother, and worse than that was calling his mother a bitch in front of him. Loretta now knew that she would be extremely lucky to get off with a beating, and she wondered numbly why it didn't come.

Yet they stood frozen—Mrs. Guffey with a long, noncommital gaze, Walton staring deeply past the wall. From outside came the cry of a whippoorwill, quickly lost in the profound silence of something being weighed in two minds.

The moments passed before her stricken eyes, and no one moved

82

or spoke. She realized vaguely that she had breached something sacred to this family, something of far greater import than calling a name. She had threatened to take away the child, and that threat carried into their deepest existence and passed along ancient racial nerves. No one who carried their blood and name would be removed to any place other than death, to which the others acknowledged that they did not have immediate access. The threat to take the child was a menace to the fabric of a family grown strong in time, and now these two were quiet and listening to hear and rehear her words. Their silence was significant, as though she were before a hidden jury of all the past and dead members of the family, and in this secret gallery many hidden voices were arguing and determining.

Loretta rushed back toward the remainder of the liquor. Mrs. Guffey looked at Walton. "What do we do?" she asked simply.

Walton listened to the blood in his brain as it washed clear the answer. In a motion of mind he referred the question to all those ancestors and wondered only briefly what was expected of him.

"Have him ready to go out of here in the morning," he told his mother. "You fix breakfast and let her sleep. I'll put you on a bus to Franklin. You can get off at Chestnut Creek and cut across Antler Ridge to Aunt Mindy's place."

So into the ridged stronghold of his own territory did he consign his valuable. He lay abed and listened to Loretta's deep and drunken breathing and was torn by compassion because he could always see some small part of the many personal tragedies of her life. He loved her but he could not understand her. Before he dozed he saw the many images of her that roused feeling: her face at chores, her carriage as she walked to the well, a sense of vulnerability about her behavior. In the night he patted her shoulder gently, but he was not tempted to change his decision.

They were almost through breakfast when Loretta awakened and stumbled in to sit at the table. She took uninterested sips from a cup of coffee, holding her hand over her eyes to keep the lamp's heavy glare off her hangover. She did not notice their quick, silent gestures with hand and eye. Walton bent and kissed the top of her head and went through the door. It was an hour later when Loretta was sufficiently alert to realize that the child and Mrs. Guffey were not there. She searched the house, cellar, barn, and brush before the dreadful realization came. Her pulse pounded painfully

83

across her skull as she ran to Hame Tree Gap. In the mud she found the tracks, and she plunged into the trail through the forest. Once she fell, retching, rose, and ran again until she found a diaper lying on a root beside the trail. It was wet from the drizzle, and she knew they had a long head start. She stared into the gloom of the wet woodland; then a vision of the entirety of her broken young life came, and she fell against an oak and cried bitterly, clutching the small, dingy diaper to her breast.

She made her way to her father's house in Hollytown. The information spread quickly among her brothers and sisters. They were bewildered and sympathetic. The girls were excited with the sadness of it, but the boys grew quiet and a bit sullen, as though they were now in the position of having to defend her and did not know whether her cause was just. They sought no trouble with Walton or anyone. Ultimately they decided that it was her trouble, and finding her own way out of it would help her mature. "Out of the hottest forge comes the best ar'n," said one, who had never been in a forge.

When her sister Alice came from her job, she and Loretta went to a lawyer's office in Wadenton. The counselor gave her no satisfaction—only vague suggestions and legal possibilities. He took no fee for that. A neighbor gave them a ride to Wild Cat.

Walton rented a room in Hollytown and did not try to contact her. Each day he went to his room from the job, changed clothing, then traveled through the woods and concealed himself in the foliage around the house. He sat patiently, unmoving, in the low brush beyond the front flower garden. On the fifth afternoon Loretta and two sisters came and looked around the house, then left. He followed them carefully, inflamed into wild jealousy by the sight of her and by her inaccessibility. He trailed them to her father's house to see if any men joined them. That night he moved back into the house. He wrote a note to her and had it delivered by a neighbor the following day:

Dear Loretta. I am now back at our home and the others are in a safe place. I took my boy to Atlanta and put him on the train for Denver, Colo. where Mama has family. Mama will take care of him until I can work out money to go to him. I morguaged the home that I have spent so many happy hours with you to get the money to send them. You won't ever see them again to throw off on them.
Walton

Then, irrationally:

P.S. Do not worry.

The next day he went by bus to Franklin. At a feed store by the river, he caught a ride on a logging truck to Chestnut Creek. Then he struck out across a ridge until he reached the house where his people were keeping his son. That night he caught the midnight bus back. When he arrived at Hollytown at 2:45 A.M., he went straight to the tannery.

Production had slowed in the warehouse, and cured hides piled up. The men listened to the foreman's orders attentively, grinned, and slacked even more. The days were sullen. It was not in them to go to a higher authority if the higher authority was also an outlander. But they fashioned terrible fantasies for his end: beatings, slashing his guts out with pocketknives, shooting him between the eyes (either head-on or from ambush), burning his house or barn, maneuvering him into one of the cutting rooms and sticking his head under a blade. These sprang from minor irritations with the foreman. The major provocations brought one common thought: lure him into the room where the long vats of hot acid were, throw him into one, and in the brief time he had before death came he could reflect upon his transgressions against their individual dignity, and repent in that time of ever having said a harsh word to men who accepted only orders expressed in the most courteous and obliging tones.

The foreman did not know them. He shouted and insulted them so that the department heads might know that he was doing his job. The shanty Irish and blacks in the north had bent to him because they needed their jobs for survival. To him the mountaineers seemed of an even lower and more childish order. He could not know, then, that the mountaineers would not admit to needing a job in the first place, did not respond satisfactorily to driving in the second, and finally, could live off the land if they had to.

All he knew was that production was off, the men were hostile, and he had lost more control than he had gained by his tactics. He pushed on and decided to make a spectacular example of one of them. He would upbraid one of the reliable ones, then the message would be clear to those who had grown indifferent and sloppy. His mind turned to Walton Guffey, who was always on time, was

85

always courteous, stayed past quitting time to finish work he had begun, had family to support, and finally, was not a large man and could more likely be intimidated.

Walton stood with Norton Suggs beside a cart of hides, waiting for another cart to be unloaded.

"How's it a-goin', Walt?" Norton asked.

"All right."

"Ye mama and the boy still gone?"

"Ayeh."

"They be back?"

"In time, in time. When my woman gets herself straightened out."

"Her side said anything?"

"Nothing. They know I'm trying to break her, I guess."

The foreman strode up.

"Suggs, why in hell are you standing here jawing?"

The man's face reddened.

"Why, I'm a-waitin' fer the ramp to get free."

"You'd better get your stringy ass back to work."

Heads appeared over the stacks of leather.

"Guffey, what in hell are you doing?" the foreman demanded.

Walton's face grew serious, thoughtful.

"You're not worth a tenth of what the company is paying you. You stand around doing nothing, and you're worse than . . ."

Walton's balance shifted and his eyes lit.

"That's not the truth," Walton said slowly, "and you ought to tell the truth. Back off if you can. This is not the day to start in on me."

The others came out from behind the stacks of leather and gathered in the center of the floor. The foreman stared belligerently around.

"All here, eh? Good, I want you to hear this." He turned to Walton and shouted: "Are you calling me a liar?"

"You goddam right I am. Let's fight about it," Walton said, his first blow flattening the foreman's nose, his next one gashing his cheek. The foreman fell. The others stood about and nodded wisely.

"God A'mighty!" Norton Suggs said. "Walton was on him like a rooster on a june bug."

"He swarmed him like bees," another said.

"Stuck to him like a coat of paint," another said, sharpening his

86

own metaphor for the tales which must grow out of it and be told and told again in the boiler room and drying loft, the cut-sole and the elevator.

The foreman rose to one knee, then fell against a cart.

"You come with me, Guffey," he bleated in a ludicrously high and humiliated voice. "You're through here."

Walton grinned with exaggerated stupidity on his face and drew his fist back.

"Kick his goddam yankee face in," a man shouted.

Walton rocked back and forth, his fists nervously working the air in small punches. He sensed freedom and bad trouble—they came in the same package.

"All right. Get up and let's go," Walton said. He dragged the man up and pushed him down the ramp, through the corridor, and onto the grass. They crossed the bridge over a pond. The foreman wiped at his face with his sleeve as Walton paced him with his long, rambling stride. The men poured out the door and followed. Their low laugh swelled over the distance. The procession attracted workers from other departments, and the business of the tannery slowed to a standstill except for the cut-sole, where no one yet knew and the machines click-clacked and squeaked on.

The office workers saw them coming, then saw the workers behind them. Their faces grew fearful, and they glanced at the plant manager's door. He came out in time to see the foreman turn to Walton and say:

"Yes, we're going to the office, by God."

"Keep a-goin'," Walton said.

"Now you'll get it, you hillbilly son-of-a-bitch."

Walton hit him again. The foreman offered no resistance and fell, stunned. Walton got him to his feet and pushed him across the lawn to the office. One secretary fainted and the bookkeeper paled. Walton shook the stuporous foreman.

"We're at the office, you son-of-a-bitch. What's supposed to happen now?"

The plant manager blinked and pulled off his spectacles.

"Did you beat up the foreman?" he asked, bemused.

"I shore as hell did. I am the very one," Walton said. Snake-bit and going to die anyway, he would not now say "sir."

The manager's face clouded. He looked outside at the gathering men and could not fathom it. The fear of strike came to him. There was no end. Production was down; Massachusetts was unhappy. The foreman had numerous duties, among them the handling of violent workers. Now the foreman was beaten to hell and back. The machines in the cut-sole quieted, and the crowd of workers swelled. Walton went outside and yelled at them.

"Get back to work and quit watching us."

They stared, and a gabble of laughter and talk went up.

"Give 'em hell, boy. Just give 'em hell," someone shouted as they unclotted and headed for the buildings, already weaving the legend of it, the lore, the better telling of it: "He is in there right now threatening the plant manager," because that would have been the next logical step.

"To hell with these sons-of-yankee-bitches," a voice shouted.

"Yeh, we'll feed ye family till ye git something else," another yelled.

The plant manager picked the crotch of his trousers from between his thighs. His face was concerned.

"I never dreamed they were this hostile," he muttered to the foreman. Walton came back into the office to face him. The clerical help studied the walls, evaded any direct gaze. The manager adjusted his glasses and looked from Walton's bloody knuckles to the foreman's bloody face. Then he spoke gently, but with his full authority: "Gentlemen, step in here, please."

He looked across his desk at them. Now, in the fortress of his authority, he was comfortable. Yet the mountaineer was still wild of eye.

"This is outrageous," he said to Walton. The foreman nodded and held his jaw in his hand, satisfied that sanity would now return and justice could be done. Walton said nothing.

"Why? You tell me why?" the manager said.

Walton took out his Prince Albert can and studiously rolled a cigarette. His hands trembled slightly. A ritual, thought the manager. He must be allowed to finish. He is showing that he is both a thoughtful man and at the same time one who doesn't give a damn. Walton flung crumbs of tobacco onto the floor, moistened the seam of the cigarette with his tongue, then struck a match on his teeth.

"Jesus Christ!" said the manager.

"Because he's a loudmouthed son-of-a-bitch, and he better learn who he's a-hollerin' at," Walton said, glancing about at the manager's sanctum, which gleamed with power and high decision.

"He is my representative. I told you that when you came to work here. You said you wanted a job, and you have been a good worker. But we have to have discipline. You told me you were grateful for the chance to work when you were sixteen. Now this man here is passing on to you the orders I gave him. . . ."

Walton shrugged indifferently.

"This company has been good to you."

"I been good to this company. I break my back."

"You ought to be more loyal to the company that pays you."

"For a day's pay you get a day's work and that's all. My loyalty ain't for sale."

The manager looked at him, took off his glasses again, and rubbed his neck. He stared at the slopes of Eagle's Nest Mountain, then back at Walton.

"But I like you all right as a man," Walton said, nodding earnestly and naively. The manager took his tie in his hand and stared at it, his face working in red foolishness and embarrassment.

"Thank you," he said wearily.

They talked for three hours. When it was over, the foreman had resigned and Walton had been named to take his place.

A thaw had begun in Walton's terrible quandary. He saw movement in his life, and he did not slow up or turn back. That afternoon he went to the house of his father-in-law and spoke to Loretta on the porch. They did not ask him in, but they did give him room. Members of her family withdrew to the back of the house, the back yard, the vegetable patch. Walton tried the tentative tongue of conciliation. Each sought the cautious vocabulary of compromise, yet both stood ready to bolt into bitterness and poison. Walton told her that he loved her and that that was the issue at the moment. She told him that the issue was her son.

"Do you want to try again?" he asked, his face miserable.

"Do you?" she asked.

"I asked if you did."

"I don't know, I just don't know," she said, evading his eyes. "There's just so much to think about. . . ."

"Now don't be stubborn," he pleaded.

"What? Ha ha ha . . . ." Her laugh was cynical, but it shut no doors.

"I don't want to go on without you," he said.

"I am tormented by memories of you," she said, "and I need you, but I can't go back up there. I can't. I can't." She wept a little, and he saw again her frustration, her despair, her vulnerability.

His question hung there in its dry, stubborn reality, and it was more dramatic than anything she could have staged in her wildest moment of fantasy. She was aware that the abduction of her child had impressed her girl friends and sisters more than any tale she could have invented, more than any of the previous confusing situations she had been in. In magnitude it equalled, if it did not surpass, the near death of the child. Her friends would talk of this for years, and they would feel sympathy for her. Her great need was for someone to feel and understand some small part of her pain.

"If you don't come back, I guess I'll stay drunk as long as I'm here, and when I go to Colorado I'll do the same thing," he said sadly, but both of them immediately recognized it as a bad play, and it died unanswered.

"I have to think, Walton," she said, dry now of emotion.

"If you'll come back to me, I'll come after dinner tomorrow, and we'll go to Macon County for something I have to get, then we'll go get Logan."

She sensed deception.

"Where is Logan?" she asked.

"Where did I say?"

"That's a long trip. Have you got enough money?"

"I'll get enough," he said lamely.

"I'll have to see," she said, suddenly with tears. "I don't want to promise you now."

He stared at her, leaned toward her a moment, hot and anxious for her, then wheeled and left, swinging like a tall man past the cinder piles and through the tannery grounds.

The next day he rented a friend's Ford for two dollars and came for her. She was packed and ready for anything—Colorado, Mexico, or New York. On the winding road to Franklin, some of the honeymoon was restored to them, except at those awful moments when they recalled the mess they had made of it. He drove up Chestnut Creek and parked at the mouth of the trail which led across Antler Ridge. He led her up the rooty path, around the cliffs to the top of the ridge, and down into a small clearing ringed with hardwood and hemlock. When they entered the door to Mindy's big log house, Loretta knew instantly that Logan was there, and anger stormed her. Mrs. Guffey, her sister, and some of Mindy's daughters rose from their chairs and smiled widely.

"Why, here's Loretta. How are you? We're so glad to see you."

Bright fury in a dark face. "Hypocrites," she hissed, "where is my baby?"

They were not chastened.

"Why, h'yer he is," a pigtailed girl said. She chucked the child's chin. "H'yer's ye mama, baby. Ye want to see ye mama?"

Loretta leaped to the girl and snatched the baby.

"Yes, he wants to see his mama," she spat, staring about defiantly. They fell back, not now able to separate mother and child. Yet they made a big to-do over mother reunited with lost child, as though they had nothing to do with it. They smiled quietly, unembarrassed, and she turned to them.

"Hypocrites! A den of vipers, every one of you," she sobbed. "I was a-fixin' to come and get him anyway, even if me and Walton hadn't made up. God damn each and every one of you."

Walton passed on into the kitchen, uninterested in the women and their scenes. Mindy's voice lost some of its glow, but it was slow and thoughtful.

"No, don't God damn us. We're not hypocrites, either. If Walton hadn't brought you, you wouldn't have gotten here. You can be friendly or not, but don't make any threats or call us any names. We're not mad at you and never were. Walton asked us to keep his mother and his baby and we did. We'll do that again whenever he asks, or anything else. That don't mean we're mad at you."

Walton, Loretta, Logan, and Mrs. Guffey left and drove back to Wild Cat in near silence. When they reached the house, Walton strode in, his heels banging loudly on the flooring. He lit a lamp, gently took the child, and put him on the bed. Then he turned, grabbed Loretta by the collar, and shook her until her teeth clicked.

"I love you, woman. You're my wife, but don't you ever think about taking my boy again," he thundered, pushing her onto the bed. Her spirit plummeted. Life was to continue on its dreary way.

"Another thing," he said, "get ready to move off this mountain by Friday. I've been promoted to foreman, and I've rented us a house in town. We're a-leavin', Mama, and you needn't start in."

But she did.

"Oh Lord! Lordy, Lordy, Lordy," she wailed. "What have I done? Oh Lord, what have I done to deserve this? Oh Lord in heaven, why are you treating me this way? Why, we've been so happy. You're blaming it all on me. I tried and I tried to get along with her. Oh Lord, I've done all I know how to do. . . ."

Loretta stared. So! Mrs. Guffey was a woman too, turning in defeat to tears. But Walton was not moved. Though he knew his mother was right, he would not turn back. She had done no visible wrong, and she had hewed to the ways of the family as they had been taught her. She was loyal. The women struggled in his life and he had decided. The stricken look faded from Loretta's face.

"Mama! Shut up. Life ain't ending," he said.

No, but one of the final sections of it was closing up for her, and as it did, it left the end much nearer than she had realized. She shuffled off, confused, into the back bedroom and sat alone and helpless on the cot upon which her husband had died, when he had had no more liquor and no more strength and had given up forever the will to continue on a bad road.

She heard Walton put wood in the stove, heard the fire roar. She heard him go for water. He returned, picked up a poker, and blithely struck a flatiron with it. The poker rang with the golden notes of a tuning fork. In the back room it sounded like a knell.

7

IN THEIR HIGH FASTNESS, the Skillers lived a simple life in rhythm with the land and the sky. They normally blew out their lamp and candles about eight-thirty and retired. But on the nights they made or hauled liquor, they only appeared to do that. Only Mrs. Skiller went to bed. The brothers and sisters sat quietly in the darkness for half an hour, then Earl slipped out the back door and patrolled in a circle about the house in the woods, moving silently, stopping to listen, moving again. When he returned for them, they went softly in scattered file past the cliffs and over the ridge to the still. There the girls poured the liquor into fruit jars and cased those in boxes. Earl shouldered a case and took it up on the ridge. He scouted some more, then returned for his brothers. Each loaded up and marched past the edge of an old pasture, grunting, and out the ridge. The delivery route led them eventually down a mountain and along a cow path beside the Guffey fence.

Earl arrived at a point beside the road and waited for the first brother to come. Then he stacked both cases under a brush pile. Earl and the brother went back up the mountain, meeting the others at intervals. Only Earl and the first one carried a full case. The others brought half-cases. Earl went to the still and got the girls and walked them home. He took one more case down the mountain, and they all rested in the darkness.

"What time is it now?" one asked.

"It's right at one," Earl said. "You all got guns?"

"Yes," they murmured together in the darkness.

"Jody, go get the truck."

"You want any hay or fodder on it?"

"No, we got too much likker. If we're caught we're caught."

"We can shoot it out," said one.

"No, we won't shoot cops over likker."

"Why'd we bring the guns then?"

"Not for killing cops."

He spread his brothers out in the brush while Jody went for the truck. In a while he heard a soft snore. He walked among them a moment and returned to his place.

"Spread out, I said."

The snoring stopped and they blundered noisily through the brush.

"Damn," Earl said, incredulous.

The truck's gears ground as it came on, then the headlights illuminated the clay banks of the bend. The brothers came in from their positions and started getting the whiskey up.

"Leave it alone for a minute," Earl whispered sharply. The truck stopped and he went to it, calling out softly:

"Stay here. We'll make a short dry run."

The truck left and returned shortly. They loaded the boxes on the bed of it, and Earl sent all but four of them back up the trail.

"You want us to stand in the back to hide the boxes?" Harley asked.

"No, no use. Sit on it if you want to. I just need you to help unload."

The ones on the path heard the truck pull out on the road below them.

"Ah, hell," Buddy said. "I lost my pistol."

"You better come back early in the morning and find it," another one said. "He'll be hard to live with if he finds out."

"Well, I didn't even bring mine," said a third. "If there's any shooting, I believe in running."

Earl sat in the cab with Jody. The odors of hot crankcase oil and vapors of a leaky radiator infused the air. The headlights moved through the night, revealing here clay banks and roots, there crags beside the road and ruts, now an occasional possum, then a cat or dog out in the night. They took a long circuit around Wadenton, along a quick, tumbling creek, the lights playing on small foaming rapids and dark running channels. On the highway beyond the town Jody ran it faster, and the truck shot past the Blue Moon Cafe at Clyde, crossed a bridge, and stopped. Earl took a shotgun and a high-powered rifle from the cab, and he and two brothers dismounted. They walked through woods for a quarter-mile; then in a crouching assault run they went about a hundred yards through a field. They sneaked up to the back of a barn. The night was clear and the stars were bright. While the others were prone on the ground, Earl rose to his knees, head up and turning about like a snake. A lantern glowed through cracks in the rear door of the barn. Earl dimly saw a big car far enough behind the barn that it would have been hidden from view if they had come in by the road. He waited about ten minutes, then whispered:

"All right, now. Drop back down there about fifty yards and get across the road. One get up there and watch that car, and the other stay in the ditch right in front of the barn. Billy, do that and take the shotgun. She's loaded with double-aught. Be careful if push comes to shove. We'll try to stay clear of the door if we get trapped, and you let'er go right down the middle of the opening."

"What about me?" asked the other, leaning across the rifle.

"Keep that car in sight. If it comes to a fight, put two steeljackets in the tires. Then put the rest of 'em as close to the driver's seat as you can."

"You expectin' trouble to start?" Billy asked shakily.

"I don't ever expect trouble to start, but I never doubt that it will," Earl said. They skittered away, one at a time, to their places. A very gentle whippoorwill sounded sadly in the night. Earl waited a moment, then answered it and returned to the truck.

"Godalmighty damn," Jody said. "I been settin' on pins and needles here with the biggest load of likker I ever seen on a open truck."

"Where's Harley?" Earl asked.

"Standing over here with a rifle bead near your head in case you ain't Earl."

"All right. Let's drive on in there now."

The truck went to a side road and turned down a rutted and rocky little road to the barn. Earl slipped a pistol from the bib of his overalls.

"Get out and get ready," he hissed. Then he coughed loudly. A voice came from the barn.

"Earl?"

"Yeh, it's me."

"Everything all right?"

"It is here. Is it with you?"

"Yehman. Back up to the door."

"Just a minute."

The others stood aside as Earl backed the truck up near the door. But he did not block the door, or leave the truck where it might impede the fire from those hidden in the darkness. Yet he could roll under it if a fight started.

"How many men with you, Earl?" the voice asked.

"Three, counting me," Earl said.

The door opened, and light from the lantern fell out and revealed Earl and Harley and Jody, dark apparitions at the edge of darkness. Inside stood one man in overalls and two others in suits.

"Bring it in here and put it under the hay," the farmer said. The Skillers formed a line and passed the cases inside. After it was all down, the city man opened the cases at random and took a jar from each of them. He sniffed at some, and from others he took small sips.

"That is mighty good," he said.

"Thankee. I try to make it good."

"I hear you do. I can use plenty of it. Can you get me this much about twice a month?"

"No."

"You can't?" The man's laugh was false-hearty, faintly disdainful, disbelieving. "Why not? I pay top money for this."

"I don't make it in a big way. I just did this because Weldon there said you wanted some. He's a regular customer."

"We can make plenty of money."

"After you pay me, I won't need no more."

"What?"

"I got regular customers and I have to take care of them."

"No more for me?"

"No, I don't see how I can right now."

The man's face grew cloudy. He glowered about. Earl stood calm and humble, uninsulted, untouched. Magnanimous, with two armed brothers out in the dark.

"All right," the man said, reaching into his coat pocket. They watched closely, waiting.

"Ha ha ha," he laughed. "What if I pulled out a pistol?"

His companion smiled darkly. The farmer moved back a step. Harley sidestepped quickly from the middle of the floor, his eyes wide with bucolic innocence and wonder. Even as he did, Jody and Earl moved from between the door and the man.

"That shore would be a trick," Earl said.

"Yeh, yeh," Harley hissed. Jody gripped his pistol in his pocket, his young face humorless. The farmer knew something from deep instinct. Then the man pulled a wallet and counted out eighty dollars to Earl and twenty to the farmer.

"And you won't let me have any more?" the man asked.

"No," said Earl, watching the man, the farmer, the back door, the loft. His eyes were ceaseless in their survey, his ears conducting their own sweep. Slowly he and his brothers sauntered out the door. The farmer ran to them.

"Earl, I didn't know he was going to act like that."

"Don't worry about it. Who is he?"

"Ah, he's jist a man I know."

"Which man?"

"He's a city man. He married my niece."

"What's he going to do with that likker?"

"Take some of it to Asheville, and split the rest between bootleggers in Greenville and Spartanburg."

"I ain't a-gonna sell him no more."

"I think he was joking, Earl."

"I believe so too," Earl said.

"I'd like to keep on getting a jar from you for myself now and then."

"You will, too. Come and see me," Earl said and grinned. The truck moved off slowly, and the farmer went back into the barn. Jody stopped and picked up Billy, then the other one.

Dawn had not yet come when they reached Wild Cat. They lit the lamp and roused the others and distributed the money. Mrs. Skiller got ten dollars and the rest was split evenly except for an extra five for Buddy.

"You're a-gonna git married. That's what that's fer," he said. Buddy grinned.

"Something else we need to talk about," Earl said to him, and Buddy's grin faded.

"What?" he asked.

Earl handed him his pistol.

"Where'd you find it?" Buddy asked.

"I took it out of your pocket while you snored last night in the brush."

Buddy looked about. Earl stared steadily at him, then the trial was over.

It was Saturday. The brothers shaved and the girls dolled up, and they all walked down the road from Wild Cat. At the Upper End the ladies caught the bus to Wadenton, and the boys went into Lon's place to drink beer. Earl had not taken the truck because he knew they would get high, and he didn't want anyone caught for drunk driving.

8

A FEW DAYS AFTER Walton's family moved out, Edith's foot went through a rotting plank in her own house. Big Boy arrived from work to find Edith and Sue Ann sitting on the front steps with clothing stacked and bags and boxes filled with possessions. He went back to Hollytown to rent a tourist cabin, pondering the possibilities. Big Boy was not one to linger long in one stay if the responsibility was his. He did not care to own land, house, stock, or dog. He also did not like being married as much as Edith thought he did. When he returned from renting the cabin, they went to tell Mrs. Guffey goodbye. She nodded, a stoic jut to her chin. Then she followed them to the gap and watched them go down the road with their load, her face dignified but forlorn.

Now Mrs. Callie Rose Ann Horton Guffey had come to the last of her middle years, and she looked at the bleak prospects of the time to come. She was shaken by the swiftness of the desertions. But she had the strength and determination of her tribe, and with that and prayer she struggled through the first lonely weeks. The boys returned to see to her every few days. Sometimes they brought their wives, but the visits were short and hurried.

She began to cook in the fireplace, as her old folks had done and as she had done when she was first learning to cook. It was a quest for a stable time in her life—the past—but the past was done with. Yet it had the allure of being known and certain, and the future was becoming more and more uncertain. The ritual of cooking served her with comfort. As she ate, with plate on lap before the flames and a glass of milk or cup of tea on the floor beside her, she stared through the flicker of fire and into the past.

—Her father, silent and alone at the old homeplace on another mountain years before. His children had abandoned him to his unyielding pride and his memories of Manassas and Shiloh and the Wilderness, and of the long running raids through the Shenandoah with the guerrillas until Sheridan blighted the land. He had gone to war as a wagonmaster, but he was good with saddle horses, so he was transferred to the cavalry. When his troop was scattered, he was one of those the enemy picked up straggling in the Shenandoah Valley. But he escaped and made it good because he also knew about long walks and hiding and stalking and going about hungry without fearing it, so he made it to the fastnesses of the Blue Ridge with strength of spirit to spare.

Her father had been a praying man and given to high passion in his prayers, though he would not go to church. Once he ended a fervent prayer for grace at the table by bleating spitefully: "God damn Jefferson Davis and the whole shitting Confederacy."

Years later, when he was old, his wife died, and he would not let his children take him in. They did not insist, and he was left to his memories at the old homeplace. Now Mrs. Guffey was sorry that they hadn't moved him. They didn't visit him often, and one day they found him dead, his thin old arm thrust forward with a gnarled fist aggressively out. His gray eyes under bushy brows held anger yet, but dulled by death, and rounded upon his cold lips was some stark and unspoken word.

Appomattox?

Death had tracked him down in the severity of old age on a remote mountain. So then it must come to her. If so, what word would be frozen on her lips?

Logan?

She stared into the fire, her mind flowing with thought. She had seen it approaching for a long time, but she did not know what it was she watched, and now it was hard upon her. She dreaded to identify it because she would not believe it had come. Its one cold name was loneliness.

Alone?

The whippoorwill piped by the well and the leaves rustled.

Her existence had been predicated upon the maintenance and continuation of the family line. It was a line of sensitive, intelligent, and high-strung people—willful and stubborn, yet as kind, gentle, and considerate a group as any upon the earth. Their physical features were of a singular cast, with individual variations.

Their eyes ranged from a masked and melancholy gray to dark brown, and those eyes could ignite suddenly to light their faces with strange, obscure humor, with shallow or profound laughter welling from their throats. When they reached middle years, slight dewlaps folded under their faces, and parenthetical lines were printed from the ends of long upper lips to the tops of their chins. Youth remained below their lips and beside the nose. As a group they were slow to gray, and the ages of the more vigorous ones could not be estimated with accuracy.

Within their frame of thought, they were a cautious and judicious people—deliberate in most of their daily decisions. However, nature had distributed quite freely in the men a strain of wildness, of ungovernable tendencies, and at the most unexpected of times they lost judgment, control, and perspective. Although as individuals they seemed to know exactly why they did the baffling things, they were unable to explain it. They had a tolerant insight into themselves, and they extended that understanding toward the rest of mankind, as long as they weren't being put upon or their personal code of honor being violated. They required obedience to no rule apart from family solidarity. Some of them went to church, but most did not. They were fearful before their maker, true enough, but they would tremble before no man or congress of men.

If the essence of their thought had been condensed and poured together into one man, and that man had been appointed as a judge, then he would have been exceptionally lenient to defendants who came before him charged with poaching on government lands (but not on private property), hunting and fishing out of season, killing in self-defense, justifiable homocide, assault, cockfighting, the manufacture of liquor, the nonpayment of taxes, and other like crimes, which did seem to be lumped together as vague and ill-defined misdemeanors. However, had there stood before this composite judge a malefactor who had practiced deceit, lied, trespassed, informed to the law, thieved, paid attention to someone else's wife, abused children, ignored the old ones, let dogs and stock go hungry, or killed people without cause, then the judge would have hanged him without further quibble.

In frontier times they had settled and thrived in one locale, but with the passing of generations the family had one or more households in each general township of the county. They were good neighbors, hard workers, and they paid their debts. Some chose to remain in the remote and isolated coves and upon the further ridges. These were of a fiercer candor, maintained their own stills, raised all their food, bought little from stores, and settled quarrels among themselves without disturbing the judicial system.

The older members of the family maintained and visited regularly a family plot in a cemetery. It had started more than a century earlier as a family cemetery and would have so remained—reflecting a certitude of unity in life and in death—but at some time a church had taken root, and those of authority in the family at the time had generously opened plots to others in the community and finally deeded the whole burying ground to the Baptists as a churchyard for everyone. Down through the generations certain regrets lingered. It was felt that those ancestors who had deeded the land had squandered some vague family legacy. It was not lost on the generations following that after the plots were deeded, all the other lands owned by members of the family fell away in bits and pieces and small tracts to other hands. Superstitiously they pondered the wisdom of opening the ground to receive the corpses of the general public, although in fact not many who ultimately went into the graves were not related through some branching and diverging of the blood. However, they were not close enough to the main line to rate a grave in that single and formidable line of generations that stretched from one side of the ridge, up the rise, and down the other side. The original patriarch and matriarch were at the east end of the line. Two ancient stones, big field rocks, were enchiseled:

JOHN NATHAN HORTON
1701–1790
BORN ON A FAR SHORE
AND CAME TO LIE DOWN HERE
AT THE END OF A GOOD LIFE

And next to that:

HANNAH SHARP HORTON
1708–1794
SHE FOLLOWED HER MAN
WHITHER

The earth covered all the generations except a few who had gone into the world and had not made it back to claim their last place. Here and there among the tombs were vacant plots, which were being held for some who had outlived their own generations and most of those following. But even those ancient members would come here on the homecoming and grave decorating days, look at the markers, talk about the ones whom only a few remembered, and sit for a time upon the very ground that would claim them when time had its say. Among these was the smug security that sprang from a continuing family line—the knowledge that one will not immediately be forgotten after death, but rather will be recalled in all the minds as a part of the whole.

Mrs. Guffey, with the others, had watched the decline of family strength for some time. Though she could never articulate directly what she saw, her uneasiness grew as she watched the clan dilute with later generations of young strangers who strayed from the old ways—the great vigorous flow of family pouring into dismal bottoms and spreading and losing its force. At family reunions and on homecoming days she was one of the old guard, and all about were near-strangers—young adults with children of their own, such as Walton. When they were introduced as Barton's granddaughter, Mindy's grandson, Verdell's great-grandson, she started momentarily in quiet terror, looking for the familiar markings or brand, for something recognizable in the set of the chin, the color or shape of the eyes, the texture of the hair, the complexion, the form of the face, the build, the stance, the hands, a note of identification in the voice. Usually she could see something that had been passed along, something traceable to someone in the five full generations that she had known. In these times, only at an angle, with favorable light and with great use of the imagination and suggestion, could a smile be detected as one used by Porter, a dimple from Mindy, a frown from Papa or Monroe, a wide, friendly crinkle from her grandfather. Those characteristics had held strong for the generations within her own memory and knowledge, but were fading now. At the last reunion someone had whispered that one of the later ones had gone out into the world and had been jailed for stealing or some such, and she did not want to know who it was or from which branch of the family. Her heart sank into despair and disgrace.

Mrs. Guffey sat before her fires, chewing her food slowly. There was self-pity and some anger. In the dark corners sat something waiting.

Death?

Sometime.

Soon?

The whippoorwill cried out.

The yard was empty, lonely. The old house creaked. She sopped her bread in her plate, tore at the crust with her dentures, pondered and nodded.

Though she was of the mountains (or "of an early pioneer family" as some of the more pretentious ones insisted go into obituaries), many of them had traveled and spread to the northwest of the continent, with a few strays going into Texas and Arizona. But ultimately they returned to home grounds to live out the remainder of their lives among family and friends. They turned out in great numbers for family funerals, and after the box went into the ground, the menfolk surged forward to cover the grave over, stomping on the earth to tamp it tight.

If one of an old couple died, the survivor was absorbed into the home of a son or daughter, brother, sister, or distant cousin—but no one shrank from accepting a member of the family into his own household. Now the younger ones complimented the older ones for the custom, and with that notice the older ones knew that the custom was being gently dissolved. They shook their old heads, insecure. In their youth they had cared for the old, expecting the same in turn . . . .

The older ones drew near to each other. The young did not know how life had been in the mountains before their time, and they did not seem anxious to learn. So now Callie Rose Ann Horton Guffey watched the passing of her generation. Even the next generation was suffering losses. The survivors were watching after each other.

She stared bleakly into the fireplace. Autumn was coming. The wind boomed through the trees on the mountain and carried lost voices down the slopes.

She had always comforted herself with the idea that if her life fell apart, she could return to the land of her people and live near them. She told herself that she would not move in, or be dependent upon them.

Home? Return now? She saw the dream was thirty years too old. The jarring reality came. She must remain here. She had roots sunk into this life, and into this piece of land bought by her husband. He was buried across the valley at Green Knoll Cemetery, and she did not want to leave him. He had been her life. Despite his drunkenness, she had held to him, tolerated him in those times she could not love him. She had grown to believe that she did not love him in later years when she suspected him of women. But the night he lay a corpse in his box by the window, she was surprised to discover that she had loved him, and much more than she had known.

Their courtship had been fiery and often angry but always with high emotion, and that had frightened her because such feeling was usually kept hidden among her people's womenfolk. But he deliberately and skillfully aroused it in her, toyed and worked with it, got it out, and then fought it like a cougar he had flushed, and conquered it. When he claimed her for his own, she discovered that he truly did own her, and it was both pathetic and wonderful because some of her reserve and cold self-reliance fell away. She was stunned and happy that he had reached among the filaments and fibers inside her and found the one true release of pain and joy and had mastered her. He told her that a man of intelligence and love would do this no matter how a woman fought it, so that she could know of her womanhood. He married her, and she bore Walton by him.

She grew dependent upon this manly, relaxed veterinarian for emotion, and she got it fully. Later, when he worked too hard and alcohol got to him, she resented her dependency because he was not taking care of it. It was she who had to make decisions, and she found that the capacity to do so had diminished in her. She was unable, for a time, to use judgment in even the simplest matters, and so was he. She was angry and lost until she saw how pitiful it all was, and after that she was the strong one. But when people came to get a cow or horse doctored, he mustered his reserves, because she could not do his doctoring for him. People swore by his powers with animals—and in some emergency cases, with people. They called him the best horse-doctor around, but he was also the only one around. He bragged that he could do a better job drunk than sober, but that was moot because by that time he was always drunk.

He died in his dreary old office upstairs on Main Street, on a cot under gray windows which faced against the dim light of cold dawn. When death came, it must have roused him, because it appeared that he had tried to forestall it. Perhaps he had tried to rise from the bed to fight it but had been cut down and then pitched outward, because the upper part of his trunk was bent out over the cot to the floor.

Because he had not come home the night before, Callie went to his office and found him. When she saw the gray scum of death in his wide eyes, she felt some bitterness because he had brought himself down to this. Her deep indignation gave way to strength, and she went to the coroner and later made the arrangements. Then she went home and told the boys.

She let an undertaker prepare him instead of the neighbors, because he was a professional man, and there was a certain air to him, even drunk. When he was washed and shaven and lying in the casket in his good suit, she began to think better of him. When friends came and began to remember, they did not talk of the drinking and wilder scenes, but of his ability, his wisdom, and his uncanny affinity with animals. It struck her that he was well respected, that the people had not seen him through her eyes, and that her own prestige was not tarnished. She was ashamed then that she had scorned him and thought evil of him. As he lay there clean and dressed in his coffin, she looked in upon his whiskey-weathered face and saw the memories—of promises betrayed, true enough, but of more kept than she had realized.

He was buried on the southeastern slope of the cemetery, from which point the house could be seen in the distance in the winter when the leaves were down. She saved her nickels and pennies for a tombstone. She did not sell the land and go back to her people because his will had left her only lifetime rights, and she could not leave this life behind anyway. She renewed a correspondence with the Cousins Club, and later with the Rosicrucians, and went to the Methodist church and sometimes the Baptist church.

The children were on their own and could not come back, any more than she could go to her own people. When this filtered clearly into her brain, some of the grief and resentment she felt toward the boys and their wives faded. The universe was measuring and balancing. She occupied her life with her shrubs and flowers and garden, her cow, hay, and fowl.

Trees and shrubs and fowl and beast. And she had the whip-poorwill. The boys came often enough to see about her. She overcame herself and began to visit them occasionally.

Each Friday in the spring she cut sprays of wild and domestic flowers and trod the miles to the veterinarian's grave. She arranged them on his mound like a shy girl trying to please a suitor. She stood beside the grave and let grief have a small run through her. Walking homeward, she was an old woman again.

9

WALTON WAS PLEASED with the change in his wife. She was now the mistress of her home, and she flaunted that status unabashedly before any visitors. The company did not own the house, and this was of great value to her and Walton both. She was pleased that her husband had remained free of company nets. Sometimes he bought things at the commissary, but usually he traded with P. N. Caldwell on Main Street. Loretta now received each week a household allowance as well as a small sum for her personal use.

Walton tucked secret funds back, saving for acreage in the mountains, preferably with a stream. One day he would again break free of the town. But he succumbed in a weak moment and spent his savings as a down payment on an A-Model roadster. Loretta was upset to learn that he had money he had not told her about, but still, everyone could see what a man she had. They did not live in a company house; he did not owe the commissary; he got a doctor instead of a granny-woman when Logan was born; he had a good job and a car.

The rented house sat a few feet off the Hollytown main street. This allowed Walton to sleep later since he did not have the long walk out of the mountains. There was full light when he went to work now. He returned to see about his mother several times a week. Sometimes he and his half-brother took along their wives, but they sat in strained silence before Mrs. Guffey. The two daughters-in-law had grown apart in the weeks since the moves. They had lost the sense of closeness they had had when both had lived on the mountain.

In the new house, seven-month-old Logan crawled about. There was the ever-new light. He did not look at objects; he looked at light playing over them. Light and shadow, brightness, dimness, obscurity. Along the fine rims of light he saw the world, filled with shapes of no name, with motion he could not fathom, with colors melting and forming and dissolving. He sat beside a chair and stared dumbly at the light softly infusing the room. The window was in a good place in a good room, and its light was both comforting and exciting.

The days tracked across Logan's mind, here skimming and leaving only traces, there striking deep with vivid impressions, crisscrossing event with excitement, coloring the blank places in his mind with encounters and knowledge, until a bright perimeter of comprehension formed. From this boundary he sent tentative questions into the world, probing, reconnoitering. The patrols returned with other scraps of intelligence, which raised other questions, and then a pattern took thin shape.

The town lay in a broad valley which was broken by a number of ridges jutting into it like peninsulas. The valley swept down from the steep, spruced watershed to the south, and also from Balsam Mountain. The two valleys forked in the south and were split by the rugged Pinnacles. A barricade of mountains, one of which dominated the others, lay to the west. To the east of town were lesser mountains. The mountains of the watershed appeared gentler, but that was deceptive because they were so far away. Southeast lay Wild Cat, Wolf Pen, Lick Stone, and the wilderness of the Narrows. To the north was a buttressed and ribbed mountain, Eagle's Nest, named in the old days when eagles flew and glided about, and the settlers in the valley watched their big shadows slipping along the treetops as they sailed in to nest.

The valley also included Wadenton, and the towns joined lines, although there was little development where they met, and the lines were lost in a buffer of woods. From time to time the ruling clique of Wadenton tried to annex the smaller town, with methods called underhanded and devious by the powers of Hollytown; each time, the outrage and threats of violence from the Hollytown bunch drove them off. At least the voters of Hollytown knew those whom they elected to watch the skimpy public coffers. Therefore Hollytown had its own water and light departments, its own street services, and an official governing body of a mayor and three aldermen. It was partially governed—unofficially, but in reality—by a boosters' club, the small businessmen, the baseball team, and others with civic interests.

Those who boosted the town said that Hollytown had a good elementary school, a drugstore, a doctor, a dentist, a chiropractor close by on the highway, two furniture factories which turned out quality furniture, and a tannery from which leather went to Massachusetts to make shoes. The tannery also bought tanbark from those mountaineers and woodsmen who scaled the bark and brought it to the bark sheds for weighing and sorting.

The brown poisons of tannic acid drained into Camp Branch, turning the water to a weak mahogany color. All but the hardiest minnows and tadpoles perished. The air near the tannery was odorous—sometimes pleasantly so—with the scents of tanning liquor, dry bark, and drying leather. The workers were identifiable by their brown-stained hands and the subtle, rich aroma of the leatherworks coming off their clothing.

At the furniture factories, the sawdust from the saws, planes, grinders, and other tools filled the air with its own exciting wood fumes. Tin ventilators sat along the roofs of the factories like deformed dwarfs standing watch on the town.

The industries dominated the waking hours of the town, and they influenced the sleeping. Both companies had a number of houses they rented to employees—drab frame houses of uniform construction, painted with flat gray paint. The tannery had its commissary where employees shopped, and the factories had a certain credit arrangement for their workers with some of the stores.

Yes, the eternal and wearying presence of industry. The shrill steam whistle blew at the tannery at five in the morning to awaken its workers—and everyone else not stone deaf—and again at six o'clock to let them know it was time to begin work. The whistle blew again at noon, again at 12:20, and finally at 3:10, when the workers trooped out.

Steam whistles blew also at the furniture factories, but at a much lower pitch—a jarring, deep, and anguished blast, like the cry of a mighty fogbound liner going aground. The boilermen at the factories waited for the tannery blow, then tugged their own lanyards. The whistles were used also as fire signals. And as the daily train signaled its arrival and passing to the town, the boilermen let slip brief greetings. No one set his clock by these blasts, however, because the trains were not reliable.

The streets were narrow in Hollytown, but laid out in a clean and orderly fashion. Houses clustered on some streets but on others were widely separated by grassy lots, which were used by some residents to stake out their milk cows. The railroad cut off the west side of town, but it did not mark off any areas of class or caste.

In the last of the three tannery houses that sat nearest the sprawling plant lived Loretta's family. Although Albert Walters was no longer an employee of the tannery, he was allowed to live on in the company house. He paid four dollars monthly rent, and though he had been fired because of age, he still suffered the vague fear of being fired—the phantom pains after an amputation.

When Albert Walters was not puttering about outside the house, or busy with his small agricultural pursuits in the back lot, he prowled the house in painful boredom, studied his life and where it had led.

The house was of standard company architecture—wide, squat, and mean, painted gray. Despite the racket and throb of the industries, it was nevertheless ridden with the silence and loneliness of a remote mountain cabin. There was the lurking thing of the mountains, unspeakably ancient, of brooding spirit, silent and fearful, and of days forever spent, now departing, slowly turning in darkness, lit briefly by memory, eternally threatening to return; something of time's tread, of nights wasted in dreamless lost sleep.

The unslaked mood of that house came down from Albert and Carrie Walters and tinged it, and then seeped into the souls and moods of the thirteen children who had crowded its rooms of narrow dimness. Four of the seven boys were now gone, but of the girls, only Loretta had ventured to a life of her own. Because she lived in town now, she could visit more often, but she always became a bit depressed when she returned there.

Despite the numbers of them and the coming and going, the silence of the house lay on heavily, and it told of a rigid and oppressive discipline and of something deeper and darker, a dread jail to those children who grew up there. It sprang from the need of Albert Walters to fit into the community. He was a proud man, considered himself a gentleman, and raised his children to be good and not to question him. They must not draw criticism, or even attention, from the community. Attention they feared; criticism was a whip laid upon them. He taught them to seek respect more than anything, yet that would have required action open to comment. They settled for vague acceptance by a vague element in the community. They huddled together for protection, fearing things not of their house, yet they denied each other during the times when cocks crowed truth.

A deep and abiding sense of shame . . . because . . .

They were working people.

Only that, and nothing more.

Albert Walters had come up to this village out of Madison County, where his pioneer forebears had beaten out survival in this harsh land. He had met and courted the former Miss Carrie Bell Barnet those years ago; married her one Saturday night among a gathering of friends under the first street lamp ever lit in Wadenton; came then to Hollytown.

Thirty years at the tannery, then he had been promoted to foreman. Five years later, the company sold the tannery, and the new owners released him with two weeks' pay and no pension. There was not much work left in him, and little spirit. They allowed him to remain in the house at the same rent.

His wife was of the bar sinister. She knew the hateful days of it, the tortured nights. People never got over that.

But she had a position in the community and could not be replaced. She was a midwife and herb doctor. In her youth, bastard girls had had to prove their worth a thousand times a day. She had had to learn those many things that gave her value.

She brought to Ab Walters a comfortable kitchen. In that old, squared company house there hovered the rich aroma of her cookery. From the wide wood range's oven came big biscuits, tanned to the right complexion; pies crisscrossed with strips of crust pierced here and there by fork tines in even patterns; cakes freighted with tasty assortments of wild berries and nuts.

The true artist, with a distinct style. The air about the oven stung the nostrils with sharp soda and baking powder—not enough in the dough to give offense to the senses, but rather enough to set the pastry off to itself, to impart to it a style and body that other, lesser cooks would never master with any blend of flour and water and salt and soda.

She waited, this sharp, watchful woman, for the opportunities to offer her talents to those of the community.

A death? She produced a towering cake for the survivors. (A plain one, in keeping with the solemnity of the occasion, but one unlike any ever before called plain. A plain cake of vanilla and nutmeg and ginger and the rarest combination of spices.)

Or an illness? Some cookies or a pie, always with an eye toward the degree of sickness. If it was a bad case, possibly terminal, then a brace of sedate, unpretentious pies—unspiced and held to the natural taste of the fruit, pies that would not be ostentatious or out of place at the lackluster table of a worried and tired family. Pies that they could share with the sick, to eat the same food and break the same bread with the one afflicted.

But if the illness was on the upbeat, if the last turn had been passed and the fever broken, if the days ahead were optimistic— God in heaven! what joyous pies she then created in her wide, iron oven. She would go to the cabinet, mixing bowls at the ready, stirring, mixing in her happy frenzy as if she alone must furnish the nourishment to lift the stricken over the final hurdle to health. She cajoled her stove with low, urgent talk; she blended wood as the moonshiners did to build the right temperature.

She constructed her crusts out of a beauty in her heart. She slammed the pies from her board into the grills of the oven like an artilleryman slamming a shell into the cannon breech. Then she stood triumphant, her dark eyes aglitter and her shrewd mouth smiling, a black-gum toothbrush dipped in snuff and then into her jaw. She stood with her small, strong hands on her hips, her checked apron spotted with flour, waiting, waiting, waiting. She used no clock, no timer. She merely waited, humming a high tenor melody of the mountains. Then abruptly she leaped forward, slammed down the oven door, and extracted the pies, filling the kitchen with warm, exquisite, and maddening odors of fruit fulfilled, of flour in the flow of its own destiny treated as God surely meant it to be, of spice enough and not too much, of the great talent of soda, the whisper of nutmeg, the chorale of a song sung in that oven, the sweet notes of vanilla victorious in an anthem of love.

Oh, Great God Almighty! What authority in a pie.

Modestly she bore this overpowering tour-de-force to the sickbed, veiled with soft linen.

She demanded strict obedience from her daughters. They served

113

quiet, fearful apprenticeships about the stove, the cupboard, the drainboard. They were commanded to peel potatoes, to skin onions, to set out the spices, and to observe silently. The cooking was hers and no one encroached upon her domain. The young potatoes boiling in an aluminum cooker came out better under her hand. The gravy seething in its pan—bubbles and blobs—was the sum of vast experience. Those breads and sweetmeats, the cookies fragrant and tantalizing, were wrought by craftsmanship.

Yes, the cooking was hers.

Yet the tenderness she put into food was the only visible sign of love for her children. If they but knew, if they but knew. With eyes to see, they saw not—because she was dark, and her spirit was hidden in other ways. Her face held the quick gleam of perception, touched here and there with the sharp light of paranoia. In her lost days on the earth, she had sustained a thousand inner shocks that pinched her soul in tight knots; punishment, at last disillusionment. But past the faint scars of pain, she was stamped also with endurance.

Sometimes they saw. To look upon that webbed face was to see occasionally—and briefly—a child, lost and hurt and not comprehending. The lash had been laid upon her. Her dark, grim eyes looked into the day at hand, but reflected bitterness and unfathomable knowledge from the past. She was short and impatient with her children, cutting them to raw nerve with words, with sudden rejection. But always later, in a complexity of mood, she tried awkwardly to make it up. She could not show warmth and flexibility. To regret openly was to admit defeat in her heart. She was too insecure not to be tough, too tough then to be gentle with her children.

But Mrs. Walters tried in her stiff, secret manner to make amends. When the atonement came, it was often extravagant, and the children never realized that they were being compensated for some painful rebuff of days or weeks before. She would suddenly become warm—a different person—with a gift, or if not a gift, then the granting of some rare privilege. Her children stood in awe of her, uncertain and wondering.

Her time was full with her duty to family. Daily she was in the backyard beside the creek, boiling their clothes in a great black pot, rubbing them over a washboard, wringing them out with her hands, hanging them to dry on long rope lines and low tree limbs.

Gruffly she bedded the children down while Albert rocked his chair on the porch and stared ahead through the maddening tannery vibrations and drones. Carefully she put the covers over them, briskly she patted their heads in rough goodnight, crossly she called for them to stop giggling and go to sleep.

For breakfast she served up a big bowl of thick gravy, oatmeal, biscuits, meat—sometimes bologna—rich and hot, in dawn's dim light.

To work, to work, to work.

Her husband stared bleakly across the creek, into a past of toil at the tannery.

———————

Now Loretta welcomed her sisters into her own home. The wife with a house, she postured extravagantly, heating coffee, doing things that needed no doing.

"I have to go to work after a while," Alice said grimly, her eyes narrowed in envy.

"That Logan is so cute," another one said.

Loretta set cups down. "Now, girls, we've got cream and sugar," she cooed.

Cynthia stood and stared out the window, saw Boogerman Sitner, the town policeman, standing near the fountain. He leaned to his cane, bad leg outward.

"He's got the stick today. He claims his leg hurts when bad weather is coming," Cynthia said.

"Who?" Loretta asked, pouring.

"Boogerman," Cynthia said. They all stood to stare.

"The law carries the stick," Lucy said in mock profundity, then sat to her coffee.

"Why, why," scoffed Cynthia, "he ought to be locked up hisself."

She walked up and down the floor with her cup. Sally giggled. Loretta glowed.

———————

The young women murmured in the kitchen. Logan bent his head forward to see the window. Beyond the glaze, the eternal movement of cloud across the land. As he watched the light, he grew to hear it also—beyond the noises of the town, he heard the quiet, smooth flow in the sky, felt it passing upon his skin, opened his mouth to taste it, reached out to hold, and found only the boarding of the floor. He was caught again by the vision of the window, the glazed sparkles of reflection and refraction.

———————

The plant dominated the town even past the quitting whistles. Workers went home and sat silently on the porches of the company houses and contemplated the corrugated metal buildings, sat in dull stupor and gazed at dense smokes pouring forth from the towering smokestacks, felt the phantom vibrations through their bodies as the still, hushed machinery lurked and waited until the morning. They peered into the dimming light before them, saw the plants that owned them, heard eternally and would never stop hearing the mutter-mutter-mutter of machinery deep in the angled, labyrinthian bowels of the tannery, or the steady, maddening low hum of the ventilators in the factory—a diabolical exhalation of sawdust and moisture.

Into the night, the gentle, stupefying mutter and hum, the muted vibrations in the earth under the town. As each day ceased its activities, the noise pushed beyond its own boundaries and spread through the coves and hollows, over ridges and mountains. For miles deep in the land, a steady mutter-mutter-mutter, putt-putt-putt, hummm . . . mmm . . . mmm . . . ummmm . . . hum . . . mmm . . . ummmm . . . wheeze, wheeze, putt-mutter ummm and mumm mummm mummmm

They did not protest the place where they made their living. They sat dumbly upon the porches and watched the plants, and listened, as though they were spellbound by the great, quiet, slow drama before them. Their lives. Their slack faces glinted dully in the late afternoon light.

Mutter, mutter, mutter.

Putt. Putt. Putt.

Wheeze and hummm . . . umm . . . ummmm.

———————

Logan's eyes were heavy. He stared at the fiery sill, the light as it came and the loss of it at the stove where darkness ate it; then it loomed, hovered, came and went, and he heard a bird's cry, and in a dimension deep in his heavy mind, he heard the far noises of the tannery and the factory and the temblors from a passing train. His thoughts dimmed and he was lighter. Then he breached that lost dimension and heard the quiet song of the sky and slid across a wide ribbon of liquid light, swept down long bright slopes and through fields of bold color. But it did not impede him, because he could not stop long enough to experience it or remember it; he was at a place beyond recall and the noises were fading.

Alone now in the kitchen, Loretta sang bright songs.

―――――――

Walton sat under the tree in the backyard, whittling a big twig. Loretta rocked Logan on the back porch. Walton felt vague stirrings of discontent. He was trapped, getting nowhere. He walked about the small yard of the rented house.

"Property," he said. "I need my own place."

"How?" she asked.

"Work and sweat and bring it home and watch it go into bellies. Save, save, save."

"You can't save much on your wages."

Silence.

"Walton?"

"What?"

"You mad at me for something?"

"No."

"What then?"

"We need a place."

"Yes, I want us to have one."

"There's a house for sale on McClure Street, but I want a place out of town."

"No, I'm not going back to Wild Cat."

"I mean another place."

"I don't want to leave town again. I've made up my mind."

Walton walked around the tree, stopped, and stared toward the plants. Both boiler rooms let off steam. They began with shrill blasts and died to steamy sighs.

"God A'mighty," he said. "A man can't even breathe in this town."

10

Summer surged up out of the earth, spun softly out of the sky, and plumed the trees at Wild Cat with rich greenery. The wind broke gently over the crest of the Balsams and flowed across the valleys to whisper along the cliffs. Rain enough came to fill the springs and the little branch. The garden planted by Earl came up on time, and young potatoes, onions, and beans graced the table early. The blackberries ripened, and first the Skillers picked them near the cabin. When they ripened later on Wolf Pen, the family went there to pick. All of them but Earl and his mother left early for the final day's picking. Earl spent the morning cutting brush at the end of the rocks nearest the house. The cover for snakes had to be cleared. The coming and going of the family kept the snakes away, but occasionally one of the big rattlesnakes was found in the yard or in the weeds behind the house. They could climb through the low windows better than anyone would have thought. Earl did not hate them. He knew the nature of a rattlesnake. If something warm moved near one . . . .

Occasionally the fleeting picture of a big snake's head cocked back came to him, and his pulse was cut. But only for a moment.

Sometimes he thought also of wet rocks under the earth, deep down; of water trickling slowly on rock and bone and rotten red cloth.

Earl took precautions. This family had lived through its child-hood at the cliffs with the snakes.

He stopped occasionally and sharpened his bush axe with a creek rock, then resumed his effortless stroke. The bright edge flashed in the sun. He sweated, and the perspiration rolled down his face and body and lubricated his very joints, hinges, and straps. In the short space of the morning the sun had worked upon those shoots and boughs he had cut, and from the bared earth and drying wood rose brown heady odors to perfume the air about him.

He cut a swath in against the cliff and piled his brush to the side of the new clearing. Then he raked the ground clean of roots and small rocks and went into the trees, where he got several flat rocks, which he carried to the clearing and put down. The rattlers that failed to catch the midday sun as it came straight down through the trees onto the ledges could crawl here to be in the lingering warmth of the stones after the sun was gone.

Earl walked across his cleared place and calculated a field of fire with a soldier's eye. Then he sawed a small locust pole into rungs, took a hammer and big nails, and nailed the rungs up to the crotch of a twisted oak beside the trail. From that vantage point he had a clear shot at the ledges and also at the flat rocks in the clearing. He returned to the house for the .22 rifle and a box of shells. Then he climbed up and leaned into the crotch of the tree. He did not expect the snakes to show themselves immediately because his chopping and moving around had fixed them in silent coils.

He practiced patience. Waiting, waiting and watching, and silently listening, motionless, his head tucked so that his face was in shadow. Nothing knew he was there. His slow eyes crossed the ground, the cliffs, the limbs above him. In a while the insects in the tree resumed their whirring, oblivious of him, and birds flitted near. He was now of the terrain, both absorbing and adding to it.

He noticed a movement at the cabin and dipped his head forward and to the left with such speed that he appeared not to have moved at all. He saw his mother come out, stick in one hand, the cat-fur bag in the other. He watched and noted that she did not go forth with purpose. She tottered about, then took the path to the spring.

A bird rose straight up in the air near the cliffs and flew in circles, chirping wildly. The bird made several low swings along the ground, chattering angrily, then flew back into the brush. Earl watched.

The bird shot out of the brush, screeching. It flew in again, changed its tune to a wounded cry, came back out, and flipped about on the ground. Then it moved a little further out, where it flopped all about and left its spoor on the ground. It dragged one wing as though it were broken and went into the clearing. There it beat the other wing against the ground. Earl waited. The snake was drawn forth. The bird cheeped its distress, waited a moment, and fluttered. Earl bent to the rifle sight, watched a slow, subtle movement in the weeds. The snake's head came up slowly. The bird fluttered and cried, then flew away. The big rattler came out toward the center of the clearing. The bird screeched one time on a high limb in lusty triumph, then flew off, having led the snake away from her nest of baby birds, hidden back in the brush.

It was a rattlesnake in the yellow phase, with the lesser black bat-wing patterns accented by gold velvet. It was still for a time, and though Earl was looking right at it, he lost sight of it as it melted into the ground color. When it crawled again, he saw it. It went toward one of the flat rocks, and he kept the bead of the rifle's front sight hard upon the snake's narrow neck. Then he aimed about an inch under it, waiting. It crawled upon the warm rock, and Earl studied the slant of the stone.

"I'm a-goin' to bounce one into you, snake," he murmured, and for a moment there was heat in his heart. But then the heat disappeared as though some psychic switch had been activated between his mind and deep soul. He did not hate rattlesnakes. They had their nature. He learned from them. Earl squeezed the round off, and the snake rattled wildly and thrashed off the rock onto the cleared ground. He could not sight again until it stopped moving; then he shot it in the neck, taking off the head, except for a small shred of skin which still held it to the body. Earl grinned. A good trap. The bird was luck. He had not expected it. The trap was natural, a thing that flowed from one part into the next.

Now it was noon, and the sun blazed and poured heat past the shelter of leaves and into the shadows. Earl stood motionless on his locust rung, staring at the dead snake and then for a pondering instant past it, and saw himself across the gap of years standing at the parapet of a trench in France. Earl Skiller in that year stared out in front of his position at a squad of dead Germans. He saw past the dead and the barbed wire and the mud, stared past the gray rains on French fields, past the horizon, and saw a cloud of mustard gas meant for him and him alone . . .

. . . stared past gray rains of France and the horizon. Earl Skiller stood on a parapet, leaned forward against the lip of a trench, and stared vacantly past all before him. He looked with a searching eye far into time and saw . . .

. . . Earl Skiller standing on a locust rung with a rifle pointed toward . . .

. . . a dead rattlesnake.

In a fit of rage he had once promised himself that he would kill them all. He was not bitter about rattlesnakes; it was just that he once promised himself that he would kill them. Before the time of that promise he had never killed one, and had never wanted to do it.

And now as he stood on the locust rung and looked at the useless flesh before him, stared to and fro into time and up and down the broken, wrecked years, he decided at each point that he did not ever again want to shoot anything but snakes at Wild Cat Cliff, North Carolina, and not many of them.

Then the noises of his mother pulled him back out of the cloudy passes of time. He heard her whooping and shouting and could not ignore it. He cut his eyes about the past-present fields of fire once more, saw neither Germans nor snakes moving, nor the burning mustard gas. He went to the snake, put his shoe on its head, and with a swift stroke of his pocketknife, severed the rattles.

Earl walked softly down the trail, then squatted to watch his mother. The fur bag hung on a pine limb, and the articles it had contained were scattered upon a rude altar made of a board placed across two rocks. She raised an old hawk claw onto which was attached the puff of a rabbit tail and shook it over her head. At the same time her other hand held two cow ribs, and she beat them together on her thigh in a spoon beat. All the while she chanted in a tongue recalled by no race on earth and jumped slightly off the ground in a strange, wooden rhythm. Earl's eyes ran with tears.

"Mama, Mama," he said, shaking his head.

Once her husband had gone to prison for moonshining and left her alone to raise the first four of the children. He came back a broken man, good only to breed and eat and sit mournfully about the house. He did not work for a long time, and he did not make liquor, so they were deprived of that little income. She took over and they got by. When the husband was finally killed in an automobile wreck, she went a bit daft. She told people that she had gotten a call to witch and that it was as legitimate as a call to preach. Yes, she wanted to witness to the universe as a witch. Earl didn't know where she learned her witching, unless she remembered tales from her old folks. If her methods and rituals were not authentic and fit no pattern, they did not lack an impressive knack for invention. Her little fur bag of unknown charms and talismans was a marvel to behold. She brandished it and dealt with it as devotedly as a Jesuit with his beads. Earl had decided eventually that if it gave her strength, it was all right. It caused him some embarrassment at times, but not a few people granted her credibility. Though none of them had ever heard of a person getting a call to witch, it seemed plausible enough, and they did know of the various gifts of the upper powers. The people did not argue with her about it the way they argued with the preachers about religion, and they gave her room to practice it. She was laughed at only in private, and then with trepidation and serious reservations.

Earl remembered his father as a strong man and a hard worker. None of the others remembered him quite so clearly. Earl remembered what his father had meant to his mother, and that his mother had once been religious in her way. During the hard times she had prayed, and with particular force immediately before her husband died. If one of her prayers had been answered—just one—she would have continued with the church. The witching rose up in her of its own desperate power. She found comfort in the complexities and compelling powers of the spells she cast, or tried to cast; the signs she read, or said she read; the futures she foretold; the numbers she chanted; the stars she watched. The blame was laid elsewhere if her charms didn't work, because there were other witch-women about who wouldn't admit her gift, and they used dark powers to nullify her effectiveness. These powers she did not know how to counter.

———————

As Earl watched, his mother worked herself to a high pitch, her eyes walled, and she began to salivate. She staggered and almost fell. He ran to her and clutched her arm.

"Mama! Stop this, I say."

She twitched and jerked and did not recognize him. Her mouth slack and eyes glazed, she turned on him and waved the bones feebly. He talked her down toward awareness.

"Mama, h'it's Earl, here to help. Simmer down. Come down,

now. You know better than to get worked up like this. Here, here, Mama, here . . . here . . . look at me . . . here . . . ," he said, rubbing her back and shoulders with one hand as he held her with the other. She calmed too suddenly and sobbed. Her watery eyes were confused, lost. Earl slowly led her up the trail.

"Now you go rest awhile, Mama. Ever'thing's all right now."

"Git my charms, Earl honey. Git 'em fer me."

"Mama, you don't need them now."

"Yes, I have to have 'em."

He released her, waited to see if she would fall, then returned to the spring and put her charms in the bag. He came again to her and led her gently to the house.

"Don't die and leave me. Oh God don't die and . . ."

"Mama, Mama, now. H'it's all right."

"No h'it's not all right and never will be," she said, and there was a hopeless thing in her voice, as lost, dire, and lonely as an old passed shadow. Earl had just gotten her to the steps when an unkempt man with whiskers came into the yard.

"Are you Mr. Earl?" he asked humbly.

"Yeh, that's me," Earl said, uneasy.

"I wonder if ye'd sell me a jar?"

"A jar of what?"

"Likker."

"I don't keep no likker. I don't fool with no likker."

"Well, I'd shore like to have a little lasher of h'it. Man tol' me you make h'it good and pure."

"What man where?" Earl asked in such subtle gentleness that the stranger's jaw fell.

"Man down the road. I can pay right now."

"Man down the road lied."

But then his mother shrieked from a tongue rooted deep in terrible fears of old midnight hungers.

"Yes, pay us. We're a-starvin' to death up here on this mountain. I'll git h'it fer ye," she yelled and stumbled hastily into the house. Earl stared at the man and did not move. She ran out with a jar, the bead of it afoam under the lid. Earl raced to her, pulled at the jar in vain.

"Pay us. We need the money," she yelled. The man laid a dollar on a rock, and she took it.

"Mama. Turn this goddam likker loose," Earl yelled. "We got

plenty of food. You're just all worked up. Turn it loose, I said."
He yanked savagely, and it came into his hands. He turned and
saw that the man had a golden badge in his hand.

"Mr. Skiller, I'm a federal revenue service agent, and you are
under arrest," he said coldly. Earl balanced the jar in his hand. He
suddenly dropped it, and with this distraction, he pulled a pistol
and pointed it at the man. The agent went pale for a moment and
moved his lips soundlessly. Then he stared at Earl ruefully.

"Don't do that," he pleaded softly and regretfully, as if he were
not now afraid at all. There was the honest tone of solid advice in
his voice. Earl knew then that he was ringed.

"H'it wasn't her that had it, h'it was me," Earl said, a subtle
plea in his voice as his eyes searched the man's face.

"Right! That's right. That's all right with me," the agent conceded in good humor. "Not her. You. It's you we want. You're a
hard man to catch."

Earl looked at her. She was still entranced. Slowly she crumpled
to the ground. "I'll git you out, Earl," she said, her voice strangely
sober and clear.

"Mama, don't worry," Earl said. He turned to the lawman. "Can
she sign my bond?"

"That'll be up to the judge. Does she own this property?"

"Well, h'it's in her name."

"If it's in her name, then she can sign a bond, I guess. We don't
need you in jail, Mr. Skiller. We just need for you to stop making
whiskey that you don't pay the taxes on."

Earl turned to her, his face now bland and unworried. "Mama,
when they come back from Wolf Pen, come on to the courthouse
and sign my bond."

She nodded slowly. "Can I sign h'it now?" she asked.

"We don't have it now," the agent said. "You'll have to come to
town."

In the time between being caught and being tried, Earl showed
them how to get by until his return. He was brought before a
federal judge in Asheville and drew thirty months in the Atlanta
federal prison.

II

THE WAREHOUSE ran itself. The crew there did their jobs at their own speed. All that Walton required of them was to keep the work flowing in and out. A system of signals evolved so that when one of the top executives arrived on the scene, the men were always quite busy at whatever pleased the management. Each Saturday morning one man or another brought a jar of moonshine, and they sipped and worked and were relaxed and in a good humor when they drew their pay and quit at noon.

Walton had new pride in himself, and with confidence came ambition, which brought the realization that he did not know very much and that he must prepare for other employment eventually. The car was now paid off, and he had secret savings building up again, and they were for a purpose. For weeks he carried around an ad he had found in a newspaper. He took the clipping out of his billfold and studied it from time to time.

Mechanical Drafting and Design
American Correspondence Schools
Chicago, Illinois

Self improvement.
Your path to a secure future.
Write immediately for details.

He wrote. He studied the deal they offered, and after he had extracted the promises, fantasies, and dreams, he worried with the price. Eight dollars a month for twenty-four months. He did nothing except fold the letter and carry it in his pocket with the ad for several weeks. Finally he mentioned it to Loretta.

"Well, why did you ever quit taking lessons from that other school? It was the same thing, wasn't it?" she asked crossly. Life had staled for the time being. She spent periods sitting in the kitchen brooding and letting the child do what he would.

"No, it ain't the same thing. I learned from that school, but it was just drafting. This is a bigger and better school."

"Well, how can we pay for it? You tell me that."

"I don't know," he said, keeping his fund secret.

"Well, think of that before you get any more ideas," she said.

Walton had nearly grown sour to the idea when he got a letter from the school, in which they expressed concern about his loss of interest—adding, by the way, that a special arrangement would cost him only $6.50 a month. Later the mail brought a brochure listing impressive testimonials. Another letter brought the price down to $5.00 a month. In two weeks the tuition dropped to $4.00. Walton guessed that this was the lowest point it would probably reach and enrolled. He did not mention it to Loretta until the books and lessons came. She saw he meant to do it, so she faced about and became a nuisance with her prodding.

It took a while to discipline himself, but his brain was quick. A vein of talent opened, and he ran through the lessons with such enthusiasm and skill that he got ahead of his schedule of study. Soon he began to prowl about the machinery in other departments at the tannery when the warehouse was running apace. One morning he was caught at it by some northern inspectors. In midafternoon he was summoned to the office.

The manager was doleful, uncertain. He looked as though he had been betrayed. He sat behind his desk and cut his careful basset eyes about. His assistant sat across the room, solemnly happy that a man had been caught cheating. Walton was as alert and wary as a cougar.

"Well, Walton, here is this report. It says you were away from your job," the manager said.

Walton stared back at him.

"What do you have to say?" the manager asked.

"It says the truth, then. But the hides are going out of the warehouse on time."

"That does not answer the real question."

"Who told on me?" Walton demanded abruptly.

"I did. I got it from the inspectors," the assistant said.

"Don't weasel now, Walton," the manager warned, sharp with him for the first time. "We know and you know."

"Well, I was down at the engines," he said lamely.

"Specifically, what do you consider the duties of the warehouse foreman to be down at the engines?" the manager asked.

"Not any."

"Well, I don't know what to do. I promoted you. True enough, the warehouse keeps up production. Is that because you're foreman or because the other man isn't foreman anymore?"

Walton frowned. "I don't know."

The manager studied him. The assistant studied the manager.

"Why were you in engines?"

"I had to see something."

The assistant snickered. Walton glared at him. The manager also stared sullenly at his assistant.

"What did you have to see? You have no business down there."

"Well, about one of the pump arms . . . ," Walton said.

"Pump arms? You may explain that to me," the manager said, a slight edge of impatience to his voice. "It is sometimes a trying experience to try to pull information from a mountaineer, if you don't mind my saying it."

"Well, in this lesson I got confused about ratios and strokes. I know what the answer is, but I still don't know what makes it right, and I had to know," Walton blurted. There was an extended silence and the manager's face remained frozen.

"I see," he finally said. "The lessons. Of course."

He waited again, then asked guardedly, "What lessons?"

"Well, this school, these lessons . . . ."

"What lessons, man?" the manager demanded.

"The goddam school," Walton said, and they both stared at him. The assistant laughed. The manager smiled timidly, shook his head, and then laughed too. Walton grew red in the face and shouted, "What the hell you laughing at?"

The manager's sensitive face reassumed the managerial mask.

"What school, Walton?"

"The American School."

"What is the American School?"

"Drafting and design. Machines."

"What?"

127

"A damned mail-order school," Walton said, gritting his teeth. "Drafting and design. I can increase my salary . . ."

"Not here, buddy!" the assistant said. The manager held up a hand.

"Is that right, Walton?" he asked in genuine interest. "What is it you are taking lessons about?"

"Drafting and design, I said. Mechanical drafting."

"I do say. Well, how are your grades?"

"I'm doing good."

"How are you with mathematics?"

"Good. I've always been good."

"How far did you go in school, Walton?"

"Seventh grade at Chestnut Creek School."

"I say! I do say. Have you learned a lot at this?"

"Yes sir," Walton said. The assistant's face now showed proper amazement.

"Let me tell you something," Walton said in his candid, abrupt way. "I don't cheat the company. I come in early and I leave late. I get the work done and you know it. The warehouse is ahead for the rest of this week. Everything is in good shape. I just had to see the pumps and engines while I was studying about them."

The plant manager closed his eyes prayerfully and made churches-and-steeples with his fingers. Then he turned to the assistant.

"Bring the engineer in here," he said.

The engineer questioned Walton, and when the conversation became technical, he nodded to the manager to indicate that Walton's answers were correct.

"Well?" the manager finally asked.

"He has some background in this," the engineer said. "He knows some elementary things and some advanced things in theory. I don't know how practical he is. He's not a college graduate, by any means, but he's getting there."

Walton fixed the assistant manager with a sardonic eye.

"Walton, do you really want to work with the machinery?" the manager asked.

"Yes, indeed I do," Walton said.

"Well, you certainly can't be a foreman in the machines."

"All I want is to be in there. How much is the pay in there?"

The manager sent for pay sheets and studied them. He conferred in whispers with the engineer, then said: "You lose about $2.50 a week right now, but the pay is much greater later on."

Walton pondered. Ten a month. Savings would have to pay for the lessons.

"I'll take engines," he said.

He left, and they watched him through the windows as his tall-man stride carried him across the cindered yard, across the bridge, and up the stairs to the warehouse. The manager sat back, stared at his assistant and his engineer with a curious smile.

"I think the whole thing is unprecedented," he admitted.

"I need a good man," the engineer said.

Loretta's mood swung and shifted. She transmitted tension to Walton, and life became difficult again. Daily she silently rebuked him, following behind him with a wet cloth to pick up bits of cigarette ash, mud from his shoes, other things he couldn't see. He was aware of it, but he ignored her. He knew it grew out of some small, unsaid resentment, because he had seen her too many other times leave the house untidy and cluttered for days at a time.

Logan became cross with one of the many small illnesses that worked at him. He was feverish and cried out in his sleep, and they moved his crib into their bedroom. Loretta fumed all day, and in bed that night she tossed and turned. Then Logan began rubbing his feet over the oilcloth at the foot of the crib. The noise grew on her and she tossed and turned all the more. Finally she sat upright, jerking Walton out of his own restless slumber.

"Now what is the matter?" he asked.

"The baby is gritting his teeth too loud," she said.

"By God, Loretta. The baby ain't got that many teeth."

"Well, some other people in the baby's crib are gritting their teeth too loud, then," she replied.

She arose at two o'clock and made coffee. She banged the pot and cup around so that Walton could not sleep. He was red of eye when he left for work. He did not speak when he returned in the afternoon. He changed clothing and left. The longer he was gone, the more her uneasiness grew. When he finally returned, she was exhausted with worry, but submissive. The remainder of the night he maintained his silence, and he did not return home from work until late the next night. She went finally to tears.

"What is it? Oh Lord, what is the matter?" she wailed.

He stared at her a moment.

"I bought us a goddam house on McClure Street," he announced with a smile, then went to bed.

Saturday after work, he brought Big Boy home to help him move. Big Boy had not changed clothing, and he reeked of wet leather. They loaded the furniture in a borrowed truck. Logan waddled among them in a soggy, drooping diaper, stumbled to the back door, and stared at the ground under the tree where light danced in speckles on the dark earth. Feeling ran through him, a bright quick river. He strained to remember something. His father under the tree?

Clouds gathered, glowered. Thunder rumbled in the distance. Logan ran to the front room and took a final look at the northern sill where light splashed off the glass and ran across worn boards. Beyond the pane he saw lightning leap from cloud to mountain. He blinked.

Walton scurried about, loading the truck with the help of his half-brother. Loretta bustled with bags, putting them down, picking up others, then putting them down. She went everywhere, did nothing.

"I'm coming," she yelled happily. "I've got it all ready. It'll be so good to own instead of renting. About the same money, but we'll be paying on our own place."

"Yes, come on. I want to get in there before dark."

"Well, it's just a little way, Walton."

Walton tripped over Logan on the porch, picked him up, and hugged him. Paul Fortune appeared on the sidewalk.

"Well, well, so you're moving out?"

"Yeh, but just to a house on McClure Street," Walton said proudly.

Fortune stepped forward. "Let me help load," he said, giving a boost to a chest of drawers going into the back of the truck. Then the storm came on. Lightning flashed and snapped, and the explosion broke on top of them.

"God damn it to hell!" Walton shrieked on the sidewalk, trying to lash a tarp over the truck bed. The rain came in slashing sheets of water. Paul Fortune fled into the house, his face dimly visible in the door.

"It takes a brave man to cuss like that in a thunderstorm," he said with awe.

Walton covered the truck, and they all went to the kitchen to smoke and drink coffee still warm in the last pot. Logan grew tired and sat against the kitchen wall until sleep came. He awakened in a chair in the new house. Loretta chirrupped and danced about the house.

"I'm so glad. I'm so happy."

The men wrestled the furniture in. Loretta stomped on the planking of the back porch to test it, checked the door-facing of the kitchen, ran to check the bedroom windows. She had not had the courage to do so before the house had legally passed into their hands. She ran to Walton and hugged him tightly.

He grinned. "You like it all right, then?"

The house was halfway down McClure Street, not very far from the tannery houses. Up and down the street, faces lurked in the shadows behind other windows.

The Guffeys. His people came from Macon County. He took on the foreman and is foreman.

Walton got the final chair into the house, alone. Big Boy had wearied and headed for the Western Front in company and sporting mood with Paul Fortune. Logan thumped across the strange boards to seek his mother. She was kindling a fire in the stove.

Logan explored the house for the abiding places of light. As he reached the living room, the sun's waning power slipped from the crest of Plott Balsam in the west, rode broad, deep avenues of beams off the mountain until it struck the raw, resinous boards on the wall, was reflected in gentle gold, and diffused on the front wall. The child felt alone in a strange place, lost and bathed in an alien light which held scant comfort. In the soft glow he saw that someone had carved a round, crude animal into the narrow beading of the wall. Then night fell, and he felt the incessant pounding through the air, the wheeze and mutter that underlay even the ancient noise of cricket, frog, and nightbird.

Over the next days, as they settled into their new home, the random parade of Hollytown passed before them. The whistles at the factories and tannery gave forth their last shriek and blast for Saturday, and as their reverberations returned from far hollows and coves, there was the movement of those last Saturday workers away from the buildings and sheds and toward the dim cheer of kitchens in the company houses. Old man Jolly stood in the door of his store, sucking cinnamon candies. Taffy Suggs, twelve years old with a man's body, strolled out of the drugstore and smiled gently upon the world. He licked his ice cream, strolled homeward. Tatterdemalion Alex Fore passed on slow, beaten feet, toes rank with grime in flapping shoes, his rags fanning old foulness in his wake. He looked up to see the Guffey tot standing on the porch staring at him. He grinned wanly, lifted a sooty hand, and waved in tentative gesture.

Heading towards the furniture factories, Alex Fore shambled along in a broken limp. His chin worked in low, muttered plaint, answering to himself idle and unfounded charges brought by God-fearing, hardworking townsmen.

Worthless. Does not work at a job, will not work; picks up beer bottles to swap for beer, liquor bottles to swap for liquor, drink bottles to swap for whatever they'll bring.

—Yes, some truth to that.

Ingrate! Will not pay the community respect for living in it.

—Does not live in it.

Nevertheless, lives among them.

—Yah! In a pig's ass. Not in a million years. Live with wild dogs first.

Will not pay his dues.

—Owes no man dues.

Bum, tramp, hobo.

—Kiss my goddam ass.

Filthy-mouthed old man.

—You heard what I said.

Comes from a good family.

—There ain't no good families.

Won't pull his load.

—Ain't got no load, don't want no load.

Got caught screwing a sheep one time.

—Everybody's got to have somebody.

"Baaa . . . baaa . . . baaa . . . ." The hateful echo. He wheeled about, an old man outraged.

"Who done it? I'll kill the son-of-a-bitch."

A daring, frightened boy darted under a porch. His voice was a faint, muffled echo:

"Baaa . . . baaa . . . baaa." The cruel bleat.

On lots beside each of the furniture factories were high stacks of drying lumber, to be taken inside in time and turned into quality furniture. The narrow alleys between the stacks could accommodate the passage of one man only, and where short lumber had been stacked with long, there were niches big enough to hide a man.

Alex Fore, limp-legged, dragged his broken and malnourished body into the lumber stacks like a wounded cur. The air about him was thick with stench. Nobody loved him but the flies and gnats, who swarmed in a dark, close, and protective mist.

Has withdrawn from human society, eats from slop buckets.

—You lie, you lie foully. Pork and beans, crackers and cheese, and potted meat. The bane of a man is his stomach and his pecker. Damn human society, their pious bleating.

Bleating? He crinkled his eyes, rimmed with poison.

—It's a goddam lie somebody told.

He found a shelf, ducked to avoid the rough, splintered ends of new boards, slid in, and lay upon his back. He patted the lumber, seasoned, almost dry. Soon to the saws and lathes of the factory. He grinned, his gaunt, whiskered face broken with ironic humor. He laughed with short, shallow, idiocy.

—Haw, they'll make a bed, fine brown bed. He patted the planks with a stained, grimy hand. Fancy ladies will recline. Perfumed.

—Haw, tell 'em Alex Fore slept here first.

He slept in the afternoon, twitching occasionally in the drowsy drone of flies.

12

EMERGING FROM diapers, Logan was a runty, puny child. He grew into the clothing Loretta stitched for him on her sewing machine. He also received hand-me-downs. The women of the town carried on a lively commerce in outgrown clothing.

Logan played behind the house in a stack of old lumber and factory slats Walton kept for firewood and kindling. He burrowed in the dirt under the front porch. Frequently he wandered out of the yard and onto the street, into other yards, under other porches.

He had little appetite. He nourished himself with cornbread and water between meals. Richer foods nauseated him. He never got hungry, only sick. In these periods of fasting he became moony, prone to meditate upon vague and unformed images and thoughts. At night his dreams fed upon the confusion of the day.

Loretta learned to control Logan with music. When he was outside, she put the radio in the window and turned it up loud. Music! Speechless thought swirled madly. A single phrase reduced him to happy delirium. When some of the mountain musicians were at the house, the random stroke of a hand across the strings released unplanned melodies within the child.

Music and light. These things mattered most to Logan Guffey. His mind was imprinted with light, shapes, the moods of windows and rooms and clouds. His attention focused upon the strange and secret places that no one else watched—those unnoticed places that brooded with the silence of time. His bemused eyes fastened on the corners of the room. His gaze lingered in the area under the stove, swept clean daily but never seen; on the light on the sill, the shadow under a weed, the brief crest of a ripple in the brook beside his grandfather's house.

Wan, freckled, he played listlessly in the front yard. The clouds rose over the rim of the mountains, and the shadows of these great sky fish fell onto the far slopes as the wind moved them under the sun. From somewhere down the street, a woman's voice sounded as she cleaned her house. A clear tenor.

> In a quiet and country village
> Stands a maple on the hill,
> Where I sat with sweet Geneva long ago.
> When the stars were shining brightly,
> You could hear the whippoorwill
> As we vowed to love each other long ago. . . .

Heartbreak in song and voice.

> Don't forget me little darling,
> When they lay me down to die. . . .

Bittersweet, coiling among the other impressions in his brain.

Logan grew stubborn—wrongheaded, his father called him when he bucked. The boy was not yet four, and Walton felt a tinge of pride when the lad bucked. Walton watched Logan and sometimes felt the faint tug of his own boyhood, buried deep, heard a brief, anguished cry, felt the stir of himself as a child deep in his own breast. When he could, Walton took the boy with him on his various duties and diversions.

The rich color of his father's day:

Saturday again at the tannery. His father held onto his hand, led him through the cavernous plant, through the room of vats. Acid, be careful of that boy, Walt . . . man fell in there and almost melted before they could pull him out. Lofts, filled with racks of drying hides; the warehouse, where the hides were stacked; candy at the commissary.

Saturday's work done, Walton and son sauntered with the loose column of tannery hands past the depot and onto the sidewalk, where small groups formed. Two drinks on the sidewalk, then Walton and Logan walked on to the Western Front, in its brightest mood of the week—early Saturday afternoon. Walton drank a cup of wine at one joint, then moved toward Lon's, clucking and praising his fine son and feeling good. They stopped to chat with a logger of Walton's acquaintance, and Logan stared about.

A lone preacher occasionally stood against the arrayed forces of the devil on the Western Front. Only when the denizens of the joints reached the besotted edge of remorse and self-pity did they hearken. Teary, stinking of alcohol, they turned, faint echoes of a poor mother's teaching ringing in their ears. They came as he stood beside the highway urging repentance.

"Ah preacher, the words are the ones I was taught as a boy."

"Now is the time, brother."

"They sound in my head, those very words my dear old gray-headed mama used to say to me those years ago."

"Stop and think. Did you ever wonder how and where she got those gray hairs? I didn't know your mother, friend, but I can see her now, praying for you. Now is the time to turn from Satan. Throw yourself at the foot of Christ's cross and be forgiven."

"Yes, preacher, I was taught . . ."

"I mean right now, brother," the preacher demanded, his voice desperate. "Oh, brother, if I could just get one to repent and stay repented here on this lost battleground of the devil, the others might come. Let it be you, brother."

The drunk swayed, gazed around, stared at the fronts of the two taverns.

"Decide now where you will spend eternity," the preacher said.

"Can you sing 'The Old Rugged Cross,' preacher?"

"I am not here to sing. I'm here to preach the word. There will be singers a little later."

The drunk licked his lips.

"Well, I think they got it on the jukebox in Lon's. I know they've got 'The Wreck on the Highway.'"

He spun and lurched toward Lon's.

"No, my brother, wait."

Too late. Each time he lost. Then he shouted on, reading now and then from the Bible. In a while the ladies of the choir arrived in two cars, dismounted, and began singing. Faces appeared in the windows of the joints.

Lon looked out and frowned. "Them people are going to ruin business one of these days," he confided in worried tones to Paul Fortune, who sat in blinking stupefaction before seven Ram's Head ale bottles and one pint of liquor. Fortune nodded. Sweatbee raised his head from the bar, shook it, then cocked an ear to the choir music. He went to the window and looked. He had always admired pure, holy church women. He yearned for their attention.

"The pore girls are wasting their time here," he said and walked to the door as the hymn ended. The women stared about selfconsciously. The preacher began yelling again.

Logan blinked, stepped behind his father, and hugged his leg.

Sweatbee decided that someone must stand with the church people. He stumbled out of Lon's door and fell on his face. He recovered swiftly and stared at the group.

"Brother, come here," the preacher said, holding out his hand. Sweatbee went, his stride confident and dramatic.

"Brother, do you know that the Lord sent you here to this place of evil today?"

"Right!" Sweatbee conceded, looking at the women.

"He sent you here that we might find you."

"Right again," Sweatbee said spiritedly.

"Brother, the Lord tumbled you out of that door at my feet . . ."

"Yes, yes, yes . . . ." Sweatbee smiled and looked to the ladies and the angels for their favor.

". . . put you here before me . . ."

"How right you are. Yes, hallelujah, you are right," Sweatbee crooned.

"He brought you here for me to save."

"H'it's the very truth," Sweatbee cried ecstatically.

"Now, brother, what has the devil ever done for you?" the preacher screamed.

"Nothing. No, nothing. Fuck him," shrieked Sweatbee.

His move toward Paradise was suddenly thwarted. The gates slammed shut, and the boulevards of gold shrank to rocky paths. In the stillness Sweatbee backed away, aghast, and fled into Lon's, his face pale.

Paul Fortune was in the door. He stood out of Sweatbee's way, then walked out and glared angrily at the preacher, who was trying to get the milling women reorganized.

"You don't know what you're preaching about," Fortune spat in mighty hostility. "You say man was made in the image of God. Then God must have been made from the beasts, for it has all turned out to be a fine lot of savagery."

The preacher looked at him, bewildered and myopic.

"Well, I didn't say that man was made in the image of God. I shore didn't, but I'll say it now," the preacher said determinedly.

Fortune belched and went inside. The preacher stared at his companions as they loaded into cars and left.

Inside, Lon sagged against the counter and shook his head sadly.

"Now, by God," he said to no one in particular, "it is exactly shit like this that gives my place a bad name."

Walton was now as high as he wanted to get, so he and Logan left and walked up the road toward Wild Cat. They cut through the golf course, in patches of pine and beside little stomped-down clearings in the brush and weeds, feverish with activity: a cockfight here, a poker game there, a blackjack game, a crap game. The caddies and roughnecks. Well-packed little paths ran under tunnels of boughs, brush, and blackberry briers. The ground was littered with bottles, Prince Albert cans, cigarette packs, a cud of chewing tobacco, the card box and jokers, and Bicycle decks torn in half by angry losers. The torn cards lay on the ground, bright-colored confetti, faces of the royal family staring blankly to the sky—the weary king, the suave, sinister knave, the sorrowful face of the queen. Bottles and caps, and now and again, stains of human blood. Around the roads near the golf course cruised John Shirley and Clyde McDonald in an old sheriff's department car, patrolling, patrolling.

Another autumn faded, and the clear wind rustled the curled, dry leaves against the limbs. Mrs. Guffey's sons came to chop her wood and see to her. As December made its cold advance upon the earth, they laid in piles of oak, locust, and hickory. Fireplace wood was corded on the front porch, and the stovewood was stacked on the back porch. Old obligation, guilt, drove them to offer this care. They found it hard to look her in the eye. Inside her doleful face was hidden a terrible ironic smile. She knew, she knew. Once she had been where they now stood.

Walton brought Logan. Mrs. Guffey held him, cooing in his ear.

Weekly her sons came to work, their voices flowing about the house as though nothing had happened or would happen, and yet it had happened, and she watched ice floes drift away in her back mind.

Those who had once walked in her life—gone!

Mountain cabins entombed in twisted dreams.

She watched them walk up the trail with the boy, leaving, then she turned and stared silently at the wood they had piled.

Cold wind howled in the trees on the ridgeline, and leaves fluttered through the yard and piled and flapped dryly in the rose-bushes and hedges.

Her own parents would not move in with any of their children, and in due course they had perished on a cold mountain. She grew to think, in torturous obsessiveness, that she had not done enough for them. In this culpability she turned down toward a certain paucity and poverty of spirit which neglect of parents brought. It caught up with her in her lonely nights, and she did not quail at a similar fate. In apathy, she dimly felt it was fitting punishment.

The house was growing old with her, and she did not know when it parted from its plumb and resettled through warping wet storms and fierce winter winds. One day the doors to her china closet sprang; and only when the secretary desk tilted a bit did she know that the floor was crooked. Many spiders dead and gone had left webs high in the loft and in the upper corners, and those nets had caught dust, and the webs and dust together had aged and hung in flimsy black festoons of old, dark midnight festivities celebrating the grief of time. Also in the loft, rat turds petrified by the years rattled across the planks as the wind howled down and through the vents.

When the kitchen was warm and coffee was upon the stove and the aromas of spiced cakes arose from the oven, the house was comfortable and homey. But when it had cooled and the stove had not been used for a few hours, the stale odor of old meals came on like decay.

Her fare had always been simple, yet now there came the insidious encroachment of destitution upon her table. She was careless in the preparation of food, let it sit long in pans, and picked at it before she rid the house of it. Yet when Logan came in from the fresh air, the stale odor of her kitchen seemed to him strangely permanent and thereby comforting. There was a security to it. He belonged to this ancient small kitchen with its clutter and odor. It had always been in his life.

They came to chop the wood, and Logan played in the trail above the house. Mrs. Guffey watched him with a keen, bright flash of her eyes.

"Time is feeding him and killing me. Not much is left," she whispered dolefully to herself. They finished again and left. She smiled, unwilling to show her loneliness, her martyrdom.

Frequently at night she took the kerosene lamp into the front bedroom and prowled through her old trunk of keepsakes: Confederate money, old letters and postcards, tintypes and the stereoscope, a picture of the leaning tower, a quilt top her grandmother had given her in her youth.

Lonely, bereft, forsaken. Happily one night she discovered some of her old correspondence with Uncle Charlie's Plan. She opened it and read it and stared curiously at the names.

In his youth, Walton was seeking education through the mail from places beyond the mountains. In her youth, she had sought friendship, comfort.

She read:

Comfort's League of Cousins, Augusta, Maine.
Our motto—Love, Virtue, Mercy, Brotherhood.
Note: Always be sure to write your membership number after your
name in all correspondence with Uncle Charlie or the Cousins.

Uncle Charlie's picture was at the top of the letterhead, framed in an ornate oval.

Herewith Uncle Charlie sends you, with his very best love, the card of membership and button of our society, and congratulates you on now being one of the League of Cousins and a member of the happiest, jolliest, nicest, most helpful and biggest-hearted family on earth. Wherever you go you will now find relatives and friends, and no longer need you dread to go far from home, for no matter how far distant your journey, you will always meet a cousin and receive a warm welcome and a hearty greeting.

She sighed. She had not sent in since 1908. She stared at that December's List of Cousins Desiring Letters: Ellen Milford, Jacksonville, Calif.; Cleo C. Smith, Laredo, Texas; Miss Artie Henson, Gade Hill, Mo.

Nearly thirty years? Perhaps the League of Cousins had disbanded. Uncle Charlie must be dead. Did anyone try to carry it on? She had run through a life since then.

Before she slept she lay and listened to the rising, lonely wind, stripping away the leaves and flinging them madly over the cold ground outside her window.

———————

Loretta and Mrs. Guffey had settled into a grudging acceptance of each other. As long as she did not have to live under the same roof with her mother-in-law, Loretta could see many fine qualities in the older woman. She did not resent the strong gravitational pull of family as she once had, although she suffered some uneasiness from time to time. In her turn, Mrs. Guffey felt a dim admiration for the girl, who was of the flesh and spirit and passion, and it was not lost on Mrs. Guffey that Loretta's temper and spirit were wrenching her free from the ancient servility of mountain women to men and custom.

One Saturday Walton and Loretta took Logan to Mrs. Guffey's so they could go to a house dance. They remained to talk awhile. When they were ready to leave, Logan grew panicky and began to cry. Walton tried to soothe him, but the boy cried louder. Cajolery, bribery, threats—nothing worked. Then Walton yanked him up and began beating him. Logan screamed louder, and Walton's face grew redder. He stopped spanking the boy and began shaking him, his face contorted.

"Shut up, God damn it, you shut up," Walton yelled.

Logan was wracked by sobs and he snuffled. Mrs. Guffey and Loretta evaded each other's eyes. Logan caught his breath and screamed again. Walton savagely jerked down the child's pants, and as his calloused palm met the soft flesh on the thin little hips, the loud smacking sounded through the room. Abruptly Walton stopped. A strange, troubled ray struck his eye, and he stared at his hand and the raw, red buttocks. Logan tried not to make any sound, but he whimpered, swallowed his breath, hiccoughed, sniffled again, and put his tiny hand over his mouth to muffle the sound. He stared in fright and betrayal at his father. The women left the room, white-faced.

"Son, son, you have to shut up. Mind Daddy," Walton muttered in sudden weakness, his own face anguished and filled with self-loathing. He strode quickly into the dining room where the women were. Loretta sat in her dancing dress and shoes, her black coat open at the front. She smelled of soap and perfume, and she was cloaked in the raiment of high fun, but her face was infinitely sad. Mrs. Guffey stared straight at her son with pain and anger. Her apron was flecked with blades of hay, which she had been reaping and piling in the sun.

Logan stood at the window, pulling the cloth of his pants from fiery hips, a hurt and stubborn little boy.

"I will not say anything," Mrs. Guffey said, but in her terrible face Walton saw himself condemned past redemption. Loretta's eyes flashed anger and dull sorrow in turn, and she opened her mouth to speak, closed it, and looked out the window at the neat rows of corn in the garden. Beyond that she could see where the older woman had been cutting hay and piling it in an unused corner of the fencing. She smelled the low colognes of drying grass coming off Mrs. Guffey's person, and for that instant she was very fond of her mother-in-law because she was hardy and meant to endure. She gazed at the green straw on Mrs. Guffey's apron, and again outside at the piles of hay, and felt keen admiration for an old woman who took a reap hook and stooped into the ground where rattlesnakes and copperheads waited. Before she turned to her husband again, she realized one thing: she would get drunk if she went to the dance.

"Well . . . well . . . well . . ." but Loretta could utter nothing else.

"Well hell, we're going to the dance, that's all," Walton blurted.

"The dance?" Her voice was detached.

"Yes. Do you think I like it when I get like that?"

Mrs. Guffey looked about the room, not at Walton. She stirred among her worries like a seer among the entrails, then spoke.

"I hate to tell you what you've just done," she said. Walton flinched. She had not recently spoken to him with such authority.

"Now, Mama, I've not hurt him," he said.

"No, he'll get over the pain. It's what you just now taught him."

"What?"

"To beat down whatever bucks up on him. You taught him that today."

They were silent, and she sat in her chair, looking at the floor. She had seen the violence in most of the men of her family, and she was not surprised to see it in Walton. She had tried in her way to train him away from it when he was young, but it had skulked back into him as a demon creeps into its lair. And if it was in him, then it was also in the boy, and if the boy lived to be a man, he too would meet anything that thwarted his will with a violent force. She had always accepted it in the men, knowing sadly that one day they would come up against a greater force—either man or beast or circumstance—and if that force did not kill them, it might break them forever, because they never learned the necessity of accepting defeat. Vengeance seared their brains. Very few of them with that wild power ever lay down to die in the beds of old age.

Walton and Loretta did not try to approach Logan before they left. He stood backed against the wall, his small dark eyes looking defiantly ahead.

Walton had won. He and his wife danced, but dance through the night, chatter foolishly, drink deeply if they would, the boy had come with them. The child with the dark, hurt eyes was in every drink, at every table, standing in every corner, staring fiercely.

13

THE YEAR PASSED, then a letter came for Mrs. Skiller at the Hollytown post office. No Skiller came for mail, so the postmaster sent the letter to Wild Cat by Walton. He left it with his mother. She waited beside the road until one of the Skiller girls came by. Later Mrs. Skiller brought the letter back to Mrs. Guffey to read. Mrs. Guffey adjusted her reading glasses, held the letter at arm's length, and read it to Mrs. Skiller.

> Moma hir is to dolors im sory i dot hav mor far yu. the sed hir i git out in to weeks, maken to ther about sateday on elevn clock trane en holeton dipo if ye wont to com ther far me. all be cerful the no whot i meene. Earl

Mrs. Guffey deciphered it slowly, and Mrs. Skiller pondered Earl's words, the claw of her thumb and forefinger clamped to her lower lip.

"Now, when did he say?"

"He'll be here, let's see, postmarked the fourteenth, not this coming Saturday but the next, on the eleven o'clock train."

Mrs. Skiller folded and refolded the money that had fluttered out. Then she put it in her bosom. Her harsh, red features shone in pleasure at the news.

"Earl'll be home. H'it's been awful hard. The rest of 'em mope about and cain't be counted on to work ha'f the time. H'it's shore been make-do up thar at the cliffs."

"Well, if he acts right, maybe he won't have to go off anymore," Mrs. Guffey said.

"You mean not make likker?" the old woman asked, her eyes like big blue coins.

"Yes, Earl's good. He don't have to do that."

"Well, Earl'll make his likker. Why, h'it's about our only living. If h'it worrent he'd make 'er anyway."

Mrs. Guffey nodded. "Yes, some of the men in my family do it. They don't see any harm in it."

"I say. Yes, law me, I say. But if they will, they will, and you cain't stop 'em short of jailing them. It's enough to break a mother's heart to see 'em go off to the road."

"I thought Earl was in federal prison instead of the road."

"Prison. Road. Chaingang. Jail. Workhouse. County Farm. H'it's all the same. Devil's camps set up to snare and hold the good and the pore."

Mrs. Guffey wheeled about impulsively and went into the kitchen. She returned with a cardboard box with some food in it.

"I want to share," she said.

Mrs. Skiller looked in the box: a small bag of corn meal, some pork, oatmeal, butter, a can of blackberries, and some coffee in a small paper bag.

"I don't want to take this," Mrs. Skiller said.

"Go on. Go on. Take it," Mrs. Guffey said. "I've got enough."

"Well, I hate to take it but we can use it."

Mrs. Guffey watched her walk up the path. "Poor, poor soul," she muttered.

Walton came that afternoon. After he chopped the wood, he looked at her food.

"Is this all you've got left, Mama?" he asked irritably.

"It's enough, son."

"Well, it's not and you know it."

"Don't fuss so much."

"Where did it all go?"

"I probably ate it up."

"Well, you didn't. You gave some away. Who to?"

"What makes you ask that?"

"I found the coffee at the gap."

She dropped her head. "Well, the Skillers. They don't have any."

"Oh," he said, chastened. "Well, I'll bring more Friday."

"No, no, son. Now, I can get by all right."

"Well, like hell you can. Here you are, giving away what you have. I can't afford it and you can't. By God, I'll say . . . listen, by the way, I'll bring Loretta and Logan up this Friday . . . no, I have to work ... we'll come a week from Friday, but I'll bring some groceries Friday ..." and on he yammered uncharacteristically. She knew he needed a reason to come home for a weekend.

They walked out into the yard. The sun faded behind a thin palette of cloud over Balsam, and old leaves blew off a nearby Lombardy poplar in a swirling flurry. A ray of sun found a weak place in the cloud, slanted in low, and hit the big poplar's rich yellow leaves. They reflected the light, and for a moment the yard was a bright golden flash.

A week from the following Friday Walton came with Loretta and Logan. That night they popped corn in his mother's fireplace and knew that some of the wounds had healed. Logan was bedded down on a featherbed pallet in front of the fire, and Walton and Loretta slept again in their old bed. They woke early to cold, blue skies. The chill in the house was sharp and invigorating. Gusts in the chimney puffed aromatic woodsmoke into the room. At mid-morning they all left to return to Hollytown. At the corner of the sidewalk below the school the Skillers came into view, and the two families slowly came to meet.

"Howdy do," Walton said.

Logan stared up and found a great brooding face, watchful eyes, a hidden smile. The man bent to him.

"Logan, I'm Earl. I've known you all your life. I was there when you came."

Logan backed away a step. Earl squatted, radiating infinite gentleness.

"How you, little man?" he asked with a deep, kind chuckle.

Logan flushed and crooked his neck. Then he looked at Earl and grinned. Earl laughed, straightened, and looked at Walton.

"I'm glad you made it, Earl," Walton said and held out his hand. Then each of the Skillers stepped forward to shake hands solemnly with Walton, his wife, and his mother.

"Anything I can do for you?" Walton asked.

Earl, guarded, courteous, proud. "Not nary a thang," he said.

"Well, if there is ...."

"I'll be back in business in the spring of the year," Earl said.

"I'll be to see you. Be careful."

Then the families circled each other courteously and backed away. They nodded, made choppy, awkward salutes with their hands, and went their ways. Logan straggled, watching the Skillers go.

Earl was the tallest. Mrs. Skiller had her arm through one of Earl's, and a sister held him on the other side. The brothers circled now and again as they walked, pulling at him. Nobody had ever seen such affection from them.

As the Guffeys neared the fountain in Hollytown, Walton grinned. "By God," he said, "they fixed Earl's teeth at the prison."

Earl had planned to stay quietly drunk for a week when he returned, but he settled for Saturday night and Sunday, alone in his back room washing out the prison memory with old yellow liquor. On Monday morning he arose and took his place as leader. He tightened the discipline of the family, imposing his terrible quiet control. He led by example, with very few orders.

First he repaired the fence.

"Do you know why?" he asked the brothers.

"No, we had to sell the cow and horse."

"We're fixing the fence because we're going to get some more."

For a while they set posts and restretched the wire.

"How much did you get for the cow?" he asked.

"Five dollars," Buddy said.

"Five. Do you know that cow was worth twenty-five?"

"Five was all we could get," Buddy said lamely.

"Who did you sell it to?"

"Plutus Edwards. He bought the horse too, and he wouldn't give but eight."

Earl put down his tools and stared in exasperation toward the locust trees clustered along Cryme's Gap.

"Eight? Well, when did you have to sell them?"

"The week you left."

"God A'mighty! What did you do with the money?"

"Groceries," Buddy said, his face crimson, his eyes darting. He stretched a bony finger to his chin and raked it across a dimple. The others shifted nervously on their feet, afraid that Earl's questions would whip them raw.

"Groceries?" Earl said, staring at them. They looked away.

"Well, we did buy some beer too, now Buddy, so tell the truth," another said.

Earl nodded incredulously, turned to the post, and began hammering staples over the wire. They worked the morning away and went home for the noon meal: potatoes, beans, biscuits, collards, and a bowl of old grease. Later Earl took out a sack of tobacco and rolled a cigarette.

"Mama, who offered to help while I was gone?"

"Some people brought things."

"Who?"

"The Guffeys. Preacher Wharton come once and brought a little and prayed a lot. Crockett was good about letting us have stuff if we asked, but he didn't volunteer. Sometimes we found boxes of food at the trail and didn't know who left 'em, but one of the girls saw Walton and Big Boy leaving something once. They was bound to been the ones who left the other stuff too."

"What stuff?"

"In hog-killing time some fresh loin and liver showed up oncet, wropt so nothing could git in to h'it."

Earl weighed her words, muttering to himself, "Who helped? Who didn't?"

The family sat and waited on his judgment.

"Now, who done things against ye?" he asked, leaning forward.

"The law come here four times. They sacked the house a-lookin' fer likker, and they beat the bushes lookin' fer ye still."

"Find it?"

"No, but they held guns on us all till they got through searching."

His face grew still. "Guns on ye?"

"They didn't exactly point 'em at anybody, but we knowed . . . they had 'em out."

Earl leaped up and ran into the yard. They followed in an excited, stumbling swarm. He stared about the mountain as though taking something into his heart and brain.

"All right, by God. All right," he muttered, striding about in the yard. One by one, in loose, lank motion, they lowered themselves and slouched against the bottom log of the house.

"Git up," Earl barked. "Git up and start gittin' wood."

They leaped up, fearful. "Fer the still?" one asked. "We h'ain't even got any mash."

"Fer Mama's cookstove. She's been a-gittin' h'it all herself, I guess."

That afternoon he began going over the terrain. On many long nights of imprisonment he had made his plans. He climbed to the top of the cliff and took a sighting of the valley below. At the boundary line of Crockett's property, where a small branch ran among laurel, he saw a full, tall tree towering above the others. For a long time he studied the lay of the land—the approaches, the defiles, the places of concealment, and the openings. He circled the cliff and stared again into the valley. Again the tree was prominent. From here the road was open to sight in short lengths, and he could see an open spot on the slopes sweeping up toward the cabin. Then he went through the brush to Cryme's Gap and looked.

"If they come, they come this way," he whispered. It was the harder way, and he knew they never took the harder way, yet someone might be that smart. He looked in the direction of the planned still site and plotted possible courses into it. Again he could see the tall tree. He wandered down the ridge, letting his eyes and intuition run across the land. From there he circled below the house and explored the slope until dark, noting the easy walks and the harder ones. In the forest below the house, they would take the easier, softer routes. They would not get quiet and devious until they got closer to the house. He then switched his trail, heard a voice, and fell behind a log. He looked at the road. Coming from the cabin were four men. Soon they faded from sight on the sweeping road. He went home.

"What did they want?" he asked.

"You. They said they wanted to see you," his mother said, her face old and weary.

"What did they want?" Earl asked again.

"They said to let you know they'd be watching."

He stood erect, his head moving about silently as though he were scenting winds blowing deep in his brain. He ignored the fearful faces of the others. Yet Earl slept well that night. He had a program now, and he knew his enemy. He had the ground. Early the next morning he rousted all of his brothers out and took them toward the old still site. One hundred yards short of it he showed them where to cut brush.

"Get all this down in here, make it clear, and pile the brush on a line that'll circle three sides of the still," he ordered. They stared at him.

"Do it now," he said softly, and they labored. He climbed onto the ridge above them and looked into the valley for a long time.

By the afternoon of the following day, the circle of brush had been made. They sat and talked while Earl wandered the ridges in an aimless fashion. When he returned, he ordered them to begin cutting the brush near the still, and after that to begin hacking brush from higher on the mountain and dragging it in. With this brush he had them almost close the circle.

"Leave it open enough for a big cow to get through," he said. "Plenty of brush, high and thick, so brambly that even a squirrel can't get through nowhere but the opening."

They labored for him, daily adding to the high gray wall of brush and limbs. It rose above them, bouncing in the wind and swaying precariously. It would settle in time. As they chopped and dragged and piled, Earl took a mattock and shovel and cut a trench three feet deep and three feet wide. It ran from the center of the clearing, straight through the hole in the circle, and on to a downed log about fifty feet outside the circle. One day he took the truck off the mountain, and when he returned, he had it loaded with cull boards from a sawmill. He sawed them into short lengths and placed them carefully over his ditch. Then he covered them up with a layer of earth until there was a small tunnel running from the still to the log.

Earl then built a squat cabin of poles around the still, and when that was done, he had a curious fortress: the little structure surrounded by the great circle of brush. The tunnel ran from the dirt floor of the cabin. He chopped a small, Z-shaped cutback in the wall of brush, so that it might be breached by a smart man who wanted in. The fortress took a month to complete, but Earl was satisfied.

"Earl, I just don't see how that's goin' to protect the still, or how we're a-goin' to git water to h'it," said Buddy.

"It h'ain't. We're going to move the still."

They stared at each other.

"Where?"

He showed them a place even more inaccessible—almost impossible to find by anyone who didn't know. They sank a pit into the bank of the branch, then dug a big cave. From there they tunneled a vent into the slope.

"Let 'er smoke out that vent," Earl said.

They covered the pit with planks and left two smoke holes on the sides. Earl knelt, drank the water from cupped hands. "Yeh, this is it. The right water," he said.

The winter was old, and on they labored. They cut a clean trail along the spine of the ridge and another up from the bed of the little stream. The one from the creek forked; one path went toward the pole shack and brush, the other toward the still. Then it tapered off into nothingness—a blank wall of rock and tree. More brush, sprigs small and portable, was piled along the trail, so that if it became necessary, one of the forks could be closed off by sticking the brush up so that it looked as if there were no trail at all.

"The time will come when you can close off one trail or the other, so they'll have to come on the path I want them on," Earl explained to his brothers.

"Who'll come? Who?"

"The law. What do you think I've been studying over?"

"I jis' thought you was teched, that's all."

"Not that you'll know about."

"We worked all winter," Buddy yelled. "Fer what? Fer what?"

"So they can take whichever trail I want 'em on. And they're going to come, son. They've been and they're going to come again."

They grinned and nodded wisely.

"What about that big brush pile up yonder?" one asked.

"Ye fight with what ye've got. That brush pile will make somebody mighty sick, if it comes down to it."

He led them to the several overlooks on the mountain, where they could see the big tree in the valley and the trails and spines. He assigned each a vantage.

"From now on, they won't be as many working at the still as they is out here at the lookouts. We'll never keep likker right at the house again. After supper, go to ye places and watch that tree. I been down there fixin' some ladder steps up that tree. I'm goin' to take a lantern down there tonight, and I want to be certain ye can all see it. I got a big torch fixed up there at the top of the tree, and I got it waterproofed. I'm a-goin' to teach ye some tricks. That'll be our signal one day."

Following their meal, they gathered around the fireplace for a while to heat their haunches. Outside, the winter wind roared in barren trees. Reluctantly they went into the raw weather and took their places on the heights, where they waited and watched in the darkness. Then they saw it in the valley—a far globe of light swinging back and forth.

14

THE CLEAR SKY of April caught the sharp dawn. The sun burst in the east behind the trees on the ridges, and clouds rode into the sky from the west. Outriders, long and thin, were spaced across the jagged horizon as they probed the sky, and the sun tinted their forward edges a rich tan.

Logan, up and about, watched the sky from under the porch. He had scraped out a tiny, twisting roadbed with a wood chip, but he abandoned his work when the light gently swelled across and through him. He stretched forward and put his chin in his hand as the shades, glitters, and streaks flashed across his inner landscape. Then a big body of cloud entered the sky and spread apart, flanking and holding, moving quietly forward to ebb and drift in high tides and currents of wind.

His mother's voice shrilled on the porch above him: "Logan! Logan! Where are you?"

His brow wrinkled.

"Oh, Logan . . . Lo . . . gaaannn. Where are you?" Now her voice was sharp and alarmed.

The wind moistened and swept the ground and blew upon his face. He turned dark little eyes to the steps and saw his mother's feet and ankles. He waited, watching the mountains. Another white tip of cloud rose over the peaks and caught the sun. The wind ruffled the small new leaves in the maple. Rain was coming and he knew it. He was in a dry place, and the very dry dust beneath him was cozy. He felt a great harmony with all that was and all that would ever be.

Loretta's voice grew angry, urgent. She walked into the yard and searched about. When she spied Logan under the porch, relief brightened her face.

"Are you all right? Why didn't you answer me, honey?"

He stared at her as though she were insignificant. She bent to him.

"Is Logan all right?" she asked softly, smoothing his hair. He nodded impatiently, then ignored her.

"What are you doing? Building a road?" she asked. He stared into the sky.

"You're the funniest little boy," she said, pinching his cheek. Then she straightened and went inside.

Heavier reinforcements of clouds came out of the west and spread into an inverted wedge high over the mountain. The outriders had advanced to the east and were beginning to interfere with the sun. The light that escaped was split into small shafts, and yet some wider fans of it struck brightly upon the forward elements in the second wave of cloud.

Alex Fore passed slowly down the sidewalk, looking neither right nor left. Logan kept his eyes to the sky. Bright splashes of sunlight struck down along the trees near the Plott Hole at the creek, advanced quickly across the field, and then lit the street in uneven slashes. Alex reached the maple and stopped suddenly. His eyes cast about wildly for a moment, but his head did not move. The cow in the field across the street stopped picking at grass and lifted her head to stare blankly at Alex. The old man did not see her. Rather he looked straight at Logan, then at the front door of the house. He slouched across the yard and squatted beside the steps, staring fiercely and defensively at the boy. His chin was stained with tobacco juice.

"You scared of me?" he whispered.

Logan watched the top of a tree, washing in the wind and colored by the sun's glare. He did not reply.

"Well, why ain't you scared of me?" Alex demanded.

Logan turned his head and stared at him with dark, somber eyes.

"Do you like me?" Alex inquired tremulously.

"You smell funny," Logan said. "Why do you smell funny?"

"It's a lie," Alex said. "It's part of the lies they tell about me. I don't give a damn whether they tell them or not, and I don't want people to like me."

"I like you all right."

153

"You're Walton's little boy, ain'che?"

"I'm my daddy's boy."

"Are you a truth-sayer?" Alex asked. "I've just been thinking about the truth bird."

Logan was again watching the sky.

"I'll tell you what I know about the truth-sayers. They're hard to find, and you can't recognize them when you see them half the time. I been sitting around, and I got it figured out."

"Let me alone," Logan said.

"Children are truth-sayers sometimes," Alex said, "but they don't know what it means. What are you looking at?"

"I'm watching that," the boy said and pointed his finger at the world. Alex turned and stared vacantly. He chewed his tobacco for a moment. Then he reached into an unspeakably filthy pocket and pulled forth a bunch of grapes.

"I want you to have this," he said. "Sometime we might get to be friends and you can remember that I gave you grapes. What are you looking at, I said?"

The wind came in low and did not ruffle the leaves of the maple, but the grass and weeds lay flat, then rose again.

"Did you know this house is hainted? There's a ghost in there. I remember the night she died. She wanted to go to the bathroom before she died, but they wouldn't let her. Somebody said they was good to her most of the time, but it is mean and low-down to not let anybody go to the bathroom, especially right when they're dying. They say that sometimes at night now they can hear her get up out of bed and go down the hall and into the bathroom and shut the door and do whatever it was she wanted to do. Sometimes she flushes it too."

"What is a ghost?"

"Well, you might find out. It might get you. I said what are you watching? Do you do much watching? If you do you might see a truth bird, and maybe it'll land on you and make you a truth-sayer. Truth-saying will get you hurt or killed, just remember that."

"What does that bird look like?" Logan asked.

"Oh, you'll not mistake it. It's not so much what it looks like as what it sounds like. I'm trying to tell you a lesson. Truth-saying and lie-telling can both get you killed sometimes."

"Is it a red bird or a blue bird? Why don't the bird get killed?"

"That is the very thing they are trying to kill, and they can't.

But if they can't get at the bird . . ." and he laughed hoarsely, ". . . then they just kill where the bird has been. They never do get the bird. It always lights somewheres else. Sometimes it lights on a lot of people at the same time, then there's hell to pay. Then the truth bird kills back. Don't you see?"

"What is getting killed?"

Alex's loose lips worked and he muttered to himself a moment. Then he asked, "What all can you see from here?"

Logan's heart was leaping. The second wave of clouds was beyond his sight, and a big section of the sky was filled with small, broken clouds, all moving east with the same speed, like a great troop of riders moving toward destiny.

Alex stared about, then looked at the spellbound boy.

"You are a strange boy," he grunted, and he rose and walked down the street in a disorganized shuffle, the soles of his shoes flapping against his feet at each step.

In the west, new clouds appeared. Anticipation and tension sang through Logan. The wind flowed in warm, wet currents, the leaves and the grass moved, and the tops of the trees at the creek whipped about. The cow raised her head and plodded toward her shed. Logan's small, still face was that of a devoted acolyte silently watching those things in the air, the sky, the light. Next door a window slammed shut, and a woman's voice came to Logan.

"Eddie, bring the lawnmower to the porch and come in."

Its clacking was quick and furious, adding to the sound and the light and the movement. Logan's eyes shifted slightly. The dark weather moved forward in the sky over the mountains, solid and unbroken, with a slow curve in its mass above the watershed to the south. The sun was high and bright, and it dropped its broken, fragmented light to the earth before the advance of the storm, but its power was lost in the western sky as darkness consumed it. The earlier clouds, which had passed to the east, had fought the sun and won. The bright patches faded into huge, shifting shadows on the ground, and the wind blew in several directions. As the power of the air and the pressure in it increased, a deep feeling stirred in Logan's heart, and along the several sanctuaries of his secret thoughts he felt a wild and warlike cry gathering itself. His joy rose to a fierce and unstoppable force which leaped through his nostrils in a light snort of breath.

The western sky lowered and the mountain was obscured. A

linked chain of fire jerked brightly and struck a tree on a near slope. The sound of it sizzled and banged sharply across the town. Logan smiled as his soul responded. The sun's light was weak, and the few rays that got through the clouds lay dim upon the land. Logan watched curtains of rain blowing down the mountains and into the town. He leaped to his feet and ran to the sidewalk to meet it, laughing loudly at the conflict. He played in the rain for an hour before Loretta thought to see about him. She found him in the yard, wriggling happily in the mud.

The rain steamed away, leaving the earth fresh, the grass green. Along the several creeks, peppermint plants filled the air with enchanting aroma, and the birds swooped and lifted and circled above the streets. It was spring again, and the creatures moved into it as though it were a new land and they had traveled a hard journey, and here would be no grief.

Boogerman Sitner left the rambling white house where he lived on Main Street and walked slowly to the fountain, flipping a knotty walking stick before him. He stood a moment, shifted his weight to the bad leg, winced, bit the wet end of a cigar.

"B'god!" he grunted, staring at the sky. His eye caught a movement on the street near the railroad tracks. Sweatbee Hardy came off the tracks and walked toward him.

"Now, b'god," Boogerman croaked hoarsely to himself, suddenly apprehensive. His leg started to throb. Sweatbee did not intend to dodge him. He came on, casually aggressive and in a taunting manner, to Boogerman.

Boogerman frowned, wished Sweatbee would swerve off from the collision course and go on his way. Boogerman braced, then started it:

"What are you doing off the Western Front?"

Sweatbee stopped in feigned surprise, hunched his shoulders. "I'm a-doin' what I please, Booger, but that ain't none of yer business, is it?"

Boogerman swallowed, ducked his head furiously.

"Maybe I can't get you up there, but I can here," he said.

"Is 'at right? What fer?" Sweatbee asked in exaggerated courtesy.

"B'god, I can do it."

"Yeh, but you ain't goin' to even try it, are ye?" Sweatbee drawled.

"You ain't drinkin', are ye?" Boogerman demanded.

"Not right this very minute, but I intend to shortly. Why?"

"Where you goin', b'god?"

"Goin' where I please, Booger, goin' where I please," Sweatbee said and rocked about. Boogerman felt for his blackjack and pistol.

"All right," he said. "Don't cause no trouble here."

Sweatbee grinned craftily. "Nobody causes trouble, Boogerman. It just starts where it will. I don't trouble about trouble, and I don't trouble trouble. Trouble does its own stirring when it's ready. I got some work here now, unloading boxcars out yonder at the tracks, so you'll see me around."

"Unloading boxcars?" Boogerman repeated crossly. "That's work. You won't last long."

Sweatbee slouched on away. The sun bore down and scattered leafy shadows across the street in front of Boogerman's house.

Sweatbee arrived at the railroad siding in Hollytown at ten-thirty. The boxcar was open and the other workers were waiting.

"Well, why in hell ain't you started?" Sweatbee asked.

"Damn if you ain't got crossways of the job already, Sweatbee," a man said. "We been waiting on you. You're a-goin' to do your part."

"You damn right I am."

"Well, we get paid for unloading the car . . ."

"Yeh, but not by the hour, and not by no certain hour. We got all day if we want to take it."

"We just want to make sure you pull your load."

"Who is we? You pregnant or something? I don't hear nobody else bitching. You pull your load and I'll pull mine. Don't worry about it. They ain't gonna give us no regular job nohow. They'll pay us just enough to get drunk on. What's in that car, anyways?"

"Cement."

"Cement in bags?" Sweatbee asked incredulously, aghast.

"Shore is." They all laughed loudly.

"To hell with it," he said and walked back up the tracks.

In the back room of the office of a lawyer in Wadenton, a deal was being negotiated that would place the golf course in new hands, and a suitable compromise was in the air. The negotiators decided to have a drink until the head of the buying combine arrived. But that man, being in a hurry to get from Balsam to Wadenton, found his last moment. As he reached the intersection at the Western Front, an old pickup truck pulled into traffic and so frightened the Florida businessman that he hit his gas instead of his brake. His car left the road and hit a tree. His throat was cut when he went through the windshield, and he died there in the window.

Sweatbee wandered upon the scene at that moment. Stricken, he swore off forever, then ran into Lon's place and offered to sweep up in exchange for a pint of wine. Lon gave him an apron and broom and walked out to the accident scene.

Walton checked out with his supervisor and started to the store to buy a new steel chisel. He arrived just as they cleaned the blood off the man's face for identification.

"Jesus Christ Almighty!" Lon said. "Ain't that the man who was heading up the bunch trying to buy the country club?"

Walton's gorge rose. "Damn, I've got to go home," he said.

The plants were greening. Mrs. Guffey walked among the jonquils, rubbed their cool petals with her fingertips. She stared across the valley to where her husband slept. Her eyes were still sharp enough to see, even across the distance, the warm light of spring glinting dully along a thousand tombstones. Slowly she cut some flowers and took them into the house. She tied an old newspaper around the stems and soaked the paper in water. Then she put on her best dress, powdered herself, and put on her good black shoes, whispering her thoughts. She picked at a dish of cold bread pudding with her fingers, nibbled, then locked the door and began the long walk to the cemetery. There was a strong wind at her back as she went. It was warm and stirred the leaves.

Mrs. Guffey met the ambulance as she trudged along the shoulder of the highway. She was not far along when it passed her on its return. This time it was not fast and the siren was not wailing. She went into the cemetery and came to her husband's grave.

"They will bring me here. When?" she murmured. She sat on a low concrete wall near the grave and thought. Across the distance she could see her house. The greening spread upward from the lower elevation, divulging the several new strands of the season advancing into the altitudes.

She muttered on. Well my dear here I am again and I miss you more than I can tell you but I've told you haven't I? The day will come when I sleep here beside you and those things of the flesh that broke you down will not matter then.

Then she pondered upon the years when he had indulged in those things of the flesh, and her mood shifted abruptly, and a chill hit her as a great insult at last cleared. In her mind was a white screen, and there she saw the graves of her old folks, in another county, deep in time. She stared sadly down at her husband's mound.

"I'll take care of your grave for as long as I live," she whispered and rose slowly to her feet. "But this is not where I'm going to be buried."

At the boxcar, the laborers had unloaded half the cargo. They slowed in anticipation of lunch. From his vantage behind a lumber stack, the straw boss saw that they were not hustling. His management instincts were offended. He went to the workers.

"Here, men, what's the matter?"

"Oh, we jis' restin' a minute, cap'n," one man said. "We ain't workin' by the hour."

The others stared curiously at the boss.

"Well, we have to get it unloaded."

"Don't worry, cap'n, don't worry."

"Well, I mean faster."

Then a man known to them wandered down the tracks and stopped.

"Boy, that was a bad'n up at the Western Front, wasn't it?"

"What was a bad'n?"

"Some rich feller got his throat cut."

"Aw, the hell he did," the straw boss said. "Is he dead?"

"Yeh, already getting stiff when I left there."

"Well, by God," a worker said, "you can't go messing around up there, I don't care who you are."

"Dead?" the straw boss asked again, shocked.

"Yes, I say. Blood all over the place."

They watched their informer wander down the tracks.

"Hmm. I wonder who done it?"

159

"He didn't say."

"By God! Sweatbee. You don't reckon Sweatbee . . . ?"

They exchanged apprehensive glances.

"He's a dangerous man when he's riled," one said.

"I always thought he was a little crazy. He was madder'n hell when he left here."

"I wonder if they arrested him."

"I never heard of him cutting anybody."

"No, but he'll bust ye head with a grayback, as he calls 'em. It's a wonder he ain't killed half a dozen or more."

Another man wandered down the tracks.

"Hey!" one worker called. "You been at the Upper End?"

"Yeh, that was a bad thing, all right."

"What was it that man done?"

"What? I don't know."

"Have they got Sweatbee in jail?"

"Sweatbee? In jail? Not yet, I guess. It's way too early. I seen him up there where the dead man was. He ain't in jail."

"Was his throat cut wide open?"

"Hell yes, I seen it. Gashed open like a pig-killing."

"Oh good God!" the straw boss gasped.

The man left, and they stared at him as he went.

"He was mad at us too," one finally whispered hoarsely.

"Shit, I'm a-goin' home," a young man said and leaped off the dock. They watched, then leaped down also.

"Hey, where are you going?" the straw boss asked.

"Home, give us our money."

"You just unloaded half this car."

"Give us half the money, then."

"Why, no I won't. We have to have . . ."

"Kindly shove it up your ass, then. I ain't staying around here without no gun."

"What do you need a gun for?"

"They is a wild-assed maniac running around cutting people's throats, man. If he comes he can get yours."

The straw boss watched them go and pondered their retreating backs. Then he slipped quickly into the lumberyard, picked up a brick in each hand, climbed upon a lumber stack, and sat. Eyes wide, he bit his lips contemplatively.

Logan played in a pile of slats in his back yard. In his hands one of the slats changed into a rifle. He walked around the house cautiously and looked up and down the sidewalk. His lip was set in a stubborn tilt. He crept to the Compson's hedge and on to the next telephone pole. He looked back, then walked to the next pole. Then he risked another.

He went from pole to pole, stopping at each to look back at the maple tree in his front yard. As long as he could see it, he was not lost. He kept walking until he reached the creek where it ran swift and deep beneath an arched footbridge. He walked to the high center and looked down. It made him dizzy, but it was not too bad.

Loretta's sister Lucy was over for a visit and walked out onto the back porch. "Where's Logan?" she asked.

"Isn't he out there?"

"No."

"I guess he's in the bedroom."

"No, he's not in the house or out front. I looked when I came in."

"Oh Lord!" Loretta shrieked. She looked under the house, then ran through the hall toward the front with Lucy behind her. When they reached the door, they found Taffy Suggs standing there.

"I better tell you something," he mumbled shyly.

"What? Is it about Logan?"

"Yeh. Yes'm," Taffy said, grinning foolishly.

"What about him?" she yelled.

"I've got him here," Taffy said.

Loretta looked around. "Where?" she asked.

Taffy looked, found Logan cringing beside the steps.

"Where was he?"

"He was swinging on the handrails on the bridge."

"Oh my God," she said weakly.

Logan climbed the steps, cramming crackers into his mouth.

"Where did you get crackers?" she demanded.

"I gave him my pack of crackers if he would come off the bridge with me," Taffy said.

"I thank you so much," she said formally. "Let me get you some money."

"No ma'am. I don't want nothing."

"Well, I'll pay you for the crackers, then."

"If you want to. I ain't got no more money."

Walton ran into the yard.

"Walton, let me tell you about something very bad that has happened," Loretta said.

"Hell, I seen it myself."

"Seen what?" she asked.

"That feller on the Upper End. The rich man. Got his throat ripped open. He died. I was right there."

"He did? Oh God! What was a rich man doing there? Who done it? See, Walton? I want you to stay away from that nest of cutthroats up there in the beer joints. It is a thousand wonders they've not cut your throat. I have said and said . . . cut his throat, you say?"

"No, God damn it. He wrecked his car and his head went through the windshield."

"I declare. I declare. You seen it, Walton?"

"I was right there. It was the worst thing I've ever seen. Don't fix much. I won't be able to eat much."

She was putting the meal on the table when she remembered Taffy.

"Walton, go out there and give Taffy a nickel or a dime. He earned it, I tell you."

Walton handed her a nickel. When she got to the door, Taffy was gone.

15

LOGAN LAY UPON his cot, and from far away he heard strange friends sounding down the wind. They were the prismed multiples of himself spread in parallel rank. They rode upon great roars and were drenched in sprays of light. Voices swam upon a sea of old hours, brackish in their depths, and midnights sailed ancient routes toward dawn. Logan Guffey went again toward death. This was the time: he could not last much longer. Enemies burrowed in his bowels. They fatted silently on his blood. There was nothing else for them. The child had stopped eating. Life ebbed to the dim, deep drains of his heart; the patterns of memory disarranged and floated upon a great heaving tide, and he could not draw them together again because the surface slid away.

The strong face of Mrs. Walters was above him, her eyes dark and sharp. She laid her hand upon his forehead. Loretta bent to watch over her shoulder.

"Yes, yes," Loretta said, pale and frightened, "I noticed yesterday that he was acting puny. Last night he just wouldn't eat at all. He does that sometimes. Sometimes he just eats cornbread and water . . . he slept badly last night. But when Walton went to work this morning, Logan got up and came into the kitchen. He didn't seem too sick. . . ."

Walton walked quickly in, pushed past all of Loretta's family, and went to the cot. Logan's eyes were heavy, lidded with stone. The face of his father, bending close, was suddenly split by fierce shafts of dazzling light, and a wave of pain swept him up. When he sank again, he saw them across a vast distance, their faces infinitely sad. The space between him and them was alive with a dense, active force which distorted his view. Briefly he became lucid and called out happily to them, but as they came toward him he lost them from sight and found himself following a bright, tonal bird song down a bough-arched path. He stopped for a moment to take a drink from the gourd dipper at his grandmother's well; then he looked at her house and saw that the doors were closed and he was alone. A great rushing of wind came to pull him away and fling him a great distance.

Loretta's family crowded into the bedroom, hallway, and kitchen and talked in soft, muffled deathwatch tongues. Walton strode about, paying them little attention. It was not that he disdained them, rather that he did not need them. Then one of Loretta's older brothers spoke to him, and Walton nodded and turned the car keys over to him. The brother drove to Wild Cat and returned with Mrs. Guffey. Loretta's brother rejoined his group and it seemed that everyone was compelled to belong to one ill-defined faction or another. Mrs. Guffey walked to Logan's cot, laid her hand upon his brow, turned with an inquisitive lift of her forehead. Then she saw Loretta's mother.

"Oh, how are you, Mrs. Walters?" she inquired politely.

"Tolerable, jis' tolerable. Are you all right?" Mrs. Walters's face was impassive and the conversation stopped there. Mrs. Guffey went to Walton at the foot of the bed and stood with him to share the silent, ruthless, and remorseless strength that radiated from her in matters of blood and kin. She stared at her son without speaking.

"Well, I'll give Mrs. Walters a few more minutes and then I'm going to get Dr. Rawson," Walton said. He was frightened, and courtesy was nearing its end. There was hardness and threat and fear in his voice, and it was properly conveyed to them all.

"Well, now Walton, you get him right now if you want him. It won't hurt my feelings none. I'm not your enemy, and I want the boy well and you think about that," Mrs. Walters said, abruptly but with understanding.

Walton turned to Loretta's youngest brother.

"Charles, go get Rawson," he commanded. The boy leaped, searched faces anxiously. A stir moved through Loretta's family. Other relatives had arrived, and they watched with a close but neutral interest. Charles swayed, uncertain.

"Move!" Walton said. Charles turned.

"Move now, Charles," urged a sister. He ran through the door.

Logan saw flickers and was wrenched back toward them. He shuddered and grew nauseous, was drawn again onto the dense cushion, and rose upon that gelatinous pulse of noise and color and heard their voices and saw them across the abyss in the room . . . familiar faces, a confluence of voice, the movement of feet upon the floor, the putter-putter-putter of the town . . . but all that was not why he listened. Rather, someone was trying to tell him something important. Then dimly he heard the far song coming off the big mountain to the west, and the low whine and hum of it grew stronger and came fast past the creek and little pasture, and then it was upon him and he saw the whirling, glittering shards of light and smiled.

"I don't know," Rawson said. "Has he been too hot or too chilled recently? I know he's been sickly. I see him now and then, but there's nothing I can do until he comes down like this."

"Well, he's down like this now. Do something," Walton said.

"I don't know," Rawson muttered. "I don't know. Let him get some more rest."

Walton stared in disbelief.

"Then later I can give him a stimulant."

"A what?" demanded Walton.

Rawson's face tightened into sarcasm, then relaxed as he faced their gaze. The multiple, humorless eye of a grim, complex beast was upon him.

"Something to help him," he said and left.

Neighbors came and went, bearing food, drink, comforting words. Big Boy sat in the kitchen. He grew apprehensive and sauntered to the Western Front. He drank two bottles of beer, then hired a man to drive him to Hame Tree Gap. From there he walked on to Wild Cat and bought a pint of whiskey from Earl.

"Boy's sick, ye say?" Earl asked.

"Bad off. He might go this time."

"No, he'll make it," said Mrs. Skiller. "I seed a bad time fer him."

Earl thought a moment, then said, "I better go down there. I want to see that boy, and I want to let Walton know we're thinking of him."

"Why shore," said Big Boy. "Jis' come right on."

"We might do it. I don't know. The law is a-doggin' us all the time. They come up here searching for likker, and Doice and Jody has to hide because they accuse them of breaking into the summer homes at the golf course, but they didn't. Harley and Buddy got into a fight at Lon's place and they got warrants out fer them. They watch us all the time."

Big Boy stared around uneasily in the darkness. "Well, come on down. Walt'll be glad to see you."

He returned to the gap, where his ride was waiting. By the time he went into the back door at Walton's house, Big Boy was staggering drunk.

"Bud! Listen, Bud," he said to Walton. "Earl'n them might come." He slumped heavily into a chair. Walton stared at him and shook his head.

Great auroras burst, then glimmered away to afterimages. The boy listed to his left, then tilted forward and slowly drifted downward through the sky. He tried to speak, managed only a small smile on numb lips. There was a tiny chill on the back of his neck, and he fell backward through it and grew very cold. A black maw swallowed the light and something of futility came, and he felt the finality of the darkness. Nearby was an ending. Existence became bleak, and he did not have the strength to move up through that cold hole where the long drop had commenced, and he did not know, did not know, did not know . . . .

When the Skillers came, their arrival was quick and unnoticed. The old truck rolled under the big globe swinging off the light pole at the end of the street and rolled to a stop at the curb at the upper edge of Walton's yard. As soon as it stopped, one of the Skillers moved quickly across the street and into some high weeds along the fence. He hunkered down with the shotgun and its deer loads. Two more of the brothers trotted around each side of the house, met, and came again to the front and nodded to Earl.

They entered the house silently, their sudden presence over-

166

powering. They took up a stance in a loose cluster in the sickroom, the main of it near Walton. At the edges they mingled with Loretta's family and the neighbors. Control was theirs. They had split apart the people and were in position to do immediate and savage damage if it must come to that. But no one thought consciously in such terms. So there stood the Skiller brothers, silent in watchful humility and of one mind.

People wanted to leave, yet their duty was to be there a while longer. They hoped that whatever it was the Skillers portended would not ignite. A small tone of old savagery and carnage rang through the room. Alice was chilled with fear, and she did not know why. She gasped, and everyone's eyes turned to her. She bowed her head and silently prayed for the boy to be spared because she was afraid that if he died, these fearsome gaunt men who were Walton's allies might decide it was the fault of her mother who doctored with herbs, and she was afraid there might be several funerals—all in her family—because these quiet, murderous men, who smelled faintly of moonshine whiskey, had more knives and guns than the National Guard.

The Skillers dispersed as suddenly and as silently as they had arrived. The night wore on and the child endured. Most of Loretta's family went home. On the way to the street, they noticed two Skillers at the truck, where a 1903 Springfield military .30-06 rested in the cab. Another brother stood in the shadows at the side of the house, and another sat in the darkness of the back porch, his thin legs pulled up against his stomach. Yet another stood politely against the wall in the hallway with Earl, and another sat in a chair in Walton's bedroom, staring out a window. The others maintained occasional traffic between all these posts, carrying sandwiches and coffee, and now and then taking a small drink of liquor from the truck. Their peculiar placement did not register on others that night, and even if it had, it would have meant nothing except that this was the way these ignorant, dangerous hoojers were.

At the truck, on the porches, and in the weeds, the Skillers watched, and as the town sank into deep slumber they watched on, both for the death of the boy and for the coming of the law because the law came best at this time. They did not know which warrants might be brought, and on this strange street they wanted to leave their options between fighting or running open until the last moment. If it was a nothing warrant for the fighting in the joints, they would run in all directions, and the few caught would not fight. But if it was for assault or threats or blockading or breaking and entering—one of the bigger matters—then they would fight their way clear at all costs. It was one or the other because they were growing desperate about the harassment, and they did not want to stand and surrender.

Earlier in the night, Paul Fortune had learned of the sickness, but at the time he had not thought it appropriate for him to go. He felt that he should not intrude on this private family matter because he did not belong here in this land and was not one of them. The death watch was personal and none of his business. He had gone to his house and fallen asleep. When he awoke at midnight, he suddenly realized that he liked Walton despite his aloof and independent ways, and he wanted to go in his own lostness and express some regret. Surely that would not be held against him. So he went to check on the boy.

At the head of the street he stood under the streetlight, his face pale and bloodless under the naked bulb. The lights still burned at Walton's house. Fortune felt the brief, deep pains of loss because he knew the child was again near death.

He moved slowly down the street, and as he did he heard the brief, melodic cry of a whippoorwill. He thought that was passing strange since he had never heard one in town before, and besides, it was not the right time of year for them. He was past the truck and on the steps when he found himself facing one of the Skiller brothers. Paul Fortune stuck out his hand and asked:

"How is the boy?"

In the light that came to them from the high, swinging bulb up the street, he saw that this Skiller was not looking at him but was watching the street and the far light.

"I have not seen you or your family lately," Fortune said. "I hope things are going well with you."

The gaunt young man's dark eyes moved restlessly about the street. Fortune saw the dim form of another face in the window, and he wheeled to see one man slouched loosely beside the cab of the truck and another hidden near the truck bed at the back wheel. The light glinted briefly off a small, dull tube, and having been in France in 1918, Fortune knew the stance, the silence, and the atmosphere. He realized that if these were enemies, he was deep within a trap. Alarm shot through him. He looked again at the

168

strained face before him and felt dismay. Briefly he saw death. He cleared his throat nervously.

"Is Walton awake?"

"I believe so, I believe so," the man said in his slow accents, his deep-sunk eyes worrying with the darkness beyond the light at the end of the street.

"Good! I'll speak a word with him," Fortune said, then awkwardly, in some compelling, desperate effort to communicate with this man, "I hate this about the child." The man only nodded absently and shrank back into the darkness. For an instant Paul Fortune recalled machine guns, the early hint of mustard gas in the wind, and captains bloody and dead on soggy earth, fallen on their way across cratered fields.

In the hallway he met Mrs. Guffey, and since he was this far into a fortification, he became all the more courteous.

"Please," he whispered, "how is the boy? I could not sleep until I found out."

She stared tiredly at him. Her eyes were of such strength that he felt she was examining him for something false.

"Please . . . I hope I'm not in the way. I wanted to know," Fortune said.

It was the best thing he could have said. Her face relaxed as if she felt that all the concern they could gather would count heavily while the Lord was making up his mind.

"Come in quickly if you want to see him," she said, "because if you come back tomorrow he might be gone . . . he's a sickly child and maybe he shouldn't have to suffer anymore."

"I am sorry. I am very sorry," Fortune whispered, nodding his head. A neighbor woman stepped up to them.

"It just seems like a time of death," she said. "They say it comes in threes, but there has already been four deaths that I know of around here today."

"Who else is dead?" Fortune asked in surprise. "I've been in my place all day."

"Why, a man up on Eagle's Nest. He was a big shot. He used to be the governor of Florida. He's got a summer place up there, and he dropped dead today. Another one was that feller who owned a store in Wadenton, whose family had so much money. He was on a big drunk and shot hisself. Then old Colonel Sykes of the Guard was found dead in his bed, but he was old and sick anyway, and then there was somebody else. Give me a minute and I'll think of it. Oh, I was counting . . . you know . . . Logan . . . ."

Fortune blinked, frozen in thought.

—We are the sound of big rivers rushing down.

He stared into the room, at the boy's sweaty, tiny face, then at Walton, slumped in a chair asleep with his own face on the boy's pillow.

—The lesser streams also go their way to the sea, and neither do they come this way again.

He stepped inside the room and gently patted Walton's slack shoulder. Walton moved slightly, moaned thickly, and slumbered on. Loretta was curled asleep in another chair.

Christ Almighty! Fortune felt the irony of it. The boy was dying, and they were all too worn out to watch him go. He felt a presence behind him and turned. Earl had leaned against the wall and was staring at him.

—The wind skirls and goes upon its path; it carries fear to the east and west.

"Are you all right?" Fortune asked. The quiet, ugly man stared at him from under a low hatbrim and nodded.

—There is no north wind. If you want to lead men, keep your mouth shut and do the things you have to do. They will come along. Why do I think of war around him?

Fortune walked out the door, saw the men outside, and noticed that they had not changed their stance. When he was almost back up to the street light he heard the soft countersign. The cry of a bobwhite, out of place in the darkness. But he knew that the outposts were relaxing.

———

Loretta woke and went to her son. Walton slept on. She reached and felt the boy's head, bit her lip, and went into the hallway. "I tell you," she said to Earl Skiller, "It might have been a mistake to put his cot in there where that woman died that time."

His face was devoid of expression, as it was when his mother had spoken of witchcraft.

"Everyone's heart is with him, 'specially mine," he said humbly.

At four o'clock in the morning the Skillers got back on the truck, drove down the street, turned left, and made a circuitous drive over many dirt roads. They hid the truck across the ridge from

Wild Cat and walked home, where those who were not wanted by the law went to bed in the house, and those who were found a place to sleep in the woods.

About 5:00 A.M. a car with one deputy and three revenue men drove slowly down the street past the Guffey house. Other officers at a roadblock at Hame Tree Gap stood about, impatient and sleepy, until after 8:30.

"He must not be coming," one grunted, and they left.

A million miles and falling fast, then a far gleam, a burst, a flame, ten suns firing long beams like arms and hands all the way to him across those eons and pulling him gently toward brightness. He smelled leather. His father. He smiled. Feet scuffed across the floor. Low voices, weeping women.

Now his life was a bare flicker. His breath came extremely slow, shallow. Noon approached and he lingered. They all knew it would not be long.

Loretta was strong and rose to it. There was no doubt this time that he would die. She met the crisis with drama. She would last the night. She would not yield him without a fight. No, not as long as there was breath in her body, or his. She was now at her best. The eyes of the town were upon her. The people marveled.

Walton was in the front yard, cursing God and shaking his fist at the sky. His billfold shook loose from the bib pocket of his overalls. He picked it up and flung it against the maple, scattering papers over the yard. His agony was heard up and down the street. People listened inside their doors and shook their heads.

Dr. Rawson came again, in a hurry. He examined again. He did not know what was wrong. The boy's health had been slipping all along, and when Rawson saw that this illness could be the last, he flooded the locks in the family's hearts with bad hope and doubt so that he could float them down to the hard floor of certainty, slowly drain away their remaining hopes and prepare them to accept the limitations of doctors.

"Well, it is not good, not good at all," he said and waited awhile.

A bit later, more worriedly: "Things are bad, I say."

And later: "Maybe a prayer would help."

Walton glowered at him. Finally Rawson took them aside and said, "Get ready for the worst. There is little I can do now. It is in the hands of God. He has been a tough boy, but death is coming, I think." He noted that they clung desperately to any doubt in his word.

"I have some other calls to make," he said, "but I'll be back."

"If he is still here," Walton said numbly, bitterly.

The doctor drove away in his clanking little car. Inside a tired mind which sped furiously out of control he thought:

"Has this boy been put here solely to hound me and test my skills and faith? There is never a clear reason for this child to be sick; yet he is regularly at death's doorstep. God damn it to hell, I am overworked and underpaid and I want some sleep and food, and I am sick and tired of a child who is pulled away from the pit only to run headlong back toward it. Does the child want to die? God damn the boy. He is a malignant and thin-faced creature of fevered eyes, which seem always to be looking at nothing and seeing everything. This child has no known thing wrong with him but the look of death, and if he does die, I shall send more flowers than anyone, because God Almighty Your Blessed Honor and Excellency I realize now that I can't save them all, and this one journeys back and forth between me and death on a regular schedule. If you are testing me with him, then let me concede failure, because I now have the wrong attitude toward him, and I personally think now that the only way he can be helped is to die, and I hate myself all right but even more I hate this demanding, baffling child, and a man must have at least one good enemy to hate. I used to hate sickness and death, but they have come together at one place and that is in him, and so therefore, God, I choose him to hate and hate and hate. . . ."

Then Rawson's car swerved off Camp Branch Road, plunged down a bank into thick brush, leveled off, and stopped. Rawson could not turn off the ignition because he was finally fast asleep, and so the motor ran on for an hour before the gas was gone.

As night fell again, Mrs. Guffey sat in a chair in the shadows away from the bed, her face sad and truly humble. She stared at the child and experimented with trying to project her will to live and her strength into his tiny heart. She tried to offer herself up again as ransom, but God was not dealing, and her loneliness sharpened because there seemed to be no place that she had influence.

Mrs. Walters took a chair next to Loretta near the head of the bed. She felt the boy's brow, placed her deft, competent hand upon his chest, and let it rise and fall with his faltering breath. She patted Loretta's shoulder awkwardly; in times like these she tried to show affection. She looked at Loretta's face and saw the terrible strain, the guilty, haunted eyes.

Loretta wiped her face, composed herself, and talked with her sisters.

"Why, Loretta, we'll be glad to stay all night with him," Lucy said.

"Law yes, I say! Yes indeed," said Cynthia. "You know that. You can get some rest."

She looked at them, her eyes brimming again. "Stay if you want to, but I'll get no rest. No, as long as he's alive I'll stay up with him. I thought all day about how he's pulled through the darkest times. But he got to where he couldn't walk day before yesterday. The shine went out of his little eyes and I knew then that something was bad wrong. He told me in his own little way, 'Mama, I love you and my daddy and my grandmas and my grandpa and my uncles and aunts,' and it crushed the very life out of my heart and the breath out of my lungs because I said to myself right then, why, little Logan's trying to tell us something in his own way, and I see now he was trying to say goodbye. . . ."

Everyone in the room heard it and broke into sobs, and Loretta herself almost collapsed when she got to the last part. They fell eagerly into the story and listened attentively, courteously, and sympathetically to her every inflection. They owed her this: to listen and to cluck, to nod and look sad of eye.

Mrs. Guffey shook her head angrily and left the room. Mrs. Walters took no time for such extended dialogues. She sat back, working her black-gum toothbrush in her snuff can. She studied the boy's face in the low light. The overhead electric light was out, and the soft illumination of the kerosene lamp held the bed afloat in shadow. No one noticed when Mrs. Walters suddenly sat upright. She stared closely at Logan's face. The tip of a worm slid slowly down onto his lip from a nostril. He turned his head a bit and the worm crawled on out. It was about seven inches long. Shortly another appeared in the nostril and slid out a little. Mrs. Walters' face tightened a moment and her eyes flared slightly. No one was watching her. She leaned to the boy, her hand patting his

173

forehead and rubbing his cheek. Quickly she pulled the worm from his nose and picked up the other one from the pillow. She put them in her apron pocket and turned to her son.

"Git here Charles! We've got to go. Loretta, don't worry, honey. We'll all try to do our best, and that's all the Lord's very angels can do."

Walton walked through the house to the front porch.

"God damn it, where's Rawson?" he bellowed in anguish. Several neighbors jerked their heads inside their doors.

"That son-of-a-bitch Rawson," Walton wailed.

But Rawson, born of human flesh and heir to its manifold limitations, was yet deep in exhaustion and slept soundly in a brushy ravine at the head of Camp Branch. His stomach did not bother his mind with its hungers, and his mind knew no other puzzles. He had not slept for the seventy-two hours preceding, nor had he eaten in twenty-four hours. He had reached the end of his endurance, and now he slept like a baby in the seat of his car near the purling small cascades and currents of Camp Branch, and no one knew where to find him.

When Mrs. Walters and Charles returned, Walton was silent and subdued at last. He stood alone on the front porch, his eyes red. He watched his mother-in-law's relentless stride—she always walked as though she breasted deep snows on missions not known to mortal man. Suddenly Walton was frightened of her. She midwifed some and dispensed some herbs, she fed the sick and offered sympathy in the community, and sometimes she officiated at laying out the dead in the more backward and old-fashioned homes.

—The winding-sheet, the winding-sheet, bring my son the winding-sheet.

—And the cooling board, the cooling board, lay him out on the cooling board.

—Wash his face, his pallid face, and comb his soft dark hair.

Through his tears Walton meditated upon the tiny hands, curled beside the boy on the bed. The hands remained in his mind, and when he was no longer angry at God, he began hoping that God was not mad at him. On Mrs. Walters came with Charles. Walton was not in control of himself when they reached the porch. Mrs. Walters had something in a paper bag.

"Howdy do," Walton said in bright tears. "What have you brought?"

She patted his arm, and he grasped her hands desperately, as if to wring from her the assurance that she had not come with a winding-sheet, and he was suddenly afraid that she would ask, of all improbable things, for Loretta's ironing board to use for a cooling board.

"I've got some chicken broth," she said softly and passed him, and those watching from the hall knew that he was now not dangerous. His grief had been tamed, and he was accepting death at last. They made way for Mrs. Walters to get to the bed. She bent to Logan and cried out in her bleak, sharp voice:

"Boy! Wake up! Raise your head."

The boy's tongue moved across his lips. She slapped him sharply. His eyes opened and rolled wildly. She shoved a spoonful of warm broth at him, the deep mystical kindness of hard reality upon her face.

"Drink this, Logan," she ordered. He shook his head feebly, perplexed. She slapped him again, as loudly as a shot. He flinched, his eyes open and alarmed. He opened his mouth, and she emptied the spoon into it. Mrs. Guffey came awake, saw, and rose angrily from her chair. Big Boy pulled her down gently.

"Sit down, Mama. Just sit down," he said, watching Mrs. Walters closely. Others in the room murmured.

"Swallow, Logan," she commanded. He struggled, took it down. She looked around in triumph, a power in her that would brook no interference. Her very strength and indignation made her right. Again she commanded, fed him. Sweat poured from his face. Fingers and thumbs stirred and reached out. He drank. Again, again, again. They watched in awe. Then she placed two tan wafers in his mouth and fed him again. She quit only when the quart jar was half gone. Then her dark eyes cut about sharply, slashing the watchers like an eagle's beak.

"Ye'd let the boy die, would ye?"

Their eyes fell to the floor, and they were silent and still. They did not know how to respond. She sat beside the boy for a while, speaking to no one but holding Loretta's shoulders with an arm. Finally she rose and stood beside the bed.

"He's not puked. We'll see."

She rubbed her brush deep into her snuff can and placed it in her mouth at a weary angle. Then she jerked her head at Charles.

"Let's go. I'll be back."

She left Loretta's house and went briskly to her own. Family and neighbors, sensing that they had stayed their duty tour, now fanned out to home and bed. Cynthia and Lucy remained behind, keeping the long watch.

———————

Logan roused and saw an ancient woman sitting beside him. She spoke and he strained to hear.

"I'm here to see about you," she said, or seemed to say. He stared.

"Do you want to go with me?" she asked.

His small face pouted. He was too tired to care or to be frightened. Then he realized that she was not so old, and he was not so young.

"Don't be afraid to go," she said. "It is not a strange place. It is as familiar as the old homeplace. You will hardly notice you've gone. We come and go there all through time."

Her face was weary yet alive with currents of tidal energy, sometimes coming, sometimes flowing off.

"Are you hurting?" Logan asked.

"No, I left my pain in this very room. You can see it if you will."

He looked, almost saw something, saw nothing at all. He heard the steps of his aunts in the hall, heard his father snoring and his mother moaning in their room across the hallway. He saw that he and some old woman had been riding on a sea of light. She rose from beside him with an easy movement.

"You can come with me," she said. "Do you want to come now? Sooner or later . . . ."

He stared at her. She slipped and flowed and faded, and again his mind whirled down to nothing.

Coming back from the kitchen with a freshly-filled lamp, Cynthia stopped in the door, aghast. Lucy felt coldness descend, and her face rammed into the back of Cynthia's head. The globe rocked perilously on the lamp.

"What?" pleaded Lucy.

"Did you see that?"

"I felt something. Oh God in heaven. What?"

"I saw somebody in there beside his bed," Cynthia said.

"What? Who? Oh God!"

"I thought for a minute it was Mama or Mrs. Guffey, but she was older."

"Who? Who?"

"That old woman. She had her head against Logan's, or in his head, and then she disappeared."

"Oh God it was her," Lucy cried weakly and fainted. Cynthia grabbed the lamp before it fell, but the globe shattered on the floor. Cynthia stood a moment, her face lit by the smoky wick, and she screamed.

Walton and Loretta were up and quickly past her to the boy. Mrs. Guffey and Big Boy ran from the dining room. Lucy sat up, and Cynthia was white and shaking. Walton had the overhead light on. Logan breathed regularly, a faint smile on his lips. They turned to the girls.

"The ghost." Cynthia nodded solemnly. "We saw the ghost."

They looked at Lucy, who glanced at the broken globe.

"Cynthia saw the ghost," she said. "That's what she told me."

A warm wind blew through the town in the false dawn. Tentative pipings arose from birds in the line of trees along the creek. Tan clouds, with some undercolor, stood on all horizons. The mutter, wheeze, and ponderous clunking fell outward from the industries and pulsed through the town. Here and there a light went on.

Walton stood on the porch, the breeze warm upon his face. He looked at his watch. Ten minutes until the first whistle. A man came down the street in the weak light. Up from her pallet on the dining room floor, Mrs. Guffey projected her will with all her might. She had struck no bargain. No trader came.

Walton stared at Rawson as the doctor mounted the porch. He had no bag and his face was puffed. He spread his hands in hopeless, wordless explanation of that thing which he could not explain. He walked quickly to the boy's bed. In high professional pretense he pulled a stethoscope from his coat pocket and listened.

"Coffee," he commanded.

Loretta stood at the door, red-eyed but agreeable. "Coffee? For Logan?"

"No, for me. Fry me four eggs. I'm starved to death."

Cynthia, in worship of the doctor, ran to the kitchen. With loud rattlings of iron, she banged wood into the range. The air in the house was close, stifling with tobacco, coffee, and hot grease. Then Mrs. Walters barged through the door. She went to the bed and took a small paper bag from her apron pocket.

"Get me a spoon," she ordered. Rawson stared at her, his eyes wild and nervous.

"What are you going to do?" he inquired, his tone that of conferring with a colleague of wide reputation. His face was foolish, as questioning as a student's.

"Shut up and get me a spoon," she said. Loretta brought it, and Mrs. Walters opened a bottle and slipped another of the tan tablets into the boy's lips. Then she unscrewed the top of another bottle in the bag and poured something dark and vile into the spoon. Rawson snapped alert.

"Just a minute, here. What is that you've got?"

She slapped the boy. "Logan, swallow this."

He did not respond. She slapped him again, and his eyes opened. She thrust the spoon at him. The boy received it and swallowed. Some of it ran from the corner of his mouth, and he coughed. His face was contorted.

"Oh God! Fool!" Rawson rasped furiously. "What have you put in that boy?"

She cast an impersonal eye upon Logan. He did not vomit. Rawson noisily slurped coffee.

"By God! What do you think you're doing? You'll kill him. What was that?"

"Black Draught. Shut your mouth, doctor. Where have you been?"

"I've been asleep," he said guiltily.

"Yes, well, we've not been, you see," she said sardonically, her eyes accusing.

"Black Draught?" Rawson mumbled. Loretta handed him a plate and he began eating.

"Sit and wait," Mrs. Walters said.

The whistle blew, and its echo volleyed through the coves and subsided. The men moved up the street to their work. Some stopped briefly to inquire about Logan.

They waited. The sun came up, flat and dull. There was the early hint of changing weather in the air. The boy suddenly twisted violently.

"Get him up. Get him onto the toilet," Mrs. Walters shouted, rising quickly. She pushed them all out of the way, gathered up the child, and ran down the hall with him. She lifted his moist gown and stuck his scrawny butt over the seat. A great gush poured forth. The child's body buckled with pain and exertion. Then he pitched forward into her arms and wide, warm breast, trembling and helpless. Rawson stood in the bathroom door, staring suspiciously. Mrs. Walters cleaned the boy's rear, which was raw and drenched. She turned to Rawson.

"C'mere, you," she said.

Rawson stared into the bowl. Long, fat worms, thick with rich, dark blood.

"Christ!" he said reverentially. "Worms! Worms?"

He stared at the boy, rubbing his nose reflectively.

—Always something you can't anticipate gets into this boy's gut. How did I miss this? How? How? With this one, it could be anything. This old woman beat me. In the very sacred name of God.

He stalked back to his plate. A moment later he was elated. The boy lived, then.

—Forget what I said—he said to God.

Mrs. Walters was on the bed with Logan, petting him as he trembled. She cajoled and scolded playfully and got another wafer into him. She set the vial down, and Rawson grabbed it and looked. Tabor's Worm Medicine. Christ Almighty! Patent medicines.

She fed the boy more broth, waited, and poured more laxative. Shortly afterward he moved again. Floating in the bowl was an entanglement that appeared to be several living hair nets.

"There," she said to Rawson. "Their nest. We cleaned out their nest."

He nodded. Bullshit. They do not have nests. He did not say it aloud.

"Now feed him more broth," she commanded Loretta. The boy was even whiter and trembled uncontrollably, but Rawson knew the worst was over.

Worms?

"Say, you're not going to feed him any more Black Draught, are you?" he asked, merely an interested spectator.

"No, that's going to do awhile. He can get strong now."

Rawson got to the door, then dared to say it: "That boy's lucky to be alive, by God. I'm goddamned if you haven't nearly killed him. Jesus!"

Then he strode briskly up the street. Mrs. Walters chewed contentedly on her brush.

"I wonder why he's walking," she muttered. "He's got a car."

16

Red rivers of health flowed through Logan Guffey. He ate oatmeal and fatback.

"Why, you're just a little pig," Loretta chided. "You'll get fat." He smiled and ate more.

He gained sufficient health to enter school. School days sprang forth like a river from the ground—a bright and bursting flow of apprehensive, joyful days, a parade of ringing activity, an outpouring of sight and sound. His heart nearly burst with love for the teacher. It was the mixture, the amalgam of school, that stuck so firmly in his memory. It was the early rising and excitement of dressing and setting forth alone in the September mornings; the bracing lotion of the air, the cobwebs dewy along fences, the smells from the waking land, the bird songs and the sun rising; the girls and boys turning toward the bell in the hand of the janitor; the Pledge of Allegiance and the patriotic songs. Each day for the first week Loretta met him after school; then she softly released him to make it through the squared routes of Hollytown on his own.

Businessman P. N. Caldwell came out of his store.

"Hey, boy! Hey, Logan," he croaked. Logan stopped.

"Ol' Alex Fore is right down there. You watch out. He's done things. Nobody is safe. . . ," he warned darkly.

Logan turned his thin, dark face, saw Alex slouched upon the sunny grass past the railroad tracks, muttering dark imprecations, dire threats. The boy stared at P. N. Caldwell, the tracks, the old man in the grass. His young eyes swung here and there. He smiled briefly, strode on.

"Hey, boy! Hey, little Walt!" Alex called. Logan turned timidly.

"What?" he asked.

"Did he say somethin' about me?"

Logan stared, did not speak at first; then: "Not much."

"He is one of the ones who tells things. One day I will begin to tell things. When I tell, it will be the truth, and not many will be able to stand it. The people may or may not want to believe me, but the time of truth will come about. It's up to them if they want to hear or believe it, but the time of truth is on its way. One day the truth bird will land on me and squeeze its claws into my mangy old head and I'll tell it all. That is the day the angels will testify in heaven and that is the day the shit will fly, and some of these so-called Christians will hunker down and start trying to beg out," Alex said, a certain light of anticipation coming upon him as he spoke.

"Why do they baaa at you?"

Alex's face flushed darkly. "Because they're a sorry bunch of sons-of-bitches," he said.

"I'll hit them for it."

"Oh, wouldja? Wouldja? Don't worry about hitting 'em. Just hold 'em till I can git to 'em."

Paul Fortune set up a tenuous discipline. Some things in his mind cleared for him in an otherwise boozy haze, and he stopped drinking again, shook out the vestiges of his drunks with the aid of Dr. Rawson, and put pen to paper.

In the times in which Paul Fortune sought reason for living, he saw life as a great notebook and rough draft, with atrocious punctuation, obscure allegory, and metaphors that did not fit. Life was an art form, must always be rewritten and polished, and Fortune was the editor, trying to absorb form and sense into his brain and put it onto paper. Or perhaps he was only the typesetter for the tomes the earth was writing, as life fell through his days like lino-typed lead, in long novels, short stories, ringing little poems, paragraphs, sentences, appropriate little fillers. The endings were the hardest to set. An inner sense told him when something was shifting in time; the end was near, everywhere, anywhere. He had to look closely to see when it was time to turn from those nearby whose parts had ended.

So that his life might not fade entirely in the leaps of time, Fortune kept a long, rambling diary in which to salvage and store some of the incidents and thoughts of his days. He was aware of the many little episodes, vignettes, and poems opening around him, closing into denouement, opening again to wider interpretation and further study, but he could not capture them. He began putting down some abstractions of things he had observed in the town and in the mountains. His words looked strange and false to him, and he hated what he had put on paper. But he knew that he must let it sit awhile and cool, and when he read it later, perhaps he would find something of truth in it.

The months went by, and on the last day of the year, Fortune wrote in his ledgers until dawn. He slept until noon, ate a bird's breakfast, then left his place for the first time in two weeks. He stopped at the rock fountain and bent to drink. There was the sharp report of a gunshot at Boogerman's house, and Fortune jumped. The few people on the street were still and watchful, alarmed. They did not move for the two minutes it took Boogerman to lurch out the door, his face guarded and embarassed. Fortune looked across the street and saw Doc McCall in the door of his pharmacy. His face brightened. Doc grinned, waved him over. Fortune went to coffee with the druggist. Rawson joined them.

"Oho, Rawson! Where have you been? Did Boogerman shoot his wife or what?"

"Well, if he did, I wasn't asked to see about it. I guess he let it go accidentally. He's done it time and time again."

"What is the news from the medical section of the world?" McCall asked respectfully.

"Misery. Torment. Aches and pains. Eventual doom for the entire population."

"I see!" Fortune said. "Do you expect us all to go at once?"

"Frankly, I do not foresee simultaneous departure, but I could be wrong."

"Yes, yes, but I don't think so. You are a smart man. What is the epidemic that will get us all?"

Rawson sat back and pondered the wall soberly. "Death," he said.

For a moment Fortune was strangely comforted; then suddenly he felt a flow of dark mood sweeping him toward a bend beyond which lay bright and unspeakable oblivion. A weight was upon him. New Year's Eve. The year itself began to plunge toward death, and Fortune's mind also began another of its terminations. Old guilts rode in like tired horsemen, and behind them fears came like wolves at dark. Slow panic spread and smothered him with the gaseous climates of death.

Time, like a dusty portico, rumbled and collapsed around him. Destruction loomed, and again a weary old man stepped forward inside him asking for surcease, freedom from the flesh, and passage on to the next place of the soul. Fortune had seen it all. Nothing important remained. Sweat beaded his brow. Without further notice of his cronies, he ran into the chill of late December's air toward the Western Front.

"Oh, h'yer he is, h'yer he is," exulted Sweatbee as Fortune entered Lon's. "I thought we'd lost 'im, he's not been around in so long."

Lon looked up, gloomily studied Fortune, then turned on a wide, counterfeit smile.

"Ready to start, are you?" he asked.

"Give me a big cup of wine to start with," Fortune said, defeated. His voice was shaky and formal.

"Hell yeh, hell yeh," Sweatbee whooped. He swaggered to the bar and goggled his eyes comically. "Gimme a Ram's Head ale and call the law."

Fortune laughed, lifted high his wine, looked around at them. Four others sat in quiet stupor.

"Down it now!" Sweatbee shrieked. Fortune drained it, waited for the blood to warm and shoot about. He had been sober for a long time.

As night fell, the Skiller brothers came the long dark way down from Wild Cat and hunkered quietly in the pines on the golf course above the Western Front. They waited for Earl to think and feel it out. He turned his face toward the lights, but he did not look as much as scent the air. His brothers lay on pine needles in the darkness. Then Earl rose and went to scout the Western Front. He stationed himself in dried weeds near Lon's place for a few minutes. No sheriff's car prowled. He returned to the pines.

"All right, let's go drink and hear the music," he said.

Except for random creaking in the wind, the house was still. Walton watched Logan play on the floor. He walked about rest-

184

lessly. Through the kitchen window he studied the moonrise on the east ridge of the town. Then he turned to his son.

"I tell you what, old boy," he said. "Let's put on our coats and go shoot some pool or something."

"Where's Mama?"

"Her uncle is home from the army. They're at your grandmother Walters'. She'll be gone until midnight."

"Can I see him too?"

"Maybe tomorrow."

"Where are we going tonight?"

"Why, boy, we're going abroad in the world. We'll go to the poolroom in Hollytown or maybe to the Upper End. How do you like that?"

Logan's face lit with a quick smile. Walton counted out money, hid some in a cabinet, then folded other bills into his pockets.

Up the glum street, unlit yet by moonbeams, to the Western Front. All roads lead to the Western Front.

Three whores came into Lon's as the jukebox played the "Brown's Ferry Blues." It was a night for a party. Sweatbee put a pint on a table for all to drink from. It lasted only a moment. The girls giggled and tried to get the men to dance, but the men were not ready. Lon cast a dubious eye into the night and felt his stomach twitch with a short pain.

"There's a bad sign," he said, staring at Paul Fortune. "He held out a long time."

Fortune sat with his back to the bar, his legs spraddled and his body hunched. Defeat and agony were upon his face, and his eyes were fearful and self-pitying.

"I've done it," he said. "By God, I've done it now. I fought . . . ."

He sobbed, wheeled around. "Give me more wine," he ordered.

Sweatbee left a whore and came to him. "I'm gonna git more likker," he said.

The door opened and in walked the several Skillers. No sooner were they seated than Lon had beer before them. He poured wine for Sweatbee and Fortune, then went into the back room, lost his own fight, turned up a quart, and drank deeply. He marveled at the quick change of atmosphere. While he continued to serve his

185

customers, he began sneaking back frequently to his own bottle. Then he came out and grabbed one of the whores and danced about the floor. The atmosphere of gaiety so intensified that when Alex Fore stumbled in, he was served without hesitation and treated as a fellow, a colleague, and a gentleman. The reek and stench of him came before and with and after him, but it was part of the old man, and tonight nobody was disqualified. When Walton and Logan entered, the night of the bright cut moon was in full swing, and drinks were being served grandly without regard for who was paying. Two of the whores were making sandwiches on the grill, and the other was being put upon by Sweatbee. He had her dress up to her underwear.

"I'll swear, I'll swear," Paul Fortune said. The spirit of excess rode strongly in the night. Lon, lost to misery and good intention at once, sat in a chair near Earl Skiller and sang lusty whorehouse songs, cursed all women, grinned slyly at a naked thigh.

Logan looked at his father. Walton smiled uncertainly, his eyes glistening.

"Whhoooo . . . haaawwww," he yelped. "Gimme a drink."

Sweatbee handed him a full pint. "Now, Walton, I never seen you git plumb drunk. Go ahead and git drunk."

"I don't know," Walton said. "I might ought to take Logan home."

"He's old enough to begin the enjoyment of a full life," Fortune yelled.

Walton had two drinks of moonshine and two cups of Old Maude wine before he saw the Skillers. He moved Logan to their table. The air was rich, ripe with fermented drink. Earl looked at Logan and slowly sipped beer.

"You been a good boy?" he asked.

Logan nodded.

"Does he want to sip my beer?" Earl asked Walton.

"A little won't hurt. Don't tell Mama," Walton said.

Earl held the brown bottle to him. Logan raised it and swallowed the bitter, brackish beer. He frowned.

"Good?" Earl asked.

Logan shook his head. Walton held out a cup of wine, and he sipped again. It was musky, rich, sweet. He drank it all.

Sweatbee danced with his whore and slugged more nickels into the jukebox. At the end of each record they came to the table to drink from brown bottles.

Lon locked and shuttered the front door. The club was now closed to all but the present membership. The owner leaned heavily against his bar, not drunk yet, nor sober. Paul Fortune muttered a thing profound:

"Death. Each drink is a little death. I die as the light of day seeps down to grayness, and the fawns leap wildly from the deep thickets of me."

Lon rolled his head, frowned, and fixed his eyes upon Fortune.

"By God, you can say that again," he said.

Sweatbee and one of the lesser Skillers were up and bristling at each other.

"Ah, hell. Hell!" Lon moaned, but he did not move. Sweatbee bit his upper lip with fierce lower teeth, growling unintelligibly. The Skiller's voice rose.

"Say what you mean or I'll stomp yore ass," said the Skiller.

"You'll stomp nobody's ass," Sweatbee said. "You're not man enough."

Lon raised his head. "I'll have to ask ye to hush," he said in profound disinterest, then let his great head loll again onto his chest.

For Logan the room gathered momentum and whirled in wide, rising stripes. He tilted forward and would have tottered if Earl had not caught him. Walton raised a cup of wine and stared about in a wine-shocked gape.

"Whooooopppeee!" he shouted.

"I said to hush, b'God!" Lon said.

"Who? Me?" asked Walton.

"No, not you. Them great fighters there. Them and that son-of-a-bitch a-singin' Dixie in my ear."

"What fighters?" Walton asked.

"The two skinny ones there," Earl said, grinning.

"Take it back, by God," Sweatbee said to the younger Skiller.

"I'll not do 'er," he said. "Take what back?"

"What you said."

"What did you think I said, you son-of-a-bitch?"

"There, fer instance. You called me a son-of-a-bitch."

"You lie. You're a goddam liar."

"See? You called me a liar and a son-of-a-bitch."

"Where do you get all that crazy shit, Sweatbee?"

"By God! My name's Mister Hardy to you, you low-living cock . . ."

Alex Fore stumbled between them, stared owlishly, and loosed upon them a powerful grin of immense yellow evil.

"Ho, boys," he said. "How ye doin'? Let's have a drink."

"Git out of the way, Alex," said the Skiller. Alex leaned into him.

"What fer? Why not?" Alex asked.

"Why not what?"

"Why not . . . why not . . . why not . . . why, well, let's put it this here way . . . let's see now," Alex said, his face puzzled. When the Skiller looked again, Sweatbee had unlocked the door and was gone.

Earl sat quietly, watching everything; then he asked, "Lon, has the law been here tonight?"

Lon's confused eyes lit on Earl. His brow was heavy with worry. He thought a moment.

"No, they don't come here. I'll kick their asses if they bother my customers," he boasted. His head lopped sideways on his shoulder. Earl grinned, lifted his bottle.

"You want some wine, Earl?" Walton asked.

"No, beer's all," Earl said. "Wine is crazy."

Logan watched them split into doubles and triples of themselves. The chair upon which he sat raced down through space, and the current of it was gray and dense with a thousand voices. Overhead, the ceiling and light swirled and separated and then mingled and fused again, and the long high music broke through to him.

> Way back in the hills,
> As a boy I once wandered . . . .

Fortune wheeled abruptly, tilting on his stool. He stared at the Skiller and the whore dancing.

"What did you say?" Lon asked.

"I said nothing worth repeating or even rethinking. But I can phrase it differently, if you like."

"Ye can, can ye?"

"Yes. Listen. The dawn comes up like thunder outer China 'crost the Bay."

Lon squinted. "Well, what's that got to do with anything?"

"My man, my man," Fortune said, "have you not been to other places?"

"Yes, yes indeed," Lon said uncertainly.

"I do love conversing with a man of your caliber," Fortune said.

> Very deep in the grave
> Lies the girl that I love. . . .

Lon's eyes clouded.

"I mortally love that goddam song," he sobbed. Paul Fortune shrugged, leaned forward, and patted Lon's shoulder comfortingly. Walton reached out and caught Logan, who was sliding from the chair. Earl stared blankly at them all. The young Skiller danced with Sweatbee's whore, and others brought chairs to the table where the brothers were. Earl rose while they arranged the seats, and none saw him leave.

> She was called from this earth,
> A jewel in heaven . . . .

Lon and two whores wept.

"I hate that part of that goddam song," Lon blubbered, wiping his cheeks with a handkerchief. "Hell," he said belligerently, "I'll tell you what let's play. Let's play 'Will the Circle Be Unbroken,' and for a goddam nickel we can break down and cry all night for our mamas."

> Very deep in the grave
> Lies the girl that I love . . . .

Sweatbee paced up and down beside the highway. Then he picked up two rocks the size of teacups and returned to Lon's. Past the shutters he could see them stumbling and weaving about. He fingered the rocks. He listened to five songs, then stood to rest his haunches. Suddenly he felt sharp steel on his throat.

"Drop them rocks, Sweatbee. Right now, I mean, or I'll hide your head in a deep hole at Wild Cat," Earl said. Sweatbee let them fall.

"Now, Sweatbee, I know he was wrong and I'll apologize for him, but you ain't going to bust his head. My brothers ain't everything they ought to be, but I'll keep care of them. If you want to come on inside, I'll buy your beer the rest of the night. Just don't pay attention to my brother anymore."

"Shore, Earl, shore. That's fine with me," Sweatbee whispered. "You're a good man, and if you say to let 'im off, then I will."

"Ah, I thankee fer that," Earl said and removed the blade from Sweatbee's throat. When they went inside, the brother glared at Sweatbee.

"Aha. Here you are," he said. "I wondered . . . ."

Earl stared grimly at him and he shut up. With dignity, Sweatbee walked up to him and offered his hand.

"I'm ye friend. I'm a friend to all you boys at Wild Cat. You know that. You know me, boy."

The brother shook hands.

"Bring Sweatbee a cup of wine and beer," Earl commanded.

"Let him git his own, like everybody else," Lon said.

One of the whores went to tend the bar. Lon slouched heavily on his stool. Paul Fortune swayed about in befuddlement. The girl carried drinks to Sweatbee, took Earl's money, and put it on the cash register. She looked timidly at Lon.

"Put it in the drawer," Lon said. She rang it up.

They drank to spinning records. Logan drank more wine and puked.

"God A'mighty, what time is it?" Walton asked, holding Logan's head up.

"It's even midnight, up and down," Lon said.

"I'm going home if my boy ain't dead," Walton said mournfully. He staggered sideways.

Alex Fore rose from his lonely chair in the corner. "Better let me help ye," he said to Walton, who swayed and stared confusedly at him.

"All right, old man, if you want to," Walton said finally.

"Wait a minute, wait a minute, wait a minute. I'm going that way. I'll help with the tyke," Fortune said.

Lon raised his head and stared woefully at the back door.

"You're all going home?" he asked.

"I've got to go home," Walton said, holding Logan under the arms. Alex Fore had the boy's feet. Logan's face was slack.

The Skillers stood. "Are you drunk, Walton?" Earl asked.

"I'm drunker'n forty-nine hells," he said.

"We'll go with ye, then."

"I ain't got room for you to sleep there."

"We're not going to stay."

"The law looking for you?"

"Yeh, but not hard."

The entire party left, including Lon.

"Where are you a-goin', Lon?" Sweatbee asked.

"I'm going to help take this poor little drunk boy home, by God."

"Well, if Boogerman's up, he'll try to git us all."

"He can try if he wants to," Lon said confidently, "but try is all."

They wound their way down the street, staggering into each other, breaking into sporadic song, feeling the whores, and drinking. As they approached Main Street, Earl's hand went out, and his brothers faded out to flank along the sidewalk and establish some distance between themselves. Fortune stopped to look at them.

"Ah, that way one shell can't get you all," he said.

Earl's voice sounded from the darkness ahead of them.

"Or one cop."

As they came into the curve above Loretta's father's house, they sang many songs lustily in many keys. When they were even with the small bridge, Walton saw Loretta coming across it. He stopped, shot through with fear. He tried to think, but could not. Loretta ran on into the road.

"What is this?" she shrieked. They milled about in boozy consternation.

"My boy. My little boy is in the arms of Alex Fore," she yelled.

Alex shrank from her anger and put the boy on the ground. Logan staggered a few steps and fell sideways into the grass. The stars spun behind dim faces. He gasped and shut his eyes.

"Drunk," she said to Walton. "You're as drunk as hell. You! The very one who takes on about somebody taking the slightest little sip. What's the matter with Logan?"

Walton cackled insanely. "He's drunk too. He took me out against my will and got me drunk."

"What? I have never seen the likes of this. I have never seen such a parade. Have you been with these . . . these . . . these . . ." she stopped, gritted her teeth, stared at the women again, ". . .these goddam sluts?"

"Whores, not sluts," one of the girls said pleasantly. "He's not been with us. We don't have to mess around with married men.

191

We got our boyfriends here." Each one was arm-in-arm with a Skiller.

Loretta picked up Logan and cradled him in her arms.

"Let me say this," she said with pressured restraint. "Just let me say one thing. Alex Fore, Sweatbee Hardy, Mr. Fortune, the Skillers, Walton, Logan, and three whores. Now! That's all I've got to say."

She stomped her foot angrily upon the pavement, then wheeled and ran down the street toward the house.

"Waal, I reckon so," Alex said slowly, turning a hideous grin to them.

"The baby in the mama's arms is the baby home at last," Earl said pensively.

Walton staggered thoughtfully down the street. Alex faded from among them, disappeared into the lumber stacks, his foul wake falling away from him.

Lon turned to Paul Fortune.

"Listen, can you put me up for the night?"

"Why can't you go home?"

"Don't be a goddam fool. It ain't that I can't go home. It's that I ain't about to go home. I'll catch hell."

Fortune's face assumed an attitude of profound thought.

"How long do you stay drunk when you start?" he asked Lon.

"As long as I can, while I'm at it."

"Me too. Let's get about two gallons and see how long that lasts," Fortune said. They turned to Earl.

"It's time to get away from beer and wine and get down to serious business. How about it?"

Earl grinned at them. "I don't personally know nothing about it," he said. "But I'll go talk to a feller. Give me the money, and he'll have the likker at your place in an hour."

They gave him the money. With Sweatbee in tow, they reeled across the town to Paul Fortune's quarters.

Friends, companions, money, liquor. I'm a lucky man, Paul Fortune thought.

The holidays ended and school resumed. Logan stopped at the pharmacy daily. Occasionally Rawson and McCall sat for coffee, chattered on, stared down the street toward Fortune's little house.

"Do you go see about him?" McCall asked.

"No. Lon was in there with him for a week. Someone finally came and hauled Lon off. This is a fearsome toot that he is on. I shudder at the thought of it. The man's liver is not of this species or even this world. He is a dead man for all practical concerns. Dead and stinking. What a stink."

A few days later Logan drifted down the street, turned, and stood at the walkway of Paul Fortune's squat little house. A pale, drawn face appeared at the window, blinked, disappeared, and reappeared immediately at the door.

"Logan, son, Logan, c'mere," he said, weak and hoarse. Logan went to the door.

"What?" he asked.

"Tell me," Fortune rasped, "what are they saying?"

"Who?"

"Anyone. Everyone. The town. The people. Are they for me or against me or what?"

Logan shook his head. "I don't know," he said.

"Ah God! Come on in. I'll give you something. I'll find a dime."

Logan entered. Fortune stumbled weakly about.

"Here, boy, here. Here. Sit here. I need company in a most terrible way. A mind by itself is a crazy mind. I need somebody to talk to. Don't leave me, son. Stay. Look, look, I'll show you around my place."

He scurried about, his face anxious. His bed was on a raised platform of plank and close to the roof. Other things in that room— files, papers, books, food—were set up high.

"Here! My bed is near the tin roof. On nights of bad weather I can hear the wind and rain close to me. Ha! But I am safe, you see?"

Logan nodded in perfect agreement. Fortune turned and pointed to the floor.

"No flood can reach me. If one comes, I am up high. Now, you see my little port of a window at the head of my bed? I can look out, but who can look in? It is hidden outside by the eaves. It is only a part of the shadow."

Fortune swayed, his face pedantic. "The way one's place is fixed is much more important than people might think. In this bed I am a ship's passenger on stormy waters. I am a traveler in a Pullman berth. I am a sick man in a restful hospital. When any mood strikes,

I am safe. Lastly I am a child in my father's house. Ye must be as a child, a small child, you see?"

Logan stared silently, uncomprehending but comfortable with it all.

Fortune's face turned dour.

"Oh, what the hell? I'm explaining craziness to a child. It won't save him from it. I'm not here to save the world. I'm here to survive a little longer. I hold up my share of the world's load by just surviving."

He paced the room feverishly. "Listen, listen. I know about you and old man Alex Fore talking about the truth bird. Well, I have thought and thought about that bird. There is an avalanche of lies sweeping the earth daily. The old man is right. Who is telling the truth? Who dares to tell the truth?

"I was near that teeming sea of sleep, that vast fishpond of slippery ideas and questions and answers, and I heard a voice saying that there are a great many truth-sayers around here, but nobody knows who they are because not many know what truth sounds like. Those who speak it do not speak in everybody's language. They stay hidden, and their effect is slight because they are afraid of being found out, and their tongue is bitter and their ideas pass off as wit. But whoever says truth in wit says only half-truth, because humor clouds the rest of the truth.

"I am not a truth-sayer, because I don't know much truth, and if I did, my words wouldn't say it. Now, there are some in the middle of the people. They are not preachers, because preachers hide the truth with their utter sincerity and they are tiresome. Nor are they teachers, although truth-sayers do teach. They are scattered among us, one to each certain number of people, and we have to listen to everyone to find out who is saying truth and when they are saying it. Sometimes their gift changes hands and the bird lands on someone else, and it takes people awhile to find out who the new truth-sayer is. The gift is like a deliberate slow bird that is careful to light on something strong enough to bear it. The bird is not afraid, but the people who receive it are. They are afraid of the bird when they find out it has picked them. Sometimes they hate that bird and are afraid that people will learn that it has picked them, but they are now truth-sayers, and they are more afraid of the bird than they are of the people. Then they get afraid the bird will fly away from them as quietly as it found them. There is no other way to deal with the truth than to be afraid.

"Always say truth, boy, if you know it by name and can say it. But it is hard to decipher. Much truth has blossomed in a bed of lies. Truth is not religion, though religion guises as truth. If you know truth and can't find the words to say it, then you are cursed in the brain and tongue—and if you can say it, then mad blood has been splashed upon your brain and you are cursed of man.

"And the truth-sayers have been licensed among us, but not by man or plan. And when you get all this figured out, then you won't ask anymore who the truth-sayers are," Fortune said, spinning wildly about on the floor.

Fortune's drunk went on and on. The days tumbling past outside his window were no longer counted. Nonetheless, he hit slow places where his mind found a certain cool clarity. Logan came again one day, and shortly behind him came the doctor, who was as concerned for the boy as he was for Fortune. They found him bearded and bleary, leaning into a stack of books on his table. The scents were winey and ancient, but the rooms were tidy. Everything was clean and in place.

"Here! Here!" Fortune said, stumbling to his feet, scrubbing his chair across the boards. His breath was strong, his jowls gray and aged. Rawson did not try to engage his eyes.

"I've got it now. I've got it."

"What?" Rawson asked.

"The secret of the universe."

"What is it, then? Tell us frankly. We can stand it."

"Here it is," he said, fumbling and getting two books open. "Some new things about creation. There was once, in the beginning, one small dense mass, and it exploded with great force and became the universe, which is still expanding."

"Aha," said Rawson. "Good. Except I've heard of this. You are late with the discovery."

"Don't get smart. I'm thinking of something else."

"What?"

"That time runs with it, hand and glove."

"Runs with what?"

"The planets, as they stretch out."

"Well, tell me sometime after you have sobered yourself up, if you live," Rawson said.

"I have a cosmic hangover, part of a great purpose. At last my drinking has amounted to something. I have a result. A hangover like this will not come again to mortal man. My brain has burst like an egg. It turns out that all the inspiration I have ever sought remained hidden like a yolk in the center of my brain. God, what a glorious tremens this is."

"I am going," Rawson said. "Come on, boy, get away from this madman. This could be infectious. We'll come back later when he has finished this."

"Maybe I'll die now that I have received this revelation," Fortune said shakily.

"I can't wait to see inside the body. It'll be a medical marvel."

Fortune watched them go from his lonely tenement. Then his nervous system surged and sparked again.

"Fools!" he thought loudly, so that his skull ached and he felt that perhaps his brain had indeed burst. "There was more to tell you. There is a limit to the expansion. The pieces will contract and shoot backward again toward the original mass, and time will contract with it, re-reel and run backward. The secret is mine. The day of the burial is also the day of resurrection, and to live we must die to rise again; time runs backward from there and we do not know which way we are going. Imprisoned in the passing bubble in the fluid moment, we grow backward into youth and are swallowed up by . . . death? No, the womb again, and go back back back . . . The human race contracts and subtracts again into nothingness, and its zeros and misery are erased from our records as backward we run. Today we do not remember tomorrow, and yesterday we do not recall today, and yesterday will also grow pale and blank as we fall down through our memory. Tomorrow! Tomorrow? We do not recall what happened tomorrow. As we form in our mother's womb from the seeds of the past, so also do we take subtle form in our graves from the dust and rot of the centuries ahead. The day is forming, even now, folding, unfolding— nothing is edited or cut.

"Quickly, quickly, yesterday is coming.

"In the rot of the tomb we are forming. Yesterday is quickly coming, throwing us softly toward the pain of the womb. As time

196

reverses and pans toward us in its glittering planes, our torment turns to joy and we head again toward our mothers.

"These bones shall rise again, and we shall be upon the old lost streets once more. We shall return to that lost home, to the cabin in the vale at dusk. Yesterday we will go once more homeward . . . ."

As he pondered, he also saw that light was with time as mother with child, and he became enamored and enchanted. Fascinated and obsessed, he grew afraid of the light for a moment as it stripped him open of soul for examination.

Light, the one great god with all the lesser godlets under its rule. The chief prince is time. Light and time run together down the cindered tracks of the universe.

Without light there is no time. Timeless darkness. Light beating down upon us, harrows of time dragged through our days, laying them open, crumbling them into dead, sterile furrows. Light coming upon us, light and time and great hooves in the night, running away with our lives.

In the tombs there is . . .

No light.

Light reflects off the planet and glances into space, as though the earth were the lens of a great projector shining our lives down the dark auditorium of space. Giant pictures of us and our days flicker out beyond Pluto, and among the stars we are young again and shall hear the songs that died on stone lips sung again in bright new skies.

In the night old voices call, and in the light we see again our lives, and at troubled midnight the voices come again.

The east light is the most painful. A new day crashes through the window, and the voices of yesterday die in the night.

The noon light is the harshest because day is losing, spilling off the earth in a turbulent wake of image, flowing fast through sidereal fields.

And the soft, decaying, and golden light from the west is the saddest because a day is done and will not come this way again.

Light burns away our day. Waters drain through tombs in lonely time. Seas of light wash the skies. We die our deaths and in the tomb we find no time. We drank our time from cups of light.

Paul Fortune trembled with his vision. He watched light pour through the room like fast wind made visible. He had searched for light and time, had feared and hated them, had known that to catch truth was to be eaten by it. God is light and in that light works protean time and it is those three that are one.

Time and light and a path homeward through the stars. Into light we are born.

Do they lay us sadly down in darkness?

Fortune raised his burned eyes to peer out his window and up the street. He saw Boogerman. Sweatbee passed, a faint sneer upon his lips.

Boogerman! Boogerman? Fortune did not mind dictatorial policemen as long as he stood in good stead with them.

The weeks passed, and Paul Fortune's spree drew near to no discernible end. He lay sick, wondering in broken consciousness how much more of it he had to take. He grew weary, saw with faint hope that he would somehow once again get better, grow older.

"I will die," he whispered, "but not now. The world will go on to the end and come back again."

Weary, weary.

He felt vitality stirring faintly. He knew dull, buried expectancy, anticipation. There was more life to come; more to come on its wearisome track.

In a few days McCall broke his policy of not going to Fortune's place. The great bald pharmacist swayed awkwardly in the room as Fortune guzzled a glassful.

"I'm glad to see you, old man," Fortune said.

"It's March the fifteenth," McCall said.

"March? March?"

"You started about New Year's."

"To be frank, I'm afraid. If I try to come off, will you give me some pills?"

"No!"

"Why not?"

"It's not good. Maybe if Rawson wrote a prescription. Why, what the hell would people think?"

"What? What people think? People think? Ah God yes, there you have touched upon the spike in the human heart. What will people think? You would be a rich man if you knew what people thought. All you know is what a few people say, and what is that? People will tell you anything in the goddam world except what they really think. People may not even know what they think till they see it or hear it, but everybody goes about trying to fit acceptable thoughts into the frame of what they think people think or ought to think . . . ."

He paused reflectively and in some defeat. "Even me, you see?" he said with a brief, wry grin.

"No pills," McCall said and lurched heavily out the door.

It was this final rejection that spun him toward sobering up. He felt very small. It was not that he felt himself an insignificant atom in creation, but rather an excess atom left over and lost, a nuisance in an otherwise well-ordered universe. He was sick of rolling around and bumping into the other well-placed atoms.

At last the great apocalyptic spree drew to its frightful close for Paul Fortune. The dimensions of the hangover compared closely with the complete set of visions in the Book of the Revelation. Several times he caught himself wandering off the edge of the known universe. Hags, angels, beautiful and loving young courtesans from the Court of the Hapsburgs, two Egyptian devils, an angry Comanche warrior, and at one vivid point, Joan of Arc riding a buffalo visited him as he passed through his delirium.

Then, incredibly and quite suddenly, one morning he was restored to an uncertain grip on sanity. He trembled his last and noticed that his health was back. That week he somehow turned from his deep personal problems to other concerns. He fell into a curious lassitude. Intuitively he recognized it as an ebb that would later rise again to accomplishment. The bothersome moods were gone. He grew into an eerie contentment.

After an appraisal of possibilities, he took a train to New York. There an acquaintance with a publisher was renewed. He remained in the city for some time to adapt to the different atmosphere and rhythm of it. For a while a suffocating and frightening sense of rustic inferiority came over him. His enforced exile in the mountains had wrought certain social damage upon him. He found himself saying "sir" to imperious subalterns and office help. In time the city became less formidable. Finally he reached agreement with some editors, and when he left the city he had a contract to turn out a dozen pulp westerns a year.

The first week back in Hollytown found him relaxed and marveling at the sea change that had swept the deeps of his heart. The town had a fresher light and hue. The buildings stood out sharper and higher. The streets seemed less shabby and more important. Though he had many depressing memories of Hollytown, it seemed at this time that the light that cleaned his heart and mind of dirt and pain also flashed back through those bad memories, relieving them of stress and ache and imbuing them with inexplicable but definite purpose.

At night he studied his books and journals. In the afternoons he sometimes met with Rawson and the pharmacist in the drugstore, and they let their minds play over questions Fortune raised. He began writing the pulp formula stories. He limned the superficial qualities of the people around him. The mountaineers fit easily into old-west frontier scenarios. In stories never to be distributed in or around Hollytown, Boogerman became the prototype of a dogged, indefatigable constable in the Canadian Rockies. One of Loretta's sisters became a pining, sweet charmer in a number of cowtown romances. Alex Fore spoke his slow, bitter wisdoms to sidewinders and Mexicans and Yaquis deep in the south Mojave. Loretta's mother became a kind mother superior in a border convent. P. N. Caldwell assumed the role of a greedy, plotting sutler in the gold fields of old California. Logan Guffey, here and there, became an Indian child, old of eye, ears pricked. Silent.

Earl Skiller glided in and out of his mind like a shadow in the deep forest, occasionally breaking free, faintly defined as a shimmering ghost. Earl haunted Fortune. He evoked vague outlines of warriors, chiefs, generals, shamans.

Death on the open fields and in the forests of the earth.

But as Earl's images rose to the edge of Fortune's consciousness, a heat and threat arose from the hidden part of himself as though a furnace had been opened or the sun was breaking free. Something in his psyche quailed before the hinted forms of Earl. He was afraid and could not write of Earl.

Life was fuller for the writer now. The checks arrived, and he was elated by the encouraging letters he received. A new beginning—he saw it in finer detail and promise now. His heart surged.

He found himself musing incredulously when his streak of sobriety extended into months. Curiously, it was not hard. No temptation came. Life visited upon him its normal miserable collection of frustrations and small adversities, many of which would have once sent him reeling to the bottle. He did not mention his situation for a long time; then he spoke to Rawson of it. The doctor, busy with a surge in his practice at the full moon, stopped to puzzle over it and to say that he had not heard of such a precedent in the annals of the archetypal low-down, worthless town drunk. He did want to be kept apprised.

17

LOGAN WENT INTO his seasons and through his life and time. His brain was a great tiered hive. Larvae of ideas struggled to hatch and take wing. He went forth into his world to see, stared with mute wonder.

Another autumn came, and the air itself was breathing. Autumn, and Logan knew he was young. He had been ancient and tired in his many sicknesses, but he was young again in the fall. The air bit the soul, the songs would not cease, and he could not stand it further. He blinked in the full, rich, and golden light of the season. Summer died an old death. Old man summer, fat and dead. But Logan was young again.

Strawy fields, fragrant, were bathed in memory's light. Apples red, and then pies in the autumn air. Cinnamon and cloves and warm cow's milk.

Logan came to notice, here in his young years bursting forth, the thing about a certain day that seemed to come at intervals and seemed the very jewel of time. It was always a bright day, and no matter if it came in summer or winter, it always had a sharpness, a quick, cutting pain. On this rare day the light was correct, and it glittered down through the air and was pierced by the day. It was better if he was in the midst of a task and happened suddenly to notice, then let the back of his mind and senses gloat in the day while he remained at his task. If he stopped and did nothing but enjoy the day, it was disappointing because when full awareness was battened on, the mystery and magic and chemistry of it fled and would not come again.

And there was this about his secret, magic day: It was so powerful that he must recall it in the nights of his life in distant places.

There was the clear sky, the cold creek, the swift movement of bright wind across his face, and fresh youth bubbling his blood. But not for that alone must he recall it, but for this also: The day found him able to dissolve the accumulations of pain and fret and to take a brief, glad hope for himself as a person. His spirit leaped, exulted. There was that about the day.

Logan drowsed in the cadenced lessons droning from the teacher's lips. He jerked awake, stared out the window, saw the clouds above the ridges, felt the lure of everything outside. He raised his hand, walked to the teacher's desk, and said softly:

"I better go home now. My grandpa is dead."

Her hand flew to her face in shock. "Oh Logan . . . I'm sorry. I didn't know . . . I just didn't know . . . hadn't heard. Why didn't you tell me earlier, child?"

"Because I like school so much. But I've stayed too long now."

His classmates watched him silently.

"Yes, yes, run along, boy," his teacher said and hugged him. He left the room with head bowed reverently. Once he was upon the sidewalk, he ran to the drugstore, to the rack of funny books.

When he arrived home, his teacher was there, silent rebuke poisonous in the atmosphere.

Loretta, sharply: "Logan! You have lied. You have told a lie, and now you are caught up with. You said my daddy was dead. What if your lie caused him to die? Sometimes the evil we do brings down torments on another's head."

"That's not what I said."

The still, straight eye of the teacher was upon him. She said, "Do not compound this, Logan. This is a serious matter, lying to me."

How to explain now? The sun was bright, the clouds were dancing gaily, the classroom was drowsy. How to tell them that?

The beating began. There seemed no end to it. Loretta laid on fiercely. It was for the benefit of the teacher so she might see that Loretta raised her child right. The teacher promised that he would get it from her tomorrow in front of the class. That was not only to provide the class with an example, but to show Loretta that her son was in firm hands. She also promised Logan a visit to the principal, who did not hold with lying.

Walton came home from work and laid on with vigor. That night Logan snuffled and sobbed, and flinched when they came near him. Walton finally picked him up and held him.

"Son, do you know why?"

"I didn't lie."

"You said your grandpa was dead."

"He is."

Walton set him down, struck with the fact of it. Then he began to laugh. Loretta came to the door, wringing her apron in her hands.

"Hell," Walton said, "he said his grandpa was dead, and he is. I went to his funeral myself. He didn't say which grandpa. He didn't lie. He just didn't finish telling the truth."

"Well, he's going to get it from the teacher and principal both tomorrow."

Walton quietly reflected. "No! No, by God, he ain't either. I may take a day off and take him fishing. Don't send this boy to school tomorrow. Wait till I can go up there and talk to them."

Hollytown celebrated the incident. Some laughed and dismissed it. Others applauded the swift action of the mother and teacher in sticking by the standards. Men knowledgeable of life agreed with Walton.

Days later the clear wind moved under the gleam of the sun, and the trees in the mountains shimmered. The chill of the wind on the boy's face awakened far wonders, and for a moment he imagined the promises of ten thousand glories to come. He walked upon the land. In all his misguided energy he was trouble, trouble, trouble. He stopped asking questions for the time being. No one could answer them anyway.

He came upon Paul Fortune one day in the street. "Have they stopped beating you because of your grandpa's death?" Fortune asked.

Logan nodded solemnly.

"Ah, boy, boy. Go slowly in judging them. You grow older, and the day comes when outrage dies, and you are left with the residue of the experience in you like ashes. If you judge without compassion, then lumps of guilt are welded to the grates. But if you try to understand them, you'll have only the soft ashes, which lie quite easily, and from these soft ashes you can sift and find wisdom, and if you are lucky, some love. Boy, God damn it, do you understand what I say to you?"

Logan stared, slowly shook his head.

"Damn, you are a strange and gloomy little boy. One day a man will grow around you like a shell. But you will always be the core, and that man will have to answer daily to the demands of a dark and stormy little boy. I know. I know well."

The fine contours of one of Loretta's lesser destinies began to trace and design themselves. Her feelings were strange and disoriented, yet familiar enough. Anxiety and apprehension ate at her. The more she tried to evade recognition of her dissatisfaction, the larger grew her fears. She and Walton attended more house parties and music-makings on Friday and Saturday nights. She drank too much and laughed too loud and long. She was garish in her dress, and even her dark vivacity did not compensate because the other women were more conservative and she was making more enemies than friends among them. Walton was only mildly irritated.

Logan now burdened her more heavily as he grew through his stages. Yet even as she hated him for the load he was, her heart cried out to herself to stop, to gather him to her, to hear his voice, to take an hour with him so that he might learn about her as a mother and not as a scolding harridan, and so that she might know him for more than a wailing, whining whelp.

She went about the house uneasy and angry. Once she went to her mother and talked to her about religion and praying, then tried to pray at home. But she did not see a God who treated her like all His other children. No, she had to have a special relationship with Him or none at all. She began to vent her wrath on Walton, behind his back, with curses and imprecations.

So it came that at this time, in a deep and dim place, Walton also found his life falling apart like a bundle of straws loosed on the ground by a fortune-teller. Some very gifted oracle would have to interpret the pattern. Things from the past rose now to haunt him. But Loretta was the main hindrance to Walton as he searched for himself in hidden and unfulfilled places in his life. He was meeting with an old girl friend. They shared some kisses and talk; that was all. They had a last conversation.

"Why didn't you marry me?" she asked. "You could have."

"No, I was afraid of you. I went with you before I became a man."

"If you had wanted me enough, that would have made you a man."

He thought a moment. "Maybe. But I didn't want you that much. It's hard to become a man and stay one at that age."

Loretta did not know. She escaped into the radio and the Victrola. Sometimes one of her sisters kept Logan so she and Walton could go to the theater in Wadenton for movies. Sometimes on Sunday afternoons they rode to the state trout hatchery in Balsam and watched the fish swarm in the pools. But Friday and Saturday nights, in this time when the last bloom and color lay on their youth, they went to parties and clung desperately to those others like them—married and now perplexed by it. They did not have what the old folks seemed to have.

Logan was blighted by the pain of his parents. It came down to him from their quarrels and their silence. He lay in the night and listened to their heavy, slumberous breathing. Each breath was a moment gone by, one that would not return. The moment joined eternity. Somewhere in the coilings of time a woman died in the next room across the hall, wanting to go to the bathroom. He had almost launched from there himself.

The house creaked along its beams. A gust of wind flowed briefly around the corners. A night bird fussed in the maple, and the clock ticked. The ventilators at the factories wheezed and throbbed, and the mutter of the tannery wove the night. Logan blinked rapidly, curled toward sleep, and worried about death. He looked out through the trees beyond the window and wished himself a million years forward of this night, and he floated then upon the billowing force of sleep. He dreamed rich, vivid dreams, exciting and portentous. He dreamed this:

In the colorless and indistinct moonlight his spirit, wraithlike, traveled the million years and grew a new mind; then he shot backward again and found himself in his grandmother Guffey's garden at Wild Cat with keen new sight. In the full, strong flow of his vision, he saw his grandmother, her shadowed brows twisted in wonderment, her face still and frozen. A strange light fell softly as if through a dense filtered lens, and it caught the brief flicker of her old face shaded under a bonnet. She did not seem to notice him, but stood with her handscythe as if struck in reddened bronze. This strange, silent image did not leave him, but even so he became aware of raucous fowl in the spruce, through veils of silence, and he wondered why they roosted in the great dead light, which lay upon the land as though the sky were smoldering. Then the fowl ceased to cry out because there was a deeper, hidden noise rumbling and pitching through the universe. Still the strange curtain of light did not shift. It was then that time was revealed to him as a most secret and painful dream; he had been caught in a coil of it somewhere else and had returned to see this old face, the weathered brow and the faded eyes that were caught in the tortuous current of light.

He dreamed more and saw his father's foot fixed in lockstep upon the endless road to Hollytown. The eye was hollow, and the worn, cracked shoe did not descend upon the packed road of clay.

And in the boy's shuttling vision he saw the sad young face of his mother pressing on past the doom in her soul. Pensive child herself, she dreamed the dreams of the future, and in passing through daily deaths she saw nothing at all of death but much of fear and frozen anger, which lit the cold places of her face. Caught in frightening light, she sought to stare down hell.

In the bed, Logan slept. There was great puzzlement on his small face, and in his deepest heart he saw old moonlight and could not raise ancient words to fill the wonder, or explain to his empty, hungry brain about the moonlight and the lost words.

His eyes opened, and he rose silently from the bed and went to the window. A strange thing had awakened him. He looked out into the yard, dim in the skyglow. Then his mind went the length of the street. It seemed that he watched it from a middle height, and he pondered the silence and vacancy of it. Nothing moved up the road, nothing at all, and that image floated in his mind, a dim shimmer. Logan wondered what had brought him awake and led him to stand with eyes fixed upon the yard while he saw in his mind a lonely stretch of midnight road, traveled only by a quick, soft wind. There are more phantoms in one brain cell than haunt the cold dark earth. He listened to the wind rise and hiss through the trees beside the creek, then turned and went to his bed. Walton groaned, turned in his sleep, spoke part of an unknown word, and slumbered on. The pane rattled briefly, and the house creaked.

Logan was awake. He felt the strange presence of supernatural vacancy.

Walton grew deeper into his job. He anguished over the time it took because he felt it was time Logan began learning the things of the mountains. Yet he was occupied with his job and the house parties. It was his lot. But he knew one thing: Logan could learn of the forest from Earl. Soon the three of them began going into the mountains from time to time. Then Walton quietly turned the boy's education over to Earl.

"I allus wanted a boy like you, and here I have got one, h'ain't I?" Earl asked Logan, his face off-turned.

They went into the mountains in the spring, dug ramps, and cooked them with ham. In the summer, they harvested the cool wind; in the autumn, they gathered the ripe yield—walnuts, hickory nuts, chinquapins, those chestnuts not yet blighted.

Earl took Logan into the mountains through the Narrows, a rocky pass within a brushy, laureled badland. The trail was in segments; at times there was no trail because no one traveled here save Earl and a few backland hunters. Even now, in early autumn, the coves sucked cold bright air across the ridges and into themselves, through themselves, and sent winds howling across the headlands to leap skyward and then dash and spread across farther coves and valleys.

The great rocks of the Narrows were tumbled and tossed about on the mountain, a giant's toys, and the small, twisting way through them was indeed narrow, but it saved miles of struggle through nearly impenetrable laurel hells and ivy thickets. The wind surged here day and night. Earl and Logan threaded the pass carefully and went to the other side. There the rock was not round or thick, but flat, as if it had been poured across the gentle incline aeons ago and had then cracked and weathered. In the midst of it, a member of some lost species had left its tracks while the rock was soft. The tracks stopped in the middle of the rock. Earl showed them to Logan.

"Thar," he said, laughing, "a lesson to learn. I spent long nights thinkin' about that. If you're bein' chased, let your tracks run out where you disappear."

"This one wasn't being chased," Logan said.

Earl looked at him sharply. "That's good. Tell me why you say it?"

"There's no other tracks."

"Well, maybe he only thought he was bein' chased," Earl said. "H'it's the same thing in his mind, h'ain't it?"

"I don't think that."

"Oho, then you think it might have been him chasing something?"

"No."

"What then?"

"Maybe it was just an animal out walking in the cool of the day."

Earl squinted one eye ruefully, stared across the rock. Then he said softly, "You just now told me something about my mind."

They passed over the rock and into a grassy field. At the far end of it was a low shack. There they stopped and unpacked the food from their sacks. Earl made a fire in the fireplace and set a skillet on the edge of the fire. They ate and rested, Logan chattering idly on and Earl glowing in the pleasure of his company. When night began to fall, Earl took the boy back to the flat field of stone, carrying two torches of pine pitch to light after dark. Earl placed Logan's hand on the rock.

"The air is chilly, but the rock is warm, you see?" Earl asked.

"Yes."

"The rock is east and south. It catches sun all day and holds it. Let's sit here, and I'll show you something else after a while."

They sat quietly on the warm stone as stars brightened and constellations pitched up above the horizon, reached their apogee, and fell away.

Earl asked, "Now, inside yourself, do you feel any different from when we got here?"

Logan hesitated. "No."

"Do you not feel nothin' at all, son?"

"Well, maybe something. My stomach feels funny."

"All right."

"I heard something awhile ago."

"What?"

"I don't know. A whispery thing off here beside me. Maybe it was a bug. It was scratchy and whispery."

Again they sat for a time, then Earl spoke. "Now, son, I'm a-goin' to light a torch to show you something."

He lit it and held it up. Across the rocks were a number of timber rattlesnakes, stretched out or balled together. Some crawled here and there. Logan stared and trembled, and Earl put his hand on his shoulder.

"They got here quiet," the boy whispered in awe. "How are we going to get out of here?"

"We can walk out. They won't bother us. It's gettin' chilly at night and they've not denned yet, so they get on the rocks at night to get warm. They won't hurt you if everything is quiet in your own heart."

He held the torch low. The light glinted back in ruby and green shots from the eyes of the snakes. Slowly Earl reached down and picked one up. It was thick and heavy, and Logan stared fearfully at the wide, flat head weaving about in the night. Carrying the snake cautiously, Earl led Logan off the rock. Then he turned and dropped the snake. It coiled and rattled for a moment.

"People think that rattlesnakes rattle and make noise all the time to give warning, but they don't, not even most of the time," Earl said. "The biggest warning is in the silence around them."

He looked out from the dim light of the torch into the darkness.

"It's September," he said. "They're still crawlin'. In the morning they'll be out to get more sun on the rock. Then they'll crawl a little ways into the brush and hunt a frog or something. Pretty soon they'll go deep into their holes and caves in these rocks and leave their enemies outside. They have lots of enemies—hawks and owls and other big birds. Sometimes wild pigs. Deer can chop 'em up with their hooves, and bears and panthers can throw 'em around. But they have one big enemy, and they fear it more than anything else. Do you know what?"

"No, what?"

"Cold. They hide out soon as it comes."

In the cabin the fire blazed and roared, and Earl told tales. Logan listened and smiled and laughed and watched the magical flames.

"I built this place myself," Earl said. "Nobody knows where it is but you and me. I come here through the Narrers sometimes to see into myself and what I'm about, when Mama and them get too close in on me. The mountains is a lonely place, and some goes crazy if they stays in 'em too long. I've done it myself sometimes, but I h'ain't afraid of craziness, so when it comes to me back here, why, I jis' stays with it. When it gets through rousing around through my brain and torturing me, I get better and feel burnt pure for a time, and I get out of the shack here and look kindly on brother snake and cousin hawk and aunt owl, and they look kindly on me, and I go on back home then."

The flames flickered down, and they could feel cold invading, so Earl put more wood on, and the bright yellow light danced into all the shadows. He covered the sleeping boy with quilts.

They stayed in the Narrows three days, hunting, tracking, watching the snakes come up the rocks at dawn and at dusk. Then they came back to Wild Cat so Logan could start the school year.

In a month, autumn deepened into its maturity. Frost and wind had slapped the leaves into crimson shock and yellow flare. The sloped forests spilled out heavy yields of nuts and seeds. Pelts grew thick on the creatures, and wild, clear cries of hawk and crow fell out of the sky. The air augured festival, celebration. Fall had come to completeness.

When Logan came to Earl's on Friday afternoon to stay the weekend, Earl showed him a new dog.

"This is Sol," he said. "He h'ain't a pup no more. We're goin' to hunt a bear tomorrow. This dog has got good blood in him. I paid big money for him."

The next day they took Sol and two more dogs, skirted Lick Stone, and at noon joined other men who held snarling, leashed dogs that tried to break away and lunge at each other. When some leaped free and tangled in vicious snapping and ripping, the hunters waded among them, kicking and stomping them free of each other's throats. For a moment it seemed that the dogs were doomed at the boots of their own masters or the fangs of their own mates. Then every man got control of his own dogs, and they pulled and stumbled and finally made their way to a laureled area near a small creek and turned three of the dogs loose. The dogs ran into the brush and struck scent near where a hunter had found a scratched-up area and a pile of droppings. The tone of their baying changed as they ran. The throaty bugling returned down the slopes to the others, and those dogs became furious. The hunters then loosed them all, and they raced to the scene.

Logan and Earl arrived in time to see the bear rear to his stance and growl his own rage out. The dogs hurled themselves at his throat, head, hump, and haunches, each lunge marking and ripping. Their daring cost them. A big Plott hound caught the paw of the bear on his head and was thrown dead into the rocks of a small stream bed. Another's throat was ripped in mid-snarl, and he wheezed and bubbled at the bear's feet, turning his head to nip faintly at the quarry before dying.

Earl fed Sol into the fight. The young dog fastened his fangs to the bear's ear and hung on. The bear shook his head but Sol held. The diversion was major. The other dogs went at the bear and knocked him down. But as he fell, the bear raised a front paw and gutted Sol with one rake of his claws. The young dog fell at Earl's feet. Earl pulled him quickly back out of the fray.

"Hold him, boy," Earl said. Logan lifted Sol's head and stared at the steam rising from the intestines and cavity.

The bear was down, beaten. The dogs snuffled and barked in victorious rage. The hunters shot the bear, and then the dogs fell back and leaped about and bayed and nuzzled up to their masters, frisking now and again to the dead bear and baying mournfully. They no longer fought among themselves. The hunters cut a pole, tied front and rear paws to it, and carried the bear down the mountain, where they made camp. Logan and Earl carried Sol.

"Well, you ought to go ahead and shoot him and put him out of his misery," a hunter said.

"No," Earl said. "He's hurt, but he's got life left."

"Well, he won't be much good," another hunter said.

"I can't kill him," Earl said.

In a while Earl took needle and thread and sewed the great slit shut in crude but tight stitches. He put the moaning dog to the side and curled him up.

"Now we'll see what there is to Sol," he said.

The men skinned out the bear and divided the meat. Earl took the skin and head of the bear home. In a little shed behind the house he stretched out the skin, still stinking with bear anger and gall, and the head. On a bed of rags before the bear's remains he stretched out Sol, who stared sickly at his recent foe.

"Now let him heal," Earl said to Logan. "That bear may keep him scared for a while. Old Sol can't move away, and sooner or later he'll see that the bear lost the fight and is dead."

The next Friday Earl met Walton and Logan at Hame Tree Gap, and they squatted to talk. A dog they did not know ran in and out of the brush, scenting. Shortly it treed. They listened.

"H'it's sweet music, a hound tongue is," Earl said.

"I like music. There's a piano at school. I play it some."

"Ah! Ah! Can ye play a pianner?"

"Not play. I bang at it."

"You like that better'n good ol' banjer tunes?"

"I just like it all."

"Me too. I know where they is some of the prettiest music God ever made."

"Where?"

"Very close on. I'll show you tomorrow."

The dog had settled to woofing and snarling. They went to it.

"Possum," said Earl.

"Is that your dog?" Walton asked.

"No, I don't know it."

Walton went to the sapling and shook the possum down. Then he stepped on its head while he caught it by the tail. Its mouth parted in a supremely false smile. Walton whirled it about and it hissed.

"Sometimes a possum seems to be a creature of deceit," said Walton. "When he smiles, he's not happy, and when he looks to be dead, he's just waiting to take a bite of your hand. You eat 'em?" he asked Earl.

"Well, I ain't too proud to do it if times is hard. But times just h'ain't that hard right now."

"You want him, Logan?" Walton asked, holding it up. Logan reached for it. The possum yawned and Walton swung it away. He put it on the ground, stepped again on its head, and pulled the tail upward until the neck snapped. Earl then stepped forward, took it without a word, and briefly worked on it with his knife until he stripped the hide free of the carcass. A few stray hairs stuck to the fleshy side. Earl threw the meat to the dog, which sniffed at it for a moment, then ignored it. They stood over it and looked at the patches of rich white fat on the carcass.

"H'it'll be a hard winter," Earl said. He wrapped the hide around his hand. "I'll dry it for you and maybe tan it," he said to Logan. Then he turned to Walton.

"I'm doin' a little trapping along the branch. I'll take him with me tomorrow night."

"All right," Walton said. "Good. I'll be proud to have you teach him. He can learn it. He can run his own line and make his own money someday. Let him go and see Mama a minute, then you can have him. Bring him back to her Sunday night so she can get him to school Monday."

That night Earl and Logan went to a spring drain in the woods below the cabin. The trap had been sprung but had caught nothing. Earl laughed softly.

"What do you catch here?" Logan asked.

"There's a weasel about, but I never catch him. He cuts my chickens' throats, but he don't eat 'em."

They went down the trail to the next trap. Nothing. Further down a drowned muskrat was fouled in a trap. The next trap held a fat, evil wharf rat. When Earl tried to release it, it bit at his boot. Earl kicked it and it squealed loudly. He opened the jaws of a trap he had around his neck, yoked the rat's head with it, then stomped it to death and threw it away.

The hour was late when they came at last down the creek to the golf course. Earl checked his trap, then took Logan's hand and led him through bramble and brush to the edge of a narrow yard separating them from one of the houses of the wealthy. The music was playing. Inside the window they saw the rich man walking about in conversation with someone. Then they saw Paul Fortune rise from a chair and weave about. Fortune went to the record player and put another record on the turntable. Then he opened the door out onto the sun porch.

"There!" he declared loudly. "Get some of this good brisk air in here to go with 'La donna è mobile.' You don't mind, do you, Beck?" The other man shook his head.

The music brought the autumn night to life for Logan and Earl. "He's got one there I dearly love," Earl said. "Sometimes I wait until he plays it. He plays it a lot."

'La donna è mobile' came down to its last. Fortune ran to the machine.

"Here, here," he said. "It's time for some Offenbach."

Earl's eyes lit up as the music began, and he smiled foolishly. "That's it. That's the one he plays. That's the one."

"Aha!" Fortune bellowed, stepping out on the porch. 'Barcarolle.' The song of all songs."

"'Barcarolle,'" Earl said. "'Barcarolle.' 'Barcarolle.'"

Earl and Logan watched as Fortune strode about, drink in hand. Beck joined him on the porch, and their voices floated across the yard.

"I've been quite sick, but I'm getting better now," Fortune said.

"No one knows why you do this," Beck said.

"Well, I have my own rationale. I think that all human beings are merely nerve endings for God, and that He, She, It, or They cannot experience life on earth except through us. Do you see? Filtered through us is experience for God. He leads us into a situation and protects us so that he can experience it also."

Beck held his drink unsteadily. "Interesting," he said. "Very interesting."

"God needs to know what it's like to get on these tremendous drunks. He uses me to find out. I am the nerve ending through which he experiences that."

He took a long drink from his glass. Beck eyed him speculatively a moment, sipped, then said, "Well, now I have some good Gregorian chants I want to play for you."

Fortune stared belligerently at his host. "Just a minute," he said, "just one minute, if you please. This music is all right. I don't think God wants to hear any Gregorian chants right now."

Beck shrugged, shook his head in resignation. "All right," he said. He went inside, shouting back, "Enough Offenbach? How about some Bizet?"

The strains of "Habanera" looped out into the night. Logan pulled at Earl's hand. "I like that one," he said excitedly. "That's the good one." He and Earl swayed unselfconsciously to the music.

They listened to the records, the talk. At last they faded through the darkness toward Wild Cat.

The boy slept late the next morning. When he arose from his straw pallet, Mrs. Skiller fed him and deferred to him in her strange way. Rain spattered, and odors from the burning wood lightly perfumed the cabin. Logan found Earl in the shed filing his axe and crosscut saw.

"Ho, boy! This here weather is to fix up and git ready in. If she keeps a-rainin', I got some harness to fix and some more mendin' and fixin' to do. If she lets up, we'll stretch a few skins."

They skinned animals until dark. Earl stretched the hides over willow frames. Despite the low, grim clouds, they went again down the trapline. Poor pickings: one rabbit and one possum. Earl released the possum, dressed out the rabbit, cut it into pieces, and put them in his pocket.

"That rich man, you know, the one with the music?"

Logan nodded.

"He's got a big dog he lets run around loose sometimes. Don't get uneasy. This'n h'ain't so bad. Most rich people keep mean dogs— at least the ones do who are afraid of poor people. They see evil in the poor man and laugh when the dogs bite 'im. Maybe the poor people should get to know the dogs, huh?"

When they reached the edge of the yard, the dog sensed them and ran woofing toward them. Earl tossed a piece of raw rabbit. The dog took it, swallowed it, and then came timidly to them.

"Dogs are like some women," Earl said. "First thing to do is get 'em obligated to you. Now all this dog'll recall about me later is that I'm the one with the food. I taught that once to a burglar I was doing time with on the chaingang. He sent me word later that he was doing much better."

The rich man played his records. They saw him inside sitting in his chair, sipping a drink, changing the records. The "Blue Danube" rose and fell in the chill night . . . "La donna è mobile" . . . "Habanera" . . . a piano concerto . . . at last, "Barcarolle." Earl and Logan, the music. New rain fell lightly. It streamed down Earl's hatbrim and down in front of his face. He took Logan's hand in his.

At Wild Cat, Logan relearned the soft, hidden language of the land. He had known it forever; it had slipped his mind at birth. Now it spoke to him, the wind in leaf, the creaking of bough and house, the pour and flow and beat of rain; the noises of the seasons as each passed and each thing grew into its own outline, then altered again into new form, full, fading away, filling again.

He learned to sit on a rock and wait for time to pass. He counted as his pulse drummed out the seconds, minutes. Hours moved away.

Waiting was difficult for a boy his age, yet easy enough in the company of Earl, whose practice of such skills was effortless.

Earl's stations were beside a tree, under a log, in a cleft in the rock. Logan watched as Earl melted, then fused into part shadow and part light, edges meeting and blurring. In these times of obscure woodcraft practices, Logan saw Earl move his face forward from dimness into light. A face? Or not? A planet, a star of brief display in remote skies, momentarily catching the rays, disappearing. Earl passed on silent lessons with his eyes, an impelling smile, a quick gesture of his hand. They struck into the boy as if an exciting bright voltage ran between student and master. Logan saw that the wild animals did not fear them, rather came upon them and did not flee. It was as if Earl had restrained the forces of fear within himself, had drawn down the mean wicks in his heart and now shone with a pure emanation, the controlled slow heat of something from the deeper earth. Snakes crawled close to their feet and went on their twisty way; birds flitted about; once a squirrel bounced quickly across Logan's shoulder. In this time of learning to keep still, back beyond the Narrows and Lick Stone Mountain, large herds of deer moved near and around them and stared glassily in curiosity. Bears ambled through the woods; insects came and went; nothing bothered them.

Evening clouds reddened briefly. Thunder tore down the width of the sky. Earl made a shelter of small posts thatched with spruce and hemlock boughs and turned away the rain.

On these trips they wheeled in great circles, growing tighter as they closed on Wolf Pen and Wild Cat. Earl's eyes were as sharp as an eagle's. He pointed to any disturbance on the ground without a word. Logan came to know how men left their track and he intuitively looked to his own passing and learned to be cautious. Earl left no sign. He laughed low, sat hidden beside a big rock, whistled in bird song, and raised hawks into the sky. The crow followed to dangerous altitudes.

Earl's lectures to him were infrequent and brief:

"When I was a boy your age, there was some of the boys who lived on the reservation—I mean Jake Toineet and Charley Ocoma and the Feather boys—in trouble, and they hid out on the other side of Plott Balsam when we lived over there some. I knowed 'em well, and they taught me some things you can't learn livin' away from the main tribe. Now most white men call this craziness, either that or they believe too much of it too strong, and I think h'it's beyond the white man. But your mama has got part Indian blood. I believe in your time ye'll come to know what I'm talkin' about.

"You do this thing. You learn the woods right here, and you'll know the woods everywhere, and I don't just mean the trails. I mean all of h'it—the brambles and the briers, the roots and the leaves. Take a look at rocks, now. I mean you watch 'em fer thirty years and see if there h'ain't something to 'em. I don't yet know just what, but it seems like they's watchin' and waitin' and can think just like us. And build a fire at night and study it and listen to the woods, and let them get in you where you can feel them and they can feel you, and ye'll begin to know things inside ye own head. And if ye ever learn what's in ye own head, ye'll know something about every man that walks."

When he stayed at the Skiller cabin, Logan slept on a cornshuck mattress in a small loft above Earl's bed. Earl's life at home was one of informal aloofness from his brothers and sisters, although he showed deference to his mother. She reciprocated. If Earl needed any of the others, he summoned them. His call to them was moderate, pleasant, undeniable. It could sharpen quickly.

Earl spent part of the evening with the others before the big fireplace in the cluttered, wide living room of the cabin. His air was that of the old circuit magistrates in the inn—there to socialize but also to hold petty court and to render summary judgment. Then Earl would adjourn to his spartan room and stoke up a hot fire in the narrow fireplace beside his bed. Logan sat with him, their talks low. Once Earl brought forth his firearms for cleaning and oiling.

"Here," he said, holding out a .22 Savage. The bluing on the barrel had not been scratched. He had had it for only three years. He lightly dusted it with a clean piece of linen, worked its bolt and action a couple of times, wrapped it in clean ticking, and put it aside. Another .22, this one with light rust upon it.

"I hate to tell ye how many squirrels . . . ."

A single-shot twelve-gauge shotgun. Earl rubbed it lightly with oil.

"This ile," he said. "Ye know what it is?"

"No. What?" Logan asked, his eyes alight, ears greedy.

"Snake ile. I skin the rattler out and gut him. Then I chop him into links of sich and so. Maybe four to six inches. Then I prop him up on some bright tin in the sun so as to git the heat on him coming and going. I put gauze over a bottle neck and let h'it drip down a little gutter bent in the tin and drap, drip, drap, there she goes to make the very finest ile fer all movin' parts, and h'it fights rust like a natural enemy because who ever seed a rattlesnake rusted up, huh? Did you?" And he laughed and winked at Logan. Then he became as solemn as a warning angel.

"Let me tell ye ag'in. Look out fer rattlesnakes. They is only critters, but they is also brute-beasty-minded, and they don't know how to judge the difference between what we call good and bad. They don't make a good selection when they come to strike, and they don't show no favors if you think they's agents of God. They are silent and still, they don't know nothing but what is warm and moving. They strike like fury and strike ag'in, and like the writin' hand on the wall, they don't call back what they done nor even remember h'it . . ."

Earl looked into the little fire, down through the ages, the lost years, the time that had been and was recorded somewhere beyond the sky but would not come again on this earth in this lifetime.

". . . and h'it hurts and hurts and hurts. . . ."

Earl arose, shook his head crazily for a second, then changed into someone else.

"Now, now," he said, anxiety drying his mouth and voice, "I will show you some precious jewels, my Jody, I will show you . . ."

"Earl, my name is Logan," the boy said sternly.

Earl blinked, swallowed.

"What did I say?" he asked, held out his hand. "Never mind. I don't want to know. Logan. Logan. H'it's a good name."

Earl was unsteady and uncertain, as though under the influence of something that displaced him from himself. He reached under his cot and pulled forth a small trunk. From it he took a pistol. Then from under the cot springs he pulled a big rifle.

"See, the rifle? An army thirty caliber. I had h'it in the war. H'it's proven h'itself. They's blood of many men upon her. More than many. H'it closed many a blue eye for the last time."

Logan touched it. Earl told him to hold it. "Nineteen Oh Three Springfield," he said, then held forth the pistol.

"Here, Gran'pap's. A thirty-six navy Colt cap 'n ball. He fit the

Civil War with h'it. He was in the Yankee army, by the way, but he had a navy Colt. They was some army Colts, he said, but he said they was more navy Colts in the army than they was army Colts. One of these days I'll let ye shoot her."

Earl settled into silence and contemplation. He coated the guns lightly with oil and returned them to their places. Logan climbed the ladder to his half-loft. Earl looked up at him, smiled.

———————

In the early spring, Earl took Logan once more beyond the Narrows. Sol and two other dogs came. They passed through the snake grounds.

"Where are the snakes?" Logan asked.

"They're not out of the ground yet," Earl said.

The next morning they took the dogs to a place where the ground was moist. A bear had been scratching. Earl held Sol and let the others track. Soon they bayed the bear. They nipped and feinted cautiously because they were two and the bear was mean. Earl brought Sol in close and took the chain off. Sol stood and stared at the bear a moment and whined. Then suddenly he ran at the bear and lunged for its throat. The bear tossed him off. Sol hit the ground running, spun, and went back in. He made his unique wide leap, straddled the bear's head for a moment, then snapped onto the ear. It was enough. The other dogs hit and the bear went down. Earl shot the bear with the Winchester. He turned and looked at Logan.

"Do you see I had to shoot him? The hounds wouldn't never forgive me if I'd'a pulled 'em off and let the bear go."

The dogs settled, sniffled, bayed, and fell upon the ground exhausted.

"Did you see old Sol?" Logan asked in wonder.

"I saw Sol, all right. The reason I brought him and you here was so you could see Sol. You seen him nearly dead once with not much left. Now you seen him come back to fight the bear again."

18

FROM THE FEDERAL GOVERNMENT in Washington came new directives to revenue agents in the field. Those agents put subtle, polite pressure on the county sheriffs and their deputies to work on moonshiners. But Harwell County Sheriff E. R. Plemmons, sensitive to the greater subtleties of custom, acted as if he did not notice. However, Deputy Mitchell Sanger, ambitious and twenty-three, felt the pressure. Although he was not a bright man, he began to sense a bright future for himself. Being also insensitive, he misread the mood of the public and misgauged the times. He listened to the veiled suggestions of the federals who stopped by the sheriff's office frequently to glean information from the conversations between the deputies, the hangers-on, the spies, and the politicians. The sheriff was at midterm, not an unnatural time for some of the people to mumble and grumble against him. The sheriff did not concern himself with it, but the murmuring disturbed Mitchell Sanger. He went at last to the sheriff.

"Listen, E. R., they's something you ought to know."

The sheriff looked up from documents upon which he was affixing his hand and seal. "What?" he asked impatiently.

"Sher'f, I hate to mention it ag'in, but they's a lot of talk going on."

"What about now?" Sheriff Plemmons asked.

"About how they ain't no sheriff cars a-runnin' on Johnson's Creek and out in there. They say the papers on the lawsuit in Nags Valley ain't been served. They is white likker by the barrelful being sold on Main Street in Wadenton. The Western Front is a shame and a disgrace, and Christian people hate it. They are several new whores in business on Smathers Street, and . . ."

"Is everybody complaining to you?" the sheriff asked.

"Well, yeh."

"Well, if me and my voters are having to go back and forth through you to tell each other stuff, then we're all in a hell of a shape. But if you have to answer a'tall, you can tell 'em this. Tell 'em the cars don't run on Johnson's Creek because there ain't nothing for 'em to do down there. They're all honest people, and they keep each other straight. A little bootlegging going on, that's all."

"Bootlegging is what I'm talking about. Why don't we get them?"

"Because they're smarter than us, and they've got hold of the territory and we ain't. We ain't got time or money for it. If anything goes bad wrong down there, they'll turn 'em up to me. Now the reason the subpoenas and papers ain't been served in Nags Valley is that the lawyers on both sides and the judge all told me to hold them until right before the next term of court. They know what they want.

"If they are selling likker on the main street of town here, then that's the business of Chief Springfield and his police. It ain't our business until election time. If you think I can do anything about the Western Front, then you've got what the lawyers call a grave mental disorder."

Then he grinned craftily.

"Now, how much do the new whores charge?"

"Sheriff, I don't rightfully know," Deputy Sanger answered angrily.

"It is your business to know, and whether or not it's worth the price," Sheriff Plemmons cackled. "Now they is one more thing, son. The people always vote me in, and right after that they wonder why. That doubt builds for a year or two, and they set in to grumbling and complaining—about anything at all, I mean. Some of the ones complaining are drinking the likker and visiting the women. They raise hell about all the things a sheriff can't do much about. Then something happens and they see the light, and by the time election rolls around again, they work like hell to get me and the whole ticket reelected. There's a lot of favors exchanging hands in the meantime."

But in the next weeks, further conversations with the federals kept Mitchell Sanger in turmoil. The federal men did not discourage his ambitions as they spoke of the need for a change in the sheriff's office. They suggested that the way to attain high office in the state was to take a term as sheriff, and that the best way to become sheriff was to lead the way in cleaning up moonshining. Sanger thought about it for many days, keeping counsel with himself.

One man. Yes, the king of them. A feather in Sanger's cap. To jail Earl Skiller for a long time, single-handedly, would put Mitchell Sanger on the path to recognition. He began to patrol the Wild Cat area alone and on foot.

With her mysterious savvy, Mrs. Skiller anticipated him. Miseries of deep and personal nature afflicted her for weeks, and she began to see that something from her other world was trying to get her attention. She studied the faces and forms of her children for clues. She watched the cloud formations. But each time she looked at Earl, there was a quick jerk in her abdomen, like a fetal kick. Earl perceived a new silence in her and finally asked. She told him that something somewhere was working against him.

"Earl, I want ye to learn these things I know. You are right for it. When ye git up towards forty the time is right. Ye mind naturally turns towards the deeps. You can go crazy in the deeps—ever'body does. How ye come out the other side depends on what ye do while ye're in there," she said. Her manner was highly exaggerated and melodramatic, and he watched her in his shy, sideways glance, grinning crookedly but serious enough. He had already been into those deeps.

Not long after that, Earl found Mitchell Sanger's track in the woods. The deputy left signs everywhere he went. Earl left some jars half hidden near a trail. Then he made a place for the deputy to conceal himself. Behind that he made himself a place and waited. The deputy found the jars with no trouble. He then went straight into the spot prepared for him by Earl. From his own hideaway, Earl studied him—young, nervous, anxious. He could not keep still. The birds would not go near him because of his incessant movement. When Sanger finally grew impatient and left, Earl silently followed him to his car.

Sanger habitually parked his car in the same place. Being a creature of habit, he also accustomed himself to park there about three days a week at the same time. He began to bring a woman there with him. His fornications shook the car. He was prone to open the car doors when he had finished and boast to the woman of his plans to take Earl, who was out there in the night, silent. One night Earl crawled under the car as it shook and tied two sticks of dynamite to the undercarriage. He attached no cap, did not light the fuse. Sanger did not find the explosive for two weeks. He was frightened, but he blamed it on someone from Johnson's Creek.

Mrs. Skiller's apprehension was passed on to Earl. Strangely, he was relieved, because he saw her gift was authentic. The weathers of autumn came, and as they blew into the mountains, they seemed also to blow away certain gauzes that had filmed his brain. He began to stay on the ridges, meditating on the dark land until late hours. He felt stirrings inside himself that validated his mother's practices. Witchery rode the highest winds. The quarter moon threw sorcery down through strewn clouds. Within his heart, a strange creature began to awaken and turn away from where it had hidden in the darkness; it faced the moon through Earl's eyes and headed into the rising wind. Cold and pure. Now on the land the chill gathered, made a billion crystal patterns on the creek surface, and froze it. Early snow sifted into pine and spruce, held onto brown hardwood leaves.

Earl continued his trapline. He also compulsively haunted his caches of liquor and kept a close watch on his hidden still. His mother's prediction had touched his nerve. Sometimes at dark he went down the branch and sat near the rich man's house, listening to the music.

The deputy Sanger huddled with his informer, then went to the federal agents.

"The goddam Skillers!" he boomed joyously. "Each and every one of them came out of their mammy's womb reaching for a mash-barrel. I've got Earl caught."

They set their trap carefully. Pure luck was with them, and they caught Earl with a gallon of his best at the Western Front. The federal judge in Asheville took note of his previous record, and Earl went to the Atlanta Federal Penitentiary with a three-year sentence. He had been there before. This time some dull but deep and persistent threat unfolded in him. He realized that he might be sent there again and again and again.

He underwent the medical examinations, and the dentist did new work on his teeth. He remained in the quarantine cells for the long, empty days of orientation. His mind sought the essence of the days. Each had its own climate and air. Sunday was Sunday and Monday was Monday. The late hours of Wednesday opened subtle gates into Thursday.

Earl was assigned to tend the furnace in the boiler room of the prison laundry. He bent to the coal with his shovel—he knew his fires, now he learned new fuels. As the days passed, fearful forces slowly spread from complex and obscure reaches of himself. He was unable to keep control of the taut, prowling anger of his mind. The fire! He shoveled and looked into the furnace and came to see during the stupefying hours of his task that fire cleansed as water could not.

Time!

Fire!

Yes, time is the fire of the angels! He meditated upon it, saw that everything draws down at last into the furnaces of time, and that civilizations and all their evidences burn into nothing from those slow inner heats. He came to know these things as heat and light flashed from the cherry-red grates, clanging hatches, glowing and shimmery slag.

At night the noises in the cells slowly diminished. One more day burned away, fell into its ashes. Through Earl's mind floated images of smoky tobacco beds, brush piles burning. His thoughts rose and changed and were like little creeks of flame, and his eyelids were hot from his day's work. As the noises ceased, so did his consciousness, and he slipped away into the tubeshot spew of his dreams.

Earl saw winter come—high, scudding clouds in an unclean Georgia sky. Movement, drifts and shifts of clouds, never staying. The cooler burns of time pulled apart the forms of the cloud, changing them with inner force, scorching away the moment, and the colors of the sky then melted and ran. Earl labored in the boiler room, close to the main piles of heat—great red heaps inside the big hatches.

The months passed, and Earl made his time. All the convict time he had done up until this sentence had been tolerable. Something about this one troubled him. Some thoughts were taking various forms. Each image that came to his mind was haloed with ghostly phobias. When he shook his head before the furnace door to sling off the sweat, it was also to drive away the gnatty, persistent fears.

The heat without, the heat within. The fiery angels worked from inside him slowly to burn away the elements of his personality. He withdrew from those around him. The prisoners, ever barometric in their intuition of slight change, did not try to fathom him. They left him alone, thinking that perhaps he had gone heat-crazy, like sun-crazy, from bending his head too close to the big furnace. He had boiled his brain.

And then he began to sense, in that time before sleep swept in, a dark nest of eggs gradually taking form in his skull. Had they been there always? Fearfully he sensed great eggs with dark eyes pressing against his brain, between his mind and his own eyes. In each egg, a vision, a dream.

—Back in France, he had lost his gas mask. The enemy had spread clouds of poison gas, and it came across the field and wood toward him. In it he sensed something inexorable, a destiny he had somehow missed. He seemed to be above it, then realized it was his destiny and descended to it. He headed into the gas and took it, and smiled, and nodded his head, and no longer wondered.

He snapped awake, frightened because the dream did not frighten him.

He returned to his cell late one afternoon and slept. Shortly after lights-out, he sat up in bed and stared blankly at the wall. His face was illuminated by a small patch of light coming in off the passageway. He stared through hot, puzzled eyes and saw a vision of his mother.

—A winter's dawn at Wild Cat. He heard the high wind running the ridge like a wild dog from the gods' cages. He saw his mother come out of bed at cold, gray dawn. Stiffly she tottered to the fireplace, her hard old heels thumping across the rough flooring. She broke thin twigs and piled them on weak coals. The wind rattled the door, struck quickly across the floor to her feet, and wrapped around her ankles like an icy serpent. She bent to blow the coals, her gray hair stringing in her face. Her breath fogged into the ash, flaring the embers. Death hovered now with the wintry bleakness of polar fields. A flame curled and caught the twigs, held, sank, leaped again, and spread smoke into her face and with it some warmth. Earl saw upon the wall of his cell the picture of his mother, cold and hungry and crazy, and it was as though he watched it in horror through a thousand dawns. Now the wind moved like the hard, bright steel of a bayonet, a quick blade cutting under the door, piercing and slashing and pulling out again, robbing the hearth of its warmth and carrying it across the rough floor, leaving only the red glow of coals.

The warmth went away like the last feeble flow of blood in arteries cut and drained . . .

. . . ancient, spilling, draining . . .

. . . and for the moment she seemed content because the glow was cheerful on her cold shins, and she died that way as her son sat in the dim light and saw it as a picture on the wall. She is dead, he thought in desolate rage. He was warm in his cell, and she was cut to death by the quick bright blades of January. A shapeless thing of crimson hatched and rose in him and gorged his brain. He saw dead men piled in the mountains, and he saw bullet holes and blood falling out of the sky and onto the faces of men.

She could not tell her son that she was not dead, that she endured all weathers, she of the sunken red face of vast ugliness. She was not dead—she had simply not sent a letter recently, that was all.

But he saw her die there on the gray wall of a federal cell. Black imagination was now seeded, and death sat brooding in his heart. He knew that once more he would go up that lonesome road to Wild Cat.

And when he came down again, dark blood would hatch in black nests.

———————————

He built the remainder of his time in fiery silence and went home. He walked away from the prison, looked back, and nodded solemnly.

"I'll not come back here," he said.

He stepped down from the train in Hollytown, and no one saw him. He walked quickly through the steam at the side of the engine and disappeared past it like a ghost of like substance. He faded quickly into the weeds and brush above the depot and headed toward the mountain. He traveled the ridge trail and emerged from the woods at Hame Tree Gap. A quarter-mile below the cabin, he took to the brush again and climbed the side of the ridge. He came upon the small stream, which did not now appear to flow so much as the light seemed to leap and flow on it, as if the water were molten glass. It was frozen in banks of grass and brush, and there was only the slight sound of it moving. Some crows cawed, and he stopped and looked up, slightly bewildered.

"Crows?" he asked.

He moved on up to the cabin. He came into the yard, and some brothers and sisters looked up from their leisure and saw him.

"Earl?" the oldest sister murmured.

A brother stepped to the door and disappeared, and when he came again, he had Mrs. Skiller, who was staring foolishly and happily. Earl noted her with no start or surprise. He knew it was only her shade. She had always had many powers, and it did not raise his hair that she should appear here at her homeplace among the family. She walked to him and it was merely a quirk of his perception, then, that she seemed to fade, leaving him alone with his brothers and sisters.

"Earl. Home now? Good. Ye orta let us know. . . ."

He nodded, his jaw slack and his eyes mute with wondering. It occurred to him that he was now two. One of himself was up front carrying on the conversation, and another was a few feet back, now on the ground, now levitated, and he was watching from both places and from yet a third, deeper place, wondering why.

"Earl. Earl honey. You hungry, Earl?" one of the girls asked.

"Yes, yes, he's starved," said the ghostly fraud of a frozen and dead mother's voice. He could not recall her clearly.

"Come in, come in, son. H'it's good to see ye. H'it's mighty good to have ye back," a cracking old voice said. The others packed around him, ganging, making way, rushing him through the door and into the kitchen. He smiled grimly to himself. Perhaps they were all shades. They seemed unreal from every position he occupied in space. The brothers were around him, explaining anxiously that the fences were up and mended, that the shed was patched, that two had jobs in town, and that all was well, all was well.

They ate with him, beaming proudly. He was theirs, back with them. Into the night they sat and talked. His talk was low, pensive, agreeable, and he did not notice his mother, who was dead. The one of him that kept back noted in curious detachment that a force was working inside himself, trying to form, and that it was radiant, of fire and anger and urgency.

228

The summer passed away. They put in only small crops because Earl spent a considerable amount of his time cutting and piling new brush on the old circle they had laid so long ago. The old brush was seasoned and dry. He worked at it alone because he wanted no one but himself to have part of that which must come. Serious matters were weighed in his head, yet he feared his own sense of balance. Some things ballooned into weird shapes, others dropped like small weights, and he dully noted a broken and diminished capacity for patience. Wisdom did not collect into pools as it once had, to be discharged as a controlled and beneficial flow into the main of his life.

Mid-autumn came, and some of the pain eased in Earl. He made a patrol down the creek to see to the muskrat runs. Logan came to stay some weekends. He had grown some, and they fit easily together. They went for a few weekends to check the traps and listen to the music, and then man and boy loosened their relationship in the flow of their lives, and Earl attended to other business.

He left moonshining alone. The family could live on canned goods and preserves, dried fruit and beans, wild game, and the money made from jobs in town. The brothers cut pulpwood and sold it to the paper mill, and the girls sold galax leaves for wreaths.

The lawmen came to Wild Cat at intervals with search warrants, but they found no liquor. The Skillers hacked out what they could for the year. Earl had repaired the old truck and made regular runs to Asheville with trade goods: raw fur in the fall and winter, tea and ginseng in the green months. They did not fatten, neither did they want.

The family sprawled in the yard and watched the deputies and federals come at their times. The young deputy did not come. The officers were not now contemptuous of Earl. They sensed something dark, dreadful, and close. Now they went to Earl with their rough, crude courtesy and read him the warrants. Each time he waved them on through indifferently. If they wanted to find liquor, they would have to plant it. He was neither making nor selling.

The months passed, and he did not see his mother. She realized from the first day that Earl was not right. At first she thought it was some hidden resentment on his part; then she realized there was no conscious contact with her. She tried to bring herself to his attention, but it was no use. Strangely, the others did not seem to notice it. The family organization functioned on, swirling around

Earl's blind area, flowing like a stream. Mrs. Skiller scurried about, now crippled with arthritis, pulling herself time and again to the fore of her son's attention, only to find his eyes blank and staring past her. Yet on certain rare occasions it seemed that he did see, that there was an imprisoned believer deep in his skull who had somehow crawled to the windows of his eyes to peer desperately out in a sideways fashion. She could almost hear the faint toning of "Mama." She had not heard it since he had returned. She longed to hear it and to be reborn and readmitted to the world, because, as she felt now, the others had no place to put her. Her broken gait throughout the family's day was grotesque, of lost status and least position. If Earl did not recognize her existence, then she was lost forever because the others knew only what Earl knew.

———————

The plan formed in Earl's mind. It was of malice aforethought, a malice born of desperation. By its nature it sprang forth from meditation, so it was premeditated in the exact sense of the word. But it was not cold and deliberate, because deliberation would have required an act of will on his part. Earl's only part in the planning was to remain still of mind and to entertain the thoughts as they appeared. The meditation boded that which was to come. For months he took no action. He waited, watched. The smaller patterns stretched, blended into larger outlines, which slowly filled in.

While he knew the nature of the lawmen, he realized now the need to know them still better. If he was to be their nemesis at last, then he could not remain ignorant of them. He knew they watched Wild Cat from a distance, waiting for him to resume moonshining.

One morning before dawn he circled the ridge, made a small but smoky fire, and let it fume for an hour; then he went home and waited. His family grew apprehensive. They recognized a new and strange thing in Earl. Mrs. Skiller stared at him, but his eyes would not see her; she was dead on a cold morning somewhere, on a mural in the strange, walled gallery of his mind.

He waited. No lawmen came. He built a smudge each day for four days, and then they came into his yard with the search warrant. Now they were brusque and short, but they also noted that he was not now so tired or indifferent to them. They searched thoroughly, and he smiled in grim confidence. Mitchell Sanger was there, eager, impertinent.

"We know you're making it," he said. "We know you are, and by God I'll find it. I'll git your ass and you'll go right back to the walls, and I'll keep you there, time after time after time."

Earl stared at him, a curious old regret on his face.

"I h'ain't lyin'," he said. "I h'ain't a-makin' likker; that's no lie."

In a while they finished and started filing out of the yard.

"Hey!" Earl said, and there was a command to an enemy in his voice. They turned.

"One more thing . . . I h'ain't a-goin' back to the walls, either, and that's no lie."

Then he laughed more heartily and longer than his family could ever remember. The lawmen stared at him.

"H'it h'ain't me a-goin' someplace," Earl said, still gasping with wild humor. "H'it's you. Great God A'mighty, h'it's you."

As they trooped back down the road to their cars, one of the federal agents stopped Mitchell Sanger and said:

"I've known him a long time. He said he wasn't making it and that means he ain't making it. He don't lie. Now I wonder just exactly what he is doing."

"Doing with what?" Sanger asked.

"Doing with us. He's doing it with us. He's got us watching him all the time. He baits us into it. Now, why is that?"

"He's making likker up there at night somewhere. He'll lie. He's one of these people who tells you the truth so often that if he ever has to tell a lie, you have to believe him."

The federal man looked at him.

"I wish I knew a lot of things like you do," he said with faint mockery. "I do hope you'll be careful with your wisdom."

Mitchell Sanger kept a frequent solitary foot patrol near Wild Cat. Earl toyed with him. He broke a jar on a rock and left the pieces so Sanger would find them. The deputy took them to the sheriff.

"Here. He dropped one. He's making, as sure as hell," he said. The sheriff thought a moment. It was credible enough.

"Mitchell, don't spend too much time on this. The man's making liquor. That's all he's doing. It's not a big crime."

"Sheriff, he's breaking the law and I want his ass."

"Well, I suspect if you keep pushing you're going to get all of that hoojer's ass you'll ever want. I don't know where you've been, boy, but you have to let some things alone."

Sanger grew livid.

"Politics. This is politics. This is exactly what these federal men talk about. This is why nothing gets done."

Sheriff Plemmons grew silent. There was a cold force to him.

"Politics? I never heard of the Skillers even registering, much less voting. Son, if some of these people can't make likker, then they'll wind up on welfare, and that costs the county money. The only politics connected with all this right now is you."

"What the hell do you mean?" Sanger asked.

"Well, I gave you a job because there must be five hundred Sangers and Boltons and friends and cousins out at Hemphill, and they do vote, and they asked me to hire you. Otherwise I would not have hired you; otherwise, I'd fire you right now."

Sanger stomped about. Finally, he said: "I'm going to bring him in, one way or another. If I have to do it on my own time."

The sheriff looked at him and then shrugged.

Sanger and a federal agent went. They searched the cabin and the creek, the spring drains, the ridges, and the hollows. They thought they were tracking him. But Earl, of the nature of many things, was also of the nature of a panther, and he became one. He knew that one stalks a panther only so far in the mountains; then one is not stalking, but stalked. They came in the day and they came in the night, and they never felt his nearness.

Earl crouched in the darkness one night with a foot on a rock in the branch and another on the low bank of it. He leaned forward against the higher bank and kept his head under some laurel leaves. Even in daylight he would not have been seen. He cocked his ear to the noises of the insects. The lawmen had left the trail, and as they crossed the field, the insects nearest them hushed. The men waded through fields of sound, bending the noise under as they passed. Earl charted them by the small eddies of silence until they reached the brush at the far edge of the field. A startled grouse fluttered through the brush.

A voice sounded in the night. "Hell fire. I thought it was the Skillers, or the devil."

"Shut up," Mitchell Sanger's voice came. But they had lost their silence. The sound of twigs snapping came to Earl's ears. Brush loudly whipped their coats as they moved on through the woods toward Wild Cat.

19

O N THE MORNING of the fourth of December, Deputy Sheriff
Mitchell Sanger roused from his warm bed at four o'clock,
dressed, ate breakfast, then drove his car to Hame Tree Gap. He
took out a sawed-off shotgun, dismounted, and stood in the road
just a few feet off from where the ridge gapped. Rime ice was on
some of the boughs, but it was not quite as lacy as in the altitudes
of Wild Cat, Wolf Pen, and Lick Stone. Frost was thick upon the
brush and also on the curled, dead leaves on the ground. Sanger
was not sure why he had come, but he felt a glow of optimism
that he would confront his quarry today. In the east now the light
cracked coldly and filled the sky. Some chipper winter birds hopped
about.

Deputy Sanger looked down the road and saw Joe Felton limp-
ing toward him. His old banjo was strung across his back, and his
hands were shoved deep in his pockets. Joe Felton came and went
as he would, and his meanderings could not be explained. He was
seen at curious times. Joe's eyes were faded, frozen. His breath
roped out and about, a white flow of steam. He raised his head
and spoke shyly, the deputy nodded, and for a moment they passed
a few meaningless words. Then Joe went on toward Wild Cat, his
old hard shoes knocking on the frozen earth.

At dawn Earl built a roaring fire, almost as if in memory of the
mother he saw perish on the wall of the Atlanta penitentiary, the
mother who now arose and came to the fire to warm herself with
the others. If Earl did see her, it was as a ghost; but whether or
not he saw her, he awakened with the lost and lonesome ache of
her death in his heart. He went out to the chop block and spent
some time filing the cold steel of the axe. He straightened and

234

walked down the road. He passed Joe Felton and spoke politely. He felt only faint surprise when he saw Sanger standing beside the car with one foot on the bumper and the shotgun in the crook of his arm. At first Sanger did not recognize him. He stared at the lank man coming to him with an axe on his shoulder. He smiled drowsily, as if fascinated, and murmured, "Hello, Earl." Earl nodded curtly and walked on to him and killed him with the axe. Then he strode back up the road to Wild Cat.

Logan had left his grandmother's house to walk to school. As he came down the narrow track to Hame Tree Gap, he saw his friend Earl step back from a car, whirl his axe, then turn and go back toward Wild Cat. When he reached the car, he saw the corpse, bloody across the shoulders and steaming from the gore that welled weakly yet. Then he saw the head, which had been carried across the road by the swing of the axe. He looked back at the body and saw the neckbone and windpipe sticking up. Joe Felton edged carefully into sight.

"He has killed him. He has done it right," Joe said in a low voice. He walked gingerly past Logan and looked, then plucked at his lips with gnarled fingers.

"You seed h'it, boy? You seed h'it? I seed Earl up thar on the road, but he didn't see me. He spoke but he didn't see me. He was looking straight into hell. I'm a-leavin' this country and a-givin' up my life to Christ. We are witnesses to bloody murder. Bloody bones, by God, boy. Bloody bones. Shit like this here h'ain't supposed to be seen. Earl will come to git us fer seein' h'it."

Joe whimpered and fell to his knees and the end of his banjo struck the ground. He prayed loudly a moment in agonizing tones, then rose and ran down the road quite spryly for an old man. Logan remained as he was. He did not try to look, nor did he try not to look. Finally he said in low apology to the corpse, "I have to go to school now," and he walked stiffly, formally, and thoughtfully down the road, his eyes cutting back and forth rapidly.

Joe Felton ran to the Western Front, where he found Lon sweeping out his place. Lon tried to hold Joe as he rushed through the cloud of dust, but the old man flailed the air and pushed in and sat breathlessly at a table. Lon followed him.

"Joe, I ain't selling you anything right now."

"Gimme a bock beer."

"I said I ain't . . ."

"I said gimme a bock beer. Be damned quick about it."

Lon stepped back, stared closely at him, then served him.

"Joe, it is dangerous for you to try to work something past me. Now you tell me just exactly what the hell is the matter with you."

"I am mortally scared. I have seen hot hell this cold morning."

Lon was highly dubious. "Yeh? What?"

Joe drank most of the beer immediately. He set the bottle down and watched the foam rise inside.

"I've seen the work of the devil. Old Scratch himself."

"You might get to see him in person soon. What did you see?"

"Bad, man. It was bad," he said, his old eyes wide and his voice rising. He grabbed desperately at Lon's hand. Lon pulled it back, his heavy lids narrowing suspiciously.

"You're trying to cooter me outta free beer," Lon said. "I want to know what it was you seen, God damn it."

"Hell has froze over at Wild Cat. Earl Skiller has done it. Gimme another beer."

Reluctantly, Lon fetched it.

"I do not doubt that something has scared the shit out of you," he said, "but I need to know what it is."

Joe's mouth worked soundlessly. He did not speak. He drank again. The bottle shook, he fumbled it, and it fell to the floor. They both looked at it.

"Now, Joe . . ."

"He cut his head off with an axe at Hame Tree Gap, and it rolled down the road."

"What?" Lon hissed. Then he stepped back and began to laugh.

"Joe, you get outta here now. Go get some money and come back and pay me. Durn yore hide, as the man says. I want it by nightfall."

He jerked Joe up from the chair and directed him roughly to the door. He plucked angrily for a moment at the strings of the banjo on the old man's back, then shoved him out into the cold morning. Joe fell and Lon's face softened. He went to him and picked him up. They looked and saw Logan stumbling by.

"He saw it too," Joe yelled. Logan turned blank eyes in their direction and walked stiltedly to them. He stood and stared, saw past their clothing and into flesh, and saw their bones.

"Hey, boy! Hey, Logan! Why ain't you in school?" Lon asked playfully. Logan finally perceived him, tried to speak, but his face was a rigid mask, and it was numbest at his heavy lips. He did not speak because he could not speak. He wheeled about, got his bearings, and went toward the school.

"Joe! My money before dark," Lon said.

Joe walked in a slow hunch to the bridge over Camp Branch, sat down on it where the early sun spotted it, and shivered.

Later that morning, Mrs. Guffey walked toward Hame Tree Gap, recalled a small stack of pine bark she had cached off the trail, veered into the brush, did not therefore see the body, got her bark, and returned home.

Shortly after noon, another deputy noticed that Mitchell Sanger was missing. He knew of Sanger's obsession with Wild Cat, so he drove that way. He saw it and did not even get out of his car. He drove to the Wadenton police station for some unaccountable reason—it was only two blocks from the sheriff's office—and told the town police. They called the sheriff, and together they drove to Hame Tree Gap. Later two cars of federal men came. They all stirred about, chattered on angrily, checked and rechecked their pistols. Time after time they went to have another look at their fellow officer, as if to convince themselves of the reality.

In a trance of shock, Logan made his way on to school with an exaggerated puppet stride. The teacher was reading to the others when he came in. She looked at him and noted his remote, automatic movements. The boy took his seat. The students beside him leaned over to show him the page. Logan took out his book but did not open it. The teacher stopped and came to him. He did not react. Instead, he sat still and quiet. She walked quickly away and created a gay little diversion across the room. She kept the students laughing and singing until recess; then she hurried them all out of the room. She sent a straggler to tell the principal that she needed him. When the recess bell had sounded, Logan had arisen in a feeble response, but she gently guided him to her chair and seated him. When the principal came, she quietly nodded toward the boy. The man approached him.

"Logan? Logan?"

The dark eyes did not move. They gave no hint of fear, anger, or joy. They merely glittered in contemplation of something far. The principal picked up the boy. Logan stiffened slightly at the touch, but he did not resist. The principal drove the boy to Dr. Rawson's office. He carried the boy in and held him, gently swinging and rocking him. Rawson motioned him into the examining room, sat Logan down on the edge of the table, and looked at him. The doctor looked questioningly at the principal.

"His teacher said he came in late and was like this. He doesn't speak or recognize anything. She said he moved very slowly," the principal said.

Rawson thrust his face close to Logan's.

"Son, I'm going to ask you some questions. Do you understand what I'm saying?"

Logan did not respond.

"Logan, bat your eyes or move your hand if you understand me."

Nothing.

"Son, have you drunk anything?"

Nothing.

"Have you eaten any pills or anything like that?"

Nothing. Rawson leaned close and sniffed. He felt the pulse and pushed back the eyelids. He put a stethoscope to his chest.

"God damn it," he said. "There is more medical mystery about this boy than there is in twenty-five research laboratories."

Suddenly he slapped Logan's face sharply. The boy's eyes widened fearfully, then fixed again. Rawson stared, thought, thought, thought. He went to his cabinet and returned with an ounce of whiskey. He forced it down the boy and waited. In a few minutes something that had been frozen melted.

"Uh, uh, uh," stuttered Logan.

"Say it, boy. Some words . . . say it . . ."

"Uh, uh, bub, luh, luh . . . bloody bloody bloody bones . . ."

"What?" Rawson shouted.

Logan's head jerked, his mouth flexed and worked, then he fainted. The principal danced about in wild alarm. The doctor kept his hand on the boy's wrist.

"Go to the tannery and get his father," Rawson ordered.

Shortly Walton rushed into the room, reeking of wet leather, grease, and tanning acids. "Now what in the hell is the matter, doctor?" he yelled.

"I don't know. They brought him here from school. He's just in a helluva shape. I can't find anything. It has to be shock. It's hard to get to him. You try, please."

"Logan!" Walton said. There was a faint stir on the boy's wan, pinched features, and his hand moved slightly. Walton's face dissolved.

"Logan, Logan," he whimpered. The boy's lids fluttered, and he looked up, tiredly, anciently, from behind his screen of numbness. The men hovered over him. Then his face wrinkled, and he held out his arms to his father. Walton lifted him up, smiled.

"Tell Daddy what happened," Walton said.

Logan opened his mouth, held it, could not speak, shook his head weakly. He tightened his eyes and trembled.

"He said one thing and that's all," the principal said.

"What?" asked Walton.

"He said 'bloody bones.' Does that mean anything?" Rawson asked.

"Bloody bones? Yes, we say it some along. It goes with ghost stories."

"Do you reckon he saw a ghost?" the principal asked, his voice shifting to a fearful, rural tone.

Walton glared at him. Rawson shrugged, worked again on the boy. He rubbed his cheeks briskly. The response was inadequate.

"Do you think he ought to be in the hospital?" Walton asked.

"Do you?" Rawson asked pointedly.

"What the hell are you asking me for?" Walton exploded. "You're the doctor."

Rawson watched Logan stir again as Walton's anger radiated.

"No," said Rawson. "I'll have to be here all day and night. I've got a room fixed up here with a bed for me and a cot he can use. I'll keep the shades pulled. I want him kept quiet. I'm going to put him back here. I need to doctor my other patients, but I want him here. Do you keep any pills or medicines handy at your house that he may have gotten into?"

"No, but he spent the weekend at Wild Cat with Mama."

"Does she keep medicines where he could get at them?"

"No, she uses herbs and teas mostly. But Papa had some old veterinarian medicine around the house. God A'mighty, no telling what. But he knows better."

"Go up there now and look around, and see if any of that stuff is open. Hell, bring it all here and let's see. Time may be important. It's past noon now. Go on."

Walton arrived at Hame Tree Gap a few minutes after all the law officers did. They had not yet covered up the body.

"Good God!" Walton shrieked. "What the hell is this?"

The sheriff walked up to him. "Well, somebody has killed a law officer here around Wild Cat. Now just who do you reckon would do it?"

"I don't know. God A'mighty damn. He's ruint for a funeral, ain't he?"

Walton's gorge rose and he puked. When he stopped he asked: "How long has he been here?"

"The body's cold and stiff, that's all I know."

Walton stared about thoughtfully. "You reckon since early this morning?"

Then he ran across the gap to his mother's. She was churning when he entered.

"Mama, what time did Logan leave here this morning?"

"Son, what's wrong? You look scared. What . . .?"

"Somebody killed a deputy sheriff at the gap this morning. Logan might have been there."

"Is Logan all right?" She arose, white of face. "What are you saying to me?"

"He's at Rawson's office. He's in shock or something. He can't talk. God A'mighty damn, he must have seen it."

He paced feverishly a moment, then said, "Hell, I have to go."

"Wait!" she said, running out the door behind him. "Me too. I'll go too."

They hurried to his car at the murder scene. An old blanket had been thrown over the body, but some blood had pressed through it, and Mrs. Guffey could see where blood had splashed and run at the time of the killing. They hurried on to Rawson's. Walton pulled the physician away from a half-dressed patient.

"What?" Rawson demanded.

"Listen, somebody killed that young deputy sheriff up at Hame Tree Gap early this morning. I believe it was right about the time Logan was coming to school, and I believe my boy seen that."

"What?"

"Yes, yes. They cut his goddam head off. There is blood every-

240

where. It is a goddam mess. I won't sleep for a year. His goddam windpipe is sticking up out of his shoulders."

"What? You think this boy saw that?"

"I do believe so. I'm glad it ain't something he took."

Rawson slumped.

"I personally wish it were something he took," he said dejectedly. "God damn. Who did the dirty work up there?"

"I'd guess it to be Earl Skiller. That man had it coming. He thought he wanted to track Earl down, and he tracked him down, all right."

Rawson blinked his eyes, raised his glasses.

"All right, Walton. I've got Logan sedated right now. His pulse is strong. I want him to sleep until tomorrow. Then I'm going to shoot a stimulant into him. He'll talk then. It's the best thing I can do. You be up here about noon tomorrow."

As Walton left, two lawmen came in and said to Rawson: "We need fer ye to come and announce somebody dead. Some son-of-a-bitch killed Mitchell Sanger. They cut his head off."

Rawson hung his head a moment and shook it, looked past them to Walton.

"Is that a fact?" he finally asked. "Cut his head off?"

"Yes sir."

"Well, I don't have to go up there. I can tell you from here that he's dead."

Dr. Rawson went to the gap, declared Mitchell Sanger officially dead, and listed the cause: Foul play.

"Well, it was not suicide," Rawson said aloud to himself as he filled out the form. A federal agent looked at the body, then toward the heights of Wild Cat.

"It was kind of like suicide," he said.

Foul play. Death most foul. Bloody murder. Dirty work at the crossroads. The officers turned frequently to look at the road that led from Hame Tree Gap to Wild Cat. Yet they did not move. Soon enough they would have to go up that road. At last they loaded the corpse into a hearse, and some of them puked. The hearse left, but the officers did not. In strange fear of Earl and whomever he might command, they set up a ragged defense perimeter on Hame Tree Gap. War impulses and responses formed automatically.

The information was public by midafternoon. Sweatbee learned of it and made for Lon's.

"Boy, h'it's on," he announced gravely. "I mean h'it's on for a sweet fare-thee-well."

"What?" Lon asked curtly. Two beery-eyed pulpwood cutters looked up.

"Somebody dehorned that young deputy Sanger, starting right about at his adam's apple."

Lon's eyes narrowed. "Joe Felton told you that."

"No, I heard it from a Wadenton cop."

Lon was galvanized. "What? Joe Felton seen it. He said Earl Skiller done it. He was in here early this morning running off at the mouth about it, but I didn't believe him."

"By God, a witness," Sweatbee yelled. "He's an eyewitness, then. You can believe him. Where is he now?"

"He ain't far. He's around sommers," Lon said.

Sweatbee ran out the door and trotted all the way to the Hollytown fountain, where he found Boogerman.

"Hey Booger, you heard about that killing?"

"Yeh, yeh," Boogerman snapped. "It is law business, and I don't discuss law business with a damned hoojer."

"To hell with you. I know who is an eyewitness."

"The hell you do. Who?"

Sweatbee cackled. Boogerman pulled out his blackjack.

"Joe Felton told Lon early this morning that he had seen it all," Sweatbee said.

"Did? Did, ye say?"

Boogerman lurched to McCall's pharmacy, got the telephone operator to place a call to the newspaper at Wadenton.

"All right, now," he growled. "This is Chief Sitner at the Hollytown police. My careful detective work has turned up a witness to the illegal killing this morning of a deputy sheriff. What? What? I'm going to tell the sheriff after while. I thought you'd at least be thankful . . . ."

He hung up angrily, rang the operator again, and had her ring the sheriff's office. Someone not a deputy took the information. Later in the day some officers found Joe Felton. At first he admitted that he had seen Earl do it; then he grew frightened and denied it. But that was strong enough for Sheriff Plemmons. He got the bloodhounds from the state chaingang at Hollytown and led a long double line of officers up the road. They met the Skiller family coming down the road. Earl was not among them. Their faces were guilty and proud at once. The officers surrounded them and searched them; then they led them down the road under arrest.

"You'll never git him," Mrs. Skiller said, jutting her chin defiantly.

20

A GENERAL ALERT was raised in the mountains as the news of the killing of Mitchell Sanger spread. No one doubted that the chase would be difficult. Slowly the details of the murder filtered down from the officers. Everyone knew it to be more than an ordinary killing. Each person of mature mind knew that it was complex and had been constructed over a long period of time; that it came as retribution with frightening overtones of a rare appearance of destiny and justice.

Paul Fortune got the news of the Sanger death from Boogerman at the fountain. Boogerman was quiet, less assured than usual. His information was brief.

"Earl Skiller killed that young debbity Sanger at Wild Cat this morning."

"He did?" Fortune asked, astonished. "How? Why?"

"With his axe, for his own reasons."

"Where did they take Earl?"

"They never took him anywhere. They ain't got him."

"They don't have him?" Fortune stood a moment watching the small ripples run into the fountain drain. He looked at Boogerman and found a man without a mask. Booger was not chewing on a cigar butt, his eyes were not restlessly roving the street of his jurisdiction. He was not swaying on his cane or ceaselessly fingering his pistol. Boogerman's face was still, and for the time a certain quiet dignity was upon him. He was thoughtful, and his eyes were full upon Fortune, as if he tried in some fashion to determine where Fortune stood in case there was to be a struggle for sympathizers. Fortune looked straight back at him. If one cop gets killed, the others draw back slightly into their own deaths, he said to himself.

"They ain't got 'im, and it's going to be a helluva mess before they do, I'm afeared," Boogerman said.

Fortune nodded.

"Sweatbee came here to tell me about it. He said Joe Felton seen it all. Joe is at the Western Front, in case ye want to know. It might make you some good writing."

"I thank you, I thank you," Fortune said, and he was quite elated because he realized that now the mountaineers saw a use for him. He would be expected to chronicle the case. He recognized his cue and responded to it immediately. He ran to get a pad and pencil, then went straight to the Western Front. The word was not yet well out, but the ones who had come to the joints had heard and were talking in low, somber tones. Fortune sat in with a huddled group, took out his pad, and wrote. His role was acceptable, even expected. None commented on his countless sprees at their sides.

The people were assuming their various parts. Earl had done his bloody job, and from there on out the forces were loose, both inside and outside the people's minds. The rituals were up for performance. Some acted wise, some brave, some thoughtful, some foolish, some crazy. Paul Fortune was to write it down.

It was not lost on him that this was of a certain historical significance, with sociological overtones, and of psychological moment. He had realized from his first shaky days in the mountains that there was a defiant streak in the mountaineers, that they were in favor of going up against the law and its minions. He had watched it played out in various small rebellions and mutinies along the Western Front. Now it had flared into magnitude, and he felt that something deep, hidden, archetypal was being expressed for a whole people.

Henceforth, for the community, memories would be marked and dated using the hunt as a point of reference. Occurrences would be recalled as happening before, during, or after Earl's rampage.

Logan remained silent. Both sides of his family heard of it and gathered again to him, then went away without telling of the incident. Joe Felton alone enjoyed his celebrity. And after Joe mentioned it to Lon, he did not again tell that the boy had also been at Hame Tree Gap at dawn on the fourth of December, nor that the boy had stood and stared for a long time.

Finally the sheriff learned that Logan had been at the scene of the murder. He winced, then drove secretly to Walton's house and asked to talk to the boy.

"No, hell no," Walton said. "Dr. Rawson, such as he is, said to keep him quiet and out of this. I'm sorry. He's not spoken a word."

"Walton, I have to know all I can about this. That Sanger boy was loud and rough, but he was my deputy. I have to try to send somebody to the gas chamber for this. I know it was Earl, and everybody knows it. But I have to prove it. All my men want to shoot Earl on sight, and I did too at first. But I'm ag'in' it now. But I need to get this thing proved. If this boy of yours seen it, and I figure he's seen something or he wouldn't be so jarred up, then I need to know it. I won't harm him, but I can't rest until you let me try."

Loretta stood beside Walton in the living room. The sheriff was in the chair, and Logan wandered in and out while the adults talked.

"All right," Walton said. "We'll try it. If he gets upset, you'll have to stop."

The sheriff nodded. Loretta wept softly. Walton brought Logan and put him on his knee and hugged him securely. The sheriff cleared his throat and began in a slow, awkward manner.

"Logan, you all right?"

The boy stared at him, finally nodded.

"All right. Now, son, I know you was coming down the road to school the other morning, and . . . well, you know . . . ah, you recall . . . uh, what you seen, don't you?"

Logan looked at him.

"Say?" the sheriff snapped, and Logan immediately nodded his head, his eyes wide.

"Tell me in your words what you saw," the sheriff said. Logan's lips turned white and twitched.

"Say what you saw," barked the sheriff in tight anger.

"I saw a man dead," Logan croaked, trembling.

"What else, son?"

"Bloody bones in his neck," Logan said.

"No, not that. We all saw that. You're the only one who saw who else was there. Who was it?"

"Joe Felton."

"Who else?"

"Earl was."

"Earl Skiller?"

"Yes."

"Where did you see him?"

"Beside the car, then he left."

"What else?"

"Nothing else."

"Did he have anything in his hands?"

"His axe."

"Now, think about this. Did you see him . . . um, ahm, eh . . . hit the deputy?"

Logan's eyes fixed again and he slowly shook his head. The sheriff leaned and patted his cheek.

"Well, as long as you seen him there. I do thanky. Mighty much, young man, mighty much."

Then he slouched out the door, a load removed from him.

For a time after that, Logan brightened. He played and sang and talked, and his kin came to see. They decided he was a happy child again.

Even so, often his dark eyes fixed on death's distances.

Lawmen moved on the Skiller place at Wild Cat. They went on the trails but found no trace of Earl. They left a guard, and the rest of them went to the funeral of Mitchell Sanger. By then Sheriff Plemmons had thought out his plan. He deputized some paid men and swore in some unpaid special deputies. In a high, formal ritual, he swore out a first-degree murder warrant, folded it carefully, and put it in his inside coat pocket.

Now they began to hunt Earl as they would hunt a killer cat. There was fear in the people and something dark and fearful in the hearts of the lawmen. In their minds abided the certain knowledge that this would be the nastiest, bloodiest hunt they had ever undertaken.

In France, Earl had fought the lonely war, the solitary war of sniper and patrol and knife in the night. He knew defense and offense—trench, trap, box, decoy; how to exploit ravine, ditch, and hill for cover and concealment. He was highly pitched to warrior intuition. No general pondered position and movement more.

There was a concession none of the lawmen openly made: that Earl was smarter than they individually or collectively, even on his worst day. Now he was controlled and inspired by cold hatred. He held command of the terrain. He had set snares that they would overcome only to find themselves in finer, more subtle ones. What they thought was the trap was only the bait; what they thought was the bait was the trap sprung. More than that, he could endure the land, the pressures, the stern weathers, and the grim weight of being hunted. If Earl chose to run, they could never catch him. If he chose to fight, he might win. So he had some control. Whatever they decided to do was going to cost heavily.

A week passed after the killing of Mitchell Sanger, and no sign of Earl was found. Then on Friday, shortly after noon, he suddenly appeared in the trail beside old man Fred Sales, a special deputy who had an unremitting belief in the supernatural. The old man shied in terror at the appearance, then raised his shotgun. Earl shot him in the thigh. It was his final mercy. The report from Earl's pistol and the cries of the old man alerted two more deputies who were at Earl's cabin. One of them fled down the road and got three other deputies who were on their way up the road from Hame Tree Gap.

Earl waited until they reached Fred Sales. He showed himself to them a short distance up the trail. He stared at them with a quiet, insolent grin—a judicious use of the taunt. They charged him, raising their weapons, but he fled into the brush and offered no clear target. He leaped the brook and climbed swiftly up a ridge. The deputies fired at random, their stray rounds pelting the limbs and trunks of trees. He led them easily through the openings in his maze of dried brush, then ran into the low pole cabin in the center of the clearing. The five men worked themselves through the baffles in the brush and moved with natural ease to the small depressions that he had arranged for them. Then he fired from between the cracks in the poles, and they hunkered down.

"Hey!" one shouted. "Earl. Earl Skiller. We've got you now. Come outta there peacefully."

There was a moment's silence. The wind rose.

"Start thinking about where you want to be buried, boys," Earl shouted mockingly, "then scratch ye last will and testament out on the ground fer ye families to see. H'it won't do no good to tell each other, 'cause one and all is bound fer hell right on this date."

His voice was strong, assured. They grew uneasy.

"What's the matter, Earl? Let's stop this. You come on out now."

"Yore life is in my hand and I'm a-fixin' to squeeze," Earl said. He then threw a torch into the brush off to one side of the cabin. He lit another and threw it into the brush on the other side. The wind was with him. The fire mounted and raced around the perimeter. Earl entered his covered ditch, shoved the army rifle before him, and crawled out past the brush fence to the log. Swirls of heat and smoke rose rapidly and smeared the sky. Fred Sales could see it from where he lay bleeding a mile away. The deputies in the inferno panicked and raced forward to the cabin. The heat was scorching the side of it, and some smoke curled off the poles. One deputy gasped and fell. The others saw the only opening and ran for it. Earl killed each of them with the rifle as they came. He watched awhile through the ground smoke. The heat from the wall of fire scorched their clothing and caught it afire and charred the bodies. Earl rose and faded into the forest.

After dark, two more special deputies came to relieve the ones at Wild Cat and found only Fred Sales.

"They was a big fire over yander," he told them. "They was a lot of shooting and a big fire. I seen smoke and heat going up in waves over that ridge. A river of heat and smoke."

"When?"

"Early this evening. Two o'clock or so."

"Ain't nobody come back here?"

"No, not one. They ain't coming. I thought they'd bring his body back by here, and then after time went by I thought again about that. They ain't coming. I been a-layin' here scared to death."

They sat uneasily in the darkness. Finally one of them said:

"If they was five, and not one is back, then they h'ain't no use in two more a-goin' up there, is they, now?"

"Hell no," the other whispered. "That would jis' mean that seven didn't come back."

"All right, let's jis' clear outta Wild Cat," the first one said.

"Boys, don't even think about leaving me here by myself," Fred Sales said, "or I'll take this shotgun and scatter your asses all over this mountain."

They carried him down the road in a pack-saddle grip. Shortly they came upon a flaming pine torch stuck in the middle of the road. They dropped the old man and dived into the ditches. There they all trembled for more than an hour until other deputies came. Then they all went out together.

The wind rose, fell, sighed, and passed them and went up the timbered slopes and came again, a despairing refrain. Empty land, peopled with many fearful spectres named Earl.

The sheriff swore in the entire fire department in Wadenton, and they went in with lanterns. They were nervous and nervy at the same time. They grouped, and it took some time for them to find the cove, guided as they were only by wind-drifting scents of burnt wood and leaves. They came upon it abruptly. Where the brush had been, there was now only a ring of coals, but the coals were enough to warm the little hollow against the night. Rising heat distorted the bright stars. They found the bodies immediately, but three of them were not readily identifiable. They were roasted to the point that their clothing was only fabric ash. Their weapons lay about, the bullets exploded from the heat. They began hoping that one of the corpses was that of Earl Skiller. With that small, false comfort they began to relax in that dark vale of death and heat and burnt earth. A party of deputies went out to bring in Dr. Rawson. They awakened him. He was irritable and tired, and he could not immediately comprehend. Then he impulsively went to rouse Paul Fortune. Together they drove to Hame Tree Gap and waited beside a fire with deputies until daybreak. At first light a group of men stumbled up the road and made their way to the hollow. The sheriff stood apart from his men, staring silently into the fading darkness. When he saw Rawson he went to him.

"Doctor, we have only rolled them over to look at them. They're layin' where they fell. I want you to examine them."

Fortune took shallow breaths through his throat to keep from having to smell it. He gagged while Rawson bent to them, probed, peeled back cloth and flesh, looked over each of them.

"Some of them, if not all, have been shot," Rawson said.

"Do you know Earl Skiller, Doctor?" Sheriff Plemmons asked.

"Yes, I know him quite well."

"Is one of these here bodies his?"

Rawson went again to them, looked a moment, and came to the sheriff.

"No, he's not here."

"Well sir, kindly tell me how you determined that."

"Their shoes are not burned. Now, Earl Skiller, in all these years I've known him, has never worn this kind of shoes. He wears brogans or boots."

Fortune drifted away, and in the clearing light he examined and analyzed the trap. He stopped now and then and whistled. He returned to Rawson and the sheriff.

"He pulled them in here somehow, and he closed the door on them," he said.

Sheriff Plemmons looked somberly at him.

"It was an oven door he closed," he said, "and may he himself roast in hell for this piece of work."

––––––––––

The news spread quickly, and people came by curious hundreds. But they would not pass an invisible line at Hame Tree Gap. That creature of darkness had been activated in its depths—the old creature that they recognized in Earl and in themselves and in each other. It was now out and among them, and they dreaded the old being. Was it the old beast operating from within the brain? Was it a strangely divine thing, a force of justice loosed by the higher powers? Or was there the slightest difference?

As tales of Earl's grisly work spread among them, they turned against him in their hearts. A people whose forebears had never held brief or sympathy for the crown's men or the law's men now turned their sympathies toward them. The lawmen were somehow the underdogs. For a briefly exultant moment, the people had pondered the news of Earl's axe, his rifle, his great raging fire, but they knew they could not seriously support him. Most of them would not join in the hunt, but they wanted the protection of the lawmen now, lest the dark spike plunge into their midst.

––––––––––

Earl made random, taunting sign, enough to let them see that he was roaming Wild Cat–Wolf Pen–Lick Stone. They set traps, waylaid trails, patrolled, and scouted. Then quite suddenly, nothing. Not a whisper, not a trace.

The sheriff held the Skillers in jail. He questioned them daily in the jail kitchen. The state sent expert interrogators. The federals remained out of it except to observe. It was not in their jurisdiction. The nonpayment of taxes on liquor was their business. The ambush of deputy sheriffs was not.

The sheriff despaired. He could question this ungracious bunch forever and still not draw anything intelligent or helpful from them.

Sometimes they offered information they thought might help, but it was generally incoherent and not relevant.

"Does Earl have any secret hideouts?"

"Yais, plenty, damn plenty."

"Where are they?"

"One's under a rock yander on Turkey Ridge."

"Where is Turkey Ridge?"

"Oh, h'it's up thar. Granpap seed a turkey thar oncet."

"It's the real name of a ridge or just one you people use?"

"Waal, h'it's what I said. Turkey Ridge. No more, no less."

"God damn you, hoojer. What rock?"

"Looky here. Don't cuss me. Don't take the Lord's name in vain. I found the Lord since I been in jail this time."

"Get him outta here. Bring his mama in here," Sheriff Plemmons said.

She entered, sheepish and shamed. She sat.

"I h'ain't never been done like this afore. I h'ain't no jail bird."

"Madam, just kindly tell me where to find your son Earl."

"You can't find Earl."

"I'll find Earl."

"No, son, you won't find Earl. You h'ain't got nothin' on ye hands but trouble now. You better stay outta thar lookin' fer him."

"What's the matter with him?"

"Well, if ye ast me, I think he's kind of crazy, even if he's mine."

"I'll just agree with you. I've been going to funerals all over this county. He laid out a week's burying up there at one big old party."

The sheriff rose and walked agitatedly around, past grim deputies.

"Yes, he's crazy all right. I do agree. A man in his right mind won't do such as this. I want you to think, madam. Where is Earl?"

"Oh, he's bound to still be up thar around Wild Cat somewheres," she said.

"Has he got any secret hideouts that you know of?"

"No! Now, sheriff, we want out of here. Earl has murdered, as ye say, or maybe not. Each man is innercent until proven guilty. But we've not killed nobody. We want to go. Except Billy. I think he likes it here. Let us out. We'll remember this on election day."

"What?" Sheriff Plemmons exploded. "Election day? I've never heard of a goddam Skiller voting."

She squinted her eyes. The sheriff sat close by in a cane-bottomed straight chair, tilted it against the wall, and stared out the window at the mountains around the Wild Cat section.

"If you're turned loose, Mrs. Skiller, where would you stay? Around Wild Cat?"

She thought a moment. "No, not now. That's ruint. I got a cousin at Saunooke. We'd go thar."

He let his eyes travel the range between Wild Cat and Saunooke. Then he went to the telephone and called the superior court solicitor and talked awhile. He sat again in the chair and looked out over the ridges. She waited. A deputy hovered. Finally the sheriff turned and looked at her. His eyes were quiet.

"Turn the Skillers loose," he said to a deputy. "Each and every one of them."

The lawmen patrolled without cease and with revenge in mind. They inspired some of the citizens, who got worked up and formed armed bands to help search. Three of them were seriously wounded inside a week in separate instances of mistaken identity, and the sheriff stopped recruiting.

They sought an invisible man. He left no tracks accidentally, but he left sign, which appeared as if out of nowhere. In openness high on a tree limb he went unseen. He listened to three searchers talk as they rested on the trail below him. From the tree, he tossed a twig into the brush below the trail, and they leaped up and went there. Then he dropped a used .30-06 cartridge beside a bag of food they had left. They returned, found it, and ran up and down the trail searching the ground. He dropped to the ground, took their food, and left a loaded shell in the bag. He went to a brook and from there to a hiding place as the other searchers came to where he had been.

The days passed and the sheriff did not relent. Searching parties came from as far as Tennessee and Georgia. The National Guard loaned a tent, and the sheriff raised it just off the road at Hame Tree Gap, a few yards from where Mitchell Sanger had gone down. Some Indian trackers were brought from Cherokee. They went in to Wild Cat and stayed only a day. They came out and got ready to leave.

"Why?" asked Sheriff Plemmons.

"Some more people will get killed in there," the chief tracker

253

said. "There ain't no tracks. There is sign everywhere. There is a crazy smart man in there playing with you. Whatever this is ain't our business. You said for us to come and find him. Well, we found him. He's still in there. You said for us to find him, but you didn't say for us to catch him."

"I'll tell you what," the sheriff said, "you stay and help us get him. We'll pay you."

"No. Somebody like that knows too much about forces and spirits and boogers and ghosts. I don't know much about them. We can't take the chance. You don't owe us nothing. We didn't find no tracks. Only craziness and sign. Goodbye and watch out for yourself."

The lawmen stood outside the tent and watched the Indians get in their old A-Model Ford and leave.

"When they leave, big trouble is around," a deputy said.

High winds came that night and brought wet, heavy snow. The sheriff warmed his shanks by a fire near the tent door and watched day break and snow fall. He sat there throughout the day, watching and thinking. He kept sending patrols out. The men came in off the trail, ate, and rested. He sent more men.

"I ain't going to make it easy for him. He has to know we are pushing it. And if he moves at all in this weather he has to leave tracks," Sheriff Plemmons said. Night came again and the men came in. The sheriff slept deeply in a warm bedroll and arose at dawn. The snow had diminished to lighter flakes, and the air was much colder. At midmorning, a front blew in and the skies cleared. The wind bit deeply.

"I want one man to go in there who's not afraid," the sheriff said. "He might try for one man. Who's not afraid?"

In a moment a big deputy from Georgia stepped forward. The sheriff looked at him appreciatively, somberly.

"You know the way. Stay right on the trail. Go past the cabin and out past the cliffs. The trail forks there. Take the right fork and go to that little creek. Watch for tracks. Coming back, stay out of the tracks you made going in. Look in them and see if he's walked in them. If and when you see him, shoot him down right there," he said and waited a moment. Then he added:

"And may God have mercy on your soul."

254

The man grinned awkwardly.

"Hell, Sheriff," he said, "I heard a judge say the very same thing one time to a condemned man."

Sheriff Plemmons stared at him a moment. "Yes," he said, then went back into the tent.

The deputy carried a double-barreled sawed-off shotgun in his hand and a long-barreled pistol in his holster. The freeze had glazed the snow, but the crust was not enough to hold up a man of his size. Each step he made broke the snow, and in a few hundred feet his shins were raw and freezing. Yet he made the lonely, brave trek. He was halfway back down the mountain when a heavy flung club skipped across the snow past him. He wheeled about belligerently, his gloved thumb cocking both ears of the shotgun.

Nothing. The lonely wind moaned on frozen limbs, rattled curled laurel leaves. A rock jutted grayly from the snow. Only that: the wind, a sense of remoteness, and somewhere a malignant eye watching. His Georgia soul did not understand. He broke and ran wildly down the road.

"A stick?" the sheriff asked.

"Yeah! Yeah!" he said. "It was the lonesomest, scariest, coldest goddam thing I ever seen. There was nothing up there. Nothing. Then here come a goddam whittled stick across the snow past me."

The sheriff turned to the small gathering of men. "Go on up there now. He is somewhere within a half a mile of here. Dig him out like a groundhog. Shoot the son-of-a-bitch down. Put so much lead in him they'll have to melt him down. We're going to stay in there till we find his tracks in this snow. He ain't good enough to hide 'em and he can't fly."

They went in to endure. They stayed on the road, tromping back and forth. Night fell and still they stayed in the snow. They wanted Earl Skiller to be dead by the end of the next day.

In the dark woods a dim glow arose from the snow. A shadow shifted briefly, but it went unnoticed. The next morning they found the big Georgia officer's body. He was in the snow below the road with his throat slit. There were no tracks, not even from the dead man. There was very little blood, except where it had poured down his chest. There was a slight scuff in the snow where the body had slid.

Then they found the scene of the killing. It was fifty feet up the mountain in a most secret place. They found tracks where a man had walked and dragged another, where blood had gushed onto the snow from the jugular. They found the strong birch sapling that had been used to catapult the corpse down the slope. They found no tracks leaving the scene.

They did not notice a slight ruffling of leaves under a downed tree, or the scuff marks made by a shoe going up another, smaller tree, or the bent limbs there; they did not notice that a whole line of saplings was slightly bent in one direction, toward the brook. They did not therefore go to the brook and see that a rock or two had been turned slightly, or that there was part of a shoe-heel print in the stiff mud. There was sign everywhere, but nobody noticed because they were too busy looking for tracks in the snow.

"We're a-huntin' a ghost," a deputy said.

"Ghosts don't carry pocket knives," the sheriff said.

Above them tall trees reeled against the sky like stark, tangled masts, and beyond them goosebelly snowclouds swept darkly over Plott Balsam and boiled in the sky and spread eastward. The sheriff reached under the fallen tree and bunched some of the dry leaves together. He broke off some twigs from a dead laurel and piled them on the leaves and lit a fire, and from that he lit another twig for his cigarette. He warmed his hands awhile and listened to the wind. The others stood about shivering.

"The wind is his flog," the sheriff said. "He can beat us to death with it."

The fire leaped and hissed.

"Hell, I don't know what to do next," Sheriff Plemmons said. They all watched the woods around them for a moment.

"Well, you're the goddam sheriff," one finally said. "If you don't know, we shore as hell don't."

21

THE AIR WARMED, and the snow rotted away in patches. The sheriff had tried many schemes, and none of them had worked. The outlander lawmen stayed a few days and then returned to their own jurisdictions. Out of his solitary musings in the dim tent, the sheriff hatched still another scheme. He called his few men together and made a proposal.

"All right, fellers. It's down to dog eat dog if it ain't been that way before. It's down to root hog or die. We're going to ambush this road and do it right. I've had his ol' mammy and his family watched and if he's been to them, he is a ghost, because nothing could have reached them without us seeing.

"Now we're going to flank this road with a trap. We'll be our own bait, and we'll be fixed in such a way that we can see each other at every minute. We'll be able to see all around each other. He can't rush anybody without being seen. I think he's crazy and he's going to try to kill us all. I would like to see that son-of-a-bitch filled full of holes. I don't see no need to tie up courts or guards or our jail or anything else. Fill him so full of lead that when we send for a coroner, we'll need to send for a miner too.

"We're a-goin' up this road to that deep bend below the Skillers' old cabin, and I want three men below the road looking up toward the road—in sight of each other at every minute.

"Now, above that section of the road will be two men right together, looking down onto the road and onto you three. Back to back with them is two more looking at the road after it bends, and across the road will be three more. Down at the bend across the road, setting in that tumbled pile of logs and tree laps, will be one more man—Hugh Stepp, here—and he will have a sawed-off double-barreled twelve-gauge shotgun and a thirty-thirty. Everybody will be looking at Hugh—he'll be right there in plain sight of us since we'll know exactly where to look, and that'll make sure nothing happens to him.

"The rest of us will go in a file on up past the cabin and to the cliffs, and then we'll come back down to Hame Tree Gap. Then we'll turn around and go back up there, and we'll come back again. I think he'll be watching, and he'll start following, and he'll come right into it and through it, one way or another. Now, whatever you do, don't fire into each other. But don't take a chance on him getting away, either. I think he's up there, and I doubt that he can resist this chance to tangle with us."

At daybreak the next morning they went to their ambush. Hugh Stepp climbed up on the pile of logs and limbs and sat on a log with his feet hanging down to within three feet of the ground. He leaned back and stared around. The tangled thicket was behind him and to the sides, and beyond that was the forest. But he could not see clearly the road and the hairpin turn in front of him. He set the butt of the shotgun under him on a log so that he could grab it at once if he needed it. Then he leaned across the log in front of him and stuck the muzzle of the thirty-thirty out in front. He waved. The others could see him clearly from the chest up, even though he was in some shade and his hatbrim threw more shadow onto his face.

They took their places and signaled and adjusted their positions until all were visible to Hugh Stepp and he to all of them. Hugh took a chew of tobacco and leaned back to wait. Shortly, Sheriff Plemmons led a procession of eight men into their view and then past them on toward the cabin and cliffs. In a while they returned. Hugh raised the pale palm of his hand and flashed it. The sheriff saw it and went on. Later they came again and passed and returned, and after they passed, the ambushers leaned forward to try to detect any movement. The day grew warmer, and on the ridges the crows quarreled with other birds. The earth's noises rose and fell, but there was nothing but suspicion and heavy doubt at Wild Cat, and the strange force of that land arose and prowled.

In early afternoon Hugh Stepp dozed only a moment, and when his head jerked slightly to wake him, he let his hand drop to feel the shotgun barrel. The gun was gone. He straightened to stare down, and he stared into the muzzle of his shotgun. It was in the left hand of Earl Skiller, who was hidden below him in the logs. Hugh froze for a second and dully noticed that Earl's right hand darted forward to his thigh, and a blade flashed, and it was so sharp it brought no pain, yet Hugh Stepp felt the heat of his own blood. He was too shocked to utter a sound, so he stared silently into the shotgun's tubes while his life pulsed quickly out his femoral artery. He blacked out and died sitting, and no one noticed from the road because his position was almost unchanged. Earl unloaded the shotgun, pulled the rifle down, unloaded it, and put the guns where they had been. Then he slipped between the logs like a snake and silently crawled away.

The sheriff continued the patrol on the road. When the men looked toward Hugh Stepp, they saw him in place. The shadows lengthened and evening fell. It was dusky when Sheriff Plemmons stopped at the bend in the road and signaled the others out of hiding. When Hugh did not move, they went to him and saw where his bright arterial blood had splashed upon the logs and brush and into the snow before him. Now they had become veterans of a strange conflict, one where they took it all and got not even a shot at a shadow. They were not very shocked at the quiet death of Hugh Stepp.

New strength came for the search. Sheriff Plemmons led the men who wound about the woods and glades searching for Earl. The remaining snow melted; then new cold came. The wind rose, clear and cold and sharp. It swept away the last vestige of moisture, and the leaves and mulch became wide carpets of tinder. For three days there were gusts and prolonged wails of wind. Then suddenly one morning before dawn, as several squads of men prowled along a ridge, the woods caught fire. The wind flashed the fire up toward the men, and they fled, only to find it in front of them. Smoke rose near Wolf Pen, then Lick Stone. From the towns at first light spreading smoke could be seen. It rose in high plumes, and the wind blew it into wide lapping strata. The men found the trails and then the road and came out of the mountains. Some of the rocks had gotten hot from the fire, and snakes crawled sluggishly into the woods and stopped. The sheriff abandoned the land again and went to the top of the courthouse in Wadenton to watch. The wind was carrying sparks, and fire spread past any hope of control. The odors of burning leaves, grass, and wood reached the

259

town and stung the people's nostrils. Haze covered the fields and ridges.

"Fire and wind, that is the sign of Earl Skiller," Sheriff Plemmons said.

The search had cost heavily. He talked to an old lawyer, who told him of the wisdom of an opinion in an old case as it applied to fleeing felons.

"You are not supposed to shoot him down like a mad dog anyway," he said. "The law supposes that there will be a better time and more suitable place for his apprehension."

The sheriff nodded slowly in his fatigue.

"I see. I see," he said.

He took the warrants from his coat and put them in the safe. There they waited with a grim and inexorable intelligence of their own.

The indictment went before the grand jury and a true bill was returned. Earl was in the mountains free, but the papers awaited him. More solid than the currency of the realm, they would not devaluate; more precious than a note or deed of trust, they would not depreciate. The first-degree murder indictment was as stable as the government itself.

After the fires, and the cold weather that came in on top of them, Sheriff Plemmons sent a few patrols into Wild Cat, but they realized that Earl had now abandoned the field. The woods were charred and stank of fire for weeks. Plemmons often felt that his time as sheriff was limited; he was identified in the public mind with a sorry catastrophe, and the blame was somehow his. But to the people, Wild Cat was too painful to think upon, so they avoided it. They did not go around Wild Cat. It was not that the area still held a threat. Everyone felt that Earl had gone somewhere else in the mountains, despite occasional panicky rumors. It was simply that Wild Cat was a dead, depressed place, a land reserved for the devil.

———————

Paul Fortune recognized that if the story of Earl Skiller was to find its true size and place in society, it must be publicized wider than the region. He contacted a newspaper editor in New York and told him that the story had the appearance and feel of a developing saga. The editor authorized him to represent the newspaper in the time to come. He stopped his work on the pulps for the time being and geared for a news operation. He got himself a small camera and began tracking. But there was no real interest outside the county until the number of deaths rose.

He began at the obvious place for his first questions. He went to Saunooke to see the Skillers. They had not told the lawmen anything, but they allowed themselves to be drawn into conversation with Fortune.

A brother talked to him about the big ring of fire.

"Yais, yais. He done all that several y'ars ago. We he'ped him pile brush and didn't know whut fer. He kept it built up over the y'ars. He built that shack fer God knew what, and he grubbed rock and stump out, a-diggin' 'at ditch. Wasn't no tellin' whut he wuz a-doin' all that fer, was there?"

"No," said Fortune, marveling, "there was no telling."

Mrs. Skiller stepped up, blinked, and stared about. She waved in slight contempt at that son.

"They think Earl's gone crazy. What a word that is. H'it don't mean much. Crazy? Crazy? H'it's just that his time is here. He's a soldier, and now he's a-fightin'. H'it is like the demon possessing him, except it is the soldier from his deepest parts. They was always one in thar clost to the top. Always they wuz two or three different men you could see in his ways, but mostly it was the soldier waiting on his time. I knowed my own boy. He took his wounds well."

"Soldier?" Fortune asked. "What is he fighting for? Soldiers fight for something."

"No, not the true soldier," the old woman said. "The true soldier jist fights. If he has a reason, that's all well and good, but h'it's accidental or h'it's neither here nor there. He is jist a-fightin', and if there is anything in his heart, it's the joy of a soldier in his big fight."

Fortune sent his dispatch to New York, with a photo of the Skiller tribe standing bunched in front of the rickety cabin in which their cousin let them live. His story brought immediate and important attention to the events in the mountains.

Fortune saw clearly the direction his coverage must take. He found himself repossessed by the person who had once practiced his craft. Old images swam again in new mutation. Earl's face came and went in Fortune's restless dreams.

After his trip in with Rawson to check the five men caught in ambush, Fortune rarely joined the patrols. He saw it as a personal war, and if he was only a detached observer, no danger would come to him. He had been a field correspondent in the World War and was seasoned to it. He understood perfectly Mrs. Skiller's reference to the archetypal soldier. He had seen death around the clock, but he had never deliberately put his own life into direct jeopardy. He felt that as long as he did not intend to kill anyone, no one would kill him.

The memory of what he had seen at Wild Cat burned his mind. The Georgia deputy with the slit throat looked as if he had been dropped from the sky. He went with Rawson to look at Hugh Stepp where he had bled to death on the logs. Afterward, Fortune had tortured dreams of the place. The ridges, coves, slopes, springheads, branches, all seemed to bode a high silent threat. Perhaps it was that strange vacancy that called forth from the minds of the searchers such painful, haunted projections. Wild Cat was fearsome, a place of blood and sudden savagery, a lurking, demonic void; the abandoned ground, the silent and untenanted, the deserted. The terrain was diabolical, hostile. The air was antagonistic. The very trees took on a forbidding aspect.

Fortune was working on his dispatches at his place in Hollytown the night the mountains were fired. He watched the tides of smoke wash the ridges as great updrafts threw spark-storms swirling into more leaves and brush, and he nodded somberly.

The soldier. Götterdämmerung.

Great billows of mustard gas.

Earl Skiller knew warfare.

City reporters came, billeted themselves in Wadenton hotels, and depended on Sheriff Plemmons and his deputies for their stories. The deputies were not telling much. They did not understand the city writers and their distorting questions. In a few days the outlanders began to explore the environs and discovered the Western Front. They found a keen-witted man, a diamond-in-the-rough, who not only possessed a great repository of folk wisdom and lore, but who was also an eyewitness to the entire series of killings ascribed to Earl Skiller, and who also hinted authoritatively at several other slayings not yet laid at Earl's feet. His name was Mr.

Sweatbee Hardy. He held forth in Lon's with various accounts of the activities of the dangerous, brooding Earl Skiller. For a time, dispatches filed to publications all over the eastern seaboard of the United States were heavily flavored with the influences of that one reliable source, Sweatbee.

Lon gloried in the use of his joint as a press headquarters. While Sweatbee and certain others held forth, Lon served up libations, nodding at Sweatbee's inventions. If a new group of reporters wandered in, Lon imposed upon Sweatbee to repeat a striking passage from one of his previous versions. But Sweatbee was a creative man, not a detail man. He could repeat nothing. He couldn't remember it. He brought forth an entirely new version, eminently satisfactory.

Joe Felton sat outside on the steps, plunking his few chords and singing over and over in his monotone:

> Earl's a-comin' down that lonesome road,
> His big axe in his hand.
> The sheriff's gonna die at Hame Tree Gap,
> 'Cause Earl is a murderous man. . . .

Some of the reporters learned Joe had truly been an eyewitness and carried beer to him and had photos made. The accounts they sent to their newspapers were at wide variance with each other, and with the facts.

When the sheriff called off the hunt for the time being, the reporters also pulled back from the Western Front. That occurred not only because the hunt was being called off, but because one of Baltimore's top reporters had been stabbed; a Greensboro photographer had had his stomach ripped open in the beer joint bathroom; and a New York writer and one from Charleston were hospitalized with severe head wounds received when they rashly pointed up thirty-four discrepancies in two short accounts given by Mr. Hardy of Balsam. The reporters later could not find the sheriff to enter a complaint, so they went to Boogerman, who not only disclaimed jurisdiction but also informed them that they were exceedingly fortunate in that no one had been killed.

22

IT WAS THE FINAL THRUST of that winter when Paul Fortune decided to go to Wild Cat alone. Even as high, raw weather began building, he equipped himself and moved to set up a small camp at the first brook past Hame Tree Gap. He hoped and believed that Earl would not harm him. He merely wanted an interview about Earl's life and times. He did not care to talk to him about surrender. But after he set up his camp, he was drawn toward Wild Cat. Frightened, he walked slowly up the old, worn road. He felt the lack of welcome, the foreboding over the place. He stopped, stared back, saw only heavy festoons and tangles of grapevine draped through poplar and oak.

The land whispered old fearful prayers of doom and last thoughts as slight winds whirled in the trees and scattered leaves along the ground. He felt the deaths of men invade him, heard ancient, faded tongues twisting fey words. Vanishing thoughts surged and dimmed, blown out into the air by the last breath of dying men and held until he came, then inserted into his mind, surging and dimming, light and dark—the road from Wild Cat, sloping on past timber and into bent, broken nights. Fortune had the sudden realization that he was not afraid of Earl; he was afraid of himself on this lost mountain road with darkness coming on.

Yet he camped for three days in bad weather, waiting to see if Earl would make an approach. He did not try to walk around, lest Earl misconstrue that as an impertinence and kill him. His fire was under a small spruce, which was under larger trees, and the heat from the flames wafted the low spruce boughs. Here, he smiled ruefully, here is where every man belongs. Life, nomadic and uncertain under any circumstances, was meant to be spent this way.

Offices and desks and hard city streets are but a part of lostness. Woodsmoke in fresh cold air wrote ballads; the brook made tunes and sang them.

Fortune arose from his bedroll the fourth day, took pad and pencil, and went to see Mrs. Guffey. She was breaking brittle poplar twigs, as dry and white as old bird bones, when he found her in the brush. He came up behind her and she turned slowly, cautiously.

"Oh, Mr. Fortune. How are you?"

"Fine, madam, just fine. I trust you are."

"Yes. Are you not afraid to be around Wild Cat?"

He smiled. "Just a bit, if you don't mind understatement. I've been camped up the road for three days, and I've not been killed yet."

"Maybe you are a ghost and don't know it yet," she said.

"Perhaps. There are some schools of religious thought that present life as an illusion anyway, and they say that when you die, you never realize it but simply make a small shift in thought and then continue the fantasy of life."

"Is that right? What church is that?"

"Not churches, religions. Not the Christians. Would you expect Earl to harm me?"

"No, I don't believe he'll intentionally, and I mean intentionally, hurt anyone but the people hunting him."

"Intentionally? Why do you stress that? Has he hurt someone unintentionally?"

"Yes, my grandson, Logan."

"What? Logan?" Fortune asked. "How, for God's sake?"

"We don't know yet. The boy went down the road to school that morning. He must have seen something of it. He was in some kind of shock."

Fortune squatted, shaking his head. He saw the woman's face burdened with her grandson's pain.

"God!" he said. "If that kid saw that! Who else knows about this?"

"They're keeping it quiet. The sheriff talked to him, and the doctor, that's all. Only a few know it."

"Rawson knows?"

"Yes."

"I thought the boy was acting strange. Hell, he's a witness."

Then he turned and looked at the woods surrounding them.

"If Earl knew that, he could take care of the boy. He could kill him with no trouble," he said somberly.

She smiled slightly.

"No, he won't hurt Logan," she said.

"God, what it must be like for the boy. He must be torn up. If he saw that slaughter, or even the scene . . . ."

"He'll be all right sometime," she said. "I heard my mama and papa and their mamas and papas talk about when this was frontier and there were a lot of killings. People who got scalped and lived through it. Throats cut and hearts ripped out. Young'uns seen it and lived and done well. Made 'em tough."

Fortune stared a moment. He scribbled that down, then looked at what he had written.

"I don't really believe that," he said. "Do you think people need to be that tough anymore?"

"Well, Logan needs to be that tough, don't he?"

"I'm writing stories about all this, as you have probably heard. What do you think about all the killings?"

"I've known Earl for a long, long time. His family lived once where mine did in Macon County. He always done his best by his family. He had troubles and travails and bore them. It's been bad on him. That last time in prison did something to him, his mammy told me. He seemed to not care for anything anymore, and when you get there you can suspect that God's angels are preparing you for the next step in your destiny."

"Madam! My dear Mrs. Guffey. I am astounded at your acumen. I certainly am. Can we sit at your house and let me talk to you a bit? It is chilly, and I need a place to rest my pad."

He helped her with the twigs. She built a good fire from coals in her fireplace and shoved the kettle over the edge of it.

"I'll fix some pennyr'yle tea," she said.

While she puttered about getting ready, he strolled outside and found Logan playing quietly among the rocks in her flower garden. He walked up to him.

"Hello. I was here the night you were born," he said.

"I know that," Logan answered.

"How?"

"Grandma told me. You told me yourself when you were drunk."

"Ah. Aha. Ah well. Your grandma is a good woman."

Logan's face was watchful.

"She keeps me now."

"Yes, I know."

They were quiet for a time; then Fortune said, "The wind was high last night."

"Our house snapped and cracked in it," Logan said.

"It reminded me of something my own grandmother used to read to me when I was a boy," Fortune said.

"What?"

"A poem. 'The Highwayman.' Every time I hear wind like that I hear the muffled beat of horses' hooves too."

In a moment Logan said, "I hear and see things too."

"In the wind?"

"In the wind, but not just in the wind."

"Are they real?"

"No." He paused, then added, "Sometimes they are."

"What things do you see or hear?"

"I can't tell all about it. I look for the truth bird like you and Mr. Fore said. When somebody says something to me, I listen in case the truth bird has started talking."

"Well, that's not strange or crazy," Fortune said.

Logan stopped playing with sticks, stared at Fortune for a long and solemn moment.

"No, it's not," he said in a very aged manner. "Has someone said I'm strange or crazy?"

Fortune shook his head.

"Has someone said that Mr. Fore is crazy?"

Fortune shrugged, shook his head again helplessly.

"I've heard some people say that you're the one who's crazy," Logan said.

The wind howled in the treetops for a moment. Fortune looked up at the ridge.

"There!" he said. "There! The truth bird has spoken indeed."

But the boy was walking into the pasture.

Fortune returned to the house and sat. He drummed his fingers nervously on a table.

"We've not seen you in a while," Mrs. Guffey finally said as she poured the tea.

"I'm busy. Pretty busy. The boy seems to be all right in most ways. Is he?"

"No, not exactly," she said. "Sometimes he cries in the night, and sometimes he walks around in his sleep making funny noises."

"Does he cry for his parents?"

"Maybe. But I think he cries for Earl."

"Does he talk about Earl?"

"Not a word. But sometimes he goes out to the gap and just stands there."

"Have you seen any sign of Earl?" Fortune asked.

"No."

"Have you heard any gossip, rumors, or anything?"

"No."

"I guess he's gone from here. Do you think he's gone?"

"No."

They were silent for a moment.

"So Logan is staying here with you," Fortune said.

"Well, he is staying here *some* with me."

"Yes, that's what I meant," Fortune said dryly.

"Sometimes I wonder how you've lasted as long as you have around here," Mrs. Guffey observed.

He laughed. "Because I am as contrary as the rest of the people. Are his parents having a lot of trouble?"

She stared at him a moment. "You are reckless with your curiosity, aren't you? You don't back away from any question. Well, the fact is, everyone knows they're having trouble. I don't know why you would ask."

"Actually, my interest is in the boy. I would imagine that he has been traumatized."

"I often think he has forgotten most of it. But I guess he hasn't," she said. She rose and went to the door and called out to Logan. Then she turned back to Fortune.

"I have some soup ready," she said. "You can eat with us."

The boy came inside and sat at the table. Mrs. Guffey poured tomato soup into bowls, and the three ate quietly. Then Logan shrieked suddenly and pitched to the floor, trembling, screaming. They bent to him.

"What? What is it?" demanded Fortune.

She took the boy to his bed. In a while she returned.

"What was it?"

"The soup turned to blood in his mouth. He said he could feel it clotting up."

Fortune slumped, stared at the window. Outside, the wind rose in the darkness, and on the eastern ridges he could see the glow where the moon was going to come. The house creaked, and Mrs. Guffey slurped her soup thoughtfully and spoke no further.

Fortune returned to his camp. He found no sign of a visitation. He sat beside his fire all night, thinking. The wind howled mightily, chill and portentous. He broke camp early the next morning, went home, and slept for two days.

Spring came, and as the weather brightened, the community took on a new outlook. There was not so much talk about the killings, except for a brief time during the primary election. But the election was quick and painless for Sheriff Plemmons. He was a good sheriff and he had weathered the crisis. The sure defeat he had expected did not come. Once the primary was over, he had the reelection in the bag, because the Republicans did not field a candidate against him. The murders had hurt him personally and deeply. He had always taken his badge seriously enough, but more as a politician than as a lawman. But even as he had watched the dead deputies being carried off the mountain, a shrill cry for justice had sounded in him. The affront was not solely to him and the dead men, nor to the county, nor to the general statutes of the state, nor to law enforcement's pride. It was an open and evil threat to civilization itself.

The sheriff did his duty and administered his county and waited. He often took a straight-backed chair to the roof of the courthouse, leaned back, and contemplated the light greens of spring spreading across the rough ridges of Wild Cat. The weeks passed, and the clustered communities settled some in their fear.

Dear Mr. Fortune:

(wrote the editor of the *New York Sentinel*)

The accounts published by the *Ledger* concerning the rampage of Earl Skiller, released under your by-line, have shown more quality than anything yet written by the two correspondents we sent to your area. With deft strokes you have lent depth and sobriety

(Fortune managed a wry grin)

to what would ordinarily be just another story of man run amok. We are vitally interested in this kind of journalism and in your perspectives. We think that your writing serves the various ends of justice, society, and a profession too often branded with charges of sensationalism.

Would you file some sidebar pieces with us? This is on the condition that doing so would not violate any contracts or agreements you may have with the *Ledger* or other publishers.

Waiting to hear from you at the earliest,

> Sincerely yours,
> Jim Harrison
> Managing Editor
> The *New York Sentinel*

From the *Commonwealth Bulletin Service*:

Sir: 2¢ word per ur writing Skiller stop use 2000 words every 3 days stop advise soonest stop

cable CNY London 1215 ccaq typ ed

From the *Chicago Times*:

Congratulations on premier handling of a difficult story. Would you consider filing one or more stories each week for the *Times* at the top correspondent rates? The caliber of your writing is something the *Times* sorely needs. Please answer as soon as possible.

> Sincerely yours,
> Sidney Krokus
> Managing Editor
> The *Chicago Times*

P.S. Paul, apparently you are sober. I hope it has been a condition of some length. My best wishes on that, as you know. As you see, I have been promoted and maybe I can make some changes here now. Best. SK

Long distance calls in search of Fortune came three and four times a day to Rawson's office, the drugstore, Boogerman's house, the sheriff's office, and the Wadenton police department. All were concerned with retaining Fortune in some manner to cover the manhunt. After a week of it, Fortune at last sat down with Rawson.

"I don't know, I just don't know," he said. "There were times when I was so low I would have welcomed any assignment anywhere on the face of the earth, any interest from any newspaper or telegraph service. Now I don't know if I have the energy, the will, or even the interest. It is all very stimulating, but there is a wide area of numbness in me, and I am not motivated to begin filing copy to a large readership."

"Well, you do quite a bit for those pulps."

"Yes, well, I'm in that nice rut. It is fiction. I don't have to do any leg work, prove anything, be accurate. All I have to do is spin a little mystery by the second page, start some excitement by the fourth, and so on. It is smooth, easy work, and I can do it and draw good pay. This kind of journalism, on the other hand, requires a lot of push. Earl has faded out of the mountains, I think. I believe he ran for it. There's nothing left to do except plow old ground."

"For God's sake, don't close the door. I've doctored you through the low spots, and I've worried about your health, your sanity, and your life. You needed something to pick you up. Now, the things you've written so far were tidy but complete. We need that kind of chronicle for this event. You will notice that the people here, shiver though they may in the night, have a proprietary interest in this little legend a-building. It will not hurt you to stay half awake to this feeling."

Fortune looked out the window. "Perhaps," he muttered listlessly, "perhaps you're right, but I'm not interested or inclined . . . ."

Suddenly he sat bolt upright. "By the way," he said, his voice cold, "why didn't you tell me that Logan Guffey was a witness to the Sanger killing?"

Rawson stared at him a moment, then clamped his jaws firmly. "The sheriff thinks that might put the boy in danger."

"From whom, exactly?"

"You know who."

Yet even as the force of the manhunt dwindled to dormancy, telegrams and special delivery letters came for Fortune. Major news organizations sought him after his early dispatches reached print and spread through wide readerships. The stories with Fortune's by-line rang with authenticity, while those of noted national writers were more form than substance. Their stories might just as well have been lifted from some of Fortune's westerns. The nature of the situation limited those writers who came from outside the region. Their stories were interesting for the moment, sensational in spite of all efforts to tone them down, then gone.

In Fortune's stories, the readers heard the low, frightening snarl of something free and lawless in the mountains. They felt the spirit of a pioneer land, a time that had passed and yet a time that refused to pass, even in 1940. It was these stories that people were clipping from newspapers and keeping. In significant numbers, readers called editors and asked for more from this writer. The editors talked among themselves at bars, dinners, parties, gatherings. The writing was of something native and powerful at a time when the news from abroad was freighted with the strange, draining, occult flavor of the new Nazism, frustrating to the American soul. Here, out of a nearly unknown region of the Appalachian Mountains, was a man making mock of arrayed forces.

"Did you know that boy is staying at his grandmother's up there, and that is the last outpost in hell."

Rawson shook his head tiredly.

"No, I didn't know that," he said.

23

TIME GREW TIGHT and hard for Logan. The strain between his parents was amplified in him. Smaller despairs grew large in his heart. He did not eat or sleep well. His breath did not come easily. His face lit now and again with dark lights. What he had witnessed at Hame Tree Gap was too powerful. In the weeks following his interrogation by the sheriff, his mind desperately sought distraction and diversion. Sometimes he thought of Earl, but that memory was also painful. As the months went by, he let the shape and cast of Earl's face slip from memory. But it lurked at the edge of consciousness with a life and power of its own. He had startling visions he did not understand. Those far, hidden skies that had been revealed to him in his serious illnesses came again in stark, abrupt intrusions. Pain tailed across his mind like a comet, and he traced it across his brain knowing that somewhere before him a day must come—his own death, a dark gravity pulling the brightness of his life into its maw.

Logan too!

His universe was contracting, collapsing upon itself. Sadness infused his soul. He began collecting petty enemies at school because some of the children were reacting to a new thing in him that they did not understand. Out of the oldest part of his mind the images formed. When larger boys set upon him, he fled into the future. He had seen the spine sticking out of the deputy sheriff's neck. He had seen death and graves. Now he quietly watched those who antagonized him plunge into the future and their destiny. Time transported them to their graves. He saw their old moldy wet bones and smiled sardonically. I do not fear you, he thought. You will not last. I see your bones.

He reflected.

Mine too, he thought.

He came to the days of an ancient and tired turn of mind. His thought swelled and tossed with strong imagery. One day as he walked toward his grandmother's, he found a golf ball in the weeds beside the fairway at the golf course. He stuck it in his pocket. Suddenly a man appeared.

"Listen, boy, give me that ball."

Logan stared at him, reached into his pocket, and withdrew the ball.

"It's going to cost me a stroke, and I'm already two down for five dollars," the man said angrily. A rage rose in the boy, diffused away helplessly. Time came into vision.

"I see your bones," he said to the golfer.

"What? What the hell?"

Logan said nothing. He held the ball in his fist. He looked into the hatches and holds of time and saw the man dead and rotting.

"I said give me that ball, boy," the man shouted. Logan dropped the ball and backed away.

"I ought to kick hell out of you," the man said, lifting his foot.

A strange, cutting humor flicked from Logan's dark eyes.

"Kick," he said. "I see your bones."

In late spring the tannery manager called Walton in. His face was bright, cheerful. He shook Walton's hand and brought a chair.

"I have some exceedingly good news," he said. "It is going to give me a great deal of pleasure to tell you what I have to tell you."

Walton relaxed, a shy smile on his lips. The manager fingered an envelope but did not open it. His voice purred on and on.

". . . heard about this young man . . . actually watched you in some of . . . yes, my God, I said, there must be some way to open up a path . . . in Hollytown we have this young man . . . ."

Finally he took out the letter and looked over it at Walton.

"Walton, the new president of the company is interested in grooming people from within for higher positions. In other words, he knows about your studies, ambitions, and abilities. I have talked with him at length. Now, he is willing to make certain arrangements for you to study. There is a school near our corporate headquarters in Boston which has a course ordained in heaven for you.

We also have a small plant nearby where you can work half a day. If you are interested, the company will pay all your expenses there, your tuition, and your salary.

"You will have access to some very good brains, very good books, fine machines. This is a very good way for you to improve yourself and become a greater asset to the company. I want you to take a reasonable period of time and think about it. I trust your wisdom and reason to prevail."

Walton stared out the window, his head shaking in disbelief.

"I don't know. Sometimes Logan doesn't act himself. I just don't know."

"Well, you can take your family. The boy has always been sickly, I know. What is the matter this time?"

"It's hard to determine. The doctor can't pin it down. It's got something to do with Earl Skiller."

"The murderer? What?"

"Earl was a good friend to the boy."

"Friend?"

"Yes."

"Well, I can understand. But that's been some time. Is the boy not over it?"

"He may not get over it."

"Why do you say that?"

"We think Logan saw him kill that deputy at the gap."

The manager sat back and stared out the window at Eagle's Nest.

"My God!" he finally said. He looked at Walton sadly. "I'm sorry. I'm so sorry."

They stood, and the manager gently led Walton to the outer door of the building.

"Think it over, Walton. Take your time and think it over well. There might never be another opportunity. Any time opportunity arises, there arises with it one or more good reasons not to take it. They are always illusionary. And this may lead the company to training many more of its own men for advancement. It could be the way to keep the company vital."

It was summer when Earl returned to Wild Cat. He could not stay away. The day was appropriate for his return. It was in July, and the land had greened over the char of his burns, but the sky that day belonged to December. Heavy clouds came low and diffused the light, so that even the leaves appeared gray and ashen.

In a defile near the cliff, through which the little stream rushed and jumped, Earl made a hidden shelter from logs and poles. It was among laurel and spruce and could not be seen as anything but jumbled poles and brush. He made a rough flooring of poles, which rested on shelves he had dug in the dirt at the sides of the cut. The top was of bent boughs, which he had tightly thatched with weeds and hay. When rain came, the water dripped down the thatching and ran into the stream. The thatching fell low enough so that only a few poles and some bark were needed for the walls. Several inches between the wall and the thatching was a screen of brush, and upon that he had piled other brush and weeds and bark so that it appeared to be merely a great washup of wilderness trash left piled in the defile by high water.

Inside the shelter was a small area where he could stand, and from there he could see a long distance in all directions through the cracks. The rest of it was for sitting, crouching, or lying down. It was a peculiar cell. There was no door. He entered through a small opening in the floor.

There was no path to the hideout, and only a sharp eye could have detected the little parts and segments of a path Earl made in his comings and goings. He kept mostly to the rocks of the stream, which he had subtly arranged for his pace. Some were deliberately uneven and tilted, and tumbled noisily unless one knew where to step. On the days he remained holed up, he was quiet and motionless, watching the little stream slide below him. If people had come toward him from above, they would have disturbed the sand and mud, and their coming would have been so slow and clumsy that the muddy warning would have been downstream long before they arrived.

From there Earl prowled Wild Cat, touching nobody, nothing. It was as if he were a shade, rummaging through past times on present earth. He meditated and contemplated and sat for motionless hours in the flow of the days. In the fall, as the leaves began turning, he again abandoned the land and went further back into the mountains.

Paul Fortune went again to Mrs. Skiller. Her eyes brightened when he began talking about Earl, but she said, "I can't tell you anything else. There's nothing new."

"Some people think he's still around Wild Cat or Wolf Pen," Fortune said.

Mrs. Skiller snorted. "If you'd heard all the things I've heard about where he's supposed to be, you'd be so addle-witted you couldn't ask foolish questions. He may be at Wild Cat, he may be on Caney Fork, he may be in Cherokee, he may be in Florida, and he may be in hell. Wherever he is, he's where he wants to be, and he ain't told me, and I wish he would. If he does, I'll not tell one confounded soul. I told 'em not to fool with him. By God! I jist don't know what they expected. The sheriff hisself told me he didn't realize what that Deputy Sanger had been up to. He thought he knowed better. Well, they turned a hell-dog loose and they know it now."

She stopped, then cackled. "They say they'll get him sooner or later. Ever'body says that. But h'it's not true. Earl comes and goes as he pleases and he always has."

"Mrs. Skiller, I'd like to talk to you about Earl's life—from boyhood on. I can't find anyone who knows much about him. Will you tell it?"

"What fer?"

"I need to know it."

"You're going to write it down?"

"Do you mind? I'll give you whatever money comes from it."

"Law me. We always need money, but no, not fer this. This is beyond money. This is heart's blood. I don't know if I want to tell it."

"Was there something in his past to push him finally in this direction?"

She swung her head about and let it rock slightly, the ruddy grinning skull of her face swaying. Then she clamped her teeth and nodded.

"Damn plenty, man," she said. "They is damn plenty. He had enough pain to go around, enough for ever'body on this earth. If ye get it right—there's been so much said. I h'ain't heard nothin' like the truth yet."

"Madam! My dear woman. Tell it as you know it. I'll put it in your words."

She drew her thin feet back to her chair and bent them at the ball. She swiveled her knees about excitedly.

"Here 'tis. H'it'll take a while. Somebody with some sense needs to hear it."

"Tell it."

"He was the first one. He bore the worst of h'it. His pap always said later that Earl was the one we learned on. He got beat and kicked and yelled at a lot because we thought he was as old as we was."

She stared into old days.

"He were, too, only older and wiser. After we beat him, he'd always pet us. He knowed we felt bad about h'it. He was helping his daddy think and figure out things when he was six or seven. But that boy hurt, too. I never seen anyone feel so much of ever'-thing going on around him. H'it was good and bad. There was times when I'd feel blue and down and out, and when I'd get around Earl, even when he was a tad of a boy, I'd see h'it go to him and leave me, and I knowed he'd somehow drawn the poison of that day's mood out of me because I could see my hurt in his eyes. Then somehow or other he'd get it swallowed inside him, and after a while he'd be all right again. If you ask me, Earl was always a better healer, even when he was a boy, than all these doctors and herb doctors and midwives and granny-women put together. Why, something he said one time was what made me start witching. I knowed a power had started from him to me one day. He said something about a bird's nest, and h'it seemed that a deep person in him spoke to me. He said that people ought to go to nature for lessons, and that all eggs ought to hatch in the warmth of the mama, and that the trouble was to decide what thoughts was eggs and what wasn't. But I knowed he spoke to me, and my powers took shape in me, and the more I thought it over, why, one day they jist come out, hatched, ye might say."

She sat back, pleased with herself.

"Well and good," Fortune said. "Now, what work has Earl done?"

"He's done all you can do and get by in these mountains. His first work for money was picking blackberries when he was about five or six years old. He walked into town and sold them—but that was when we lived in another county."

"But still in the mountains?"

"Yes, in these damned everlasting ridges. He'd pick berries . . . . When he was bigger, he split fence rails and posts, and he cut and split crossties fer the railroad. He's trapped all his life, and he knows how to take the animals off their runs. He larned the moon signs, without anyone ever teaching him that I know of. He knows wood and the little tides of the saps and other waters. Earl always said they was other waters in trees besides sap.

"He's cut and hauled tanbark to the tannery. He's raised crops, and he's hunted all his life and he's the best one they ever was. The young bucks from the reservation used to go a-huntin' with him because they said being around Earl lit up new ways for 'em. Why, he taught Logan Guffey more in a little while than anybody else'll learn in their life."

Fortune stopped scribbling and leaned forward intently.

"He did?" he asked.

"He shore did."

"How do you mean?"

"Well, Walton wanted Earl to take the boy and show him things in the woods and mountains. That boy has spent many a night at our house. Earl has had him out in all kinds of weather, day and night. He said that boy could get tough and nothin' would stop him in life. They've gone back in there and laid out in the mountains and come back in with that boy dragging, he would be so tired. But his eyes always lit up when Earl talked about the next trip. Earl taught that boy ever'thing but how to run the likker."

"Mrs. Skiller, do you know that Logan Guffey saw that man get killed at the gap?"

"Pshaw! No! I doubt that. I've heard one lie after another."

"This is the truth."

She looked away a moment. Despair ruined her face.

"I know it," she suddenly choked. "I knowed that had to be true. I jist knowed it." She wiped her eyes.

"Are you all right?"

"I reckon so."

"Can you continue?"

"I guess," she said. "Earl saw his own daddy get killed."

"He did? How?"

"He was in a car wreck. It hurt him. I guess Logan's hurt too."

They were silent for a while, then Fortune asked: "When did Earl first start making liquor?"

"His daddy made it. Sooner or later ever'body made it, for a time anyway. Earl took to it like a duck to water. You've never seen anything so natural. And h'it wasn't jist the likker, h'it was all that went with it. He knowed about fires and heat, the right wood, the way to keep the coals turned, the steam, the furnace, and the pot. H'it all jist jumped into his head. He has ways of keeping ever'thing shifting as he goes along, and that makes the very best likker. They was something high and mighty and strange in Earl's head when he made likker. They was times when I'd feel the air around him change, and I'd get scared out of my wits."

"You? His mother?"

"Well, to tell the truth, I never felt like I was the mother of some of the things they was about 'im."

"For God's sake, explain that."

"No."

"Why not?"

"Shet up. I don't have to. I can't. I don't know. H'it was the way he poked at his fires and worked 'em. They seemed to be creatures themselves. He'd coax and pull and rake and scrape, he'd fool with those coals, and h'it was all so gentle and natural. The fire was alive, like serpents of some kind."

"You saw this?"

"Well, yes. You might say that."

"What did Earl say about this?"

"If I mentioned it, he'd grin and shake his head and try to make me feel like I was a little off."

"Did he mean to do that?"

Suddenly she started crying again. "I don't know. He's looked past me ever since he got back from prison the last time."

"Past you? What does that mean?"

"He acts like I h'ain't even there. H'it's true. I'm not crazy. Earl's crazy. He don't even recognize his own mama. One of the boys met him one day out by the cliffs with some flowers and asked him where he was going, and he said he was going to put some flowers on my grave if he could find it. He said he'd forgotten where it was. I just didn't pay that much attention. I thought he meant the other grave. But then my boy went on to it and found flowers already there. He always took some there when the flowers first bloomed in the spring."

"A grave? At Wild Cat?"

She nodded eagerly.

"It's a family cemetery, then?"

"No, jist a grave."

"And he thought you were dead?"

"I reckon. I don't know. It drives me crazy. He jist looked on past me and I felt like I was in a bad dream."

"Did you feel like he might harm you?"

"No, no, no. I wish I had felt that. Then he would have been knowing me. He just acted like I wasn't there. I got a little crazy myself."

"Go back to Earl's early years."

"Well, he was a good boy, humble, helpful to anyone. He never hurt nobody until he went in the army. He never said nothin' to me, but the other boys heard people say that he was a good soldier and killed a lot of the dirty Hun. I hate to call 'em that because Earl's great-grandfather on his daddy's side was a German. He come here when he was a young man. Earl said once the reason he could kill so good was because he saw the Hun as a rattlesnake. H'it wasn't that he hated the snake. Until this started, I don't be-lieve Earl ever hated anything."

"That is the great question. What has gone wrong?"

"I've seen him in all his ups and downs. In the light and in the dark. He was always so strong. Mary loved him so much, so much. She worshiped him."

"Who was Mary?"

"She was his wife."

"Wife?" Fortune repeated, astonished. "When?"

"The year before he had to go in the army. In 1916."

"Good woman, where has she been?"

"She's in that grave at Wild Cat, that's where."

Fortune stared fixedly out the window at the bright, clear sky. "What did she die from?" he asked.

"She killed herself."

"Killed herself? Why?"

"Because of the baby."

"Baby?"

281

"H'it's dead too. H'it's buried in Macon County, where we used to live. We took it there."

"Why was Mary put in a grave at Wild Cat?"

"H'it wasn't a grave to start with. About 1900 or 1901, some clay prospectors come in here lookin' for a kind of clay to make china out of. They dug some big holes. Mary dived straight down into one of them holes, onto some rocks. Earl went down in there and put her red dress on her and covered her up."

Earl was not often mentioned now among the general population. Fortune was able to let it lie for a time—then the image would rise and invade his mind: the slow, sardonic face of Earl smearing his simplest thoughts into gibberish.

He went to coffee one morning with Rawson and the druggist. As they sat talking, they heard the train whistle.

"Well, there they go," said Rawson.

"Who?" Fortune asked.

"Walton and Loretta."

"Where?"

"To Boston, Massachusetts."

"What for?"

"The company that owns the tannery is sending Walton to school up there."

"How long will he be gone?"

"Two or three years."

"What? Did they take the boy?"

"Nope."

Fortune leaped up, aghast.

"What the hell? Where is the boy?"

"He's been staying with his grandmother, as you well know. He will continue to stay there."

"My God! You know what has happened. The boy . . . ."

"Let the dead bury their dead," the pharmacist said.

"Well, the dead are not burying the dead. Have you seen that boy? The damage? Rawson, why in hell did you let them leave that boy here? You must know the psychological implications . . . ."

"I don't know much about psychology, but sometimes I try. You listen here: Walton and Loretta stay in a fight most of the time.

That may damage the boy worse than anything else. His grand-mother is as stable as the hills. I'm the one who assured them that it would be better to let Logan stay here."

They sat in deep silence for several minutes. Fortune finally calmed.

"I go up there some," he said. "I get along all right with the old woman, but the boy dodges me. When I'm there, he goes into the brush. By the way, I had another talk with Mrs. Skiller recently."

"Really? You are working at the saga, then. Did you get some spiritual or medical advice while you were at it?" Rawson asked dryly.

Fortune grinned. "Why pour acid on that old crone?" he asked.

"She represents a school of ignorance I have learned to hate. Did you learn anything new?"

"Earl had a wife."

Rawson and McCall stared at each other.

"I didn't know that," the pharmacist said.

"By God, that's right," Rawson said. "I recall something about it now that he's mentioned it."

"Where is she?" McCall asked.

"Dead," Rawson said. "Maybe she died in childbirth or of post-partum complications or something."

"The old lady said she killed herself," Fortune said. The other men stared at him silently, then at each other.

"I say. Killed herself?" Rawson asked blankly of himself.

"She told me several things. She said that after Earl came back from the pen this time he acted as if she weren't there, as if she were invisible. She said one of his brothers once found him walk-ing around with some flowers, looking for his mama's grave."

"Crazy! Crazy as a loon," said McCall.

"Crazy as a fox. He's bested the law here."

"It is not over," a voice said firmly. Boogerman stood near them, tilted on his cane. "The law is old. It has been with us a long time. Nobody bests the law."

"You are a subtle and profound man," Fortune said sarcasti-cally.

"The law is subtle and profound," Boogerman said.

Fortune ducked his head to hide a smile, looked around, then asked, "Did you know about Earl Skiller being married way back there about 1916 or 1917?"

"I personally do not give a God damn what the Skillers done before this present episode. He will be hunted down and killed and I say to hell with him. Good men have died."

The woman working at the soda fountain came to him.

"Do you want coffee, Mr. Sitner?" she asked.

He cocked a wild, querulous eye at her.

"Coffee? What time is it? I may take a cup."

24

AGAIN AUTUMN BROUGHT its wild prophecies, its exultant ex-
pectancies, as November sang old and far death songs, sang
for the mind of the boy Logan as he lay abed at his grandmother's
house. The wind surged through the mountains with the volume
and strength of flooding waters and gave off its own cold light,
shining like the moon, glistening along the curbs, the corners of
old buildings, the few drab boxcars on the siding. Logan, in the
enchantment of the night, thought upon all the things he had known
in perception as bright as the moon, as sharp as the wind, and his
mind and the wind came again to the mountain. In the deep cav-
erns of the tannery boiler room, the gnomish tender stoked his
coals, moved ashes in the cart beside the door, felt the wind, and
closed the door.

Paul Fortune sat bolt upright from a tired, troubled sleep. Had
someone called his name? He went first to the window, then to the
door. He opened it and stood outside, chilled, shaking, waiting.

Waiting?

Logan left his own bed, went quietly to the window in his room,
and looked out. Something moved in the night—fast, quick, hidden in the great light—stared at them all, whispered and rustled
in their minds, then looped away again as quietly as a great serpent.

The wind fanned dry leaves along the ground and piled them
against fences. Far in the tortured ridges, Earl Skiller awakened at
the strange current, rose, and went to where he could see the moon
and the wind swirling light across the face of the earth.

Time passed, and winter clamped shut like a bear trap, cold and sharp and tight. The ridges were first sifted with snow, then they whitened with rime lace along the twigs. Those in the towns did not yet feel the ice, but they knew it was coming. The prowling beast of cold could swerve suddenly out of the wilderness and be upon them.

Breasting the chill wind, Paul Fortune walked to Wadenton to see the sheriff, who was in the jail kitchen drinking coffee and signing legal papers. Fortune's face was raw, and the dry heat of the courthouse was unsettling.

"What is new?" Fortune asked. The sheriff rose and shook hands ritually, flashed a political smile, devalued himself with a shrug, and sat.

"New? Something new every day. Change, change, change. Nothing remains the same."

"Have you a lead on Earl Skiller, then?"

The sheriff stared gloomily at his papers, then said:

"There is nothing new under the sun. That remains the same."

"Sheriff Plemmons, how well did you know Earl Skiller?"

"I never knew him very well. He was a shadow to me, then and now. In the line of work he usually followed, it was best that he not cultivate my friendship."

"Did you try hard to catch him before the killing started?"

"Catch him doing what?" the sheriff asked dryly.

"Making whiskey."

"I never knew he made it. I thought he farmed and trapped and logged and so forth."

"He was caught and convicted several times by the federal government."

"Well, I believe you're right at that. Yes, now that you mention it, I do recollect some gossip and hearsay about that."

"Yes! Well, you kept him here in the federal section of this jail until they shipped him off."

"Well, that's probably where I heard it: from one of the jailers. That does seem right. I'm so busy that I can't keep up with the day-to-day workings of the federal section. They live in their own world, as the man says. Prisoners come and go through there all the time."

"Aha! The more I hang around here, the more of a sense of

order and efficiency I get. There is also a remarkable air of candor. Do you feel Earl is up there around Wild Cat?"

The sheriff stood slowly, pushing his pistol back on his belt.

"Let's go out here on this little balcony thing where we can see," he said.

They stood in the high wind on the third-floor parapet. The frosted sweep of the mountains and basins surrounded them. They stared toward Wild Cat.

"Is he up there?" Fortune asked.

"If you ask me so you can write in that little pad, I'll tell you one thing."

"What?"

"If you don't write it, I'll tell you something else."

"I'm not promising."

"Well, first I'm going to say a few things. That doesn't mean I'm making any kind of statement. It's cold in those mountains. I've looked and looked through glasses, and I've seen no smoke. I've driven to mountaintops on old roads and looked. There is no smoke rising anywhere."

"Does that mean he's not in there?"

"No, it does not mean that."

The sheriff stared away, then turned penetrating eyes on Fortune.

"Earl Skiller knows how to burn a fire. He knows what kinds of wood won't raise much smoke. He could burn a big fire at night in some fireplace or another, and heat the stones of it, they would throw off heat. He could burn hickory or oak down to char and let that glow all day. Then at night he could heat it up again. He knows what he's about back there."

"Then you feel that he's back there?"

"I haven't said that. You have asked me some questions, and I am answering the best I can with what good will and good faith I can muster. When you ask that question, you raise up a lot of other things. I think you're a useful man in this situation. One of the main things I like about you is that I can talk to you, despite your notorious reputation for drunkenness and other sins and shortcomings."

Fortune shook his head, grinned, and said, "Yes, you can talk and I'll listen."

"Well, it's not that I think you'll listen. I don't give a damn whether you do or not. It's that I feel like I can talk to you, and when I do, I can listen to myself and get it straight. Do you understand that?"

Fortune nodded.

"Now, then, I don't think Earl is back there."

"You don't?"

"No. I also don't think he's not back there."

"Aha! You're keeping your mind open. What do you think?"

"I think about what I know."

"What do you know?"

"Several solid things. One is that late in the fall, when the moon was waxing, someone broke into a rich man's house at the golf course. The man Beck."

"Beck. Of course. I know him. What was taken?"

"Little, if anything. But whoever it was played some gramophone records. Two of them were broken. Maybe a few were stolen. Anyway, they're gone. The next morning one of the Palmer boys found some footprints in the mud along that branch beside their house. They came to me. The prints were pointed upstream. Nobody walks creeks in this season but trappers. Now, I went up and down that stream as soon as I heard about the prints. I found not one trap. They was one old chain, years old, on a root. They was good slick muskrat runs. No traps. Who in the hell would leave footprints in the mud of a little creek hung over with brush?

"I know what I know. I hold it in my memory and wait. Early in the summer a strange man went in a store over on Caney Fork and traded a few things for some staples, and the store owner was glad to trade. For about fifteen dollars worth of food, that stranger laid down about $250 in gold nuggets, raw and out of these creeks. I just found out about that last week. I talked to the store keeper. He didn't know Earl Skiller, but he remembered all the fuss about the killings. Anyhow, he said his customer was a shaven man with clean clothes. He said the man talked like a mountain man, but he was dressed different.

"I went back to Beck at the golf course. No earlier break-in, nothing missing but the records. Then I happened to overhear a young traveling man complaining at a cafe the other day. He had passed through here in the summer and had parked his car at a lady friend's house. He said they talked late into the night about scripture and such, and when he went to his car about ten-thirty the next morning one valise was gone and with it his razor and so forth, and some clothes. I don't know what a man so versed in the scripture was doing in the Royal Cafe red-eyed and half drunk, but some workings of justice is of such hidden motion that I don't question them.

"Now, that car was parked inside the town limits of Wadenton, Mr. Fortune. That is, not Wild Cat, and not the golf course. That house is within four hundred yards of this courthouse."

"Then you think . . ."

"No sir, I don't think nothing. You asked me what time it is, and I'm telling you and me both how to make a watch, but that's how I have to do it. Now, we've watched old lady Skiller closely and only you and two other people have gone there."

"Earl won't go there. He thinks she's dead."

"How do you know?"

"She told me."

"Well, in any case, I know several other things, all of them of a similar nature. They prove nothing. That is not counting all of the everloving horseshit I have heard from all over this county every time a cloud crosses between the sun and the earth, or a pig dies. I have set traps but they hasn't been a bite. I talked to the National Guard. That captain is a lot of talk. He said they had to get ready to go to war. I told him that if they needed any practice, I could point them in the right direction. He said the only way he would go to Wild Cat would be by direct order from the governor, and even then he would drag his feet getting ready."

They both looked at the mountains. The clouds rose over the western ridges. There was a new dimension to the wind.

"Cold, cold, cold. It'll come in hard," the sheriff said.

"Well, I've got to go. I'll keep asking here and there."

The sheriff looked at him for a moment. "If you hear anything, you'll let me know right away, won't you?"

Fortune nodded absently.

"Anything a'tall," the sheriff said, "or if any kind of thought or stray suspicion comes to mind, let me know, won't you?"

The freeze did not lift. Fortune went through the cold to visit Mrs. Skiller again. Her rooms stank with staleness and poverty.

She folded her hands in her aproned lap.

"Earl is back there," he said sharply.

"I don't doubt it," she said in that infuriating way of switching her view to accommodate.

"Do you know where?" he asked.

"I kin give you some advice. Don't even try it."

"Have you seen him?"

"No! Not since the day of the first killing. That day he came through the yard as happy as I've ever seen him. He was excited and pleased. He didn't even know we was in the world."

"Perhaps you weren't. Anyway, a few days ago the boy Logan mentioned something to me. He said through the Narrows, and on past Bailey Springs, is a little shack. He said Earl used to take him there when they were in the mountains. It is in a field or bald. Do you know where it is?"

She rubbed her forehead.

"No," she finally said. "If I did, I wouldn't tell . . . I couldn't tell . . . ."

"Do you know what or where the Narrows are?"

"The Narrers? Yes. It's a slim little pass through the rock on past Lick Stone. That's a snaky place in the summer."

"That's what the boy said. Well, they won't be out for a while. Logan said Earl knew how to talk with the snakes with his hand. He said Earl could turn his arm into a snake, and then his brain, and the real snakes stayed calm, and he could touch their heads."

"Earl knows how to do all kinds of things that I don't know about. I can show you from here where the Narrers is."

"Show me."

They went into the smashed snow of her yard. She pointed toward a far mountain.

"You see the one that turns off sharp there?"

"Yes."

"The Narrers is to the right. There's a trail along the top of that ridge. When you come to some big chestnut trees that are down, you see another trail to the left through some ivy, and it goes into the rock."

"Madam, I thank you."

"Are you going to tell the sheriff?"

"No madam, I am not."

"Well, you might want to tell somebody where you're going."

"Why?"

"So they'll know where to send your stuff. You know, the arrangements. You ought to take care of that before you go."

25

EARL WAS BEYOND the Narrows, and he lay in his hidden cabin in the dead of night, listening to the continuous whistle of the wind. He had slept himself empty of drowsiness, and now with lonely, bright clarity of mind he concentrated on the sound of the wind. His mind developed no images. His nerves were taut, and when his brain was this free from stimulation, he was drawn down again into painful, vacant madness. There was nothing to do but lie within the warmth of the blanket and meditate upon the great, bright blade of wind sawing ceaselessly through the land.

He watched the wind, but he did not watch time because in time are many times, to love and to fight and to fight love and to love fight. Change and cycle. There is also a right time to die—he could feel that one truth building in his fey soul. He must live past the temptations to misread a time and wait for the one true time when it was right to die.

He considered the mysteries of his own heart. He was full of the deepest ache, and yet he did not feel he had done anything wrong. He had carried hard battle to natural enemies, that was all. A warrior fighting warriors was exempt from those penalties of soul that sent men who harmed the innocent into perdition.

Inside the darkened shack he moved silently to a port and stared down the moon-glossed snow. There was only the glow from the chunk of moon, and the shadows. The wind leaped and moaned. Earl put dead poplar on the coals in the fireplace, and shortly the tea-sweet aroma of it filled the close cabin. In the flickering fire-light he looked strangely about the place. Yes, the time was coming. There was a sense of departure upon the place. Daylight came, and Earl sat and looked out the port down the field. It was near

noon when he heard Paul Fortune's shout and saw him come out
of the rocks. Fortune came up the rise to the cabin, and Earl slowly
opened the door and looked at him.

"How are you, Sergeant Skiller?" Fortune asked solemnly.

Earl stared at him for a time, and Fortune felt the deadly emptiness, the silence, and in that silence his own mind rushed crazily.
Then Earl stood aside and let Fortune in.

"I remember you from France now. It took me a long time to
remember," Fortune said.

"France? Where?" Earl asked.

"Verdun, for one. You were the sergeant who penetrated the
lines all the time. You were 'The Silent Sergeant,' the sniper with
the medals. I saw you twice. I saw you coming back in once across
no-man's-land, and later I saw General Pershing decorating you. I
wrote stories about it."

"Stories? Me in France?"

"Somewhere in my trunks I've got those stories. They were in
papers all over the United States. I'll get them and read them. . . ."

"How did you know where to find me?" Earl asked, his voice
soft and frightening. Fortune cleared his throat and blinked his
eyes.

"I'm going to tell you the truth," he said.

"Yes," said Earl, "do that."

"A good friend of yours told me."

"Who?"

"Logan Guffey."

Earl sagged onto his cot. The strength in him was suddenly
drained. His face was despairing and his eyes haunted. They sat
quietly for a time, Earl nodding his head slowly. Finally Fortune
spoke.

"I started early yesterday morning. It is hard to climb in that
snow. I slept a little last night. I turned out my blanket roll and
tarp under a big log. I had a fire. I thought all night that you might
kill me."

Earl grinned slightly. "Not in this weather," he said.

"Well, if you don't mind my saying so, weather hasn't stopped
you before."

"Maybe it wasn't me. Maybe it was somebody who wasn't worried about weather."

"Well, I understand the different people in us. Let me tell you this, that the one who doesn't worry about weather and other things has gotten you into bad trouble."

He looked around and saw some gramophone records against the wall.

"Good music there. Do you have a gramophone here?"

"No. I took them from a man's house. I don't know why I wanted to keep them. I can't listen to them here."

"You left tracks in the creek near Palmer's."

"Sooner or later a man on the run leaves tracks."

"Well, I'm not coming under a false flag. I'm a writer and some newspapers and magazines have asked me to do some stories about you."

"What about?"

Fortune cleared his throat timidly, sighed deeply and fearfully, and said, "All the killings."

Earl's eyes bored into him with the fearful force of silence and emptiness.

"How many?" Earl asked suddenly, with a strange, insane smile, as though he posed a riddle.

Fortune was shaken, dry of mouth, but he went on. "I don't know. How many do you say?"

"I won't admit to nothin'. But maybe I let some go who could have died, and they never knew it."

"How many times could you have killed me?"

"Every time you came to Wild Cat."

"Why didn't you, then?"

"You don't mean me no harm."

"How do you know?"

"I know."

"Why did you kill those men?" Fortune asked abruptly, a strength seeming to come to him from Earl so that he could ask the question.

Earl strode to the port and looked out. Then he made tea from some pennyroyal and horsemint. The water boiled quickly on the fire, they drank, and Fortune smoked. Drowsiness descended in the dry heat of the cabin, and the unceasing pull of the wind across the land lulled them toward entrancement. Finally Earl spoke. Even as he did, Fortune saw a new dimension of the man emerging. There was now in Earl a high gentleness and refinement of emotion.

"I never have got to talk much about this. Some of it got to be too much. In the war . . . I tried to tell it to my people, but they always got it wrong. They thought I said I killed Germans because they were rattlesnakes. That's not what I said. I told them once the reason I was so good at it was that I could turn into a rattlesnake in my mind, and then I could come and go and do my damage and nobody watched. I learned a big lesson once from rattlesnakes."

"What?"

"They're silent in spite of the rattles. They're silent at the right time. They can do a lot of damage. If they're silent and it's dark, then who can see 'em?

"Some people say I'm crazy but I'm not. No."

Fortune sensed a force rising in the cabin. He grew as frightened as he ever had been in his life. He cast about desperately for something to dissipate the force.

"Listen, I've always admired you boys who went behind the lines in the war. Personally, I'm a coward. I don't believe I could have done that. If I had, I would have bungled it and gotten people killed. I was afraid I'd be killed."

Again a long silence. Earl, eternally fixed in some kind of dim half-light, stared at him, finally said, "Don't ever doubt your own nerve, mister. If you come up here where I am, you'd have gone in on Kaiser Bill hisself. You'd have a better chance of getting killed here than you would've there."

Fortune was now shaking and licking his lips.

"Are you going to kill me?" he finally asked.

"What do you say I'll do?" Earl asked.

Silence again, and two men staring at each other.

"If you did, nobody would ever know what happened to me, would they?"

Earl smiled vacantly.

"Are you going to kill me?" Fortune asked again.

"I don't know and you don't know. I don't feel like it, but you never can tell. But that's what makes you a brave man, and seasoned in the fires."

"I'm not a brave man, Sergeant. If you kill me, I will not die brave. If you don't, I will not live bravely through this. I am shaking every minute of it."

"All right. Now you're making a beginning. You can understand about me, then."

In the immense, rolling silence that followed, Fortune suddenly broke through to calmness in himself.

"Earl. Sergeant. What . . . ?"

"Ever since I was a boy, I knowed they was big dark eggs up against my brain. I saw 'em as I was going to sleep. Sometimes I didn't think about it, but I knowed they was always there."

"Eggs?"

"Something like that. I saw 'em clear later for what they was."

"What then?"

"Maybe big snake heads. There in prison I had time to see it, and I saw the big dark eggs had eyes—dark eyes watching me. They hatched anyway. I had dreams there. I kept dreaming I was back in France and I'd lost my gas mask and the gas was coming to me across a field, and the only way to do anything is to go on anyway whether or not you're afraid, so I went to it and breathed it in. Yes, I dreamed I was breathing poison gas in, and I had to face it to beat it, and I knew then that I had death to dream about. I saw my mama there on the wall, and she was froze to death at Wild Cat, and that nearly killed me because I knowed she could have been saved with just a little heat out of a little fire, and after that I saw a thousand more things, and each thing I saw put more heat on those snake heads, and they hatched into more pictures. I saw outlanders moving in here and gettin' the land and not lettin' people hunt or fish. I saw old women asking Florida people for slop and garbage for their hogs when they didn't have hogs. They ate it themselves because they was hungry. I thought about it all and got hotter.

"I've seen deputies beat men or shoot 'em for nothing. I've seen men on chaingangs whose worst crime was getting drunk, and I've seen the same judges who put 'em there drunk on the streets. They ought to know better than to keep on messing with a man. I told 'em and told 'em, but they didn't listen. When I was in town, I was in their territory, and I watched and thought. The day of change finally come. It always comes. I got 'em out here in the woods. Now they listen in the night for Earl.

"Now, down there in Atlanta working near the big fires, I learned a lot of new things right in my own head. Sometimes I used to think I could get in other people's minds, but I found out it was the other way around. They get in my mind. Then I saw that that young Deputy Sanger was going to use me to kill hisself with. That boy really wanted to die, and he told me just how to do it. Then there was the others. They took a gamble and come to see what I was like, and they come to my mind and told me how they wanted to go."

The fierceness of Earl's candor was overloading Fortune. Now he was shaking again. They sat back in silence once more, and they both knew that that part was over. Fortune felt strangely drained.

"Sergeant," he said at last, "you had a wife."

Earl tilted his face to him, and the light came down the side of it.

"That's right. I loved her. She loved me. She was the very one put here on earth for me. After she died I never cared for any other woman."

"Earl, I have to know. Why did she take her own life?"

"How did you know that?"

"Your mother told me."

"Mama? When?"

"A few days ago."

"Mama?"

"She's alive, you know."

Earl was still.

"Why did your wife kill herself?"

"Late one evening she was cooking and holding our baby boy. She took him to his crib so she could set the table. It was dark in that room. She heard the baby crying and went back in there. She had set him in the crib on top of a big rattlesnake, and it bit him in the face and neck."

Earl was standing by the port in light and shadow.

"We took him to Holly Springs and buried him there. In a couple of days she went up to that old clay pit and dived down onto the rocks at the bottom. I went down in there and put her red dress on her, and then I put dirt on her and made her grave there. I go to it now and then. I thank ye for listening. I h'ain't never talked about it before."

There was the dense flow of time, drowsiness, and wood heat, and the wind keening and crying. They drank pennyroyal tea.

"Now, that's why I liked to keep an eye on Walton's boy—so many times he almost went across hisself."

Fortune was not now afraid.

"Did you know that Logan Guffey saw you kill that Deputy Sanger?"

Earl leaned toward him, keenly alert. "Lord God," he said.

"He was on his way to school."

For the first time, perplexity came to Earl's face. "Well, tell me how he is," he said.

"Maybe he has been ruined by that."

Earl was silent; then, "Do you think so?"

"I saw him eat tomato soup and it turned to blood. There are other things . . . ."

Many minutes passed; then Earl said, "What can I do now?"

"I don't know what's in the boy's mind. But you ought to stand trial."

"Do you believe that would help the boy?"

"Yes sir. I don't quite know how, but I believe it would. Maybe justice and truth have medicinal properties."

"Trial? Do you know what will happen to me?"

"You'll be found guilty and executed."

"I wouldn't even get to the jail if some people heard I was coming in."

"Yes, you would. Don't worry about it. You can get justice."

"Courthouse justice. I don't want it. They asked to be killed, and I killed 'em. We are all even." Earl's bright face was as full of simple assurance as a child's.

"And the boy . . . ?"

This wait was the longest.

"All right," Earl said at last. "I'll be along in a couple of days. Don't tell nobody else. Get Logan and meet me at the gap about dinnertime day after tomorrow. Me and that boy is joined in our lives and souls. Then I want to hear this music one more time. I know you're a friend to that man, and you can get that done. Then me and you will go to the sheriff, and I'll turn in."

———

On the appointed day, Fortune borrowed Dr. Rawson's coupe and drove to Hame Tree Gap, then walked down the trail to the Guffey place. Mrs. Guffey met him on the porch.

"Well, you look tuckered out," she said.

"I've been stomping around in these cold mountains for several days and I'm worn out, madam. Is the boy here?"

"Yes. What do you want with him?"

"Earl is coming down from the mountains today to turn in. He wants to see the boy at the gap."

She stood unmoving. "How do you know that?" she asked.

"I found him and he told me. The last time I was up here, Logan told me about the shack beyond the Narrows, and that's where he was. I suppose he'll come in. He said he would, and I believe him."

"Yes, you can believe him. At the gap, you say? That's a bad place for it."

"It's what Earl said."

"Why is he doing this?"

"I don't know. They were friends, as I understand it. Earl doesn't think he's got any friends. Maybe he wants to apologize or something. I have no idea."

She got Logan, and the three of them walked up the trail to the gap. They stood waiting. They heard a distant bird call. Soon Earl stepped into sight up the road and came on toward them with his lank gait. Logan looked up at Earl dumbly, bewildered, then looked at where the deputy had fallen. Earl's face held its own solemn shock, as if he realized only now the dimensions and enormity of his crimes.

"Logan," he said softly. The boy turned his face to him, then began trembling and fell. Earl looked blankly at the small foot kicking the ground. Mrs. Guffey leaned forward and stared intently into Earl's face, her own without expression. Then she lifted the boy and held him. Fortune walked away a few yards.

Earl nodded, stood staring into shadowed vistas in his skull. He saw a vast region of himself that was breaking open. He nodded, nodded, nodded, and dimly saw Mrs. Guffey carrying Logan down the trail. Then she let him down and they walked, holding hands, away from Earl Skiller and did not look back.

The two men went to the Beck home. By prearrangement, no one was there. Paul Fortune showed Earl how to play the records, and Earl played "Barcarolle" and "Habanera" over and over. Earl prowled the room, listening intently, as though his mind held a recorder into which these notes were being transcribed in sound pure, rich, and clear, the notes of many dead geniuses falling into his brain, rich and subtle food upon which his own great spirit fed. He was a man bold enough to hear the song that called out the path he had to follow, no matter where it led. Earl had heard the call and had followed, and now he knew; the music told him, and he knew that he was approaching the end of a path set for him a million years ago, if one must reckon time through the limited circuits of human understanding.

Paul Fortune stood patiently, an acolyte of fate, serving at this station on a man's own secret path.

In midafternoon, Earl stopped his pacing and stood before Fortune.

"All right," he said. "Let's go."

"Just a moment, if you don't mind," Fortune said. He put on "La donna è mobile," and they listened. Then they went to the car and drove to Wadenton.

Fortune had envisioned that highly dramatic things would swirl about Earl's entry of the town, but there was nothing. They got out of Rawson's car beside the courthouse and went through the hall with no recognition. They walked through the anteroom of the sheriff's office, saw Sheriff Plemmons working at his desk in the back office, and went in.

Earl cocked an inner ear and heard the main of his life being sealed off. He was entering new corridors of existence, each with a door and a door and a door, locked. The sheriff did not recognize him.

"Yes?" he inquired tiredly of Fortune.

"Sheriff Plemmons, this is Earl Skiller."

A silence as deep as the tombs of Egypt fell over the office. The sheriff sat still and looked all around Earl, but not at him.

"I'm turning in," Earl said.

The sheriff rose stiffly, walked selfconsciously to the door, and closed it. He walked with deliberate, awkward movement to the safe, opened it, and took out the sheaf of warrants.

"Are you acting as this man's lawyer or in any other way representing his interests?" the sheriff asked Paul Fortune with abrupt formality. He still would not look at Earl.

"Why do you ask me that?" Fortune asked.

"Because I'm fixing to arrest him for murder—a number of such capital felonies, as a matter of fact. To wit, the murder of some deputy sheriffs and interested citizens, and a few other things."

"No, I'm not acting for him. Go ahead and arrest him. It's what he came for."

The sheriff unfolded the first warrant, opened his mouth, tried dryly to speak: "By the powers vested in me . . ." he said, swallowed, then, ". . . by the State of North Carolina . . ." and for a moment could speak no more. Finally he looked Earl full in the face and became himself, an honest man. "Mr. Skiller, I'm trying to do this right. This is a big day around here. You are under arrest for murder. I'm going to lock you up, and there will be no bail."

Earl nodded.

The sheriff went to a closet and took out a set of leg irons and put them on the desk. Then he took out some handcuffs.

"I ain't no stranger to them, but you won't need 'em," Earl said.

"You won't need them," Fortune said. "He came in. He's through with it."

The sheriff nodded. There was a moment's silence; then the sheriff held out his hand to Earl.

"It's a helluva way to end it. I didn't expect it to be like this. I was interested in shooting you down up there somewhere. I just don't exactly know what to do with myself now."

The three of them walked out through the office, then took the elevator up to the cells on the second floor. Earl walked into a cell and turned around.

"Do me a favor," he asked the sheriff.

"If it's not too much. What is it?"

"Just don't slam that steel door. Shut 'er as soft as you can."

The sheriff nodded, pushed the door closed noiselessly, and slid the bolts. Fortune looked through the small rectangular window, but he saw only the shadow of Earl. He and the sheriff returned to the office.

"My God Almighty!" Sheriff Plemmons gasped. "You just walked in here and handed over Earl Skiller."

"He surrendered himself. Remember that, if it'll go in his favor."

"Old friend, listen. There ain't nothing gonna help Earl Skiller," the sheriff said, waving the warrants around. "These pieces of paper may not be much to look at. They don't weigh much. But there's a name on every one of them. Now, I was a pallbearer at every one of these men's funerals. I carried those boxes, and they were heavy. Every box had a corpse in it, and in each case the corpse went with a name on a warrant. There is no consideration to be given Mr. Earl Skiller unless somehow all those deputies come back to life. They have been in the ground a long time now. I think if they were inclined to come back, they would have shown up by now, don't you?"

"Yes sir, sheriff," Fortune said wryly. "I have always admired the way you have with logic. You stack one fact up right behind the other and pretty soon you've made your case. I can see now that the jury will be drawn from just about the same walk of life as the deceased officers."

"You can almost bet on it, and before it's over the solicitor will damn sure apprise each juror of the facts surrounding each and every death."

"I knew it. I knew you'd somehow do that. Anyway, if I hadn't been convinced before now that there would be no mass resurrections, I am now. However, the reason I said that was not to save him, but so that the legend wouldn't get messed up and twisted about."

"Right. Bound to be a legend. Already is. Are you going to report this to the papers?"

"Maybe. Sooner or later."

"Damn. You walked in here and handed me Earl Skiller." Then he eyed Fortune speculatively. "Who knows he's turned in?"

"Us and Mrs. Guffey and Logan. Logan met with him."

"He did? How did he act?"

"Badly."

"Is he going to be all right?"

"I doubt that."

They sat a moment. The sheriff bit his lip and blinked his eyes for a while.

"Let me tell you what I'm thinking," he said. "I'm going to get the solicitor down here in a little while, and we're going to read off these warrants. Somewhere in all of this we picked up part of a still up there at Wild Cat. Possession of that is a federal offense. We'll get a federal warrant, and that'll let us put him in a federal cell in Asheville for safekeeping. If some people knew we were keeping him here, there might be trouble of some kind. We'll transfer him to Asheville tonight. Now, I don't intend to let anybody know about this, at least until after the arraignment. When are you going to report this?"

"Anytime or never. It's all up to me. I'd like to make some pictures of him here. I'd like to be present at all times when something is going on. I'd like to have access to him at any reasonable time. I don't know yet what all I'll need, but I'd like your assurances that I be kept notified."

"By God! Don't worry. As long as I'm the sheriff of this county, you can have any damned thing you want. You can get in that cell with him. Anything you want. If you get on any of your famous drunks, now or any time, you can count on a decent welcome at this jail at any hour of the day or night, if and when you are arrested by some of them dumb city cops, and you can count on a reasonable amount of transportation—drunk or sober—in county cars, except to the very front door of the Smathers Street whorehouses. Earl Skiller is now captured because of you, and I'll be happy to get you anything within the purview of this badge's authority, and by God, that's pretty wide in this county."

"Well, I must thank you for this great outburst of generosity," Fortune said, shaking his head sadly. "Some remarkable things happen to me from time to time. The right and good offers are always made to me at the wrong times."

SPRING, AND WARM WINDS stirred the budding trees. People began arriving on the Saturday afternoon before court opened on
Monday. They came in from the mountains and the coves. Those
who had relatives or friends in the towns stayed with them, and
the others pitched makeshift camps in and around their trucks or
wagons, wherever they were parked. The merchants were happy
because the people were spending money, and the festival of it was
in the air. Boy and girl and man and woman found each other, and
the couples walked about. In their later years, at anniversaries and
family reunions, they might recall for their progeny that they caught
each other's eye during the time that the state was trying the out-
law Earl Skiller for his life.

In attendance also was the press: the raucous, temperamental,
unreliable ones, as well as the staid, respectable, eminently reliable, sobersided ones who were there to get and present the facts
of the matter. But Paul Fortune had a deadlock on most of the
information, and he wasn't writing it yet. The sheriff gave out
nothing of substance.

However, the state's attorney, the solicitor, beguiled by the possibilities of so much newsprint, saw high office for himself not too
far in the future. He consented to interviews, gave out reams of
information on himself: the humble origins, the hard work com-
bined with a natural affinity for the complexities of the law which
had brought him this far, his political acumen, his heartfelt desire
to be of service in whatever capacity to the people of this county;
yes, this region; yes, this state; yes, this nation, if so called by the
voters.

He gave the information freely, though no one asked for it. After poring over it, the more perceptive reporters noted that they had little more on the defendant than had already been printed. Certain problems of attribution and verification arose in this phase of the coverage. They were rewriting from old clippings, and those sources were dangerously contradictory. However, most of the reporters overcame their reservations and rewrote with renewed vigor and new error.

Except for some of the more staid ones, the members of the press headquartered in the Royal Cafe in the Frog Level section of town, or established various outposts along the Western Front. Paul Fortune, for old times' sake, sauntered through the joints on Saturday.

An intoxicated reporter said, "There goes Fortune. He knows all about it. He's been here in this backwater of hell the entire time. He was doing something for some paper the day the killer was captured. He's got it all, and he's holding it."

Fortune stopped, grinned at his good old friend Alex Fore, then left with sobriety intact. The drunk reporter swayed about awhile, then summoned Alex.

"What the hell was it Fortune said, old man?" he demanded.

Alex looked about at the reporters, blinked. "He said you are the scum of the earth one and all, and you've blighted what used to be a good dive."

But Fortune was not smug. As he and the sheriff watched the situation developing, a terrible irony settled upon them. They looked over the case the solicitor had put together. What they feared had not yet dawned on the prosecutor.

———

Judge Everette Horne was on his first turn on the mountain circuit. He had been assigned from a district in the rural foothills of the state, and no one here knew him. Although he was not expected until Monday, he came incognito at midday on Saturday and went around town watching and listening. He heard or saw nothing that might cause him to consider a change of venue. Early Monday he summoned the sheriff and solicitor to his chambers.

"Gentlemen, this is going to be closely watched, especially by the press. I generally doubt their competence to understand what goes on in a courtroom, but they are here and have to be taken into consideration. They may err where they will; that will have little to do with it in the end. I must tell you, as strongly as I can, that this trial record will not err. Mr. Solicitor, I want you to be bold and cautious both, do you understand?"

"Yes, Your Honor."

"Now, gentlemen, what should I know?"

"Nothing, Your Honor."

"Does the defendant have counsel?"

"Your Honor, he has property. He said he didn't want or need an attorney, so we didn't assign him one."

The judge wiped his chin patiently. "We are going to try him for his life. We will attempt to refrain from reversible error. This man deserves to die in the gas chamber if he is guilty. I want him to have counsel, and the law demands it. Why have you not assigned it?"

Judge Horne's eyes were sharp and steely. The solicitor fumbled with papers.

"I felt the evidence was so strong that he'd plead guilty."

Judge Horne was incredulous. "What? I see now it's going to be a long ball game. I don't know how many times the state might have to try this case. I don't believe you just said that. You didn't say that, did you?"

The solicitor stammered, "Say what?"

"What you said."

"What did I say, Your Honor?"

The judge stared at the sheriff.

"I don't know what made me think that . . . ," the prosecutor finally said.

"The point is, have you really been thinking that? Where did you get your law license? This man is not allowed to enter a guilty plea. Now I am truly alarmed. Are there any members of the bar out there?"

"Yes, Your Honor," the sheriff said.

"Bring some in here."

The judge talked with some of the attorneys, then assigned one. When the judge went into the courtroom awhile later, the lawyer was standing away from the defendant, frightened.

"Gentlemen, approach the bench," the judge ordered. State and defense attorneys went to him.

"Your Honor," said the defense attorney, "he said he doesn't need a lawyer. He doesn't want one. I'm scared of him."

"Did he threaten you?"

"Yes sir, Your Honor."

"What did he say?"

"He didn't say anything, Your Honor. It was his eyes."

The judge leaned forward, his face angry. "You go sit at that table," he said. The judge then began reviewing certain documents.

Fortune wandered through the packed courtroom. An unarmed deputy stood behind the defendant. Nearby stood one with a pistol. Two armed men guarded the doors into the courtroom. The hallways were jammed. Outside, people were on benches or sitting on the grass and street curbs. Fortune returned to the courtroom. On the first row of spectators' pews sat the Skiller family. Earl did not look at them.

The murmur of voices rose and fell. Judge Horne signed papers, then banged his gavel.

"Mr. Solicitor?"

Tension rose and the prosecutor stood.

"Your Honor, now comes the case of the State of North Carolina versus Earl Skiller. The defendant is charged with first-degree murder in . . ."

"A moment, please," Horne said, then addressed Earl.

"Mr. Earl Skiller, you are charged with several capital crimes, and that means the state will try to take your life. Now, an attorney was appointed for you, but he says that you do not want legal counsel to assist in your defense. Is that right?"

Earl stood and nodded indifferently.

"Please make your answer aloud so this lady here can report it in the record."

"I don't want a lawyer," Earl said.

"Now, you have some property, or there is some in the family. That can be used to hire an attorney. You are not what is called an indigent man. Now I ask you again: do you want a lawyer to represent your interests?"

"No, I don't want a lawyer," Earl repeated.

The prosecutor smiled absently, curiously pleased and somehow vindicated.

"Well, that is Mr. Claude Atkins there at your table. I'm going to ask him to stay with you and be of any assistance you might require."

Earl nodded, turned, and looked at Atkins's cautious face. Horne continued:

"Now, Mr. Skiller, ordinarily I would ask you how you plead to the charges. The fact that you have a peculiar attitude toward a lawyer puts me in the singular position of having to hear this case and look out for certain of your interests and rights as I go along. Now, ladies and gentlemen of the court and the public, I am vigilant about his interest not because I favor the defendant and am partial to his case, but rather because I must be impartial. Any citizen of the United States has a number of rights when he is born, and we may not take them away in any whimsical or arbitrary fashion, no matter how the accusations against him may have inflamed the public. There must be a coolness to the law, and the coolness is maintained by a step-by-step process. I personally am only a rung in the legal ladder. If I do not look after the defendant's rights, then that rung above me, the state supreme court, will overturn the finding if it is guilty, and all my work and the sheriff's work and the work of the solicitor and the worry of the jury will go for naught, and the defendant, guilty or not, can conceivably go free.

"Now, I have said all of that to say this again: ordinarily in a case I would ask the defendant to tell me how he pleads. However, I am enjoined and required to do what I now do. I direct the clerk to enter a plea of not guilty for Mr. Skiller."

The crowd was still. Paul Fortune, sitting behind the sheriff, bit his lip. The sheriff turned and stared wordlessly at him. Then Earl turned and looked at Fortune and smiled, and for a moment the wildness and wiliness of a warrior was visible once again. The solicitor frowned and shuffled papers. His leg danced and jittered on one toe.

Earl's face held a taunting smile, but his eyes dulled and he only half-listened as the drone of testimony began.

The prosecutor put his first witness on the stand.

"Now, Sheriff, you were called by the Wadenton police, was it, to a place called Hame Tree Gap up toward Wild Cat on the morning of . . . yes, just go ahead, tell us what you found . . . now, who was it said that? . . . well, did he say he had seen . . ."

Judge Horne turned to the clerk: "Strike it. Hearsay."

"All right, Sheriff Plemmons," continued the solicitor, "it was cold and frosty that day, did you say?"

"Yes sir, it was," the sheriff said.

". . . the decapitation was complete, was it?"

". . . the men, or some of them, got sick at it, and . . ."

". . . investigation showed . . . now, when did you first suspect . . . you came to realize . . ."

"Strike that. Leading the witness."

"Let me rephrase the question . . . I see, I see . . . now, Sheriff, how many times have you had to run liquor investigations up there? . . . in and around that set of rock cliffs . . . now, I need this to be as complete as we can possibly make it, so try your best to recollect that morning . . . Mitchell Sanger, was he a reliable and good man, a member of a church . . . ?"

"Now, Mr. Solicitor," Horne finally said, "we're going to call a short recess here. Let the jury remain seated."

"Yes, Your Honor."

There was the murmur and flow of talk among the spectators, craning, twisting, and watching with interest from their profane seating outside the tabernacle of justice, from which they were separated by a rail and a bar.

The trial resumed. Earl did not cross-examine the sheriff. He paid lawyer Atkins little notice.

". . . yes, I see. I see. Dr. Rawson, it was your unhappy job that day to . . . you did act as coroner on this occasion . . . did the examination . . . say it in medical terms if you have to, then translate it, ha ha, to English to clarify it for the jury . . ."

". . . windpipe protruded . . ."

". . . could one swing . . ."

". . . if the axe was broad and the axeman competent . . ."

". . . do you have an opinion satisfactory to yourself as to who . . ."

". . . heard the sheriff and others say that Earl Skiller . . ."

"Sustained," Horne said, leaning forward.

"Your Honor, the defendant did not object," the prosecutor said.

"Well, I object," Horne said. "The whole judicial system objects to that, and you know it. This is the third time I've had to object, in effect, and that should not be—and you know that, too," he added, glaring at Atkins.

The solicitor reddened, wheeled about.

"Mr. Sheriff, take the stand again, if you please. Now, there was an armed posse deputized by you on the day of . . . and they must have gone . . ."

". . . yes, he was shot in the leg . . . lucky one, the only one spared . . ."

". . . drew the others on up the trail like a fox . . ."

". . . yes, yes, a wall of fire . . ."

". . . not the only time this defendant created an inferno . . ."

"Objection sustained," Horne barked again. The solicitor paused to wipe his brow; then the testimony resumed.

". . . no, not recognizable . . . it was Dr. Rawson who said . . . only the families could tell . . ."

". . . Dr. Rawson, please take the stand again . . . no, you have been sworn once and that'll do for the duration of the trial . . ."

". . . yes, Mr. Solicitor, bullet holes . . . no, no bullets were inside the bodies . . . the postmortem showed . . . it could have been . . . yes, military ammunition or steel-jackets . . . can pierce the entire bulk of a thick man . . . I wouldn't have known where to look . . . the whole place was burned . . . ashes . . ."

"We now call the sheriff again . . . and did you feel the situation was such that you actually set up a field headquarters in that community from which to direct a manhunt of major proportions for this monstrous killer wolf . . ."

Atkins's voice shot through the courtroom. "I object to that."

Every eye turned to him at this first move to assist Earl Skiller. Horne looked at him and nodded slightly.

"It is inflammatory, Your Honor," Atkins said. "The solicitor has slipped in a number of these things . . ."

"Yes, Mr. Gatlin," said the judge. "I am pleased to see you take a strong adversary stance at last."

"It's Atkins, Your Honor, a-t-k-i-n-s, and if Your Honor is being sarcastic . . ."

"You have decided to oppose us all at any rate, and I am glad to see it. Objection sustained. Now get on with the questioning."

"Well, Your Honor, I must say," the prosecutor stammered, "I have called no names. We have offered evidence that purports to show, and as a matter of cold fact, does show that a number of honorable men of the community—family men, neighbors—were found dead near Wild Cat Cliff at various times and that they did not expire from natural or unknown causes but rather were stilled in their tracks by violent means, in other words, bullets or knife blades and not by any divine agency and not by heart attack or cancer or anything else, and that it is not hyperbole or exaggeration to suggest a monster or killer wolf . . ."

"All right, all right," Horne said, grinning slightly. "Mrs. Clerk, strike that objection sustained."

Earl looked at Atkins for a moment, then straightened and looked away. Testimony continued.

". . . patrolled that road in the snow . . . the body was below the road with no tracks around it . . . thought the devil hisself had done this one . . . believe now that it was slung there by a tree . . . throat cut . . . plenty of blood above the road around a birch sapling . . . no tracks . . . scuffle in the snow . . ."

". . . doctor said what? Then put the doctor on the stand . . ."

". . . any good hog butcher would know the same thing . . . human jugular or carotid not that much different . . ."

". . . knowledge of knives and throats, eh? Such as Earl Skiller might have . . ."

"Objection sustained."

". . . come down, doctor . . ."

". . . next witness . . ."

". . . you are deputy sheriff . . . yes, now, how much later when you set up the ambush . . . Stepp in the logs . . . you could still see him? So he was not hidden, then . . . oh, I see . . . went up and down and saw him sitting there guarding you against ambush and felt safe . . ."

". . . yes, he had been dead long enough to get stiff . . . all his blood ran into his shoes . . ."

Horne made a note now and then, drowsed on. At five he recessed for the day and went to his room. He declined an invitation from the solicitor to have dinner. Lawyer Atkins went to the jail to speak to Earl. Earl stood up to the bars.

"Well, I don't exactly trust you, man, and I don't need you," Earl said.

"If anybody ever needed a lawyer, it's you."

"Needing a lawyer and needing you is two different matters."

"That is quite unnecessary. I want you to know that I'm trying to help, and I feel I have endangered my own life by sitting at that table with you. Somebody might try to get us both."

Earl's eyes lit with subtle mockery. "You mean you're afraid something might happen?"

"Quite frankly I am."

"Well, you're getting into the spirit of this shindig. I know of two of us who look at things that way."

"What way, Mr. Skiller?"

Earl laughed ironically. "Somebody might get killed and it'll probably be us."

"This isn't funny."

"Well, I told you to get out of it."

"For one thing, Judge Horne won't let me. Another, I want to stay with you. I'll do what I can."

"Well, I'll appreciate it if you let them go on with what they're doing."

"All right. You just remember that it's not only you now."

The next morning the solicitor clumsily went through a few additions to the evidence; then he stood and said with a wide smile:

"That's the case for the state, Your Honor."

Horne jerked upright, staring fiercely and malignantly at the prosecutor, his eyes bright and alert. He looked at the sheriff, at Atkins, at Earl.

"Are you quite sure, Mr. Solicitor, that this is the case for the state?"

"Why, ah, yes. Yes sir, Your Honor."

Sheriff Plemmons and Fortune stared at each other in quiet horror, nodding slightly. The sheriff whispered apologetically to Fortune, "I can't find Joe Felton. He's been holed up somewhere for weeks."

Earl stood suddenly and knocked on the table with his knuckles. Heads swiveled toward him, and numb silence spread like venom through every heart.

"You've not proved any of it was by me," he said, and stared around with a diabolical flash of his eyes.

Horne's voice sounded in slow, ominous cadence. "Mr. Solicitor, I do believe he has a point. You will not now close this evidence. You'd better get busy, and I mean quickly."

"Your Honor, it is the strongest case of circumstantial . . ."

"Circumstance is weak," Horne said, still in his dangerous, slow voice. "I do not want this going for review on circumstance. Do you understand what I am trying to say to you? Well, do you?"

"Yes, Your Honor," the solicitor said, looking about in panic. The excitement spread through the courtroom. One of the deputies ran forward.

"If that crazy son-of-a-bitch goes free . . . ," he screamed, waving his pistol. People squatted, ducked. Earl did not flinch and Horne did not move. The judge slowly tapped his gavel, and the insistent beat of it rose through the uproar and took control of the courtroom. Slowly the hysterical racket subsided. Earl sat quietly on the edge of the table, staring calmly at the deputy. The sheer force of Horne's authority prevailed, and the spectators were rooted where they stood. They stared now to the front of the courtroom.

"Mr. Sheriff, disarm that man," Horne said.

Sheriff Plemmons stepped forward and wrenched the pistol away.

"Stand him here in front of me, please."

The sheriff guided the man, in quiet shock now, to the bench.

"What is your name?" the judge asked gently.

"Sir, I'm Norman Suggs."

"Are you indeed a deputy sheriff?"

"Yes sir, I am."

"I understand how you feel, Suggs."

"Thank you, sir," he snuffled.

"Now, sir, I hope you understand how I feel."

"What do you mean, Judge?"

"That it is up to you to keep the law and enforce it."

"Yes sir."

"Now, an outburst like this can conceivably result in a mistrial. Did you know that?"

"No sir, I did not."

"Yes. Enough has gone wrong here. This has been poorly done. Do you now have a better understanding of what we face in trying Mr. Earl Skiller?"

"Yes sir."

"Do you have a wife and family?"

"Yes sir."

"I hate this, but for your contempt of these proceedings I sentence you to six months in the county jail. Take him there now, Mr. Sheriff."

"Judge! Judge! He's . . ."

"I mean for you to take him there right now, Mr. Sheriff. Be quick about it."

"Yes sir," he said and hurried Suggs out the door.

Horne continued: "Now, ladies and gentlemen, this trial is not over. It may be just beginning. It could bounce in and out of courts for years to come. Any further outburst, and I will lock people up in wholesale numbers, in gross lots, if need be. This is a court of law, and if procedure is followed, justice may be invited and may show up. We are going to try to keep conditions favorable for its arrival and functioning. I will brook nothing further."

The sheriff was back. He went to Horne and spoke quickly. The judge snapped straight again in his chair. Then he said, "Mr. Solicitor, come up here."

When the solicitor reached the bench, Horne said, "Why have you not called eyewitnesses?"

The solicitor stared at him earnestly this time. "I don't have anyone who saw him kill anyone. The only ones who saw the killings were the ones who got killed. There might have been two, but . . ."

"I want you then to call Mrs. Skiller and go over her good."

"Your Honor, for God's sake, she is the mother of the defendant and she will not be credible."

"Well, whether or not she is credible I don't know, but she had better answer some questions."

"We cannot depend, Your Honor . . ."

"Well, it is all the state has right now, so go ahead. Bailiff, call Mrs. Clementine Skiller."

"Clementine Skiller, Clementine Skiller, you are called."

She raised her head. "What?" she asked.

"Call her, Bailiff."

"Clementine Skiller, step up and be sworn."

As she came, Fortune stared at Earl. There was no change of expression, but the unnameable force shifted in his eyes. The presence emanating from Earl seemed to be falling back into itself, turning inward to his terrible distant meditations. Some part of life was sucked out of the room.

"Do you swear to tell the truth, the whole truth, and nothing but the truth, so help you God?"

She was skittery, her eyes darting, her hands fluttering, her mind both here and there and neither place.

"Yes, yes, I do. The truth and the whole truth, yes, and so help me God and all the rest."

"You are the mother of Earl Skiller, the defendant in this murder case . . ."

". . . yes, yes . . ."

". . . you were there at the cabin that morning when Earl was in the yard before he went down the road . . ."

". . . yes, yes, yes . . ."

". . . see him with an axe . . . ?"

". . . no, no . . ."

". . . you were there when he came back up the road . . ."

". . . no, I didn't know he was gone anywhere . . ."

". . . well, saw him in the yard, then . . ."

". . . yes, yes . . ."

". . . what did he look like . . . ?"

". . . happy as I ever did see him, joyous, saved . . ."

Suddenly the courtroom was in a vast, deep silence.

"Saved, Mrs. Skiller?" the prosecutor asked in sudden discovery. His eyes were watchful, and he seemed to hold a lever to a cage door.

"Objection," shouted Atkins. The solicitor turned, smiled enigmatically, and asked, "Objection to what?"

"To where this is leading . . ."

"Objection overruled, Mr. Atkins, for God's sake. Answer it."

"What was it he asked?" the old woman said.

"You said he looked saved. Is that right?"

"Did I say that?"

"Yes. Now, exactly what did you mean?"

"You know the old song . . . found . . . he'd been lost and now he was found."

"Redeemed? As we speak of it in church? The Bible?" The solicitor was very relaxed now, secure with the Baptist and Holiness jury. He pressed on. "Is that what you mean, Mrs. Skiller?"

"I meant that's what he looked like. I've seen people before who say they've been saved at some of these churches. There was a new light about his face . . ."

The solicitor sprang, his voice quick and sharp, loud. "Never mind lights on his face. Did he have a double-bitted axe in his hand, and if he did, was it dripping with blood? That is what we now want to know."

The courtroom was electric, snapping with a battle of forces. The solicitor looked sideways at the angry jury. Mrs. Skiller beheld her son, and he beheld her not. Fortune watched as the living air again drained away, boiled and dead. Horne stared about incredulously.

"No," Mrs. Skiller said. "He hadn't gone nowhere or done nothin'."

Atkins was on his feet. He spoke in careful measures and with some authority.

"Now, Your Honor. I object here. I want you to warn the solicitor about this. He has asked her some questions, and she has answered. She is the mother of the defendant, and she is hostile, but she is entitled . . ."

"Both of you come up here," Horne said. When they stood before him, he said only, "Slow down, gentlemen. Slow down. Now, I'm going to recess until tomorrow morning, but I want her to finish first. Get on with it."

"All right, madam," the solicitor said, "I want you to try carefully to recall the day that Deputy Mitchell Sanger was beheaded at Hame Tree Gap. Now, I believe that every last Skiller up there but Earl came off that mountain that afternoon, and you met a sheriff's posse going in there. I believe you told the sheriff's men that they ought to have known better than to mess with your son, and that they ought to know better than to be on their way up there right then. Now, that was a strong warning to them, and that shows that there was dirty work afoot and murder in the air, and that you knew it and knew it well."

Atkins was up, angry. "Your Honor. I am astonished at this speech or essay to the court. He is bouncing it off her and into the jury."

"Sustained," Horne said, glowering at the solicitor. "You can argue to the jury in a more direct fashion later." He turned to Mrs. Skiller. "Answer that. The question, not the speech."

"What?"

"Did you know he had done anything out of the ordinary, let us say?"

"No, I did not. I didn't know he had gone anywhere."

The solicitor resumed: "Now, madam, the sheriff and several deputies have testified . . ."

"I don't give a good God damn what they said. Now, what else do you want to ask?"

The solicitor sputtered and pointed his finger to the ceiling. "Madam, I have plenty. Your Honor . . ."

"Objection, objection, objection," Atkins shouted.

Horne leaned back tiredly. "Gentlemen, come here," he said. They came before him.

"Mr. Solicitor, she's not helped you a bit," he said. "You get with the sheriff and find out a few things."

Then he sat back and said to the public, "Court will recess until nine o'clock in the morning."

When court convened the next day, a number of lawyers were in attendance to observe. The word had spread that an aberration was at work in the legal system. The entire population of the county knew that Earl Skiller had killed the deputies, but there was now something approaching doubt. The gentlemen of the bar, and the gentlemen of the press, now perceived the dimensions of Earl Skiller. He had out-generaled his foe in the mountains. Now he sat and was beating them with little effort at the bar. No one had realized what gaping holes had been left in the case. His guilt had been so certain in the public mind that assumptions had been taken for ironclad evidence. Now the small questions were ballooning into monstrous, taunting possibilities. The prosecutor stalled, went to the bench to confer with Horne, who ran him away time and again.

Then suddenly Sheriff Plemmons, Paul Fortune, Mrs. Guffey, Mr. and Mrs. Walters, and Logan entered the courtroom quietly from the rear. They made their way slowly to the prosecution table. The solicitor put Mrs. Guffey on the stand first. She told of sending Logan toward school that morning, and of the damage.

"Objection."

"Sustained."

"Your Honor, I'm laying the foundation . . ."

"Go ahead, then, but do it right."

Earl put his hand on Atkins's arm. "Let it alone," he said.

"You may cross-examine."

"Mrs. Guffey," Atkins said, "Were you at Hame Tree Gap that morning?"

"Well, yes. I went out that way to get some wood."

"Did you see the body of Deputy Sanger?"

"No."

317

"Now this damage . . ."

". . . well, I'm his grandmother and I know how he was . . ."

". . . you're not a doctor or have you had any training . . ."

". . . I know what I know . . ."

". . . has this boy ever . . ."

". . . I've had to hold him in the night . . . yes, Earl's friend . . ."

Earl could look every man on earth in the eye, but he could not look at the boy. They swore Logan.

". . . the truth, the whole truth, and nothing but the truth?"

He nodded. "The truth bird," he said.

The judge allowed his grandmother Guffey to stand near him. His other grandparents stood so he might see them.

"Son, one cold morning about two and a half years ago, about daybreak, did you see your friend Earl Skiller?"

After a time, Logan nodded numbly.

"Let the record show that he nodded in the affirmative," Horne said.

"All right, son, was he with another man at the place called the gap?"

Shortly he nodded again. Horne leaned forward: "Son, can you say it out loud?"

Logan nodded.

"All right, now, this is the question—was Mr. Earl Skiller there with another man?"

Tears came to the boy's eyes, and he nodded.

"Answer it," said the judge.

"Yes, another man."

The solicitor: "What else did you see?"

Logan was bewildered. He looked at Earl, and his face clouded.

"Answer it, son," Horne commanded.

"Nothing," Logan said.

"Your Honor, I'll have to lead him."

Horne sat a moment, then looked at Earl. There was a curious glitter on Earl's face.

"We've gone this far, Mr. Atkins. I'm going to let him lead the boy."

Earl nodded. Atkins frowned.

"Did you see Earl Skiller with an axe?" the solicitor asked.

Time passed. Logan cleared his throat. "Yes."

"Did he hit anybody with the axe?"

Time, then, "Yes."

"Did he hit the other man?"

"Yes sir."

The solicitor leaned forward, certain. The boy trembled briefly. "Blood. His head . . . ."

"The other man's?"

Earl and Logan had locked eyes, and Earl smiled and nodded. "Yes."

The judge sat back.

"Cross-examine."

"No," said Atkins. "The defense calls Dr. Rawson."

As Rawson went up, Logan came down and walked past Earl's table. Fortune noticed a barometric lift in the atmosphere.

"Now, Doctor," Atkins was saying, "I remind you that you're still sworn."

"Yes," said Horne, leaning forward, "this is a good move. Doctor, we need to nail this down as securely as we can. We want to get at the truth, and the state's case is a shambles now. Go ahead, Mr. Atkins."

Atkins was on his feet, his spectacles in his hand and his face grave. He had at last risen to it.

"Doctor, this boy's grandmother has painted a picture of instability in the lad. Is there a chance the witness may be described as psychotic?"

"I don't want to get into that definition," Rawson said. "I don't know too much about those terms, to tell the truth."

"How long have you known him?"

"I pulled him out of his mother's womb, and I've pulled him off the lip of the grave several times—at least I've been present when he returned."

"Can you give me an opinion . . . let's see . . . is he as stable as or does he act like other children his age?"

"No."

"Then he might be described as unstable?"

"Maybe."

"How about hallucinations?"

"I would estimate, ah, um, so. Yes."

"Severe?"

"I don't know. A hallucination is a hallucination."

"At any rate, an unreliable witness, then?"

"No, he's not unreliable. I believe he told the truth. If he's unstable, it's because he saw a bloody murder, and I offer that as informed and expert opinion."

Horne leaned forward and asked, "As a matter of interest, the prognosis?"

"I don't know. He may get worse."

Again came that unremitting knock on the defense table. Earl was standing, and he held high authority in the cavernous courtroom.

"I want to tell you that you have not proved me guilty of anything. But that boy has lit and spoke, like the bird he says he's seen. Now, I have tried to plead guilty and of my own free will confess to killing those men, and I will try again. This ought to save some time and trouble."

The silence, the terrible emptiness of Earl, which was a living, leaping substance. Horne leaned back, sighed in great relief and wonder.

"All right, put this in the record. Now, Mr. Skiller, I can and must prevent you from pleading guilty in a capital case. But I cannot and will not restrain you from making a courtroom confession. Take him to the jail, Mr. Sheriff, I need to read a little law."

The next morning Horne let the courtroom fill to capacity. The people came and gawked and sat silently. After the judge's charge, the jury ruled quickly, ritually. Earl stood before the bench, and all saw him. Faces appeared at windows.

"Mr. Skiller, by the evidence of your own confession . . . eight counts of first-degree murder . . . anything to say before I pass sentence?"

Earl turned slowly and looked at the people. He was not defiant, not beaten, not proud, not humble. Just Earl. He turned back and said, "No."

The judge looked at the law book before him.

"Earl Skiller, you are hereby sentenced to be taken to Central Prison in Raleigh, and there at a time to be determined . . . to be placed in the gas chamber and administered enough cyanide gas to take your life . . ."

He sat back a moment and stared upon Earl, and Earl upon him.

". . . and may God have mercy on your soul."

27

THE EDITORS in the north did not understand Fortune's reluctance to file stories. He read one letter:

Dear Paul:

When the sheriff, the judge, and the warden at Central Prison agreed to accredit you fully, we thought we would be receiving good copy in reams. The information you have sent has been skimpy.

Since the trial, you have been to the prison four times to talk with Earl Skiller. You are allowed to come and go as you will, and apparently you serve almost as priest to the condemned man. This gives you incredible entree.

What is the block and what may we expect?

Sincerely,
Eugene Morris
Managing Editor
The *Philadelphia Advocate*

Seven other complaints were piled on his table. He pulled his chair to a window where he could see past the buildings and to the mountains in the west. Clouds rose over the ridges like woolly heads.

"God, how do you write this for a newspaper?" he moaned, slouching deeper into his predicament. Then he rose and went to the table, moving as slowly as an old man. He wrote one letter to them all, typed the copies, and went to the pharmacy. Rawson saw him going and followed him. McCall put aside his pestle. They had not talked recently.

"Here!" Fortune said. "Let me read you this letter I have written to some editors. It is hard to get a grasp on a story like this. It is too much, and I've become too deeply involved in it."

Then he read:

Dear Editor:

I cannot begin to tell you of the complications arising from trying to cover this event. Each time I try to write it, a major part of it eludes me, and I harbor the suspicion that Earl Skiller can somehow affect this too. His influence is upon so many things. I do not yet know in what terms I will have to couch the story of Earl Skiller. Good God! It may have to be done in the language of metaphysics, theology, or mass psychology. There is so much there, yet anytime one tries to sort it, the skeins take on such curious colors and defy the effort. With all of that said, now let me say this: that he is Earl there as he was here; that he is Earl in the death cell as he was Earl passing on the street outside. The Earl who sits behind bars is the same Earl who was so concerned about the baby Guffey, or the child Guffey.

I realize that you do not know about the baby Guffey, and your ignorance leads us to this point: The story of Earl Skiller was strongest long before he killed Deputy Mitchell Sanger. He is a special man among the people.

In my manhood, such as it has been, something has fought in me to leap into form, and it has almost killed me. Only recently, since I have been involved in the Earl Skiller matter, has a thought clarified itself, and it is this: It is the job of the artist to let greatness identify itself to him, let it form into a simple structure, and then present it so that people may awaken to it and reach for it.

I know now that I cannot aspire to such an achievement. I am too frail. But I believe Earl Skiller to be of greatness. In what I know of him, he has done what he must. He loved his country and fought for it. He tended those lesser ones charged to him—his family—and did it without chagrin. He served man where he stood, and he served well. He bore personal grief in silence. He entered his destiny as it unfolded. He destroyed his enemies. He did not select them out of his own bias. They named themselves and came to him. He won clearly. Then he saw that his time had passed and that he had inflicted a hurt on a boy he loved. He came down then and stood to his fate. Destiny and justice are upon him now, and he does not flinch.

I talked to the warden several times. He told me that he had gone to see Earl in his cell a number of times, and that when Earl stares at him, he feels as though he were an accomplice and also condemned. I know what he meant, because Earl does that to everyone in one fashion or another. He said that he is afraid of Earl, not because Earl is a vicious killer, but because he feels he is somehow included in whatever Earl has upon him. The warden is not a stupid man, but he is not a smart man, and I don't think he is acute enough of mind to realize what a statement he made.

The warden said that all the guards there react strangely to Earl. When I go down the walkway beside the cells to talk to Earl, I find that Earl and the atmosphere of that place have together set up a peculiar blend of forces, and if fate or destiny has a feel, it is right there. There is a strange and fearsome sense of some great constellation now completing an alignment in the sky. Earl seems aware of it. It works through him and loops out and around and through anyone who gets near him.

The sheriff is to be included among the witnesses to the execution, and he went in to talk to Earl once about remorse. The sheriff is a good Baptist, and he said he felt he owed it to the widows, children, and kin of the dead law officers, but he got no contrition to bring back to them. He said that he did not find Earl to be a defiant man, or wrongheaded, or angry, or crazy, or smug. He said that Earl simply stood at the bars, relaxed—poised, I suppose, and probably patient, if I know Earl—and answered questions and smiled occasionally, never in a manner calculated to cause adverse feelings.

The sheriff said he felt that a man in Earl's position ought to register something to which we could respond with hate, or disgust, or sympathy, or something, yet Earl acts as if he's waiting for a train out of there and it's just another day in the life of the universe. So awe is upon the sheriff. He said he did not like to feel that way about a condemned killer.

If you care to turn this letter over to a rewrite man and let him try to make a story, I do not object. The letter was the only format in which I could address you in a sensible manner. I shall continue sending you spot news, and perhaps something after Earl is put to death, but do not expect anything major out of me.

Sincerely,
Paul Fortune

They stared at him while he uncomfortably sipped coffee. Finally Rawson spoke.

"True enough, that letter is a good story itself. How much longer is it before he takes the long walk?"

"Three more weeks. There's been no reversal, no error, no clemency or request for it. Lawyer Atkins has been down there with

323

him twice. Earl thanked him and dismissed him. Atkins told me he had never been so confounded or frustrated, and further, he never knew why he took such an interest in the case anyway."

"Do you think Skiller will crack?" McCall asked.

"Hell no, not now," Fortune answered. "Do you?"

"No. He's tough."

"It's not toughness. It's not bravado. It's not grit. It's not blood and guts."

"You seem to think it's something. What is it, then?"

"A rare thing—a man watching the approach of his death like a man."

In the final days, Fortune was frantic and distracted. He was now obsessed with the saga. His energy was drained. He could think of little else, fantasies swarming in all levels of his mind. He considered one possibility after another: Earl would become a hero in a disaster at the prison and his sentence would be commuted to life; he would escape through the connivance of sympathetic guards; he would be taken to the prison infirmary and escape from there; he would fake death, hold his breath like some accomplished yogin, and escape after the gassing. Earl must not yet die. There was no way in his mind for Earl to die. Fortune saw life as a series of measured, metered, and clean literary events. He felt that truth could be recognized in one sure way and that was by its completeness in form. Earl must not yet die. The situation tugged and raked at his nerves.

During this last waiting, Logan's mind also murmured. Earl's face came and went in his thoughts. One evening he ate supper with his grandmother. She washed the dishes and then read to him from a biography of Kit Carson. For a time he played absentmindedly beneath the dim fall of light from the lamp. Suddenly he grew drowsy. His ears rang, and his face grew heavy and numb. He arose and marched woodenly to his bed. In the moments before sleep he listened to the soft, ceaseless sibilance of the wind, and hearing that, heard all things of the planet. They sang to him in haunting presentiment, and he carried the bewitching melodies and the ominous dim mood on into another land. He ran eagerly toward the vivid dream.

Earl stood clearly before him, his hands bloody. His eyes fixed expectantly on Logan. Then he picked up an axe and chopped through a wall of smoke. He cupped his hands, which began to fill with glistening liquid from a springhead within themselves, and that fluid began to sing and hum in a curious high frequency; then it swirled down a strange drain to nothingness. Logan was detached, unafraid.

Earl turned to him, his face alert and his eyes alive with the essence of himself, and motioned for him to follow. Logan went with Earl through the gap in the smoke. They walked together, thinking with one mind. They went rapidly across a well-ordered and clean forest floor, where great trees towered into infinity and the sky endlessly changed color.

On a clear, pastured slope, beyond which the skyline sharpened and grew stable, Earl began digging a hole. "It is not a grave only," he said, and Logan grew apprehensive. But it was a well, lifting sparkling fluid in artesian spouts, and there was the singing of many wild waters. The notes went through Logan and registered on Earl, and the man nodded in understanding. Water and sound swirled, as blood had, to nothingness, and Earl strode on and away from the boy toward a place unbearably bright. Logan followed a few paces behind and saw that the light was one he had followed across measureless distances in his fevers. Earl turned, rolled his sleeves up, and showed Logan that his arms were brilliantly tattooed with a rattlesnake pattern. Then his hands struck into the light. His lips curled back, and his hands were lost in the light and his arms looked like stumps. When he drew his hands back and held them forth to Logan, the boy saw that while they were indeed hands, they were also goblets of gleaming silver. Earl held them out to Logan, his face mutely pleading.

A beautiful woman stood beside Logan. Her voice was clear, polite.

"He wants to know if they are all right to you," she said. Logan stepped forward stiffly, like a very young inspecting officer, and looked. He nodded to the woman. She smiled and said, "Tell him, then. Tell him not to worry. He is going home, that's all. It's like the old homeplace."

A muted light fell throughout the land, and colors dappled the sky. Logan stared at her. "Have I seen you before?" he asked.

"Yes. I am with you. Tell him."

He turned and said, "Earl? Earl!"

Earl's eyes were like sockets. Logan turned and walked back through the strange wood toward the wall of smoke. He still heard the woman's voice from a remote place. Then he awakened. It was not yet dawn. He slipped from his covers and padded to his grandmother's bed and lay beside her. Partially awake, she hugged him and murmured: "Were you humming something?"

In a moment he said, "No," and fell away to dreamless sleep.

Fortune went to the pharmacy and found McCall busy. The pharmacist wordlessly handed him a sealed envelope. Inside was a note from Mrs. Guffey:

Mr. Fortune, could you come to see us very soon? It is important.
                                                    Mrs. Guffey at Wild Cat

He found it difficult to take the arduous walk up to Wild Cat. There were endless stretches of old, hard time. Mrs. Guffey was in the pasture gathering dry locust bark for the fire when she saw Fortune's shambling figure briefly on the skyline at the gap. She joined him at the top of the hill.

"Mr. Fortune, you have not come in some time," she admonished.

"Madam. I apologize. I have such strange feelings about this place. At any rate, I've been busy."

"I know. You've been with Earl."

"Yes, that's right. Does that trouble you? Do you hold it against me?"

"No, it's all right. I need to speak to you about that, as a matter of fact."

He leaned against the fence to catch his breath.

"Mr. Fortune, Logan wants to go see Earl."

Fortune whistled in a low pitch. He detected a brief, dim movement somewhere.

"They won't let him," he said. "I know they won't. I don't believe anyone but the family can visit the death cells."

"Well, Logan is like family."

"That's right enough in its way. But there would be a lot of complications. You understand that departmental regulations would not likely fit Logan in as blood kin. Not only that, he's probably too young."

326

They wandered down the trail to the house. Logan was in a chair on the porch, the vines above him. Fortune unaccountably recalled the hornet episode.

"That was years ago, by God," he blurted, stunned. She nodded, reading his thoughts. Logan arose and walked toward them. Fortune put his arm around the boy's neck.

"Little boy, let me tell you something. Earl Skiller loves you, and he wants to see you, but I don't think they'll let you go into the place where he's being kept."

Logan's face remained hopeful.

"God, I don't see how," Fortune said. "Hell, I'll go ask the sheriff."

"I had a dream about Earl."

"You did? Did it scare you?"

"No."

"Do you dream about him much?"

"No. Not in a long time."

"Now you dreamed of him?"

"For two nights."

"Was it the same dream?"

"Yes, he was going to a good place."

"A good place? That's a good dream."

"A woman and me and the trees were there too. It was a bright dream."

"Bright? With light?"

"And a well. He got clean there. He went on without us."

"On? On where?"

"Down the valley where the old people were waiting."

"Then what?"

"I had to come back here. But that woman said that I had to tell him."

―――――――――

The sheriff rocked back and forth in his chair, nodding, cutting his eyes about.

"I need it as a favor, if nothing else," Fortune pleaded.

"Well, I owe you some favors. This state owes you some favors. The warden at the walls owes the governor a favor for his job. The governor owes me several things because I deliver this county's votes to him. He owes me and wants to pay me. But I was thinking

327

in terms of some paving on the Fines Creek Road, and the governor knows it. How am I going to tell him that I'll settle to get Logan Guffey into the death house for a visit? Then how in hell am I going to explain to those people on Fines Creek that the debt was paid in that way? This is too much here all at once. I thought that boy was scared to death of Earl Skiller."

"No, no. There's more between that man and the boy than we'll ever know. Logan needs to see Earl before the execution."

"That is trouble, trouble, trouble. Tell you what! Have that boy write Earl a letter. We can get that in with no trouble at all. Will that do?"

Earl stood close to the bars, watching Fortune approach. They shook hands, then Fortune held up the envelope. Earl seemed suddenly apprehensive.

"It's something you want," Fortune said. "It's from Logan."

Earl's eyes glittered; then for a fleeting moment there was something profoundly sad upon his face. He seemed afraid of a last rejection, and he stood near collapse and defeat at last.

"It is from your great friend Logan," Fortune said, sensing the importance of it to Earl's spirit, framing his words carefully and speaking in tones of hope.

Earl's eyes came alive again, and he pulled childishly at his chin with his fingers.

"My great friend?" he asked. "Logan is my great friend?"

Fortune handed him the letter. Earl tore it open and stared at the markings and moved his lips. Then he handed it back.

"Read it to me. I can't read too good."

Fortune took it and looked. "Mrs Guffey wrote it for him," he said, "but Logan signed it."

Then he read it. When he finished, Earl repeated happily and foolishly, "I say . . . I say . . . I do say . . . I say . . . ." His face was aglow. "Was that heaven he dreamed about?"

Fortune cleared his throat, shrugged. "Well, he said the woman called it an old homeplace."

Earl nodded. "He knows. Logan knows it's the same thing. I've always known that. But Logan dreamed it for me. I say. I do say."

Fortune marveled. There was a movement toward completion.

Three times a week Earl was taken down the passageway to the shower, where he was allowed five minutes in the water. Then he returned, ten paces behind one guard and five paces ahead of two others, down the gallery of gray bars, gray walls, gray faces of other condemned men. He spent his hours sleeping, pacing slowly about the small cell, or reclining on his bunk.

A preacher came several times, saying the same things time and again in a low, pious voice.

"Brother Skiller, are you ready?"

"Yes, I'm ready," he answered tolerantly.

"You are right, are you? You're going to the other side under bad conditions."

"True enough."

"Are you sure you're ready?" the preacher asked, peering at him closely. He knew that in his future ministry he would often refer to this one case. He sought in Earl's answers his own shuddering views of mankind in transit.

"Yes."

"The Good Book says that you must repent, that you must confess. That is the way to the Lord."

"Thankee. I'm ready."

"Ready for what?" the preacher asked, suddenly sharp. "Brother Skiller, you must listen. There are a number of things you must do to be saved. I don't believe you are automatically saved because Christ died on the cross for you. You are not too far from death's door, speaking literally and figuratively. It's right down the hall. The time is nigh. As far as I can tell, you've not confessed."

"I owned up in court."

"No, I mean you've not confessed the sin of it."

"What?"

"You have not repented."

"You think I've not paid for it?"

"That's right."

"Well, I'm a-fixin' to, ain't I?"

"Brother, I don't mean that. I mean in your soul."

"How do you know?"

"I can tell by the way you act."

"I was paying off as I went, preacher. Have you ever killed a man?"

"No, God help me, no."

"Have you ever seen a man killed?"

"No, no, no."

"Well, you're going to be here when I go, ain't ye?"

"Yes, I'm the prison chaplain for a while. I have to do it. You're the first," the preacher said, trembling and weak before Earl.

"Let me tell you that when you kill a man, you shut a door in your heart, and the more you kill, the more doors you shut. Soon you are by yourself in your soul, and it's like this death-house cell here. You just wait for your time to come. I've been in the death-house many a year, even before I got here. I don't know what it is you want, preacher, but you don't know much about this. Don't worry, people are paying even when you might not think they are. They are paying and paying and paying. Everybody pays up. Are you in the clear, Reverend, about everything?"

The preacher stared in silent horror into Earl's eyes, which seemed briefly to be faintly tinted, like crystals through which some power was refracted in leaping, glittering arrays. He backed slowly out of the cell. The guards stared in perplexity at Earl.

The night before the execution the chaplain came again at eight o'clock. Earl stood at the bars and nodded to him.

"Everything is all right, preacher. All the debts are paid. The old accounts was settled long ago, as they say. God does all things well. Now I hope as you go along in your life God goes with you."

The preacher cried quietly for a few minutes. "I hope it's you who goes to God, Earl Skiller," he said. "I won't see you anymore until daybreak. I'll pray." He wheeled about and strode down the corridor into dimness.

Shortly afterward, by prearrangement with the warden, Paul Fortune was allowed some time in the hallway. He shook hands with Earl through the bars, then nodded to a pair of guards. They brought a gramophone and set it on the floor. Earl's eyes were watchful, expectant, and Fortune played "Barcarolle." After it played once, Earl asked:

"Did you bring Logan's?"

Fortune nodded, played "Habanera" a couple of times.

"Now for this occasion, Sergeant, if you don't mind, I have a favorite growing out of all this. It sort of marks a great experience in time and space for me. I'd like to play mine."

Earl nodded eagerly, and Fortune played "La donna è mobile." The two men stared at each other and nodded in some strange recognition. Then Fortune played "Barcarolle" again and again until surely madness from it must spread through the prison. Earl was in a loose, childish trance, and the guards were pensive, nodding to the music. Sheriff Plemmons and the warden came down the corridor, and Fortune stopped the music. Fortune leaned close to the bars and felt that an unnameable force had moved and was now expanding and contracting in the walkway like the great breath of the earth. Earl spoke then, and they all heard it.

"I ain't sorry or glad about the killings. That all come in its own time, and I didn't start it and I couldn't stop it. I'm here to pay, but I don't need to because I paid as I done it. I know about God. God does all things well. I told that to the preacher. I always have believed that.

"Now, Logan Guffey got hurt. I'm sorry about that, and that's all I'm sorry about. To tell the truth, he's not hurt too much, I don't believe. He'll get over it better than you think he will. When you see him, and he wants to talk about me, tell him I said for him to remember the old bear dog named Sol, and to remember that dog no matter where he goes on the face of the earth. That's all he needs to know. Now, for you to understand that, Logan and me and the others put the dogs on a bear way back in the mountains. The bear got Sol and he nearly died. But we got him well and took him back to a bear. Sol flinched for just a minute, then he went in and got the bear's throat, then he held onto his ear until we shot the bear."

He stared a moment at Fortune. The sheriff and the warden stepped up. Fortune held out his hand, and Earl shook it again. Fortune began choking up.

"I'll be with you, Sergeant, as far as I can go in the morning."

Earl nodded. "Thankee. Your day comes."

———————

The executioner released the pellets from outside the gas chamber, and they plopped into the pan of acid between Earl's feet. Earl took it as it came up between his legs, and as he inhaled the first of it, lights switched on suddenly at the edge of a way that was opening behind his mind. With the next breath there was a sensation of expansion, and new lights came, and many things in his memory opened. The first surprise was the music, and it was even clearer than the light—"Barcarolle," in chimes of celestial origin, and that gentle knelling remained with him into new vistas and opened new areas of pleasure. Then many tunes and melodies played, and he heard them on separate levels, and his lungs swelled once again, his ears attuned themselves more acutely, and he was much larger. As he entered the way he heard a great howl and rattle in his throat, and a stroke of color flashed through his brain. The old blood ran cold and new power surged and freed him, unpinning him from tight membranes, and the scabbard of flesh with which he had encased his soul, now too small, split and fell away.

He plunged down through the terrible phalanx of vivid imagery out of times past and yet to be, and he heard a great voice whispering through the universe speaking of the last way of men. On a quiet path ahead he saw Deputy Sheriff Mitchell Sanger, who smiled and patted Earl's shoulder as he passed, and then he came to the other men he had killed at Wild Cat, and as he reviewed their ranks they smiled also.

Then the fields of France, and him alone facing the angels of death, and suddenly he saw truth—a cloud of luminous gas arising from the German lines. He went to it rather than letting it come to him. Without a gas mask he entered it breathing deeply and then floated above it, realizing with a happy, numb jerk to his lips that he had died in early 1918, and that everything he had experienced after that was merely a death dream. Before him now was a great form, and he recognized it as an ancient being who had checked his soul before he had gone down and accepted the caterwauling, bloody, gross, dense, odoriferous, and painful challenge called earth, and then he saw her, and she was nearing, nearing, nearing, and he began to tell her that it had not been her fault that snakes were silent in the darkness, and he at last began completing himself, completing himself. . . .

The witnesses watched as the frame of the man slumped imperceptibly in the chair. Fortune's head shook slightly. He is making the night crossing, he thought. He is journeying the aeons.

332

It was not yet daybreak. Fortune went into the streets of Raleigh. It had not taken long once it began. As he walked, the sun was striking on yellow clouds in the east and bouncing light down onto the earth's sea-bottom night in wide, prism-cut flashes. He looked around, but none of the witnesses had followed him out. He went to a hotel and numbly slept away the day. That night he boarded the train to the mountains. He stared blankly into the darkness beyond the car windows and wondered if he would get drunk at last. The great humps of the mountains rose out of false dawn east of Asheville. From Asheville he caught the bus to Wadenton, then slowly trudged through the midday streets to his place. He set his bag down and went to the drugstore. Rawson and McCall were there, and the sheriff.

"I saw you on the train, but you didn't seem like you wanted to talk," the sheriff said.

"That's right. Thanks," he said and slumped. Rawson put his hand on him.

"Are you all right?" he asked in profound kindness and concern.

"Yes."

"How did it go?"

"It was like Earl. He walked straight down the corridor. He looked out that little window at us for a moment and nodded. He may have smiled; I'm not sure. He sat in the chair and they strapped him in. They put the cyanide to him, and he didn't go down to get it, and he didn't try to back away from it. He moved a little. He was there and then he was gone," Fortune said.

The sheriff nodded in agreement. "Well, I stayed awhile," he said. "I went in and looked at the body. I wanted to know for sure. I mean I had to see it as it came out of that gas chamber when they cleared the gas out. I needed to know in the worst kind of way. I didn't hold hatred then. I just wanted to know. But even as I looked, I knew the man on that table there wasn't him. Something was gone. It seemed like the body was a lot smaller. He was a slim man, did you ever notice?"

They were silent a moment; then Rawson said, "Yes, now that you mention it."

"I have to go see Mrs. Skiller and the family," Sheriff Plemmons

333

said. "I'll tell them he went easy. The casket will come in on the baggage car day after tomorrow."

The arrival of Earl's coffin was an occasion on which the people in and around Hollytown and Wadenton drew together and differences were put aside. They knew themselves to be one people in one time frame, and it was clear in their minds that they might remember this day for the rest of their lives. The day before the arrival there seemed to be an air of high expectancy. Upon the time was an archetypal formality, as though a strange era that had never been fully defined or fully visible had now accomplished itself somehow in them. They had always sensed the working of something vast in the episode, as had Fortune, but it had gleamed only on the surface of their minds. There had been a great play in the sky, its scenes performed also on earth, its echoes in the streams and winds, and they had known only parts of it. But the coming of this train could draw it to a haunted, spectral close, and they must not miss that.

In the early afternoon of the day preceding the train's arrival, people came in from the country. There were not throngs of them, but there were enough of them, and each intensely interested. That night under the street lamps the vigil was kept. People clustered and talked, and the women in the company houses cooked and made food available on the porches and in the yards, and people came to eat without apology or selfconsciousness. They were warm and unafraid. Some of the musicians who played at the house dances brought their instruments and made music appropriate to the occasion.

It was not a wake; rather it was a watch. Not for the death of a man, because death had taken its own and had gone. It was a watch for a finale that would somehow open into something wider for them all. The town waited. There was the low and hidden mutter of the tannery, the quaint whisper of wind in creekbank willows, the wheezing exhalations of factory ventilators, the low murmuring of the people telling stories, the minor skirls up from sawed fiddles. People stood on the porches in the early night and looked at the first rim of a waxing moon in the western sky. Then, exhausted in the night, their moods ran to quickening memory, now vivid and now gone, of the generations of their race and people and the spirit of them, which had been in Earl, the man of their land and their time who had died choking in a gray steel box, pinioned to an oak chair.

The day dawned brightly, and the mood was fairly festive. In midmorning they all went to the depot. It might never be determined how Alex Fore was inserted into a clean shirt and trousers, though he did remain innocent of a razor and washcloth. Nor would it ever be ascertained how Sweatbee Hardy came to reek of soap.

Pulpwood trucks came in and parked off the main street as the rich warm sun deepened the morning. There was the smell of moonshine whiskey, but not one boisterous note. In a while the tannery workers left their jobs and came in somber little groups to mingle with others at the depot. Boogerman, in a blue serge suit and vest, strode in his stiff, solemn gait in and out of the little groups, rocking and swaying as he went.

"Do ye want a chew?" Alex Fore asked, holding out his filthy pouch to Boogerman.

"No, no," Boogerman growled—then, agreeably, "Yes, Alex, yes, and I thankee."

Unflinchingly he pinched out some of Alex's tobacco and poked it into his jaw. He walked away a moment to shake a hand, and when he could do it unnoticed, he spat out the tobacco and inserted some of his own.

Now as the hour approached, down the street from Wild Cat came the Skiller family, dressed in shabby clothing, matched as well as it could be in its various pieces. They made their way silently and gracefully to the depot platform, where they stood in pride and dignity. Paul Fortune silently noted that now, as always, Earl's standing draped his family with a peculiar but solid honor.

The sheriff drove slowly up the street and parked. He was not accompanied by deputies. He walked to the end of the depot dock and stood comfortably with his colleague Boogerman, and Boogerman's friends Alex Fore and Sweatbee Hardy.

P. N. Caldwell came out of his store, took off his apron, and put on his coat. He drove his pickup truck to the ramp, where he stared out the window at Sweatbee and Alex for a moment in weary exasperation. Then he said loudly to anyone:

"They don't have any way to get him to Wild Cat. I told 'em it would be my great privilege to do it."

Then, staring fiercely around, he got out of the truck and let the tailgate down. Alex and Sweatbee nodded, mutely approving.

The girls from the Western Front and the whores from Smathers Street collected across the track and twisted their handkerchiefs. Occasionally one of them would catch the eye of the Skiller girls and wave in timid sympathy. A dark mood fell upon Boogerman's face, and he detached himself and walked away.

In the bright sun during the final moments before the train came, Fortune saw the people standing still as if posing for a great, slow lens in the sky, which examined them externally and internally and found they were yet intact as a part of the race of man.

The train whistle sounded in the distance; then the locomotive came into view around the curve. It came on and jerked slowly past the depot until the baggage car drew up to the platform. An old, solemn conductor slid open the door. For a brief time there was only a shadow in the door; then the drab state casket rolled into view on a low dolly. The Skiller brothers, now grim and not foolish, efficiently snatched it off the wheels and turned abruptly and carried it to Mrs. Skiller, a queen in an ill-fitting robe. She looked upon the casket, her face tired and as ancient as a valley floor. She nodded slightly, and they carried the casket and set it gently in the back of P. N. Caldwell's truck. Then all the brothers got into the truck bed and stood silently beside it while Caldwell put up the tailgate. The women tried to load into the truck cab, but there was not room. Suddenly Rawson ran forward. "Wait," he said gently, "ladies, take my car. Where's Paul Fortune? Here, Paul, take my keys. Drive them to Wild Cat."

Sheriff Plemmons stepped forward. "I can take them. I can haul some of them."

The Skillers turned to look at him, then past him in profound silence. It was a moment before Mrs. Skiller shook her head. The sheriff's face wrinkled in private, sensitive agony. He stepped back. With stiff and exaggerated courtesy Fortune helped the Skiller women into Rawson's coupe, seating Mrs. Skiller beside himself. Caldwell held back and let Fortune drive away first. The two vehicles drove slowly out Main Street.

At the school, well out of sight of them all, Mrs. Guffey and

Logan stood on the steps, watching Earl go by on his way to Wild Cat Cliff.

At the intersection above the school, Boogerman stood secretly alone. He straightened, removed his hat, and held it over his heart as the casket passed.

28

A YEAR PASSED. Paul Fortune, career lurching forward and spreading, went north on business matters for several months. He wrote frequently to Dr. Rawson of his revived literary reputation and acceptance in journalistic circles. His tone was subdued, yet that of an eminently satisfied man to whom recognition in full measure had come. Then, with contacts strengthened and purpose renewed, he took the train back to Hollytown and reopened his residence. He talked to no one but Rawson and McCall about his amazing new lease on life, preferring to remain in other eyes the slightly disgraced Paul Fortune of Hollytown, an identity that provided him with a solitude conducive to thought and work and also proved deeply harmonious for his inner life.

Summer passed. Within a few weeks of his return, he walked slowly up the road toward Wild Cat. At Hame Tree Gap he stopped to look about, found memory faded and fading still as he looked on. Like one of his pulp stories, the story of Earl Skiller had not happened except on the pages he had written about it. He stared for a long time up the old, rutted road leading toward the cliffs. Then he went on to the Guffey house.

Mrs. Guffey and the boy were at work on the porch stringing apple slices for drying. They raised their heads and stared myopically as Fortune entered the yard from the path. Then their eyes brightened, and they put down the pans and came to meet him. They hugged like old friends. Talk burst forth in torrents. Logan bounded about happily for a time, then went to play.

"Yes, yes, it has been good for me . . . I made numerous contacts who want my writing . . . yes, a study on mountain people is in the works . . . to be finished . . . and how have . . . ?"

"... the boy is fine, so good. Walton and Loretta are still in Boston doing fine, he's making money and studying his lessons ... be home early next year ... yes, came home once to see about him ... good, good, no, he's all right ... does not cry in his sleep or jerk like he did ... we're going to see my people Saturday if you want to go. ..."

He met them Saturday on the highway above the Western Front. They flagged down the bus, boarded it, and settled into their seats. For a time they traveled without speaking, and Fortune reflected wordlessly upon the movement of the bus against the timeless backdrop of the mountains, dark cove floors, roaring and pitching creeks, tall timbers.

Some of her people were waiting for them at the Rankin bus station. Amidst high and loud bucolic gaiety they loaded the three of them into the cab of a logging truck and delivered them to the home of her brother, Monroe. Her sisters greeted them, served refreshments, hastily launched into the conversations needed to catch up on lost time.

Fortune nodded agreeably to everyone, sat finally in a chair in the corner. Logan sprawled on the floor near him. Fortune winked at him as the others talked. The past—they dwelt upon it, turned eternally toward it, doubling and folding back into the years. As they talked, they presented mementos, souvenirs from the pioneer past. Each had his or her own little museum: Great-uncle Elijah's adze or awl, Granny Horton's old flatirons and dutch ovens. They had their own private archives of letters sent from various points in the nation, the last heard from this one or that one two generations ago, safe conduct passes through Civil War lines, old postmasterships, old notary commissions. There the old people sat, talking of the days gone, days they could scarcely recall, and then only through the faulty hearsay of time flowing through flawed memory.

"Yais, yais, Nathan's old cabin set thar beside whar the well house is now," a sister said. Together they regressed to old patterns of speech, archaic accents. They stared out the tall windows in Monroe's house at the lay of the land, recalling. ...

"Nothin' left of h'it now," Monroe said.

They nodded sadly.

"All that wuz saved from h'it was some ol' pags and cut nails. I got 'em from the floor and a wall," he said.

The sisters' eyes lit. Fortune looked on with hooded gaze.

"Ah? Did ye save some of the ol' pags?"

"Yais, yais. I knowed that someday ye'd want to look at 'em," Monroe drawled pleasurably.

"Well, let's look at 'em now, Monroe," Mrs. Guffey said. "My land, I wouldn't of thought of saving them pags. I'd like to see 'em. Mr. Fortune here, I know he would."

Fortune nodded agreeably.

From a deepening drowse, Logan heard his great-uncle Monroe rise creakily from his rocker, cross the squeaking floor, and mount the stairs. The sisters sat back, their big, strong hands limp in their laps. Monroe returned with a small package of old, wrinkled brown paper and unrolled it.

"Thar!" he said in small exultation, holding out the pegs. The others looked on. Then they reached and plucked about in the small pile.

Hickory pegs, and oak, old and brown and smooth with wear. Time had worked on the wooden pegs. The ancestors had pegged and tamped, and some of the old life remained like a low heat upon the pegs.

It was late Saturday afternoon, and they sat in the close, dim parlor. Fortune and Logan stared, took in impressions. The old folks sat like old tintypes. Ancient images rattled in the throats of Monroe and Vadey, spilled out of their lips in slow, measured reminiscing: old gossip and rumor, obsolete jokes, musty tales told of people dead. Voices, gray voices carrying the living tone of dead time. Irish wit, Scottish wisdom, Elizabethan inflection, abrupt Cherokee truths.

Logan drowsed in the murmur around him. The old folks rocked evenly together in their chairs, and time was ticked off by the creaks of their rockers. Light fell feebly through the window and scooped up their movement and fled with it. Logan opened his eyes to slits and watched and wondered. Then he slipped over the edge of consciousness, found himself afloat on a far, warm sea, saw his people from the reaches of time, saw them birthed, reared, winding down the slopes of their lives toward death, saw them dead and buried. He marveled for a moment before he traveled on to the places of his sleep.

The next morning they slept a bit late. Fortune came down from his room to find Mrs. Guffey and her brother and sisters at coffee. Logan played in the yard, dodging the rich squirms of chicken manure. After lunch Mrs. Guffey took Logan and Paul Fortune up the muddy road to the cemetery where her family dead lay among others. A strange, motionless mood of autumn noon was upon that little rise of earth.

The three of them strolled among the graves. Mrs. Guffey's voice was low, muttering to herself and to others not visible to Fortune and Logan.

"These are our many mansions, our many rooms, the home of the entire family."

History flowed over the ancient burying ground in the slow pour and drain of time. In the land of the dead, the sun flared and fell softly on stones gleaming with the gray past. They trooped the solemn ranks of tilted stones, and by those stones they knew the people and their travails in a life they could not know.

Rocks had been excavated from fields as they were cultivated, shaped and fashioned into tombstones. Many a patient, weary winter night had been passed with the careful chiseling of names and dates and simple words.

Mrs. Guffey turned and said, "It was the custom: Carve your stone and make your box, for the time is coming. Life was hard, Mr. Fortune, very hard. Some endured."

Fortune studied, finger to chin.

Here to sleep in this wrinkled old land, pioneers lay down in soft beds of death, and carved headstones told brittle stories of old, tired life lived out in distant mountains. Life was hard. Yes, yes, he saw now. Was death sweet?

They had not known that a whole world spread beyond these mountains. Known? No, nor cared. They sleep deep.

And keep for the great dawn coming.

Along the mountains, autumn winds blew the trees, and the drowsy slope was lit by the soft, high sun.

Briefly Logan saw the fusion of time with light, both fading into death. All things were passing away.

Very slowly Mrs. Guffey guided Fortune to a weedy, neglected spot and showed him the small stone:

341

SKILLER CHILD
SON OF EARL AND MARY
DEAD BY SNAKEBITE
GOD GAVE. HE TOOK.
HE WILL RESTORE.
HE DOES ALL THINGS WELL.

Fortune stared about, the strains of the music—"Barcarolle," "Habanera," "La donna è mobile"—rising sharply in him. What was it about? What was it all about? A tear slipped from his eye and coursed down his cheek. Mrs. Guffey looked at him and nodded, then gently took his arm again, led him to a newer grave nearby, and pointed to the undertaker's tag. A stone had not yet been erected.

CLEMENTINE SKILLER

Fortune stared wearily at Mrs. Guffey. "The old woman? Old lady Skiller? In God's holy name. How? When?"

Mrs. Guffey smiled, shook her head.

"No one thought any Skillers were near Wild Cat after they buried Earl. Last winter Logan went hiking into the cliffs. He looked in the window and saw her sitting in a chair in front of the fireplace. There was no fire. He went in and found her sitting there dead. Dr. Rawson said she had frozen to death."

Fortune sat on a tombstone and looked at the sweep of the mountains. He nodded his head in deep thought for a long time. Logan was at the edge of the cemetery, and Mrs. Guffey walked down toward him. In a few minutes Fortune rose and walked slowly toward them through the tombstones.

———

On the bus going home, Fortune and Mrs. Guffey sat and chatted in great high humor, old friends of the best kind. She had revealed to him the secrets of her people and their hard lives.

Logan sat in the front of the bus beside an old man. He felt acutely the bus hurtling toward a sharp curve, and in that curve a great outcropping of rock shone. In the seconds that the bus shot toward it, a thing came to Logan's mind.

—We are approaching that rock, and this is the only time this moment will be. We can go toward that rock a billion times, but never again for this time because this time is dying.

342

All of big and small history rolled across the earth, and all of time glistened like water as it slid across the face of the big jutting rock.

Then the bus made the curve and left the rock behind.

"What's the matter?" the man sitting beside him asked sternly. "Did you see something on that rock?"

A chill passed over Logan. He did not know. He did not know.

"Did you see a snake or something on that rock?" the man asked. "You sure were staring."

Light and time. Light and death and old fading time gleaming on a passing rock.

"No sir."

Only the light, and nothing more.

THE END